THE PREACHER

NATHAN BURROWS

1

The sun broke over the horizon, revealing a cluster of people huddled together on a small boat only just big enough to take their weight. They were split into two groups. The smaller group, formed of only two people, was distinguishable by their dark clothes and hair. Both male and somewhere between twenty and thirty, they were seated at the stern of the boat. The older of the two with his hand on the tiller of an outboard engine. His companion was smoking, blowing a plume into the new day before flicking his cigarette into the almost still waters of the English Channel. It disappeared with a hiss heard only by the seagulls circling the boat, looking for food.

The larger group was, with a single exception, female. There were eight women, ranging in age from twelve or thirteen to perhaps mid-sixties. The matriarch of the group, if she was indeed that, was bowed. She clutched a shawl around her head with arthritic fingers. Her bright orange life-preserver gave the elderly woman a grotesque shape. The next youngest, by perhaps thirty or forty years, was sitting ramrod straight, staring at the coast that could now finally be seen in the distance. She couldn't see much more than a dark line on the horizon above the sea, but she knew it was there.

Being so close to it filled her heart with joy and trepidation in equal measure. This was her promised land, and perhaps the promised land of them all. She only knew a couple of her fellow passengers. Ana and Elene were sisters from the same village as the woman, a small collection of houses called Nakra in the north-west corner of Georgia. The village had been overshadowed by Mount Elbrus since man had first settled there. In recent months, it had not been the mountain that overshadowed the local population, but Russian forces building on the border between the Republic of Abkhazia, eager to take back what they thought was rightfully theirs.

"Katya?" a girl's voice whispered. It was Ana, the younger of the sisters, speaking in their native Georgian. The woman looked away from the horizon and at the young girl. Ana was only twelve, but already showed the striking beauty of many women from the area. They both shared the same features. Blonde hair, so fine it was almost wispy, and light green eyes, which in Katya's case were surrounded by worry lines. Oval faces with rosy cheeks.

"What is it, Ana?" Katya whispered. The man at the stern of the boat looked at her sharply. Katya was sure he only spoke Albanian and, of course, English.

"How much longer will it be?" Ana said. She shivered and pulled her thin coat tighter around her narrow shoulders.

"You see there?" Katya replied, nodding at the horizon. "That smudge above the sea? That's England. We're nearly there."

Katya watched as Ana exchanged whispers with Elene

before turning her attention to the other passengers. The first rays of sunlight meant that she could finally see them properly, and her gaze was drawn to the solitary male of their group. He was wearing some sort of long robe, dark gray in color, and sandals over his bare feet. Seemingly unconcerned by the cold, when he met her eyes, she saw they were the same gray as his robe. His head was shaved, and the light glinted from the skin on his scalp. Between his sandalled feet was a small cloth bag.

As they had boarded the boat on the coast of France the previous night, she had noticed him but paid him no attention, more concerned with securing her own single bag with everything she thought she needed crammed into it. Katya nodded at the man, but he didn't respond, preferring instead to just look at her. She was used to men looking at her in a particular way, but this man's expression wasn't one of lust, or even interest. He was just looking at her. Katya opened her mouth and was about to say something when there was a loud voice from the stern.

She turned to look at the two men just as the noise of the engine increased and the bow of the boat lifted in the water. The movement caused the old woman to cry out and grab at a lifeline that led down the side. The younger of the two men was half-standing, his hands on the casing of the outboard motor. Through the gloom of the receding night behind the boat, Katya saw a silhouette. It was another boat. A much larger one with a black rubberized gunwale and a squat gray superstructure interspersed with windows.

The two men at the stern shouted to each other in their own language over the noise of the outboard engine. Katya looked past them at the now rapidly approaching vessel, perhaps two hundred yards behind them. As she watched, it turned slightly and she could make out the words stenciled onto the side of the superstructure: Border Force.

What happened next took only seconds. The younger man took his hands from the engine casing and turned, taking a few steps into the boat. Then he bent over as if he was about to pick something up from the deck. As he stood, Katya realized with horror that he had his hands clasped firmly around the old woman's ankles.

With a grunt, he continued to raise his hands, tipping her backward and into the inky sea beyond.

2

The captain of Her Majesty's Coastguard Nimrod, a former Royal Navy Lieutenant Commander known by his crew simply as "Skip", lowered the binoculars from his eyes. He couldn't believe what he'd just seen.

"Man overboard!" he shouted, his voice deepened over the years by a full pack of Benson and Hedges a day. "Man overboard!"

The cry was picked up by the other members of the ship's crew and a well-practiced drill on HMC Nimrod sprang into life. The crew member farthest aft on the ship was pointing directly at the location where the small rigid inflatable boat had been when Skip had seen a passenger being rolled into the water. Another member of the crew was preparing a life ring.

Beneath them, the boat lurched as the twin Hamilton Waterjets and Caterpillar diesels sprung to life. The ship accelerated from its cruising speed of twenty knots to its top speed of thirty-two knots in what seemed to Skip like a lifetime. His hand slipped to the GPS where he stabbed at the

MOB "Enter" button, but he didn't think putting out a Mayday was needed. They should be able to recover the man overboard but, Skip realized looking at the orange boat speeding toward the shoreline, it would be at the expense of picking up the other refugees.

Earlier that morning, before the sunrise, the HMC Nimrod had been lazily patrolling the area. It was one of a small fleet that tried as hard as it could to either guard the shore or rescue migrants when the weather was favorable for small boat crossings. Which it was depended on the newspaper being read. Given the English climate, this could change several times in a single day. There was another coastal patrol vessel, a sister ship to the Nimrod, and two larger cutters.

Elsewhere in the channel were three distinctive orange lifeboats, and they had eyes in the sky courtesy of the Royal Air Force's Shadow R1. The small twin-engine turboprop's sensor turrets could see a mouse from miles away. At dawn, the Shadow had returned to its base to be replaced by an unmanned aerial vehicle. It was this Thales Watchkeeper that had picked up the small boat that Skip could now barely see. But beyond spotting the boat, there was nothing else that the Watchkeeper could do. The coastline was vast and remote, and the resources available to the authorities were very thin.

"Have we got visual?" Skip said to his co-pilot, a taciturn man called Williamson, who he had worked with for the last two years. He was standing next to Skip, his own binoculars clamped to his eyes.

"I can see a buoyancy aid," Williamson replied with a grim face, "but I can't see anyone in it."

Skip swore under his breath. He knew what the people smugglers had done; he knew why they had done it. And he knew they had been successful. Searching for a man over-board was always going to take precedence over chasing a small boat, which meant that the crew and passengers almost certainly weren't refugees.

He pulled his phone out of his pocket and, after checking he had a signal, called the control center in Lydd, a small town in the Romney marshes. As he spoke to the operator, the Nimrod slowed as it approached the location where the person had gone in.

"They were heading on a bearing of about three hundred and forty degrees, which would put them some-where between Pett Level and Winchelsea. Can you send the Old Bill?" He swore again when he heard the operator's response. "No police anywhere near the area," Skip said to Williamson after ending the call. "They're all tied up at Camber Sands with a beached boat and an incoming tide." Camber Sands, while being a popular tourist destination on the southern coast of England, also had some of the fiercest and fastest rising tides in the country.

Skip made his way out of the bridge and onto the forward part of the ship. As he arrived, one of the crew was fishing a bright orange buoyancy aid from the water with an extendable boat hook. He put it on the deck and Skip bent over to look at the sodden piece of equipment. One thing it didn't have was functioning clips for the straps that were supposed to secure it to a person.

"Any sight?" he asked. The remaining four crew members were all facing out to sea, arranged in a horseshoe shape to scour as much of the water as possible. None of them replied, which told Skip all he needed to know.

He had just watched someone being murdered.

3

Katya gasped as the rigid inflatable boat hit the sand at speed and lurched onto the shore. Across from her, both Ana and Elene, who were still crying from what they'd seen moments before, crashed into each other with some force, almost losing their balance and pitching over the side.

"Move, move!" the older of their pilots, if they could be called that, shouted in heavily accented English. He was gesturing toward the front of the boat with one hand, pulling a knife from his belt with the other. A second later, Katya heard a loud pop followed by a hissing noise, and she realized he'd thrust the knife into the soft skin of the inflatable boat. His accomplice was throwing their bags onto the sand, some of them falling short and ending up in the water.

Fighting her rising sense of panic, Katya made her way to the front of the boat and sat down, swiveling to throw her legs over the side. She noticed the man in the gray robe already standing on the shore, his hand extended to her. She took it gratefully, and slid off the boat, landing awkwardly on the compact sand and twisting one of her ankles.

"Are you okay?" the man said, focusing his gray eyes on hers. As before, his expression was impassive. He just looked at her as behind them there was another loud pop and more hissing.

"I'm okay," Katya said, turning back to face the boat to help Ana and Elene get out without hurting themselves.

"I'll help them," the man said. Katya realized he was speaking English with an American accent. She watched as he strode to the side of the boat, almost up to his knees in the water, and put out his arms. He beckoned to Ana, who was staring at him from the boat and, a few seconds later, he had one girl in each arm and was walking up onto the beach, seemingly unconcerned by their weight. He placed them down on the sand before putting a palm on each of the girl's heads. Katya could see he was saying something, but he was too far away for her to hear.

A few moments later, the group was standing higher up the beach, next to a narrow road. Katya looked in both directions, but all she could see was the boat, sand, and the road running next to it. The sun had lifted itself from the horizon and Katya saw the boat that had been following them earlier in roughly the same position as before, but now facing away from them. As she watched, it turned slowly and reversed its course. It was looking for something, and a lump formed in Katya's throat when she realized it would be the woman they were searching for.

She turned to look at the two men, who were now deep in conversation, having manhandled the remains of their inflatable boat back into the sea. One of them—the one who had pushed the woman over the side—was talking rapidly as he stabbed at a mobile phone with an angry finger. She wanted to walk over and slap him across the face, call him a coward, and had decided to do just that when she realized the man in the robe's gray eyes were on her. His eyebrows went down by a fraction, and he shook his head slowly from side to side. It was the most emotion she had seen from him since the sun had come up. Even when the old woman had gone over the side, when Katya had turned to look at the man, there was nothing in his expression. It had all happened so fast there was nothing anyone could have done, as they were both on the opposite side of the boat.

Katya stood still for a moment, wondering what to do. She wanted to punch the man with the phone, but didn't think that would achieve anything other than make her feel better. Then she noticed an engine noise. A few moments later, a dirty green van pulled up on the narrow road. It looked like the Russian-built GAZelle vans that were commonplace on the roads of her hometown.

"Get in, get in!" the man with the phone shouted. Ana and Elene started walking toward the van as its driver, a man who could have been a brother of the other two, flung the rear doors open. Katya picked up her bag, which dripped seawater from the bottom, and took a few steps toward the van before realizing that the man in the robe was talking to the man with the phone. Again, she couldn't hear what he was saying, but as she watched, the man with the phone took a few steps back and put his hand behind his back.

The next time Katya saw his hand, she recognized the squat black shape of a small pistol pointing directly at the man in the robe.

4

C aleb, to give the man in the robe his Christian name, glanced at the small pistol in the hands of the man he had nicknamed The Smoker. His colleague, The Non-Smoker, was standing about five feet away from them, watching the exchange with interest.

Caleb had just been explaining to The Smoker that he didn't need a lift anywhere and was happy to walk. In the distance to the east was an orange glow in the rapidly lightening sky that would be civilization of some sort. It couldn't be more than four or five miles away, and Caleb could walk ten times that in a day. Then The Smoker had pulled the pistol.

The gun was black and tapered toward the business end. On the left-hand side was a safety, which Caleb could see was off. The Smoker's hand was wrapped around a brown stippled grip and was rock steady, his index finger coiled around the trigger. That concerned Caleb more than the gun itself. The Smoker was obviously comfortable with its weight and, as he had killed already that morning, Caleb knew he would have little hesitation to do so again.

The pistol was pointed directly at Caleb's abdomen. It looked to him like a Makarov, a staple of many Eastern Bloc militaries since the fifties. If Caleb was correct, and he usually was, it was a simple gun with only twenty-seven moving parts and so well made it could be dropped on its muzzle without discharging. It had a poor first shot accuracy, but that would not make any difference at this range. Caleb knew he was at the worst possible distance from The Smoker, which would be why the man had taken a step back. He was too far away to make a grab for the gun, but close enough for even a child not to miss. Caleb swayed a couple of inches and saw the pistol follow. The only moving part he was concerned about was the bullet that could emerge from the end of the barrel. If the pistol was fired, it would be a gut shot. Survivable if you didn't mind shitting into a bag glued to your abdomen for a while, which Caleb had no intention of doing.

"Okay, okay," he said, keeping his voice level and his gaze fixed on The Smoker's. "I hear ya."

"You work for us now," The Smoker barked, his words staccato and clipped. He inclined his head toward the white van. "Get in the back of the van."

Caleb held his hands out, palms up. Not quite in a gesture of surrender, but to let The Smoker know he was going to comply. He took a couple of steps back and then turned his back on the man to make his way toward the van. As he did so, he saw the terrified face of the woman he had helped down from the boat. To his relief, the two young girls had already climbed into the van before seeing the gun. Caleb adjusted his position slightly so that if The Smoker decided shooting him in the back was an option, the bullet would hit him and only him. The other three women who had accompanied them on the journey across the channel were standing to one side and made no movement toward the van. Neither were they encouraged to, and Caleb realized they weren't coming with them.

A few moments later, Caleb, the woman, and the two children were sitting in the back of the vehicle, which, according to the lettering on the back, was a Ford Transit. The interior was bare with a wooden floor and Caleb noticed as the doors were slammed shut that the interior handle had been disabled. Caleb could detect a musty odor that smelt familiar, but he couldn't quite place. Was it blood, perhaps? There was none on the floor that he could see. As the van moved away, the odor was gradually replaced by another smell that was definitely human.

Fear.

5

Aleksander swore in his native Albanian as the cigarettes spilled from the pack and fell to the filthy floor of the van. Then he swore again as he heard his brother, Mateo, chuckling next to him.

"You should give them up," Mateo said. "They're bad for you."

"Not as bad as a bullet in the back of the head, Mateo," Aleksander said as he bent forward to pick them up. When he had replaced all but one of them in the packet, he exchanged the gold box for a lighter from his pocket before cracking the window open by an inch. A few seconds later, he was puffing contentedly on a cigarette.

"Have you spoken to the peshkop?" Mateo asked. Aleksander rolled his eyes in response.

"Yes, Mateo, I have made sure word gets to him that we have the package."

"Good," Mateo replied with a single nod.

"Why have we brought the man?"

"To replace the Bosnian."

"What happened to the Bosnian?"

"He died."

"How?"

"His heart stopped beating," Mateo replied with a sideways grin at Aleksander. "It had a bullet in it."

Aleksander looked out of the window to his left, not wanting to continue the conversation. He wondered what the Bosnian had done to earn a bullet to the chest. Trying to escape, most probably. Aleksander was unsettled, as he often was on these trips, but this one was worse. The woman who he had pitched into the sea had not made a sound as he pushed her to her death. He would have preferred it if she had screamed, or at least acknowledged the fact that he had ended her life. Perhaps, he thought as he rubbed at the tattoo of the sun and the moon that was inked on the back of his hand, she was a Bushtra, a bad omen-wishing witch. The time was right for them to be active.

It was approaching the end of April and Walpurgis night would soon be upon them. Aleksander thought back to his childhood, when he and Mateo would watch as their father lit a bonfire to keep the devils and the spirits from their home. An involuntary shiver ran down his back and he wondered if the last thought in the old woman's mind as she silently entered the water was a curse on him and his family.

Outside the van on the opposite side to Aleksander, a grassed bank the same height of the van blocked their view of the sea. They drove past a set of steps leading to the top of the bank and, when Aleksander saw an orange life ring set on a stanchion, he laughed, partly in irony and partly through nervousness. The sky ahead was a deep orange color that gradually gave way to dark blue above their heads and he could smell the salt in the sea air filtering through his window. The road ahead, and the accompanying bank to keep the sea where it was supposed to be, were dead straight.

"In three point two miles, take a sharp left onto Sea Road," a woman's voice intoned from the sat nav.

The first sign of civilization a couple of miles later was a small cafe with an empty parking lot and a sole light in one window. Outside the cafe were a series of dark green picnic benches and a wooden structure with a gray roof for customers to shelter when it rained. Aleksander was surprised the wooden structure wasn't larger. It rained a lot here from what he had experienced over the last few months. Outside the window, the cafe gave way to static holiday caravans, hundreds of them all lined up facing the sea. There were lights on in a few of them, hardy souls who were early risers, perhaps. On the other side of the road, a few hundred yards later, were proper houses that wouldn't shake in the wind or be noisy in the rain. They passed a church, an ugly red brick building whose purpose was only obvious from the large wooden cross on top of the roof. Aleksander crossed himself, prompting a laugh from his brother, which he ignored.

Aleksander pitched his cigarette through the window and watched in the wing mirror as it hit the road and created a small flurry of sparks.

"Will we stop on the way?" he asked Mateo, deferring to his older brother's authority. "It's what, four hours?"

"No, it's too dangerous," Mateo replied.

"What about them?" Aleksander nodded his head in the direction of the back of the van. "The peshkop won't be impressed if we deliver them stinking of piss and shit."

"There's a hose at the farm," Mateo said, looking at his brother with a wry smile. "You can wash them down with that. You'd enjoy that, wouldn't you?"

Aleksander laughed before closing his eyes and resting his head back on the seat. He imagined the woman in the back, the blonde one, screaming as he turned an icy hose on her naked body. His brother was right.

He would enjoy that very much.

6

K atya was jolted awake as the van hit a pothole and lurched to one side. She was exhausted, not having slept in what felt like days. In fact, she realized as she wriggled to try to get comfortable, it had been days. She had worn clothes that she thought would be comfortable for the journey, a pair of slacks and a loose blouse, but if she'd known how chilly it would be on the channel, she would have worn something more substantial.

Next to her, on the hard wooden floor, Ana and Elene were curled up, almost but not quite touching, both fast asleep. As was the man in the robe. He was sitting upright, his head inclined forward slightly, and nodding with the van's movement. Was he asleep, she wondered, or was he just sitting there with his eyes closed? She studied him in the dim light from the small bulb in the roof.

He was, in Katya's estimation, somewhere between thirty and thirty-five. She had noticed on the beach that he was a few inches taller than her, which would make him around six feet tall. The way he had effortlessly carried the girls up the beach made him strong, but he wasn't muscular. It was more the wiry strength of a long-distance runner than the bulk of a footballer. He wore no jewelry, and had no tattoos or marks that she could see, although the simple gray robe covered most of his body, apart from his forearms and lower legs. His bag, currently nestled between his feet, was made of the same material as the robe. Some sort of linen, she guessed. From the size of the bag, there couldn't be much in it. Katya closed her eyes, opening them again a moment later to see that man in the robe staring at her. His face was expressionless. He was just looking at her.

"Where are you from?" Katya asked him when it was obvious he wasn't going to say anything.

"America," he replied, the briefest look of amusement in his eyes. "Texas, originally." They looked at each other for a few moments, his gaze never leaving hers. Katya would normally be uncomfortable being under such scrutiny, but the look in his eyes was somehow reassuring. "You?"

"A town called Nakra. It's in—"

"Georgia," he replied, cutting her off.

"You know it?" Katya asked, her eyebrows shooting up.

"I know of the town," the man in the robe replied, "but I've never been there."

"Have you ever been to Georgia?"

"I've been through it, yes."

"When?"

"A long time ago."

"Why were you there?" At her question, Katya saw the corners of his mouth move in an approximation of a smile. He paused for a few seconds before replying.

"God sent me."

"Did He send you here, too?"

The man in the robe's mouth returned to its starting position.

"I guess He must have. Why else would I be here?" Katya sighed. There was no answer to that question. "You speak very good English," he said.

"Thank you," she replied automatically. "So do you, for an American." This time, his smile was more pronounced, almost reaching his eyes.

"Thank you. My name is Caleb, by the way." He extended a hand for her to shake, a curious gesture under the circumstances. She took it and was surprised by the warmth in his fingertips.

"I'm Katya. Short for Ekaterina." They shook hands, and Katya didn't want to let go.

"Katya," he said slowly, rolling the final vowel with his breath. "A beautiful name." He blinked twice. "Pure."

"I'm sorry?"

"It's from the Greek for pure," Caleb said, taking his fingers from Katya's and returning his hand to his lap. She rubbed her thumb over her fingertips. "Ekaterina." Again, he extended the last vowel of her name, his Texan accent accentuating it. "What do you do?"

"For a living?" Katya asked. When he nodded his head, she continued. "I was an English teacher before the Russians came." Caleb inclined his head toward the van doors.

"And here in this green and pleasant land?" he said. "What will you do?"

"I'm to be a nanny for a rich English family. They have two boys, both four. Identical twins."

"I see," Caleb replied, his brow furrowing almost imperceptibly.

"I have to pay back the cost of the journey." Katya looked at the panel that separated them from the three men in the front and then back at Caleb, focusing on his gray robe. "How about you? What do you do?"

"I do whatever He tells me to do."

"God?"

"Who else?"

"Are you a priest?"

Caleb made a sound that was somewhere between a laugh and a cough. Katya wasn't sure.

"No."

"A monk?"

"No."

"So what are you, then? A preacher?"

A slow smile spread across Caleb's face and he looked at her. She could see amusement dancing across his gray eyes.

"Yes," he said, slowly. "You could say that, I guess."

7

The first thing Aleksander did when he woke up was reach into his pocket for his cigarettes, partly to irritate Mateo but mostly because he simply wanted one. While he had slept, fitfully and propped up against the window, the narrow roads they had been on had given way to a divided highway.

"Where are we?" he asked his brother as he held the lighter to his cigarette.

"Approaching the expressway in a few miles."

Aleksander sighed, realizing they weren't even past London yet. Although this was the fourth time they'd done this trip in as many months, it never seemed to get any shorter. He jumped as, behind him, someone banged on the partition.

"What is it?" he shouted, switching from Albanian to English.

"The girls." It was the woman, her voice muffled. "They need the bathroom." Aleksander swore under his breath.

"There's a lay by ahead that's set back from the road," Mateo said. "We can pull in there and take them into the woods." Aleksander's mood improved at the thought of watching the women urinate. A few moments later, he heard the rhythmic clicking of the turn signal as the driver prepared to pull off the road. "Take the girls first, then the other two, one at a time," Mateo instructed, as if Aleksander would be unable to manage without his direction. Then his brother kicked at a plastic bag in the well of the van. "And give them some water when they get back in."

When the van pulled to a halt, Aleksander got out of the van and crushed his cigarette under his shoe. He looked around to make sure they were the only people in the area before pulling his pistol out of his trousers. When he opened the van door, four sets of eyes stared back at him. Three of them showed fear; one of them showed none, just a curious interest. Holding the weapon loosely by his side, he gestured to the two girls with his free hand.

"You two first," he said. The girls stepped down and, with a glance at the man in the robe, Aleksander closed the door and turned the lock. Beside him, the girls were looking around them. One of them, the older of the two, said something in a language Aleksander didn't understand.

"Speak English, or don't speak at all," he barked at her, causing the girl to flinch.

"Bathroom?" she said, her voice heavily accented. He pointed at the woods a few yards away from the road.

"There. Go."

The girls mumbled to each other under their breath before gingerly making their way a few yards into the woods. The younger one started crying as she realized Aleksander was going to watch her, but her sister consoled her as she pulled down her jeans and squatted in the grass. A moment later, the other girl did the same thing.

When they got back into the van after finishing their business, Aleksander pointed at the woman.

"You next." She looked at him with disgust, but she couldn't hide the fear in her eyes.

"I don't need to go," she replied, her chin jutting forward a few inches. On the other side of the van, the man in the robe raised his hand.

"I do," he said when Aleksander looked at him. When he nodded, the man in the robe started to get to his feet.

"Leave your bag there," Aleksander said. At least it would discourage him from running if he would have to leave his worldly possessions behind.

The man in the robe paused, staring at Aleksander for a few seconds. Then he slipped the strap of the linen bag from his shoulder and handed it to the woman. Aleksander took a few steps back and, as the man in the robe got out of the van, raised his pistol. Ignoring him, the man in the robe took a few steps toward the trees and lifted his robe. A few seconds later, Aleksander heard him urinating, seemingly unfazed there was a man pointing a pistol at his back. Aleksander was half-tempted to put a bullet in him. He'd never killed a man relieving himself before, and Aleksander thought it would be an amusing story to tell back home. But if the Bosnian was dead, then there would be work to be done on the farm, and Aleksander certainly wasn't going to do that, so he lowered his arm.

A moment later, unaware that his life had been saved through Aleksander's laziness, the man in the robe was done. To his surprise, as he returned to the van, the man thanked him. Cursing under his breath as he locked the door behind him, Aleksander returned to the passenger's side and got in.

They were back on the divided highway when Aleksander remembered the bottles of water in the bag at his feet.

8

Caleb made himself comfortable in the back of the van and closed his eyes to process what he had just learned. They were heading almost due north, so were probably somewhere south of London, according to the crude map in his head. The trees he had seen were all broad-leaved, predominantly oak and ash, and the forest had seemed wild, not managed. This in itself told him nothing, but he couldn't help but tuck the knowledge away at the back of his mind.

He wore no watch, but Caleb knew it was almost midday, both from the position of the sun and the mild ache in his belly. He had not eaten since a hurried canned meal in France and neither would have the others. The next time they stopped, if they were not at their destination, he would have to ask for something, if only for the children.

Opening his eyes, he turned his attention to the two girls who were sitting side by side in silence. When he had laid his hands on them back at the beach, he could sense not only their fear but also their resilience. The older one in particular was a strong-willed young woman, more so than her sister. When he had taken Katya's hand, Caleb had sensed the same fear and the same strength, but the two attributes were overlaid with a deep sadness. He regarded her, taking advantage of the fact she had her eyes closed. Caleb hoped she was sleeping. People had a habit of realizing when he was scrutinizing them.

Katya was, Caleb realized, one of the most attractive women he had met in a long time. She had a high forehead, her blonde hair framing an oval face that was offset by a determined jawline. Her light blue eyes matched the blouse she was wearing, which Caleb knew was covering a lithe body with little, if any, excess. When he had stood to leave the van earlier, he had momentarily placed his hand on her shoulder and had felt the architecture of it through the thin material. He ran his eyes over her body, feeling a familiar sensation as he did so. Even men of God had urges and desires, and there was no true way of suppressing them.

Looking away from the woman, Caleb thought about the men in the front of the van. There were now three of them. Although he had not heard the driver speak, he shared many of the same facial and physical characteristics of the other two. They were Albanians, of that he was sure from The Smoker's tattoo. Caleb was sure he had read of a demigod in Albanian folklore who was the daughter of the sun and the moon. If he remembered correctly, and he usually did, she used points of light as a weapon. Caleb had many skills, some of them natural and some learned and honed, but that wasn't one of them.

When he had been standing by the woods, answering an unrequired call of nature, Caleb knew he could have escaped. The Smoker had relaxed his arm, Caleb had noted from his shadow, and by the time the Albanian could have raised it again, there could have been several large trees between Caleb and the weapon. But he would have to leave his bag behind, and there were things in the bag that he treasured. Not many, and much of its contents could be replaced, but there were some items that couldn't. It wasn't just the contents of the bag, though. It was also Katya and the two young girls.

Caleb had come to England for several reasons. One was that he had never visited before. Others were less obvious, but no less important. But Caleb was a believer, if not necessarily in an omnipotent being with a plan, in a higher purpose. A God of sorts is how he usually described it on the rare occasions he was asked about it. And Caleb's God of sorts had introduced him to these women and these men.

Caleb rested his head back on the cool metal side of the van and shut his eyes. He allowed a brief smile to cross his face, relishing in the unfamiliar sensation it caused in the muscles of his cheeks.

The three men in the front of the van had no idea how much trouble they were in.

9

Around twenty minutes previously, Katya had noticed the cadence of the van had changed. It felt as if they were now driving on a track of some sort. It was certainly moving more slowly, and every few moments it lurched to one side or the other. She glanced at her watch and stretched, hoping they were almost at their destination. In her lower abdomen, her bladder was like a hard ball, but at the same time, she was thirsty. It was now almost three hours since their bathroom stop. If there had been a bathroom, she would have used it, but there was no way she was going to demean herself in front of the Albanian with the gun.

"I'm hungry," Elene said from her position on the other side of the van. Her sister nodded in agreement.

"I think we're nearly there," Katya replied, smiling at the two girls to try to reassure them. "You'll be able to see your new home soon."

They had been told that they would live in an apartment on the edge of a town and shown some pictures. The apartment was small, but had two bedrooms and a postage-stamp sized garden that Elene and Ana were looking forward to seeing. But Katya was getting concerned. If they were going straight to their apartment, then why were they driving down what felt like a dirt road?

"Where do you think we're going?" Katya asked Caleb, switching to English. He stirred before replying.

"My guess is we're in a forest," he said.

"How can you tell?" It wasn't as if there was a window they could look out of.

"The sound of the engine is more muffled than it was, as if it's being muted by trees," Caleb replied, a half-smile on his face. "Plus, I can smell terpenes."

Katya sniffed. Other than her own body, she couldn't smell anything. "What are terpenes?" she asked.

"They're chemical compounds. I can smell pinene and limonene. Pine and citrus. So my guess would be we're driving along a track in a conifer forest."

When the van pulled to a halt a few moments later and the rear doors were swung open, Katya saw Caleb had been spot on. They had stopped in a clearing surrounded by dark green conifer trees. In front of the van was a squat, run-down house with a sagging roof and faded red walls. There was no town in sight, let alone an apartment. The two girls were looking around, confused, while Caleb was standing with his face angled toward the sun, his eyes closed.

Katya watched as the driver made his way toward the house and the other two men from the front of the van walked over to join them.

"Where are we?" she asked the younger of the two. "Where is the apartment?"

"We're going to be staying here for a few days," the man replied, his face neutral. "The apartment is still being prepared."

Katya looked over at the house, realizing that although it was shabby, it wasn't in as terrible a shape as she had initially thought. Next to the building was an enormous pile of logs, all sections of trunks, with an ancient chainsaw propped up against them, and an equally old tractor was some distance behind the log pile.

"I need the bathroom," she said, looking hopefully at the Albanian. He said something to the other man in his native language. The older man nodded in response.

"Follow me," the younger man said.

The interior of the building was in much better condition than the exterior. As Katya followed the man into the house, she looked around to see it was sparsely but adequately furnished. He led her through a kitchen with a large, heavily scarred table, mismatched and equally scarred chairs, and an enormous metal stove. In the corner, the driver was squatting down in front of a small white fridge, putting something in a carrier bag. Dust motes speckled in the sunlight streaming in through the window, and the air smelled musty but clean.

"In there." The man pointed at a wooden door leading off the kitchen. Katya pushed it open to see a toilet, its seat raised, and a sink. Both were like the rest of the house. Functional but clean.

Katya closed the door behind her, noticing that there was no lock. She took a step over to the sink and looked in the mirror above it. The reflection that looked back at her was exactly like her, but looked much older than when she had last looked in a mirror. Katya ran her fingers through her hair before pulling her lower eyelids down and leaning forward. Her eyes were red and raw.

There would be nothing to stop the Albanian from opening the door when she was using the toilet, but knowing there was nothing she could do about it, Katya lowered the seat, unbuttoned her jeans, and sat down. Seconds later, she was sighing with relief as her bladder emptied.

When she had used the toilet and washed her hands with a minute, hotel-sized piece of soap, Katya scooped some water up in her palms and splashed it on her face. The cool water went some way to soothing her tired eyes, but what she really needed was to sleep.

Caleb sat with his legs crossed under him, mirroring the positions that the two girls had taken up on the dusty ground in the van's shadow. He placed his palm on his sternum.

"Caleb," he said slowly before pointing at the older girl and raising his eyebrows.

"Ana," she replied a moment later, her hand on her own chest. Then she pointed at the younger one. "Elene."

He repeated their names, nodding at them in turn as he did so.

"Sisters?" he asked them. Neither replied. Elene said something to Ana that Caleb thought was a question, but she just shrugged her shoulders in response. Any attempts at further conversation were interrupted by the arrival of the driver. He threw a white plastic bag onto the ground between them and muttered something in his native language before wandering off to join the other two men standing by the front of the van.

Caleb leaned forward and opened the bag. Inside was a variety of sandwiches, wrapped in cardboard and plastic, some chips, and bottles of soda and water. He took everything out, smoothed the bag out, and placed the items on top of it. Then he held his hands out with his palms up, closing his eyes briefly to thank his God for providing them with sustenance.

"Eat, eat," he said when he reopened his eyes. The two girls were looking at the food with suspicion but made no movement toward it.

A moment later, Katya returned from the house and joined them, folding her legs and sitting so they formed a square around the food. Caleb watched as she picked up a sandwich, looked at the wrapper, and said something to the two girls. Ana nodded, a smile forming on her face, and Katya handed her the food before repeating the translation for the next sandwich. Elene, Caleb realized, was fussier than the other girl, but eventually Katya was able to give her something she liked. As they ate, the two of them chatted rapidly, and Caleb saw Katya looking at them with a smile on her face.

"They're talking about the new friends they're going to make when they start their new school," she explained to him, switching back to English. Caleb looked at her, wondering what it would be like to be able to swap languages so effortlessly. He only knew fragments of words in other languages. Some in Arabic, some in Pashto, even some in Dari, and so by extension, Farsi. All commands rather than conversation. "Cheese or chicken mayonnaise?"

"I don't mind," he replied. "Please, you choose." Behind them, the three men were carrying Katya's and the girls' bags into the house. Caleb watched the children eating. Their movements were measured, almost polite. The younger of the two dabbed at the corner of her lip with a serviette.

"How do you know the girls?" Caleb asked Katya.

"They go to the school I used to teach at," Katya replied. "I don't teach them in any of my classes, but I know them from there."

"And their parents?" A dark look crossed Katya's face at his question, and she shook her head.

"They're from the orphanage in the next town." He saw her cast her eyes down at the sandwich but knew she wasn't looking at it. She didn't want to look at him. "The war," she continued, almost in a whisper. "Or a leftover of it, at least. Their parents drove over a Russian mine which had been dislodged by a flood. They stood no chance."

Caleb looked again at the girls, trying to imagine how much pain they had already gone through in their short lives. It was probably more than him, but he had brought most of his on himself. He would ask his God later why that had happened to them, but he didn't think He would answer.

Katya ripped open the cheese sandwich and took a large mouthful, making a humming sound as she chewed. Caleb picked up the chicken sandwich, closed his eyes briefly to offer a prayer for the soul of the chicken, and opened the wrapper. He hated chicken, but fuel was fuel.

Ten minutes later, his stomach not quite full, Caleb finished his bottle of water as The Smoker returned from the house. As he approached, he gestured to Caleb that he should get to his feet. Caleb stood, brushing some crumbs from his robe as he did so.

"Now you work," the Albanian said, pointing at the pile of logs next to the house. Caleb followed his finger to see a chopping block with a wooden ax leaning up against it. "Firewood."

Aleksander sat at the kitchen table and pulled his cigarettes out of his pocket. He put one in his mouth and was about to light it when Mateo spoke.

"Not in here."

"Why not?" Aleksander replied, the flame a couple of inches away from the end of the paper tube.

"Because the peshkop is coming later."

"He's coming here?"

"Yes." Mateo glared at Aleksander until he relented and released his thumb from the lighter. He would have to go outside in a moment. "He wants to see what we have for him."

"We should have brought more," Aleksander replied. "Instead of those other women and the man."

"Those other women and the man paid for the journey. The ones we have didn't. Plus, we have a replacement for the Bosnian and we have his money."

"The man, what is he? Some sort of monk, do you think?"

"I don't know, and I don't care. Was there much in the bags?"

Aleksander tucked his cigarette back into the packet and regarded his brother.

"Not much. But they're clean now." He didn't mention the undergarments in the woman's bag that he'd very much enjoyed searching through. Now, the next time he looked at her, he would know what she was wearing beneath her clothes. Much as he loved his brother, Mateo's complete lack of interest in women disappointed him. "What time will the peshkop be here?"

Mateo glanced at his watch before replying. "An hour, maybe slightly more. Gjergj is going to collect him." He looked through the window to where the driver was standing by the van, watching over the women.

Aleksander scraped the chair back on the stone tiled floor and got to his feet. Saying nothing to his brother, he walked to the kitchen door and back outside to smoke his cigarette. As he smoked, he first watched the women for a few moments. The older one was fast asleep, lying down in the shade of the van using her jacket for a pillow. Aleksander admired her physique, running his eyes over her body while he contemplated it. Then he turned his attention to the two girls who were playing a card game of some sort. He heard them laughing as the older one put a card down on a pile of others and said something before picking up the pile.

He then walked to the side of the house, not hearing any sound of wood being chopped. When he got to the area with the log pile, he could see the man with the robe sitting on the block with the ax on his lap. He was running a whetstone over the blade and didn't appear to hear Aleksander approach. When the Albanian's shadow cast itself over the ax, the man in the robe looked up. His eyes were gray, and he had no emotion on his face. He was just looking.

"What are you doing?" Aleksander asked him, wondering where he'd got the small whetstone from.

"I'm sharpening the ax," the man said, returning his attention to his work. Aleksander watched as he gripped the ax in one hand and, with the whetstone in the other, rubbed it in small circles along the blade. Then he ran his finger horizontally over the blade before flipping the ax over and repeating the motion on the other side.

"Where did you get the stone?"

"My bag," the man replied, not looking up.

Aleksander realized that he'd not gone through the man's bag when he had searched the other ones. He would have to get it off him later, although he doubted there was much in it at all.

"Don't take too long," Aleksander said. "That wood won't chop itself."

"But if it's sharp enough," the man in the robe replied, still not looking at him, "it'll take much less time."

"Have it done by five," Aleksander replied, turning to walk away. As he did so, out of the corner of his eye, he saw the man in the robe glance at the sun before nodding.

"I will, don't worry."

Caleb ran his whetstone in a clockwise direction, moving in small circles from the toe, across the blade, and down to the beard. The ax itself was a wood splitting maul, with one side of the wedge-shaped head being a traditional ax head, albeit with no hollow ground concave section, and the other like a sledgehammer. It had a straight handle made of hickory that was close to round, and would have been a fine piece of equipment when new, or had it been properly looked after.

He reached into his bag, which was leaning up against the block he was sitting on, and pulled out a small tin of beeswax. With an index finger, he scooped some out and ran it across the blade of the ax. It was now sharp. Not too sharp or it would become embedded in the block, but it was more than sharp enough to get the job done.

Caleb got to his feet and balanced the ax in his right hand to locate the centers of gravity, both of the vertical and horizontal planes. Then he examined the handle but, apart from some minor imperfections in the wood, there was no chipping, cracking, or other defects. Given the amount of attention that had been paid to looking after it, this was a testament to the skill of the ax maker. He looked over at the house, but the Albanian was nowhere to be seen, and the man by the van looked to be engrossed in his phone. Caleb shifted his feet so they were shoulder-width apart before putting his right foot in front of the left. Holding the splitting maul in his right hand, he swung it to practice some basic strikes, blocks, and postures.

It had been a while since Caleb had handled an ax, and a much longer time since he had used one in anger. A splitting maul was very different to the imperial guard ax he had trained with, but as he moved, he adjusted his body to allow for the difference in length and weight. To his surprise, moves learned many years ago came back to him within minutes. The weapon was heavy, and he practiced stopping the blade at the end of each move. The first few times he did it, the head of the ax wavered from side to side. It wasn't by much, but it was too much for Caleb's liking. He adjusted his grip on the hickory handle until the wavering stopped. Then Caleb picked up a log and, placing it on the block, used the ax to chop some wedges from the edge. He raised the ax in a two-handed grip above his head and brought it down sharply over his right shoulder, exhaling in time with the motion and letting the weight of the ax head and gravity do as much of the work as possible. The log on the block was split into two with a satisfying thwacking sound and, as Caleb bent over to pick up one of the pieces to chop down further, he smiled.

Half an hour later, Caleb was covered in a thin sheen of perspiration. He had adjusted his robe and tied the arms around his waist so his upper body was uncovered. Beside him, the pile of chopped logs was growing while the other pile was dwindling, albeit slowly. He paused for a few moments to rest, stacking the chopped logs into a neat pile.

There were worse ways to spend the day, Caleb thought as he tilted his head back to allow the sun's rays onto his face. He breathed in deeply, savoring the fresh air. Above his head, the sun was shimmering and there was a heady smell of pine in the breeze. A few moments earlier, the wind had shifted slightly, and he caught the distinctive odor of a pig farm somewhere to the east of the farmhouse.

Caleb's satisfaction didn't last long, though. The four of them were effectively being held prisoner in a jail whose bars were location and distance. He would have no issues walking into the woods and continuing on until he found somewhere else to be. But Katya and the girls? Caleb doubted they could make the journey, and he wasn't sure he could fend for all four of them if they were as far from civilization as he feared.

His thoughts turned to Katya as he picked up the ax and prepared to resume his task. She wasn't stupid, but she was naïve. The men who were holding them were not the sort of men who organized jobs for nannies and families for children. Unless there were others with them who were, which he doubted. He had seen the way the younger Albanian had looked at Katya and the girls. He had seen many men look at many women that way over the years, and it had rarely ended well. Sometimes for the women, sometimes for the men, if there were others who were prepared to intervene. Caleb placed a log on the block and cleaved it with a single blow.

He was being left alone. No one was pointing a gun at him. But best of all?

He now had a weapon.

13

Katya knew the instant she opened her bag that someone had been through it. She was kneeling in one of the bedrooms inside the house, a large airy room with four single beds. One of them was jammed tight up against a wall, but the other three were more spread out. The bag was lying on top of the bed she had claimed for herself, nearest the door.

She lifted out her clothes in one bundle and placed them on top of the bedspread. Then she ran her fingers along the bottom of the bag, but there was nothing there. In frustration, Katya lifted the suitcase and turned it upside down, sending the remaining contents out across the linen. Her wash bag and make-up case rolled onto the floor, but she ignored them. It was definitely gone.

Katya got to her feet and made her way downstairs to the kitchen, her anger growing with each step. How dare they? They had no right to go through her things, and they had no right to take anything. When she got to the kitchen door, she pushed it open so hard that it banged back on itself, making the three men sitting at the table jump. The two

Albanians from the boat looked up at her while the third, the driver, just looked away.

"Where is it?" Katya said, folding her arms over her chest and jutting her chin out.

"Where is what?" the younger of the men said.

"My phone. Give it back, now."

"I've not got it." He was grinning at her, which only increased her anger.

"What are your names?" Katya said as the driver got to his feet and made toward the door, obviously not in the mood for an argument. She jabbed her finger at the older of the two men, who she thought was probably the one in charge. "You. What's your name?"

The two men exchanged glances and the older one muttered something to the other in Albanian. Then he returned to face Katya.

"I am Mateo, and this is Aleksander."

"Well, Mateo," Katya said, taking a step toward them, "where's my phone?"

"We're looking after it for you," he replied. "You won't be able to get a signal out here, anyway. Not with a Georgian sim card."

"Have you got a signal?" Katya shot back. "With an Albanian one?" The look on his face told her he did.

"You don't need a phone," Aleksander said, his face darkening as he slowly rose to his feet.

"But it's my phone," Katya replied, trying to keep the anger out of her voice. "You have no right to steal it."

"Listen, listen," Mateo said calmly. "You will get your phone back. Don't worry. Like I said, we're just looking after it for you."

"But it's mine," Katya said, staring at Aleksander. "You're just a thief."

Katya gasped as Aleksander's hand shot out and grabbed her just above the elbow. His fingers dug into the tender flesh and Katya's gasp turned into a cry of pain.

"You're just a..." He then spat out a word in Albanian that Katya didn't recognize, but it was clear from his tone that it was far from complementary.

Mateo said something in rapid-fire Albanian and Aleksander let go of Katya's arm. Her other hand went instinctively to rub the skin where his fingers had grabbed her. Aleksander glared at her but retook his seat.

"How long are we going to be here?" Katya asked, directing her question at Mateo. He seemed to her to be the more reasonable of the two.

"Just a few days," Mateo replied. "There's someone coming to see the girls later on today."

"Their new family?" she asked. Aleksander laughed at the question, but there was no humor in it.

"That's right," he replied, following the words with the same word he'd used a few seconds ago. "One of their new family is coming to see them."

14

"Welcome, Peshkop," Mateo said in English as he opened the passenger door to the van. He then took a step back, his head bowed slightly, to allow the man inside to climb down.

"Thank you, Mateo," the man replied, "but please, call me Martin."

"As you wish, Martin," Mateo said.

The new arrival was in his mid-sixties, taller than Mateo by a couple of inches, and had an expanse of fat around his midriff that must have taken years of fine dining and drinking to accumulate. A spider's web of fine, red veins sprinkled his nose. He looked around curiously, as if he had never seen a forest before. The sun was just beginning to set behind the trees, casting an orange glow into the sky, and above the forest, red kites were soaring in the thermals it produced.

"Did you have a pleasant trip?" Mateo asked conversationally as they made their way to the farmhouse.

"I did, thank you," Martin replied. "He's a man of few words, your driver."

"Gjergj?" Mateo laughed. "Yes, he is. That's one of the reasons he's such an excellent driver. He doesn't feel the need to constantly talk in either Albanian or English."

"Indeed," Martin replied, slowing to a stop a few feet away from the farmhouse door. "Tell me about your guests."

"There are two girls and one woman. Plus, a man who is helping us out."

"I thought you had a Bosnian to do that?"

"We did," Mateo replied, pausing for a few seconds before continuing. "He went to work on a pig farm."

"I see. And the girls? They are as I specified?"

"Yes, Peshkop," Mateo said. "I believe so."

"And the woman?"

"She is late-twenties, perhaps early thirties at a push." Mateo saw a frown appear on Martin's forehead. "But still useful, I'm sure. She speaks very good English."

"I was told late-teens," Martin said, his frown deepening. "She is less useful if she is older."

Mateo didn't reply. There was nothing he could say. He had been surprised when the woman had arrived on the beach and she was older than he had been told. But the only choice he had was to bring her or to leave her, and he would rather have something than nothing.

"What do they know?" Martin asked, taking another step toward the door.

"The woman's waiting for her apartment to be prepared, and the girls are waiting for their adoptive family."

"Excellent, excellent," Martin replied, gesturing to the door. "Shall we go in?"

"Certainly, Martin," Mateo said, pushing the door open for the other man. "We have some Skrapar spirit to welcome you with."

Inside the kitchen, Aleksander got to his feet as Martin

walked in. On the table was a bottle of rakia, a potent spirit distilled from crushed grapes, and three glasses. Aleksander had lit the stove as instructed, and Mateo was concerned for a moment that it was too hot inside the room.

"Welcome, Peshkop," Mateo heard Aleksander say. The way he said the word *peshkop* told Mateo that his brother had already started the welcome party without them. He watched as Aleksander picked up the bottle and poured transparent liquid into the glasses. "This is a bottle from Muzhakë we brought especially for you. It's the village that makes the finest rakia in the country."

"Very kind of you," Martin said, lifting the glass and inspecting the contents. Mateo glanced at his brother, who he knew couldn't have a clue which village the rakia was from. It certainly wasn't from Muzhakë, where just the name on the bottle would double its price. "It smells rather potent," Martin continued as he sniffed the glass.

Acting in unison, Mateo and Aleksander raised their glasses and Martin clinked his off each of theirs in turn.

"Gëzuar!" Mateo said, followed by Aleksander.

"Cheers," Martin replied before tipping the glass back and emptying it. Mateo looked at him, surprised, having just taken a small sip from his own glass.

Martin coughed once and, as Mateo watched, his face began to flush.

"My word," he said, looking at Mateo with teary eyes. "That's rather cheeky."

TWENTY MINUTES LATER, after several more glasses of rakia, Mateo picked up the bottle and placed it on a counter, shaking his head at Aleksander when he was sure Martin couldn't see him.

"Peshkop?" Mateo said, waiting until the man looked at him. "Perhaps you would like to meet the guests now?"

A broad grin spread over Martin's face. He belched once, pressing his hand to his sternum as he did so.

"That would be perfect. Thank you, Mateo," Martin replied. "I am very much looking forward to meeting them."

15

"**B**ut what if he doesn't like us, Katya?"

Katya sighed as she brushed at Ana's hair. Her constant questions since they had been told a man from the adoption people was going to visit were getting on her nerves. But at the same time, she couldn't imagine what it must be like for the two girls. First to lose their parents, then to leave their homes. They were going to be starting new lives in a new country, just as she was, and Katya was nervous enough herself about the prospect.

"Of course he'll like you, Ana," Katya said in a reassuring tone. "What's not to like? Look at you. You're pretty." She paused for a moment with the brush poised in mid-air. "You're also ticklish." As she said this, Katya squeezed the side of Ana's abdomen, where she had seen her sister tickling her earlier as the girls had played. But Ana didn't giggle, she just wriggled away from Katya with an annoyed humph.

"Where's Elene?" Ana asked as Katya wriggled closer to her on the bed to resume brushing her hair.

"She's in the bathroom."

"She's taking forever."

"She won't be much longer." Katya looked over at the other side of the room where Caleb was sitting on his bed. He looked uncomfortable in the way he was sitting, and he had his blanket draped over his lower legs even though it was still quite warm.

As if she had heard them talking, Elene walked back into the bedroom just as Katya mentioned her dawdling. She was wearing a summery dress made of a light material with brightly colored flowers. Elene twirled around, fanning the skirt as she did so.

"What do you think, Katya?" Elene asked. Unlike her sister, she was smiling and looked enthusiastic about the forthcoming evening. Katya looked at her, realizing for the first time that Elene was on the cusp of womanhood. "Do you like it?"

"It's a lovely dress, Elene. You look gorgeous. What do you think, Caleb?" she asked. Caleb looked up and Katya realized she'd spoken to him in Georgian, so she switched to English. "Do you like the dress?"

Caleb smiled at both girls in turn.

"They both look beautiful," he said before looking at her. "And so do you."

Katya felt an unexpected heat rising to her cheeks at his words. She had changed into the smartest clothes she had brought with her, a light green chiffon blouse and pale tan linen pants. Both items were heavily creased, but in the absence of an iron, there was nothing she could do about that. She wondered if he was going to be involved in meeting the man from the adoption agency, but when Mateo arrived to collect them a few moments later, he made no effort to get to his feet.

"Are you all ready?" Mateo asked. He looked nervous, but Katya didn't know why. She knew money had changed hands to arrange the adoption. Not how much money, but she thought it was a lot. The girl's aunt, who lived in America, had apparently funded the adoption. Katya had initially been skeptical when Elene had told her this earlier, not understanding why, if they had an aunt, she wasn't adopting them herself. Perhaps Mateo was concerned that the arrangements would fall through and he and his pig of a brother would be left with two children to look after. "He's waiting for us in the kitchen."

After a fleeting look at Caleb, Mateo led them down the stairs. He gave the three of them a once over outside the kitchen door before pushing it open for Elene and Ana to walk through. Elene took Ana's hand as they did so, hissing instructions under her breath.

"Smile, and be nice."

The interior of the kitchen was stifling, the air redolent with wood smoke and alcohol. Katya walked in and stood behind the girls, blinking to adjust to the bright light from a single electric bulb in the ceiling that threw everything into sharp relief. Behind the table was the man from the adoption agency. To Katya's surprise, he was much older than she had been expecting. For some reason, she thought he would be closer to her own age than double it.

"This must be Ana and Elene," the man said in English, extending his arms out. He had an immense belly and a rosy face which was split with an alcohol infused smile. "I am Martin. I've been looking forward to meeting you for a long time." Standing behind him, swaying slightly, was Aleksander.

Katya felt Mateo prodding her in the small of the back with his finger.

"Translate for them," he whispered. Katya did as instructed before adding some words of her own.

"Say hello, in English. Like we practiced."

Both Ana and Elene said hello to Martin in his native tongue, which broadened his smile even further. It slipped slightly as he looked directly at Katya.

"And you are?" he asked, his tone much more business-like.

"I'm Katya," she replied. She was about to tell him she was an English teacher and was going to be working as a nanny when he cut her off.

"How old are you?"

Katya paused before replying. She'd not been expecting that question.

"I'm twenty-eight," she said, watching as Martin turned to Mateo and gave him an almost imperceptible shake of the head.

"What do you think, Martin?" Katya heard Mateo asking from behind her. The older man thought for a few seconds before he replied.

"I think they're both absolutely perfect." He was smiling and staring at Ana and Elene as he said this. There was something in the way that he spoke that had an unexpected effect on Katya.

It sent a shiver down her spine.

16

Caleb shifted himself on the bed, trying to make himself comfortable. His shoulders were aching after he had spent what had ended up being most of the day chopping wood. The unfamiliar repeated motion had caused aching in his trapezoid muscles and the tops of both arms. It was a good ache, though. Caleb missed being as active as he used to be. The wood pile of un-chopped wood was, he estimated, probably half the size it had been when he had started. He knew he could have completed it in a single day, but he had no reason to. He closed his eyes and tried to make out the conversation from below in the kitchen, but all he could hear were muffled voices, mostly male.

On occasion, he could hear Katya's voice, translating perhaps for Ana and Elene. His thoughts turned to his situation and that of Katya and the girls. The Albanians were almost certainly criminals, which wasn't necessarily a bad thing. Of the groups of hostage takers, there were worse. Terrorists had to be right up there, with a real chance of not surviving. Military and paramilitary were probably next in Caleb's opinion, depending on the reasons for capture. Criminals were probably right in the middle of the hierarchy, above the mentally ill and the emotionally distraught, although the lines between them were often blurred.

Mentally putting Katya and the girls to one side for the moment, because they weren't aware they had been kidnapped, Caleb analyzed his own feelings. He felt no panic or disbelief at his situation. It wasn't the first time his movements had been restricted by armed men, and probably wouldn't be the last, depending on where his God sent him.

Caleb had gone, he surmised, straight into the hypervigilance stage of the normal stages of adaptation to captivity. Except there was nothing normal about him. The characteristics of that stage almost described the way he lived his life. Wary and alert to minute details. On more than one occasion, those attributes had saved both his life and the lives of others.

In his head, he listed the stress reactions to captivity, remembering being taught them a long time ago. What had happened to them had been so low key it didn't feel like a kidnapping, and indeed, Katya and the girls had not yet fully realized the depths of their predicament. Even though they spoke no English, Caleb knew at some point he needed to speak to Katya alone. In the meantime, Caleb would focus on what he did best. Maintaining his composure by being low key and unprovocative.

Overt resistance would be counterproductive. Caleb had seen more than one man die of masculinity in such situations. Resistance, when it came, would need to be swift and brutal. Fortunately, Caleb thought as the door to the bedroom was opened, he could do both, but only when required. Until then, he would just watch. At least he now had one weapon, currently leaning up against the side of the house near the kitchen door.

"Hey, Caleb," Katya said as she walked into the bedroom, followed by Ana and Elene. Caleb looked at her. Her voice was strong and confident, but underneath it was an undercurrent of fear. "Ana? Elene? Brush your teeth and get ready for bed."

With exaggerated sighs, the two girls went to their bags to retrieve their wash bags and nightclothes. Katya waited until they had left for the bathroom before turning to Caleb.

"Are you okay? You've not moved an inch," she asked him.

"All good, Katya."

"Have you been meditating?" Katya said, slightly too loudly.

"Something like that, yes. How was it?"

Katya glanced at the door before returning her attention to Caleb. When she next spoke, her voice was almost a whisper.

"We'll talk when they're asleep. I want to speak to you."

Caleb nodded in reply and watched as Katya picked up her own wash bag. She looked at him again before leaving for the bathroom, and he could see the uncertainty in her eyes. *That is good*, Caleb thought as he adjusted his position on the bed. The sooner Katya realized their predicament, the better.

Outside, he could hear footsteps in the gravel outside the farmhouse. Three sets, he discerned after listening for a few seconds. There had been three sets earlier when the van had arrived, so the only occupant of the farmhouse now was

The Smoker. *That too is good*. Potentially an opportunity, subject to a couple of barriers to be overcome. But they could be overcome, and when they were, Caleb would be two things.

Swift and brutal.

17

"Come on, you two," Katya said, keeping her voice as light as she could. "Stop messing about and brush your teeth." She wanted to get them both tucked up in bed as soon as possible so she could talk to Caleb. They were going to have to do something.

Nothing had been said earlier by either Martin or the other two that was untoward. They had talked about the potential places that the two girls could live in the future, just as soon as all the paperwork had been sorted out. Katya had observed Martin as he spoke to them, noticing the occasional sideways glances he gave, especially to Elene. At least as their translator, Katya could moderate what they were told. She only changed a few things. The weeks that the paperwork would take became days, the inclination that the girls would need to work to contribute to their keep was changed to a random story about a potential house near a playground. Katya was careful to maintain the idea, at least in their minds, that there was nothing different from what they thought.

As they had talked, Katya had also kept a close eye on

the two Albanians. Aleksander, who had sat in silence for most of the evening in the corner of the kitchen, was taking surreptitious swigs from a small hip flask whenever he sensed Mateo wasn't watching. By contrast, Mateo hardly drank anything at all, but ensured that Martin's glass never dropped below half-full. By the time Martin stood to leave, he was red-faced and wore a smile only drunk men wore.

"What a thoroughly pleasant evening it has been," he had said as they all stood to say their goodbyes. His gaze had lingered on Elene again, for too long. It sent another shiver down Katya's spine as she considered what he might be thinking. "Mateo, come. We have much to discuss on the way back to the station."

The girls finished brushing their teeth, arguing over which toothbrush went into which glass for a moment before Katya hurried them along.

"Enough, get into bed and go to sleep," she told them, not unkindly. "I'll be in shortly."

Alone, Katya looked at herself in the mirror, wondering how she was going to get them all out of this predicament. As she cleaned her own teeth, she considered for a moment whether they should try to leave straight away before Mateo returned. The problem with that was she did not know how long he would be. Nothing had been said about how far away the station was. It could be an hour or more, or it could be much closer. Besides, where would they go? It was nighttime, there was no light outside apart from the moon and the stars, and she had no idea how much either would help them.

When she returned to the bedroom, to her relief, both the girls had done as instructed and got into their beds. She could hear them whispering to each other as she crossed to where Caleb was sitting on his own bed.

"Caleb, we need to leave," she said under her breath. He looked at her and nodded.

"Yes, we do."

"When?"

"Not now," he replied. "Perhaps tomorrow."

"But where will we go?" Katya asked. Caleb thought for a moment before replying.

"Let me worry about that part. Close your eyes for a second." Katya did as instructed. "Now, you're standing at the kitchen door looking straight out at the tree line. Imagine moving your eyes to the ten o'clock position. There's a small gap in the trees just there. It's about a hundred yards from the farmhouse to the forest. Flat ground. Easy to sprint over."

Katya shook her head from side to side. "I don't remember a gap in the trees."

"It's there, trust me. That will be where we will leave from. So when the time comes, if we're not together, that's where we will meet. You, me, and the two girls."

"How will I know when the time comes?"

"You'll know."

They were interrupted by a loud bang on the landing outside the bedroom, followed by a muttered phrase in Albanian. Katya looked up to see Ana and Elene, on the other side of the room, sitting up and pulling their bedding up to their necks. A second later, the bedroom door crashed open. It was Aleksander, holding a pistol in one hand. The second they saw the gun, both girls screamed.

"Shut up," Aleksander barked, rolling the two words together as one. Katya felt Caleb putting his hand on hers, but it did nothing to assuage her terror. The Albanian was drunk. Very drunk. And he was staring at Elene. "You." With his free hand, he pointed at the young woman. "Get up."

"Aleksander!" Katya said, letting go of Caleb's hand and getting to her feet. She made her way around him so that she was standing between the Albanian and Elene. As she moved, her eyes were fixed on the black pistol in his hand. "Aleksander," she said again, this time in a quieter voice. "Don't do this."

He stared over her shoulder, directly at Elene.

"Get up. You're coming with me."

"No, Aleksander," Katya said. "No, she's not."

A few seconds later, Katya was staring straight down the barrel of the pistol as, behind her, both girls shrieked. Despite Aleksander's drunken state, the gun was rock steady, and she felt her knees trembling as adrenaline coursed through her. Until a few moments before, she had never even seen a gun in real life. Now one was pointing straight at her.

"Yes, she is," he said, this time staring straight at Katya. "She needs to be taught a lesson."

18

C aleb watched as Aleksander and Katya stared at each other over the top of the barrel of his pistol. He adjusted his legs underneath him so he could see Katya over Aleksander's shoulder but knew there was nothing he could do to help her. He considered saying something, even if only to distract Aleksander's attention, but he didn't want to make an already dangerous situation worse.

The expression on Katya's face was a mix of terror and determination. She licked her lips briefly, pressing them together after she did so, and Caleb could see a small vein pulsing in her temple. Her heart was racing, that much Caleb could determine.

"Aleksander," Caleb heard Katya say. "You don't need to point the gun at me. Please, put it down. You're scaring Elene and Ana." They faced each other for a few seconds. "Please, Aleksander. Ana's only eleven."

Very good, Caleb thought. Whether or not she realized it, Katya was saying all the right things to try to de-escalate the situation. Using the girls' first names and their ages to personalize them, and trying to deflect the Albanian's attention from Elene, whom he seemed to be more interested in. Whether Aleksander was too drunk to respond, only the next few moments would tell.

"She needs to learn," Aleksander said, his voice slurring. "She needs to learn what she needs to do." Caleb saw the color draining from Katya's face as she finally comprehended the situation, but to his relief, Aleksander lowered the pistol. Katya opened her mouth to say something but closed it again before she looked at Caleb, helplessness written all over her face.

"Elene's only a child, Aleksander," Katya said a moment later.

"She's a child now," Aleksander replied with a cruel sneer, "but she'll be a woman by the time I'm done with her."

"This isn't you, Aleksander." Caleb watched as Katya took a small step toward him. Her expression had changed. She no longer appeared helpless, but resigned. "She's a child." Caleb saw Katya reach out her hand and take Aleksander's free hand in hers. She pressed it to her breast. "I'm not a child. I'm a woman." She dropped her hand to her side, leaving Aleksander's where it was. Caleb saw his knuckles whiten as he squeezed Katya, and he saw her eyes flickering in pain, but she said nothing. A moment later, Aleksander moved his hand and grabbed Katya by the upper arm, propelling her toward the door.

Caleb looked at the children as the door slammed shut behind Aleksander and Katya. They stared back at him, both with tears streaming down their faces. Elene asked Caleb a question that he couldn't understand. In response, he beckoned them with both hands.

A moment later, with Elene huddled on one side of him

and Ana on the other, Caleb put his arms around the girls and pulled their heads toward him. He made sure one side of their heads was snug against his midriff, an ear to the material of his robe, before he slipped his palms down over their other ears.

In the room next door, Caleb could hear Aleksander shout something in Albanian. He closed his eyes, not wanting to imagine what Katya was being put through. Caleb heard a slap, followed by Katya screaming. There was another slap, and another scream that was cut short. He heard male grunting, followed by more shouting from Aleksander. What Caleb heard next surprised him. It was laughter. Not Alexander's, but Katya's. There was another slap, but it only served to increase the volume of her laughter. Then Katya's laughter stopped abruptly, replaced by shuffling and banging. A scream. Katya.

Even Caleb flinched at the sound of the gunshot. With the screams of the girls still ringing in his ears, Caleb heard another sound he recognized well.

It was the sound of a body falling to the floor, followed by silence.

19

As the van bounced along the rutted track, Mateo was glad that he'd eased up on the rakia when he had. He was feeling nauseated already, and they still had some way to go before they reached what passed for a main road in these parts. Martin, by contrast, seemed unaffected by the bouncing motion of the van. Mateo eased down the window on the passenger side by a couple of inches to let some fresh air into the cabin.

"So, it was an uneventful trip over?" Martin asked him. Mateo, choosing not to mention the old woman his brother had tipped over the side of the boat, nodded in response.

"It was, yes," he said. "Mostly uneventful, and we got them all here."

"Indeed you did, Mateo, and you will be paid well for your troubles." *Just not as much as you'll be getting,* Mateo thought, but he kept his own counsel.

"Where will you be taking them?" Mateo asked. "The girls."

"The studio's set up for the shoot already. Once that's done, the older of the two will go to London, at least to start off with." Martin hiccoughed, and the air in the cabin was filled with the smell of rakia. Mateo inched his window down a bit more. "The younger one has a buyer lined up in Liverpool. But there'll be plenty of people at the post-filming party tomorrow first."

It was Martin's use of the word *buyer* that gave Mateo pause for thought. Both he and Aleksander had been under no illusions that their cargo was just that, cargo, but they'd never spoken of it in such explicit terms. Mateo hadn't known about any sort of shoot, but it was none of his business, anyway. He wondered for a few moments what sort of men bought girls, but in the criminal world, just as in the business world, cash was king. And he and Aleksander were receiving a lot for their part in the girl's journey.

"What about the woman?" Mateo asked. "Where will she go?"

"Ah, yes, the lovely Katya. She is, alas, too old and no doubt too experienced for most of my clients." Martin paused for a moment before looking at Mateo with a sideways grin. "I might keep her for myself. I could do with a housekeeper. When she has served her purpose, there're plenty of places in the provinces where she could provide value. Milton Keynes, perhaps. Maybe Nottingham."

Mateo, who hadn't a clue where either Milton Keynes or Nottingham were, kept silent. The thought of Katya serving as Martin's housekeeper, where most of her services would be provided in the bedroom, was inconsequential to him. Like what would become of the girls. He could put things like that into a box in his mind and close it.

"When is your next trip planned?" Martin asked Mateo a few moments later. Outside the van, the road was becoming less rutted as the forest became more spread out.

"Perhaps in a month or so," Mateo replied. "It will

depend on the weather. The difficulty is as the weather gets better, the price of the boats increases."

"Why don't you just get a bigger boat," Martin said. "Bring more over at a time?"

"The authorities target the larger boats first. Better return for their time." Mateo stared out of the window as the trees gave way to open farmland. There was just enough light left in the sky for him to make out isolated animal huts in fenced off clearings. "We need to keep this fairly small scale. The more product we bring, of the type you need, the more risk there is that there'll be, shall we say, unwelcome attention."

"Indeed, Mateo," Martin replied. "Very wise." Mateo looked at him as he said this, realizing that his expression had become much harder. "But you must bring me what I ask for. That woman? I can get precious little for her."

"Then we'll keep her. If you have no use for her."

"No, Mateo, you will not. I have already said I can and I will use her. But I will not pay for her."

Mateo winced at the thought of ten thousand pounds disappearing, just like that. But the prices that the girls commanded would offset that.

THIRTY MINUTES LATER, much of which had been spent in uncomfortable silence, the van pulled into the station car park. Mateo peered at the small buildings that made up the isolated halt. The only trains that would stop here would be small, local trains that stopped at every station between here and London. Martin could be getting off at any one of them. Mateo had no idea, and didn't care, where the man lived.

"Have them delivered here," Martin said, pressing a

piece of paper into Mateo's hand. He opened the door and the interior light came on. Mateo glanced at the address, not recognizing the town. "The day after tomorrow. The party's not until a few days later, but I want them under my control, including the woman. I don't trust that brother of yours." Mateo said nothing. Neither did he, but before he'd left the farm, he'd made sure Aleksander knew not to touch anyone.

"Have a pleasant trip back," Mateo said. Martin didn't reply, but just got out of the van and started walking toward the station.

Mateo turned to Gjergj, who was watching Martin. Although he wouldn't have understood a word of the conversation that had taken place earlier, he summed Martin up without it.

"What a pig of a man," Gjergj said in Albanian.

Mateo just nodded.

20

Aleksander looked at the prone form of the woman on the bedroom floor. He had sobered up almost straight away when the gun had gone off, but the fact she was lying in front of him wasn't his fault. It was hers.

"Shit," Aleksander muttered under his breath, prodding her body with his foot. Mateo was going to kill him.

He pulled his hip flask out of his pocket and unscrewed the lid, half-emptying it in a single motion. The last thing that Mateo had said before he left was that he wasn't to touch any of them. Aleksander figured the girl wouldn't have said a word about what he had planned to do to her. Or, more specifically, what he had planned to get her to do to him. Then the woman had offered herself to him on a plate in exchange. But now this.

Aleksander crouched down next to the woman and rolled her onto her back. He looked at the front of her blouse, but when he grabbed the material, he realized he couldn't re-button it, as they had been torn away. Aleksander thought for a few moments, wondering what the best story to come up with would be. He knew he couldn't leave her here, in his own bedroom. There was no version of events that Mateo would believe that involved her being in there with him.

He grunted, a plan forming in his mind. There was gas in the tractor's tank. He could take her down to the pig farm and just say that she had escaped. But Aleksander knew that this wouldn't look good for him. He would have to claim that she had overpowered him somehow, disarmed him, and then fled. Mateo, even if he believed the story, would think him weak for allowing such a situation to occur. It wasn't just that, though, Aleksander realized as he looked at his watch. He wouldn't have time, and the pigs might not have time either. If he spun that tale and Mateo found anything left at the pig farm, then that would be worse.

Aleksander sat back on his haunches and emptied the hip flask. He was going to have to put her back into her own bedroom and then tell Mateo a version of what had happened. That she had gone for his gun and they had struggled. That the gun had gone off in the struggle.

He stood, rolling his shoulders back, and winced as a joint cracked in his neck. Then he leaned forward and grabbed hold of the woman's wrists. As he dragged her across the floor, he reflected on how heavy a human body was when it was a dead weight.

As he pushed the door to her bedroom open with his back and dragged her inside, the two girls started screaming before he silenced them with a glare. The man in the robe remained silent as Aleksander manhandled the woman to her bed before grabbing the back of her linen pants. Aleksander hauled her onto it, grunting as he did so. He swiped his forehead with the back of his hand, surprised at the perspiration. Then he turned to look at the man in the robe who was sitting cross-legged on the bed, just as he had been all evening. He was looking at Aleksander with no genuine expression that he could discern, his gray eyes almost as devoid of life as the woman's.

Aleksander laughed, prompting a whimper from one of the girls. The man in the robe could stare at him all he wanted.

You couldn't hurt a man by just looking.

aleb knew, with absolute certainty, the moment Aleksander took Katya with him, that the Albanian would not die a natural death. The sound of the gunshot only confirmed that.

Ana and Elene waited until the door had closed behind the Albanian before they threw their bedding off and hurried across the room to where Katya was lying on the bed.

"It's okay," Caleb said. Even though he knew they wouldn't be able to understand him, he hoped they would pick up on the reassurance he was trying to put into his tone. "She'll be okay. Katya's just unconscious."

Caleb knew that saying this was risky. Katya could be far from okay, but he was basing his assumption on several things. The first was that there were no signs of external hemorrhage. While this didn't mean that Katya hadn't taken a bullet, Caleb had never seen anyone take one and not bleed at all. He'd seen both sides of her body as Aleksander had manhandled her onto the bed, and there was nothing obvious that suggested she'd been shot. No dark holes in her clothing with telltale powder marks from the discharge of a weapon at close quarters.

But just because there was no blood to be seen didn't mean she wasn't bleeding. A thigh could hold a liter of blood without a drop touching the floor. The chest, between three and four. And the abdomen could hold more than Katya's entire blood volume, again without a drop to be seen. But such catastrophic internal blood loss also came with other signs such as cyanosis, the telltale blue tinge of the seriously wounded. He could, from where he was sitting, see one of Katya's earlobes. It was pink and well perfused, not pale or cyanotic.

The third thing Caleb could see that backed up his assumption was the rhythmic, albeit shallow, rise and fall of her shoulders as she breathed. No agonal breathing, no gasping for air.

He watched as Elene, taking charge of the situation, leaned forward and shook Katya's shoulder. She said Katya's name, followed by something that Caleb didn't understand. There was a brief exchange of words between the girls and Ana got to her feet, hurrying out of the room. When she returned, she had a damp flannel in her hands that Elene used to wipe Katya's brow. Caleb shifted his position on the bed and Elene looked over at him, saying something in an angry voice. Caleb knew she was asking him why he wasn't helping them, but if he told them why, that would only scare them more.

A moment later, they were rewarded by a deep groan from Katya. Caleb exhaled, not aware that he'd been holding his breath. His best guess was that Katya had been pistol whipped or hit with something, rendering her unconscious. But there was still a lot that could go wrong in the skull from such an action. An intracranial bleed could cause swelling, pushing the brain stem down through the base of the skull. A diffuse axonal injury, or bruising to the brain where internal structures were sheared, might not make its presence felt for hours or even days.

Katya groaned again, and Caleb saw her moving. That was good.

"Katya?" he said in an authoritative voice that made both girls jump. "Can you hear me?" She rolled onto her back and turned her head to look at him. That, too, was good. Her eyes were glazed, and he watched as she struggled to focus on him. "Katya?" Elene made to mop her brow again, but Katya pushed her hand away and struggled to sit up. "Katya, stay where you are," Caleb said, but she ignored him, swinging her legs over the bed and sitting on the edge for a moment. Caleb could see beads of perspiration on her forehead.

Then she lurched to her feet, swaying a couple of times, and rushed across the room to the door. A few seconds later, Caleb heard the sound of retching. While that wasn't good, the fact that Katya was moving was.

But it wasn't going to change Aleksander's life expectancy.

22

Katya's stomach contracted again, and she groaned as she heaved, but there was nothing left for her to bring up. She was kneeling in front of the bowl, eyes closed, so she wouldn't have to look at what her body had just ejected. With a groan, she got to her feet a moment later and flushed before closing the lid.

Walking across the small bathroom to the sink, she splashed some cold water onto her face before regarding herself in the mirror. On the left side of her jaw was an angry reddened area where Aleksander had punched her, seconds after the gun which she'd failed to wrestle from his grasp had gone off. Her head had been snapped to the side, the blow so hard she was out for the count before she even reached the floor. Katya had never been hit like that before. The worst fight she'd ever been in had been at school and had only involved some slapping and attempts at hair pulling by the girl she was fighting with, but it had ended before it had really begun.

Katya opened and closed her jaw a couple of times. It was painful, but as she traced her fingers over the red skin, she didn't think anything was broken. She used her tongue to feel around the inside of her mouth, finding a cut with the tip of her tongue but, to her relief, no loose teeth. She was just about to splash some more water on her face when there was a soft knock at the door. It was Elene, who was peering around the jamb with a look of concern on her face.

"Are you okay, Katya?" the girl said. Katya forced herself to smile. She could see Ana just behind Elene, her face wearing the same expression.

"I'm fine, Elene," Katya replied. "I just stumbled and banged my head."

"What about the gunshot?" Ana asked, stretching up on tiptoes to see over her sister's shoulder.

"Aleksander saw a big wild pig outside the farmhouse," Katya replied, broadening her smile. "So he fired into the air to make the big piggy run away." Neither of the girls smiled, and Katya knew they didn't believe her.

"Why didn't the man help you?" Elene asked. "The man in the dress?"

"Caleb?" Katya said. "I'm not sure. But it's a robe, not a dress."

"Can we trust him?" The look on Elene's face told Katya that the girl didn't care what Caleb's garments were called.

"Yes, we can trust him," Katya said, trying to keep the uncertainty out of her voice.

WHEN THEY RETURNED to the bedroom, Caleb beckoned Katya over to him. Hesitating at first, she did as instructed and sat down on the bed next to him, aware that as she crossed the room, his eyes were running up and down her body. But it wasn't in a lascivious way.

"Look at me, Katya," he said. When she did so, he raised

his fingers and put them on either side of her face, just in front of her ears. His touch was so gentle she wasn't even sure he was touching her. "Open your mouth." She did so. "Any pain?"

"It's sore."

"Can you move your jaw from side to side?" She could. "Show me your teeth. Are any loose?" Katya shook her head. "He punched you?"

"Yes," Katya replied, her voice almost a whisper. Caleb nodded his head once, and she thought she saw a look of resignation cross his face, but as soon as it appeared, it was gone. "You couldn't help me?" Katya continued, keeping her voice low so the girls wouldn't hear.

Caleb dropped his hands to her shoulders, and she felt him pushing her to the side by a couple of inches. When he looked over her shoulder at Elene and Ana, she realized he was trying to block their view. She let herself be moved and then watched as Caleb moved the blanket that was covering his feet.

"I would have if I could have, Katya," he said in a low voice. She looked down and saw a thick shackle around one of his ankles with a heavy linked chain running under the blanket. The skin around the shackle was excoriated and bleeding. Katya gasped and Caleb put his finger on her lips.

"Oh, my God," she said. "What are we going to do?"

Caleb smiled at her as he re-covered his feet with the blanket.

"Don't worry, Katya," he said, his voice changed by the smile. "This ain't my first rodeo."

23

"You did what?" Mateo said, clenching and unclenching his fists underneath the kitchen table. Across the scarred wood, Aleksander was sitting with his head bowed, reeking of alcohol.

"I had no choice, Mateo," Aleksander replied. "She went for the gun."

"Why would she do that? What were you doing to her at the time?"

"Nothing."

"I don't believe you. Wait here."

Mateo got to his feet while Aleksander reverted to how he always was when Mateo was angry with him. Sullen and silent, just like he had been since they were children. Ignoring his brother, Mateo made his way out of the kitchen and up the stairs of the farmhouse, muttering to himself as he did so. When he reached the door to the bedroom, he opened it as quietly as he could to see the man in the robe and the woman sitting on the man's bed, illuminated by a small bedside lamp. They both looked up at him as he walked in. With a quick glance at the two girls, who were both fast asleep, he took a couple of steps toward them and looked at her face. Mateo swore in Albanian as he saw the bruising on the side of her jaw. He'd been the recipient of a few smacks from his younger brother over the years and knew he could pack a punch.

The woman, Katya, was staring at him in defiance. For a few seconds, Mateo thought about apologizing for his brother's actions. But what would be the point of that? She was, after all, worthless to them, valuable only in that she would keep them in Martin's good books. At least, until he tired of her. Without a word, Mateo turned and left the room.

He made his way back down the stairs, thinking as he did so. It could have been worse, Mateo knew. Aleksander could, even when sober, dish out quite a beating. There had been a woman, a whore back in Albania, who had angered him somehow. Mateo couldn't remember what about or even what her name was. The only thing he could remember was her smashed face and the fact it had taken her three days to die in a local hospital. By the time he got to the kitchen, Mateo was still angry but somewhat mollified that the damage wasn't too bad.

"You're a fucking idiot," Mateo said as he walked back into the kitchen. Aleksander didn't look at him until Mateo put a shot glass full of rakia down on the table in front of him. He raised his own glass in his brother's direction. "Gëzuar."

"Gëzuar," Aleksander replied, picking up the glass with a faint smile on his face. Mateo half-emptied his glass before refilling it.

"So, what happens next?" Aleksander asked as he sipped his own glass, their argument seemingly forgotten.

"Martin wants the woman," Mateo replied.

"I'm sure he does, the dirty old fuck."

"But he's not paying for her because she's too old." Mateo heard his brother swearing, but he ignored him. No thanks to him, with any luck the bruise on her face would have gone down by the time she started working for Martin. If it wasn't, perhaps it would be covered up with some fresh ones if she was a bit feisty. "He wants the girls delivered to him the day after tomorrow."

"Where?"

"I have no idea. I have the address. Gjergj will know where it is."

"And the money?"

"Martin will pay," Mateo said, sipping his rakia. "He always does."

"We should charge him more. We could probably charge him double and still get paid." Aleksander was many things, Mateo thought as he regarded his brother, but he was no businessman. "What of tomorrow?"

"We'll put the man to work and she can clean the house." Mateo looked around the kitchen, noticing the dirty glasses and plates piled up next to the sink. "This place is a pigsty. You and Gjergj can go into the town to get some supplies. There's hardly any food in the place."

"What, you want me to go shopping?"

"Yes, Aleksander. I want you to go shopping." Mateo glared at him. "Now finish your drink and go to bed." He held his brother's stare until the look of defiance on his face had dissipated.

"As you wish, vëlla."

"You'll do well to remember that, Aleksander. I am your vëlla, your brother. That position comes with responsibilities that work both ways, or had you forgotten that?"

Mateo looked at Aleksander, who was staring at the

kitchen table. Would he apologize for not respecting his older brother's instructions not to touch any of their guests? As Aleksander got to his feet without a word, Mateo realized he wasn't going to. He sighed, looking forward to a few moments alone with only the rest of the rakia for company.

Still, he thought a few moments later as he dispensed with the glass and slugged some rakia from the bottle. Knowing his brother's temper, Mateo was aware of one thing.

It could have been worse.

24

Caleb sat on the bed, aware that he could feel the heat of Katya's thigh next to his. The bed wasn't large enough for them to sit apart, not that Caleb wanted to, and as Katya did not try to move away, neither did he. They waited as the sound of footsteps going down the stairs receded before resuming their whispered conversation.

"When did they do that?" Katya asked, nodding at Caleb's feet. "Was it Aleksander?" Caleb nodded.

"I thought he wanted me out of the way and secure for the visit," he replied. "But he wanted me out of the way for more than just the visit." Caleb thought back to the expression on Aleksander's face as, with the gun pointing at him, he'd forced Caleb to shackle himself. It was unusual for Caleb, but he'd misread the man and not realized his true intentions. The chain led to a thick pipe that ran along the wall of the bedroom. Like the rest of the house, it was old but solid. Caleb had explored the other end of the chain, but it hadn't taken him long to realize he couldn't free himself. Not without the key to the shackle or a strong hack-saw, and he had neither.

"Did you see his eyes when he looked at Elene?" Katya whispered. Caleb thought before replying. He had seen the look, and he'd also seen the look in the Albanian's eyes when he had stared at Katya. It was the same.

"When he took you to the bedroom. Did he...?" Caleb asked, letting his voice tail away.

"No," Katya said a few seconds later. "He slapped me a few times. Ripped my blouse open so he could..." She took a deep breath. "Touch me. Then he unbuttoned his trousers." To Caleb's surprise, she started giggling, but the laughter couldn't hide the fear in her eyes. "He couldn't do anything. That's why I started laughing."

"What happened after that?"

"He slapped me again and tried to pull his trousers back up. The gun was on the bedside table, so I tried to get it." Katya flexed the fingers on her right hand and Caleb noticed several scratches on them. "But it went off. That's when he punched me." She took another deep breath. "I don't remember anything after that."

"You could have been killed, Katya," Caleb said. He saw her looking over at the beds where the two girls were sleeping.

"It would have been worth it," she whispered.

"No, Katya, it wouldn't. Who would help them then?"

"We have to escape, Caleb. Who knows what they'll do to them? To us?" Katya said, her voice shaking. Caleb knew from Aleksander's expression and actions earlier what was in store for both the girls and for Katya. A horror that would be repeated time and time again. As for himself, he realized he had replaced someone else. From that perspective, unlike the female captors, he was expendable. "Will you help us? Escape?"

Caleb paused before replying. This was not what he had come to England to do, but it was where his God had put him. He closed his eyes for a moment, recalling several earlier times when his God had placed him somewhere unexpected. On more than one occasion, there were several bodies left at the end of the trip, their souls in the hands of their own gods. His own had almost been one of them several times.

"Yes, Katya," Caleb said after offering a brief prayer to his God to ensure he was following His wishes. "Of course I will."

25

Aleksander hissed through his teeth as Ana put a set of hair bobbles into the shopping cart, where they landed on top of some other items she had already added, such as a new hairbrush and some bobby pins. They had decided to take her shopping with them as security. Mateo had figured that by separating the girls, neither of them would do anything stupid like try to escape. Aleksander had argued against it, mostly because he didn't want to be babysitting Ana, but also because it could be risky. Mateo disagreed, as the girl could barely speak two words of English. Who, he had said, is she going to run to?

If they were going to be keeping their four guests for a few days, they needed to eat. Also, Aleksander thought as he steered the trolley into the alcohol aisle, he needed to drink. The trolley was almost full, mostly tinned and non-perishable food, and all he wanted to do was finish up and get back to the farm. He felt vulnerable in public, more so with the girl. He decided that he had been right and Mateo had been wrong. This was a risk to the entire operation.

"Are you done?" Aleksander said to Ana as they walked

toward the checkouts. She just looked at him with a blank expression.

The bored middle-aged woman behind the checkout sighed as she swiped their items through the scanner, attempting a smile at Ana, which wasn't reciprocated. Aleksander, keen to leave, just threw them into the bags in the shopping cart.

As he got his wallet out to pay for the shopping, Aleksander noticed Ana was staring at a small group of people standing by the door to the supermarket. There were four or five of them, all gray-haired women, standing behind a table draped with a flag. The flag was like the English one, with a large red Saint George cross in the center over a pure white background. But this one also had four smaller red crosses in each corner. Aleksander saw Ana look at him, then back at the women who were collecting food from customers as they exited. A handmade banner behind them read *Food Donations for Georgia*.

"Mut," Aleksander said as Ana broke away from him and ran toward the women. *Shit.* He threw five twenty-pound notes onto the conveyor, much to the woman's surprise, and grabbed the shopping cart to go after Ana as quickly as he could. She had reached the women behind the table and was talking to them in rapid-fire sentences, but he could see from their confused expressions they couldn't understand her.

"Come on, Ana," Aleksander said, forcing a smile onto his face before looking at the women. "Sorry, she's a bit excitable." He reached down and wrapped his fingers around Ana's upper arm, but she tried to wriggle away. Seconds later, she was screaming. He tightened his grip on her arm, but this only made her scream more. Several customers were looking over at the commotion as Ana shouted something in her native language and pointed at the flag draped on the table.

Aleksander pulled Ana a few steps toward the door, steering the trolley with one hand and pulling her along with the other. He kept the smile plastered on his face, trying to reassure anyone who was watching that everything was fine. All it would take would be one customer who spoke Georgian to understand what she was shouting and it would be all over. The two of them had almost reached the door to the supermarket. Aleksander could feel the fresh air on his face when he heard a male voice speaking, full of authority.

"Is everything okay, sir?" It was a heavily built man dressed in black trousers and a white shirt. On his chest was a badge with a single word. *Security*. "What's going on?"

26

With a brief look in Caleb's direction, Mateo stooped down with the key to the shackle in his hand. The metal ring around the other man's ankle was far too tight—the puffy flesh below it was proof enough of that—and he cursed his brother under his breath as he undid the lock. When Mateo removed the ring, the skin underneath where it had been was red raw.

"Thank you," he heard Caleb say.

"It was on too tight," Mateo said, nodding at Caleb's ankle as he got to his feet. He slipped the key back into his jacket pocket before pulling his mobile phone out of his trousers. "I'll text Aleksander and ask him to get you a bandage and some salve."

"So you have got a mobile phone signal, then?" Katya said from the other side of the room. Mateo ignored her and tapped out a message to his brother.

"You don't need to chain me to the bed, Mateo," Caleb said. "I'm not going to run away."

Mateo regarded the man in the robe with suspicion,

ignoring the fact it wasn't him who'd chained him to the bed. It was Aleksander.

"How do I know that?" Mateo asked him, taking a step back and watching as he massaged his ankle. Caleb stopped and looked up at him, his gray eyes piercing.

"Because you have my word," he replied, "and I am a man of my word."

Mateo laughed and was turning to leave when Katya spoke.

"He didn't chain Caleb up so he wouldn't run away," she said. "Aleksander chained him up so he could try to rape me."

"What?" Mateo spun around to look at her. As he watched, Katya angled her face so that he could see the angry-looking bruise on her jaw. Then she raised her hand, and smiling, wiggled her little finger at Mateo. "But he's not much of a man, your brother."

Mateo felt the anger rising in his chest at her words. What she had just described was a more likely scenario than her going for the gun and struggling with Aleksander for control of it. He'd known Aleksander was lying when he'd spun him that tale. Ever since they were small, Aleksander had never been able to lie convincingly. If what Katya had just told him was true, and Mateo was sure it was, then not only had Aleksander gone against his wishes, but he had brought shame on their whole family. They might be many things, but his family weren't rapists.

"Tell her to come with me," Mateo said, pointing at Elene, who was sitting on her bed, still with the covers pulled up over her even though they'd been awake for hours. "You two get ready. There's work to be done."

"I need my bag," Caleb said. "I can't get ready without my bag."

"Okay, I'll get it in a minute." He waited as Katya translated for him. The girl shook her head twice, her eyes darting toward Mateo, but Katya was insistent. A moment later, Elene pushed her blanket off. Mateo could see that she was fully dressed already. He tried smiling at her, but she wouldn't even meet his eyes.

Mateo made his way down the stairs and into the kitchen, followed by Elene. He pointed to a chair and, once she had sat on it, got a bowl from the cupboard. Mateo filled it with cereal and the last of the milk and put it in front of the girl.

"Eat," he said, trying to keep his voice paternal. "Breakfast."

Elene looked suspiciously at the bowl, but a few seconds later, started eating from it. Mateo left her to it and returned to the bedroom with Caleb's bag. He slung it on the floor in the bedroom and some of the contents spilled out. There was precious little in it apart from some basic toiletries such as a cut-throat razor that he and Aleksander had considered keeping, but it was small and barely larger than a penknife.

"There," Mateo said. "Do what you need to do, but hurry."

In his pocket, Mateo's phone buzzed. He pulled it out and looked at the screen. There was a notification on the screen. A text message from Gjergj. With a sigh, Mateo swiped at the screen, knowing it wouldn't be good news. It wasn't.

Mateo, we have a problem with the girl.

27

I t didn't take Katya long to get ready for the day ahead. She washed and changed her underwear, realizing that she'd not seen a washing machine anywhere. After dressing and balling up the ones she had been wearing, she returned to the bedroom. Caleb was sitting cross-legged in the middle of the room, a small round mirror balanced on his knee. He was running the cut-throat razor across his head, wiping it between his fingers after every stroke. Katya watched him for a moment, intrigued by the fact he had his eyes closed.

"Do you do that every day?" she asked him, careful to time her question in between strokes. She didn't want him jumping at the sound of her voice and cutting his scalp.

"Yes," Caleb replied. There was a soft scraping sound as he performed another stroke. Another finger wipe.

"Do you not use soap or anything?"

"There's no need if it's done every day and the blade is kept sharp." She watched as he swiped the razor between his fingers again, not understanding what the mirror was for if he was doing it with his eyes closed.

"What happens to the hair? That you've just shaved off?"

"There's barely any of it," Caleb replied. "It's more like dust." Then he mumbled something under his breath.

"What was that?" Katya asked him.

"All come from dust, and to dust all return," Caleb said, his voice languid. Then he opened his eyes and Katya saw a twinkle of humor in them. "It's from the Bible."

"So is it a religious thing then, shaving your head every day?" she asked him. Caleb, keeping his eyes open, turned his attention to the sides of his face. Katya watched as he ran the blade across the angle of his jaw. She could see its careful progress in the small mirror. "Does God tell you to shave your head?"

Caleb made a shushing sound with his lips before running the razor across his upper lip and then to his chin, again wiping it after every stroke. When he had finished his ritual, he replied to her question.

"No, Katya," he said. "He has never mentioned that to me, nor I to him." Caleb folded the razor away and tucked it into his bag. He got to his feet and Katya was surprised how quickly he went from sitting cross-legged to standing in front of her. "Shall we go?"

A FEW MOMENTS LATER, the four of them were walking down the track leading from the farmhouse. Katya and Caleb were leading, with Mateo and Elene twenty feet behind them. It gave Katya and Caleb the chance to talk.

"Of the two of them," Caleb said in a hushed tone, "Aleksander is the most dangerous. He's also the most unpredictable." Katya nodded. "Mateo is in charge. There's no doubt of that."

"And the driver?" Katya asked. She'd not even heard the man speak.

"He's just that. The driver." They walked for a few moments in silence. Caleb looked deep in thought. "We'll need to speak to the girls. Let them know what we're going to do."

"What are we going to do?"

Katya's words were followed by another silence from Caleb. While she waited for him to reply, Katya took in her surroundings. They were walking down a farm track, with the forest perhaps twenty feet to either side of them. On their right was a small stream she could hear babbling, and the air was thick with the scent of the trees. Above them, the sun was warming the air.

"We'll need to wait until we're all together," Caleb said a moment later. Katya looked at him, frowning. That wasn't much of a plan. "That's why they're keeping the girls separate. They know that one of them won't run without the other. But at some point, there'll be an opportunity."

"But do you have a plan?" Katya asked, trying to keep the frustration out of her voice.

"I don't," Caleb replied, looking at the sky. "But He does."

28

D aniel McArthur had wanted to be a policeman since he was a little boy. His favorite playground game was pretending to arrest the other children for various made up offenses. What he hadn't wanted to do for a living was work as a security guard at a supermarket, but he saw it as practice for when the police accepted him. Or, seeing as he had applied three times already without success, if the police accepted him.

"I asked if everything was okay, sir?" Daniel said. He looked at the customer, trying to commit every detail to memory. The man was shorter than him, stocky without being fat, and had dark hair. He had a craggy face that Daniel studied until he was sure that he could pick him out from a series of mug shots or work with an artist to replicate in a portrait.

"It's fine," the man said. He had a foreign accent, clipped and with the emphasis on the *s* of *it's*. Daniel made a mental note. Eastern European. Polish, most probably. They were the largest group in the area from overseas.

"Is this your daughter?" Daniel asked, nodding at the girl, who had tears streaming down her face.

"No," the customer replied. "I'm her uncle." He turned to the girl and said something in a language that Daniel didn't understand. Like most British people, Daniel could only speak English, and his usual response to hearing a foreign language was to speak English more loudly. The girl just looked blankly up at the customer.

"She seems upset," Daniel said. He focused his attention on the girl and squatted down on his haunches. He'd read somewhere that when interviewing a child, it was important to get to the same eye level as them. "Are you okay?" he said, careful to speak clearly for her.

"She doesn't speak English," the customer said. He looked nervous.

The girl said something to Daniel, her voice insistent and pleading. She wanted something from him, but he couldn't understand what. Daniel wasn't very good with ages, but he thought she was perhaps nine or ten. As he tried to commit her clothing to memory, a dirty green Transit van pulled up and parked right outside the supermarket doors.

"Hey, mate," Daniel said, raising a hand to the driver of the van. "You can't park there. You're blocking the entrance." The girl started talking again, looking at Daniel with a desperate expression. Her voice became higher as she spoke. She obviously wanted something, but he didn't have a clue what.

The customer, who had one hand wrapped around the girl's upper arm, put his shopping bag down. He hissed something at the girl, who looked up at him. Then he said something else and held his hand out flat before drawing it across his throat. It sounded to Daniel like a name. Eleanor? Whatever it was, it quietened the girl within seconds.

"She's upset because I wouldn't buy her a doll," the customer said as he pointed toward the van. "May we go?"

Daniel paused for a few seconds before replying. Other than causing a scene, no offense had been committed as far as he could see. The little girl was very upset over something, but not being bought a doll made sense to Daniel.

"Okay, sir," he said to the customer. "You may go. Have a good day."

The customer said nothing, but bundled the girl into the van as quickly as he could, putting her in the middle seat in the front. Then he shoved the shopping bag into the foot well before climbing in himself, sandwiching the girl between the two men. Daniel noticed as the van drove off that he'd not put his seatbelt on. He raised his phone to snap the retreating van's license plate, even though the automatic number plate recognition system would have captured it when the van entered the supermarket parking lot. He wanted them to know he was on the ball.

"Lincolnshire Police. How may I help you?"

"Morning Lincolnshire, this is Sainsbury's on Tritton Road. I've got some suspicious activity to call in."

There was a pause on the other end of the line before Daniel heard the female operator sigh.

"Morning, Daniel. What have you got for us this time?"

29

C aleb slowed down, allowing Mateo and Elene to close the distance between them. Just after Aleksander had left with Gjergj and Ana, Mateo had told them he had work for them to do. He had led them out of the farmhouse, and they were now walking down a path that led away from the building.

"Tell Mateo that Elene's tired," he said to Katya. "Let's see if we can persuade him to stop for a while."

Katya turned around and looked at Elene. Her face was pink and hot from the sun.

"Mateo, can we stop and rest for a few moments?" she asked the Albanian. He looked at his watch before nodding his head.

"Five minutes," Mateo said brusquely. "No more."

"Thank you," Caleb said, looking him in the eyes for a few seconds. Walking over to the stream, Caleb sat on the bank and slipped his sandals off. He put both feet into the cool water, enjoying the sensation as it trickled over the shredded skin of his ankle. Katya sat down next to him and slipped her own shoes off. They sat in companionable silence for a few moments while Caleb took in their surroundings.

The track they were sitting next to was completely straight, like a Roman road. There were deep ruts in the ground from a tractor's tires, and a strip of grass was growing down the middle of the track. Caleb could see that where they were sitting would be an ideal spot for a checkpoint, with the ability to see anyone approaching on foot or by vehicle for hundreds of yards. The dense trees on either side of the path would make an approach on foot through the woods difficult, slow, and noisy. The biggest risk, were there to be a military checkpoint here, would be snipers. Taking anyone out from either end of the track would be an easy shot.

Caleb put his hand down to touch a plant growing next to the stream. It had wide, hairy leaves shaped almost like wings and small white buds where the flowers were only a few days away from blossoming. He picked a large handful of leaves from the plant and placed them in his bag.

"Is that a snack for later?" Katya asked him with a smile.

"No, not this one," he replied. "This is comfrey. It can be eaten, though. Makes a good fritter."

"What's a fritter?"

"It's like a fried cake."

"How do you spell it?"

Caleb spelled out the word and watched Katya frown as she tried to remember it. Then he tilted his head back, enjoying the sun's rays on his face. It was nowhere near as hot as it would be back in Texas, but the stifling heat was something he didn't miss about the Lone Star State.

"Where did you learn such good English?" he asked her,

conscious of the fact Mateo could overhear their conversation.

"My father was from England, but moved to Georgia when he was small. His parents were originally from there."

"That would explain it," Caleb replied.

"But I've never met him." Katya turned to look at him, and he could see the sadness in her eyes. "He died before I was born." She looked away from him and sighed. "But he had taught my mother English, so she taught me."

Caleb thought for a moment. It would have been Katya's mother's way of keeping his memory alive.

"Do you mind if I ask what happened to him?"

"He died in the war." Caleb said nothing, waiting for her to continue. If she wanted to talk about it, she could. But Caleb didn't want to press if she didn't. He did the math in his head. Her father would have died in the early nineties, which narrowed down which war it was a little. "The Patriotic War of the People of Abkhazia, to give it the proper title. Although I don't think there was much that was patriotic about it."

"He was an Abkhaz?" Caleb asked, trying to remember who was who in that particular conflict.

"Yes, but he was one of the good ones. Not that it helped him." A solitary tear made its way down Katya's cheek, and Caleb had to stop himself from reaching up and wiping it away with his finger. "He was disgusted by what he saw his fellow Abkhazians doing, so he tried to escape to the north with the Georgians. But he never made it. He was shot in the back by his own side."

"I'm sorry, Katya," Caleb said when it was clear she wasn't going to say any more.

"Why?" she shot back. "Why are you sorry?" Katya got to her feet and brushed some dry mud from the back of her jeans. Caleb remained silent, knowing there was nothing he could say to answer that question. He closed his eyes for a few seconds, hoping that Katya's father had found the peace in death that he had been denied in life.

"Because of the pain that you still feel, Katya," he murmured under his breath. "That's why I'm sorry."

30

"What's he doing now?" Aleksander asked Gjergj.

The driver looked in the side mirror before replying. "He's on the phone. I think he just took a picture of the van."

Aleksander thought for a moment, wondering what the best thing to do was. Probably nothing, but it had been a close shave. They should have left the girl back at the farm, but Mateo had been insistent that the sisters were separated. If anything had happened, it would have been Mateo's fault, not his. He was about to suggest to Gjergj that they change the plates on the van, or perhaps even get rid of the vehicle altogether and steal a new one, when his phone started ringing. He sighed when he looked at the screen. It was Mateo.

"What's going on?" Mateo said when Aleksander answered, not even giving him time to say hello.

"There's nothing going on, Mateo," Aleksander replied. "We've got the shopping and we're just heading back now. What makes you think there's something wrong?"

"I had a text message from Gjergj. It said there was a problem?"

"No, no problem," Aleksander said with a sideways look at Gjergj. Why had he done that? "The girl kicked up a fuss at the supermarket, that was all. But it's fine."

"You should have left her in the van."

"You told me to keep her with me at all times."

"Then you should have sent Gjergj to get the shopping."

"But he doesn't speak English." Aleksander took a deep breath, trying to control his temper. He knew there was nothing he could say that would mollify Mateo. "What are you doing at the moment?" he asked, trying to get Mateo onto a different subject.

"I'm taking them to the pig farm to keep them busy for the day. Gramoz called."

Aleksander hesitated at the name. There were only a few people he was scared of, but the head of their group and also their uncle, Gramoz, was one of them. He was a brutal man, quick with his fists and boots when he was angry, which was most of the time. But at least he was in Albania, not England.

"What did he want?" Aleksander asked.

"Martin called him. He wasn't happy with the woman being so old, so he's asked for a replacement."

"Where from?" This wasn't good news. The tighter they kept their operation, the better. Martin would know that Aleksander and Mateo wouldn't be able to bring any more people over for weeks, so there must be a third party involved.

"The Hajri brothers," Mateo replied.

Aleksander nodded. They had worked with the brothers before, and he knew they were good at what they did.

"When?" he asked his brother.

"Tonight, or perhaps tomorrow. It depends on how long they take to get a boat. They have already identified the packages."

"Packages?" Aleksander said. "There's more than one?"

"Two girls, both ten. Their parents are with them, but the Hajris will deal with them on the way." If Mateo was concerned about their fate, it didn't show in his voice. But Aleksander knew he wouldn't be. Mateo was only ever concerned with what he did, not others. "Do we have enough food?"

"I think so," Aleksander replied. "If it's only for a few days, we should be fine. Will we get any money for them?"

"No," Mateo said, and Aleksander could sense the frustration in his voice. "The Hajris will, but not us. According to Martin, this is a goodwill gesture on our part."

Aleksander ended the call and turned to Gjergj, who was fiddling with the satellite navigation system in the van.

"Did you get that?" Aleksander asked him. "There're two more packages." Gjergj just nodded in reply. "What are you doing?"

"Reprogramming this thing to take us on the back roads," Gjergj said. "I don't trust that security guard."

Aleksander nodded in agreement. That was a sensible course of action. He turned to look at Ana, who was sniffing every thirty seconds or so. She wasn't crying anymore. Aleksander was tempted to slap her hard to teach her a lesson for what she had done back at the supermarket, but he didn't want to put up with her whining if he did.

He sat back in his seat and looked out of the van window at the green countryside beyond. Next to him, Ana sniffed again. Aleksander closed his eyes. Soon enough, she would have plenty to cry about. Aleksander knew Martin and his friends would see to that.

31

Katya could smell the pigs before she saw them. The odor was earthy and distinctive. Not unpleasantly so, but it was strong enough to make Elene wrinkle her face.

"Ew," the girl said to Katya. "What's that smell?"

"That's pigs," Katya replied. "Have you ever seen them up close before?" Back in Nakra, her hometown in Georgia, the nearest pig farms that Katya knew of were a long way off in the mountains.

"No," Elene replied, the ghost of a smile appearing on her face. "Will there be little pigs?"

"Perhaps. We'll see in a few moments."

The smell got stronger and, as they rounded a sharp bend, Katya could see the pig farm itself in a clearing to the side of the track. It was a lot smaller than she had imagined. There were perhaps ten pigs milling around a small building in the center of their compound, which was surrounded by a small fence. The building was made of corrugated steel that was heavily weathered, and a hole in the wall served as a door. When they saw her and the others, the pigs started squealing and running about.

"They're so cute," Elene said with a laugh. They approached the fence and stood a yard or so behind it. "Do they bite?"

"I don't know," Katya replied. She switched to English and put the question to Mateo.

"They aren't pets," he replied with a growl. "But she can find out for herself if she wants."

Katya warned Elene not to pet the pigs as Caleb walked toward the fence and crouched down on his haunches. A couple of the sows approached him and he reached out and scratched the head of one of them.

"Be careful," Elene called out. Caleb turned to look at her.

"She doesn't want you getting bitten," Katya explained. Caleb just smiled.

"Why would they do that?" he said, still scratching the sow's head.

Katya watched as Mateo made his way to a wooden box beside the fence. Leaning against the box was a bale of straw. He lifted the lid and reached in, lifting out two large, empty plastic water barrels. Then he reached back in, this time to get a long-handled brush and a pitchfork. Mateo handed the water barrels to Caleb, pointing at a metal water trough as he did so.

"You can use the water in there to clean the walls and floor of the building." Mateo handed the brush to Katya. "Once the floor's brushed clean, there's fresh straw to replace it. Just leave the old straw next to the building in a pile. The farmer who feeds them will take care of it."

"Excellent," Katya mumbled under her breath. She knew she would be working when she arrived in England, but not imagined for a moment that it would be cleaning out a pigsty. Caleb, by contrast, seemed to be delighted at the prospect.

"Once the trough's empty, refill it with fresh water," Mateo said, directing this at Caleb, who nodded in reply. "The girl's staying with me. When you're done, come back to the farm." Katya saw him looking at his watch. "You should be done by lunchtime."

"Can't she stay with us?" Katya asked, thinking back to what had happened the previous evening.

"She stays with me," Mateo shot back. Then his face softened. "But she'll be safe. Don't worry." She saw Caleb incline his head a couple of inches to one side at Mateo's comment and wondered what he was thinking. There was a fleeting coldness behind his eyes that vanished as soon as he realized she was looking at him. Katya turned to Elene and explained what the plan was, reassuring her she would be fine with Mateo. In truth, Katya thought she would be. Mateo was certainly the less volatile of the two brothers.

Elene giggled as Caleb, after putting the water barrels down inside the fenced area, hitched up his robe so that he could step across the wire. He was exaggerating his movements for her benefit and, to her surprise, he laughed when one pig rubbed its snout against his bare leg. Katya had not heard him laugh before, but it was one of the most reassuring sounds she'd heard since arriving in this country. She watched him as he looked at the ground, pushing at something with his sandal before stepping on it.

"Come on, Katya," Caleb called out to her, his voice light and playful. "Are you coming or just watching?"

"We'll see you later, Elene," Katya said as she walked toward the fence. Caleb reached out his hand to steady her as she stepped over the wire, his grip on her fingers firm and comforting. Mateo was just walking away when Katya saw Caleb looking around the small compound.

"Mateo?" Caleb said. The Albanian stopped and turned. "What?"

"Where's the tap for the fresh water to refill the trough?"

As Katya watched, a cruel smile spread across Mateo's face, causing her to rethink her earlier thoughts.

"It's back at the farm," Mateo said. "Near the woodpile. The exercise will be good for you."

32

M artin steepled his fingers and regarded the man sitting opposite him. Robert, his head of security and unofficial second in command, looked back at him with a faint look of amusement on his face. He was in his mid-thirties, wiry but strong, and uncomfortable in the suit he was wearing.

"All the arrangements are in place, Martin," Robert said. "There's no reason to be concerned."

They were sitting in the drawing room of Martin's house, which was, by most people's standards, palatial. It was mock Georgian in style, although it was only a few years old. Martin had bought the land it sat on, and it sat on a lot of land, from a local farmer, and had the house built to his specifications. This included the basement, which had some rather unique specifications that hadn't been in the architect's original drawings for the local council planning committee. But they had been in the final ones, and enough money had changed hands between Martin, the architect, and the builders to make sure its existence remained a secret. After all, Martin had thought at the time, what was the point of family money if you couldn't spend it?

"But this is another group of people involved," Martin replied. "The more people that are involved, the higher the risk."

"The higher the risk, the higher the reward," Robert said, his amused expression not changing. "Besides, Martin, I've had them carefully vetted, and they can be trusted."

"Trusted?" Martin laughed. "They can't be trusted as far as they can be thrown. They're career criminals."

Robert didn't reply, and Martin knew he was the pot calling the kettle black. He and Robert were just as bad, if not worse.

"They can be trusted to deliver what they say they can deliver," Robert said a moment later. "That's all we need them to do. Gramoz has vouched for them. The packages will be here in the next few days. Ready for the weekend."

"Another man I wouldn't trust with my dog," Martin replied. "If I had a dog," he added as an afterthought, looking around at the paneled walls of the drawing room. To his disgust, he saw a large cobweb hanging from one corner of the room. "Talking of dogs. Where is Natalka?"

"I've not seen her," Robert replied. "Why? Is everything okay?"

"She missed that bloody thing," Martin said, gesturing angrily at the web. "She's a crap housekeeper. Find her. Send her here." Robert nodded and got to his feet. He stood almost at attention for a second, and Martin wondered whether he missed the military. According to his research, Robert had spent some time in one of the special forces but left under a cloud. Martin wasn't bothered in the slightest what that cloud was, but having seen Robert in action with Natalka on one of his hidden cameras, he thought he knew.

One of Robert's strengths was his ability to hurt people without leaving a mark, as Natalka had found out when Martin had lent her to him as a Christmas gift. That he'd kept on partaking of that gift since then was something Martin didn't think was playing by the rules, but Natalka would be working somewhere else soon enough. Besides, he didn't care.

Martin moved his mouse to wake up the computer on his desk and checked his secure email. There were four unread emails, all from guests confirming their attendance at the weekend. Martin nodded and smiled. They were all high profile and had some unique requirements which the packages from Gramoz would fulfill very well. More importantly than that, they were all more than happy to spend a lot of money fulfilling those requirements. Martin, unknown even to Robert, was more than happy to surreptitiously film them doing it. One of the many modifications to the basement, as well as soundproofing that would deaden the most horrific screaming, was a very discrete set of covert surveillance cameras.

You could never have enough leverage, Martin thought as he deleted the emails. At least, not in the circles these guests operated in.

33

Sergeant Mark Bush had almost ten minutes until the end of his shift, and almost ten years until the end of his career as a response officer. He was sitting with his colleague, Constable Tony Elliott, in their marked police car tucked away on a path that led to a field. It was one of Mark's favorite spots to sit. It was peaceful, quiet, and every once in a while someone would come tearing round the corner and straight into the field of view of their speed camera.

"Not much going on today," Sergeant Bush said to his colleague, who was engrossed in a game on his phone. He glanced across at him, wondering why everyone under the age of thirty seemed to have a mobile phone glued to their hands. Tony frowned as something bad happened on the screen before putting the handset on the dashboard in front of them.

"Nope," Tony replied with a resigned sigh. "It's very—"

"Don't say the q word," Bush cut in with a grin. "That'll jinx us, for sure."

Just as he said this, the two policemen saw a dirty green

van heading down the road toward them. Bush glanced at the small screen of his camera. The van was traveling at exactly twenty-nine miles an hour, one mile an hour under the speed limit. Beside him, Bush noticed Tony stiffening in his seat, leaning forward to look out of the windshield.

"Pretty sure there was a call from control about that van, Sarge." Bush saw him flicking a couple of pages in his notebook. His eyes went from the page to the van and back again. "Yep, there was."

"When?" Bush replied. He didn't remember any calls from control at all.

"You were behind a tree at the time," Tony said.

"Ah, okay." Bush had answered a call of nature about thirty minutes ago, which had prompted an unnecessary comment from Tony about the size of his bladder. "What was the call?"

"Suspicious behavior reported by a supermarket security guard. A man and a young girl arguing."

"You've not got kids, have you, Tony?" Bush asked his colleague, knowing the answer was no. He waited for Tony to shake his head before continuing. "Let me tell you, son, when you have them, you argue with them all the time."

"I thought yours were in their twenties?" Tony said.

"They are," Bush replied, "but that doesn't stop the arguments. It just means you can't send them to their rooms as easily."

The van approached, maintaining a steady speed, and Bush saw two men in the front. The passenger was busy with something in the footwell, and as the van passed, the driver raised a hand in greeting but didn't look at the two officers.

"You want to pull it?" Tony asked.

"Not really," Bush replied with a glance at his watch.

There were only a few minutes until they could legitimately return to their station and finish their shift. His wife, a senior sister in the local emergency department, was on an early shift that day, so would have cooked dinner for them both. "I didn't even see a girl in the van. Did you?"

"No."

Bush looked at his younger colleague, knowing he was itching to pull over the van, even if it was just for something to do. Apart from one female driver who had tried her best to cry her way out of a speeding ticket, they'd done almost nothing all shift. That was just the way Bush liked it, but Tony was still young and enthusiastic.

"Just a quick look then."

Tony grinned as he pressed the button to start the powerful engines of their BMW 330d Saloon Interceptor. Bush hid a smile of his own, knowing that the van wasn't going to make a run for it. Tony needed little encouragement to drive with his blues and twos on, and in this car, why would he? The quiet engine purred into life and Tony pulled out of the path and onto the road.

Sergeant Bush reached forward for the microphone to call it in to control. He couldn't see the stop taking very long, so maybe they would be back at the station before too long, after all.

34

Caleb closed his eyes as Mateo's voice drifted into the back of his mind. He was still holding Katya's hand and just needed a few seconds of concentration. Caleb couldn't always sense people this way, but he thought he would be able to see something of Katya. He was right.

Katya was scared, terrified. That much he knew already, but underneath her fear was a strength that surprised him. And buried far underneath that strength, Caleb thought he could sense something else. Grief. Not the normal grief of a child who had lost her parents. The timing of what had happened to Katya's father was far from the natural way of things. Nor was it the agonizing, constant grief of a parent who had lost a child. Was it a lover? A husband? Perhaps a close sibling?

"Caleb?" he heard Katya say, and the moment was gone. "Are you okay?" Caleb forced a smile onto his face as he let go of Katya's hand.

"I'm fine, thank you," he replied. "I was just, er, thinking. That's all." From the curious expression on her face, Caleb knew Katya didn't believe him, but she said nothing more. He watched as she looked down at the brush in her hand and then over at the pig shed. "Let's sit for a moment," he said, placing the two water barrels on the ground and sitting on one of them. Katya put the brush down and mirrored him. "We need to talk."

"Okay," Katya replied with a nervous smile. "Let's talk."

Caleb paused for a moment, thinking. "We have to leave this place," he said. "You and the girls are in danger. A lot of danger. We need to find safety somewhere close by."

"I don't think there is anything close by, Caleb," Katya replied. "We're in the middle of nowhere."

"There must be," Caleb said. "This is England. Everything is close by. But you're right, we need some more information on where we are."

"When should we go?"

"As soon as possible."

"But the only time we're all together, they're with us as well."

"Not at night."

"But the chain?"

"Perhaps I can persuade Mateo not to chain me up."

Caleb watched Katya thinking for a few seconds before she replied.

"Tonight then? If he agrees?"

"Maybe, or perhaps tomorrow night." Caleb looked at the trees for a moment. He could just leave on his own. Walk away into the trees and to safety. There was nothing to stop him. Katya followed his gaze and, as if she knew what he was thinking, got to her feet.

"So we wait for tonight," she said, nodding. "If Mateo doesn't chain you up, then we'll wait until the middle of the night and sneak out." She laughed, but there was no humor in her voice. "What could possibly go wrong?" she asked him, her voice high-pitched. "How far away do you think the main road is?" she asked a moment later, her voice returning to normal.

Caleb paused. After leaving the road in the van, they had driven on the rough track for, in his estimation, almost forty minutes before arriving at the farmhouse. The speed of the van could have been only ten to fifteen miles an hour, given the condition of the road underneath. That meant they traveled a quarter of a mile every minute. The road was at least ten miles away, if not more. At night, in the dark, with two children. And only woods to hide in if their disappearance was discovered.

"I think it's a long way," Caleb replied, standing up and rearranging his robe. "But we have no choice. We have to leave."

"Caleb," Katya said, reaching out and placing her hand on his forearm as he made to walk past her. He stopped and turned to face her.

"What will happen to the girls if we don't? What will happen to me?"

When Caleb had stepped over the fence earlier, his attention had been drawn to something on the ground that had glinted in the light. When he had examined it, careful not to let Mateo or Katya know that was what he was doing, Caleb had realized that it was a watch. There was no strap, only a short, chewed leather stub where one had once been.

He looked at the pigs who were milling about, snuffling the earth with their snouts. It wasn't their fault. They had done just what God had intended them to do. Eat.

"Katya," Caleb replied, speaking slowly. "I think you and the girls are in very serious trouble."

35

By the time he got back to the farmhouse, Mateo was perspiring heavily. It was looking as if the day would be a warm one. He walked into the kitchen, grateful for the cool air inside, followed by Elene, who flopped into a chair with an exaggerated sigh. Her face was pink and flushed, and she looked just as uncomfortable as Mateo felt. He crossed to the cupboard and took out two glasses, one of which he filled with milk from the fridge, the other with water from the tap. Mateo placed the glass of milk in front of the girl.

"Madloba," she said, but Mateo had no idea what the word meant. It could have been thank you, it could have been a derogatory slur on him. As he watched her gulp at the milk, he decided it was probably the former.

He sat opposite her at the table and reached for his phone. There was a single text message. It was from his uncle, Gramoz.

Call me, the message read. Mateo sipped his water as he looked at the screen. He didn't particularly want to speak to his uncle, but he knew he had no choice. Opposite him,

Elene had finished her glass of milk and was holding the empty glass up, looking at him with her eyebrows raised. Mateo gestured at the fridge with a nod and swiped the screen as she re-filled her glass. To his surprise, Elene then took his glass from the table and topped it up with water.

"Mirëmëngjes," Mateo said when Gramoz answered his call. *Good morning.* Gramoz ignored his greeting, as he usually did, and was straight down to business.

"The packages will be transported tonight. They should arrive at first light," Gramoz said. His voice was deep and gravelly, and Mateo pictured him with his trademark roll-up cigarette in one corner of his mouth. "You will send transport." It was a statement, not a request.

"There are two? Are the others taken care of?"

"In a ditch somewhere in the Bjeshkët e Namuna," Gramoz replied. Mateo's chest tightened at the mention of the Albanian Alps. The jagged peaks in the country's north were not known as the accursed mountains for nothing.

"They are Albanian?" Mateo asked, hoping that the answer would be no. That the packages were just being transported through Albania, not that they were Albanian. From Montenegro, perhaps, or Kosovo.

"Of course they are," Gramoz said. "Where else am I to get them at such short notice? That's your fault, Mateo."

Mateo thought for a few seconds about challenging his uncle's last statement. Katya's age was not his fault. She had been delivered to him by another part of Gramoz's filthy little empire, a team that Mateo neither knew nor cared for. But he knew there would be no point.

Gramoz ended the call without a further word and Mateo slipped the phone back in his pocket. He looked at Elene, who had finished her glass of milk and was staring out of the window. He was able to put the thoughts of what was going to happen to her into a box in his mind where it didn't matter. After all, it wasn't him who would be abusing her. Whatever men did to their property was their business, but Mateo didn't like the idea of Albanian girls being put through the same ordeal. That didn't fit so well into the box. What if they were, like him, from the Gheg region?

If they were Albanian, then so were their parents. Which meant that Gramoz had just sanctioned the killing of an Albanian man. That went against their kanun, the customary laws that his people had followed for centuries. The man's family, if they were well connected, could start a blood feud. The last gjakmarrja that Mateo had seen had resulted in the annihilation of almost an entire family, with a lucky few banished from their region. Mateo had heard they were hiding in Sweden, hoping that the blood debt was repaid. But he knew it wasn't. Such debts never were while there were survivors.

Perhaps, Mateo thought with a heavy heart, it was time to enact a plan he had been considering for some time. He had been careful with his money to the point where he had almost enough to disappear and perhaps start a new life. When they had been paid for this job, for Elena and Ana, he would certainly have enough. He knew also under the kanun he had obligations of loyalty toward his family, but he also had another box in his head that those obligations would fit into.

His phone vibrated in his pocket with an incoming call. Mateo sighed when he looked at the screen. It was Aleksander. He rejected the call, but within a few seconds, it started vibrating again.

"What now?" Mateo said when he answered.

36

Katya watched Caleb as he half-filled the barrel they had been sitting on from the trough. He seemed lost in thought as he waited for the barrel to fill. She had seen his expression as he'd looked toward the tree line a few moments previously. It had been one of longing, as if all he wanted to do was to walk into the forest and never return. Katya wouldn't have blamed him if he had done so. Prior to boarding the boat in France, they had never met, and he owed them nothing. Carrying the brush, she walked to the small building, side-stepping a couple of curious pigs as she did so.

"My God, that's disgusting," Katya mumbled as she entered the building, ducking her head to get through the hole in the corrugated steel that served as a door. She blinked a couple of times as she waited for her eyes to adjust to the darkness. The air inside was fetid. A mixture of feces and ammonia stung both her nose and eyes, and she wondered when they had last been cleaned out. The light inside the building flickered as Caleb also entered.

"Why are you here, Caleb?" Katya asked as she started

brushing the floor. Caleb had brought the small pitchfork and was using it to scoop up a pile of rancid straw.

"Do you mean from an existential perspective?" Caleb replied. Katya looked at him and saw a smile on his face in the gloom. "Or do you mean why I am here mucking out a pigsty with you?"

"You know what I mean," she said, not returning his smile. His earlier words about them being in trouble were weighing heavily on her mind.

"I have to be somewhere, Katya." Caleb had a large pile of straw balanced on the pitchfork. He slid it toward the opening in the wall. "And at the moment, I am here."

Katya sighed. That wasn't the response she was looking for. She swept the brush back and forth, making a small pile of straw that Caleb could lift with the pitchfork, and tried a different tactic.

"Tell me something about yourself," she said, not looking at him. "I hardly know anything about you, but you know a lot about me."

"What would you like to know?"

She sighed again. He was making this hard work. "Have you always been a preacher man?"

"Of sorts, yes, I suppose I have. In one guise or another."

"But you don't belong to a church?"

"No." Caleb hefted the pile of straw out of the opening that served as a door and turned for the next one. "No, I don't." Katya wasn't sure, but she thought she caught a dark look in his eyes for a split second.

"Why did you come to England?" For a moment, she thought he was about to reply that he had to be somewhere, but he didn't. "And why did you come on the boat? Do you not have a passport?" Caleb didn't reply for some moments, but kept spearing the piles of muck that Katya was creating.

They worked in silence until he stopped shoveling and turned to face her.

"Three questions in one," Caleb replied with a faint smile. "I came to England to find something, or someone. I'm not sure which just yet. And I came on the boat because although I have a passport, I prefer not to use it."

"Why not?" Katya said, mopping her brow. It was getting hot inside the shed and their exertions weren't helping. "Are you on the run from something? Or someone?"

"No, it's just simpler that way. Shall we rest for a moment?"

Relieved, Katya stooped and made her way out of the shed to rest in the shade next to it. She was thirsty, but the only water around was in the pigs' trough. She sat down, checking the ground before she did so to make sure she wasn't about to sit in anything the pigs had deposited. A few moments later, Caleb joined her. When she turned to look at him, he was staring at the woods again with the same faraway expression as previously. Katya was desperate for him to stay, but didn't want to ask him so directly. Perhaps, she thought, if he had a reason to stay, he would.

"Do you have any brothers or sisters?" she asked him.

"I had a brother once, but he died." Caleb turned to look at her, but there was no sorrow on his face. "It was a long time ago. No sisters, and my parents are both gone. So it's just me."

"No wife or girlfriend?"

"No."

"Boyfriend?"

"No," Caleb replied with a smile.

"Have you ever had a wife or girlfriend?"

"Wife, no. Girlfriends? Yes." His smile broadened. "I'm not a monk."

They sat in what was almost a companionable silence for a few moments.

"I could sleep," Katya said, yawning. Caleb got to his feet and walked to the box. Then he picked up the bale of fresh straw as if it were made of nothing. Placing the bale in the shade of the building, he patted it.

"Curl up here for a while," he said.

"I can't. There's work to be done."

"You can."

Katya got to her feet, helped up by Caleb's hand. She yawned again and sat on the bale.

"Maybe just for a few moments," Katya said, swinging her legs up onto the bale. "Will you wake me before you start again?"

"Of course I will," Caleb replied. "Now close your eyes. You're exhausted."

She did as instructed and took a deep breath. The last thing she remembered was Caleb's hand on her forehead, brushing away a strand of hair. She heard him making a shushing noise, but it faded away as sleep enveloped her.

37

"Mateo," Aleksander said, trying to keep the panic out of his voice. "There's a police car behind us."

He heard Mateo swearing under his breath down the line.

"Where's the girl?" Mateo asked. His tone was clipped and Aleksander could sense the tension in it.

"She's in the footwell," Aleksander replied, kicking Ana as he did so. She screamed, so he kicked her again, harder this time. The little bitch was far more trouble than she was worth, and Aleksander was tempted to teach her a lesson that she wouldn't forget. Maybe that night, if he could get Mateo drunk enough and stay sober himself, he could give her an early introduction to her new life.

"Don't hurt her, you imbecile," Mateo shouted down the line. Aleksander paused for a second. If he was with his brother in person, he wouldn't dare to call him an imbecile to his face. "What are they doing? The police?"

Aleksander glanced in the wing mirror. He could just make out the police car behind them. It was perhaps fifty yards back, matching them for speed. Aleksander saw that the police officer in the passenger seat was holding a microphone to his mouth.

"They're not doing anything," Aleksander said. "They're just behind us and have been for the last few minutes. What should I do?"

"Nothing," Mateo said. "Tell Gjergj to keep calm. It could be a coincidence."

"It's not. We drove past them, and they pulled out after us. I got the girl out of sight, though." Aleksander knew that wasn't going to help them if they got pulled over. Even though she could speak no English, he knew they would be more interested in her than the security guard had been.

"The van is legal, isn't it?"

"Gjergj?" Aleksander said to his colleague. "Mateo wants to know if the van is legal?"

"Of course it's legal," Gjergj replied through gritted teeth. Aleksander saw his eyes flashing to the wing mirror on his side. When they had started the venture, they had decided the vehicle had to be properly licensed and insured. It was a risk as it tied Gjergj in person to the vehicle, but the alternative was to chance it being flagged up as stolen or illegal by every ANPR camera. In a country with more CCTV cameras than people, it wasn't a risk they felt they could take. "Tax, insurance, the works."

Aleksander relayed this to Mateo. There was a silence on the other end of the line which seemed to Aleksander to go on forever. Finally, his brother spoke, but it wasn't what Aleksander wanted to hear.

"Okay, the moment you're clear, you call me straight back."

"What do you mean, clear?" Aleksander shot back. The

van might be legal, but he was still in possession of a firearm, not to mention the kidnapped child in the footwell.

"When there's no longer a police car behind you."

"What will you do?"

"There's nothing I can do to help you, Aleksander," Mateo said. Aleksander knew his brother was right, but at the same time, he hated him for saying it. "If I don't hear from you in the next thirty minutes, then it's all over. You're on your own." In fairness to Mateo, they had discussed what would happen if one of them was caught by the authorities. Aleksander knew if their roles were reversed, he would have no hesitation in doing the same.

Aleksander ended the call and looked again in the wing mirror. He relayed what Mateo had said to Gjergj, who appeared more sanguine about the possibility of their operation being terminated. But Gjergj was only the driver. He didn't have as much skin in the game as Aleksander and Mateo did.

Behind them, Aleksander saw the police officer in the passenger seat put his microphone down and say something to the driver. A few seconds after that, he heard a sound that chilled him to the bone.

It was the *whoop whoop* of a siren.

38

C aleb grunted as he took the weight of the water barrels. He knew each of them weighed twenty kilograms—they were twenty-five liters in capacity, but he'd not filled them to the brim—yet they were still heavier than he'd expected. This was his second trip and he would need at least one more until the water trough for the pigs was full.

With Katya still asleep on the hay bale, Caleb had worked hard to finish cleaning the pigsty out, working as quietly as he could to avoid waking her. She would wake soon enough, he thought as he walked back down the track. The shaded area the bale was in was getting smaller, and he knew the minute the sun hit her face, she would wake up. But hopefully she would be rested when she did.

His arms and shoulders aching from the exertion, Caleb made steady progress along the track. He was almost exactly halfway back to the small enclosure when he stopped and put the barrels down. Earlier, he'd seen a small gap in the tree line that he wanted to investigate. If he was right, and he usually was, the gap led to a path that was too regular to be natural. As he approached it, rolling his shoulders to ease the aching in them, he could see that he was right. The path was straight and no animals that he knew made true lines through undergrowth, not that there was much under-growth able to grow under the dense canopy of the pines.

As he walked along the path, Caleb was transported back to his childhood. One sunny afternoon, many years previously, he had walked along a similar track with his brother and two of their friends. They were exploring the woods near Lufkin, deep in east Texas where his father had taken them, looking for employment. As children, they were as eager for adventure as his father was for meaningful, paid work. Caleb smiled at the memory, both because of the simplicity of his life back then and for those in the memo-ries who were now gone, never to return.

The path angled around to the left slightly after around a hundred yards before giving way to a clearing. In the center of the area, a much smaller one than the pigsty was in, was what Caleb was looking for. He looked up at the tall tower and the metal stairs that spiraled up it. Although it was thousands of miles away from the one in Lufkin, the fire lookout tower could have been manufactured by the same company. Unlike the one he had climbed with his brother all those years ago, there was nothing blocking the stairs to this tower. Probably because there were no chil-dren anywhere near it to dare each other to climb to the top.

Caleb ascended the stairs, wondering when was the last time someone had actually sat at the top, scanning the horizon for wisps of smoke. He doubted the English used airplanes to look for fires. The forest was surely too small for that to be viable. Not like the forests in Texas. Even the east central forest would occupy a whole tenth of the country he was currently in, and that was a small forest, by Texan standards.

By the time he reached the very top of the lookout tower, Caleb was breathless from the exertion. He scanned the floor of the platform, but saw no signs of human habitation. No empty water bottles, no food wrappers. No signs that anyone had been here recently. Whatever way the English looked out for forest fires, it wasn't using towers. He looked at the sun to orientate himself and turned to the north. The tree line extended as far as he could see. To the east, a good few hundred yards away, was the pigsty. He could just make out Katya's form, still lying on the hay bale, and he allowed himself a smile. Caleb's eyes followed the track. Just over a mile farther east of the clearing the pigsty was located was another, much larger clearing. There was a group of red-roofed buildings arranged around a central square. Raising his hand to shield his eyes from the sun, Caleb squinted to see various items of farm machinery and a boxy car or station wagon parked close to the complex.

Caleb entertained himself for a moment by calling in an imaginary artillery barrage onto the farm in the distance, deliberately landing his initial round fifty yards to the left of the target so he could walk the rounds in for the last volley. Then he turned his attention to the west. He could see the farmhouse and the track they had driven in on, but it disappeared into the trees after around a hundred yards. His recollection of the drive along the track was that it was straight, or almost straight. That meant that approximately ten miles in that direction was the main road. But as far as civilization went, other than the farmhouse and the farm, he could see nothing but trees.

Perhaps England wasn't as small a country as he'd thought.

39

K atya's eyes fluttered as the sunlight crept across her face. She opened them briefly before closing them again and shifting her position on the bale to shield her eyes. When she reopened them, blinking a couple of times, she could see Caleb walking slowly toward her, a water barrel in each arm. His upper torso was bare, the sleeves of his robe wrapped around his waist, and she noticed the sinews in his arms straining under the weight of the barrels.

"I thought I said to wake me up," Katya said, sitting up and stretching. "How long have I been sleeping?"

"You needed the rest, Katya," Caleb replied. He placed the water barrels down next to the trough. Several of the pigs trotted over to him, but when they realized he had no food for them, they retreated. Katya stood and peered inside the small building. There was fresh straw strewn on the floor and one of the pigs was pushing it around the now clean floor, making a contented-sounding snuffling noise. "Do you want some water before I fill the trough? The barrels are clean if you're thirsty?"

Katya walked over to join Caleb, noticing his upper body was covered in a thin sheen of perspiration. He was muscular, but his build was more that of a long distance runner than a bodybuilder. As she approached, she could see several scars on his torso. Near his right collar bone was a small, puckered scar whose paleness stood out against the surrounding tanned skin. Lower down on the left side of his abdomen was a pale line so straight it looked surgical, until Katya saw the dotted lines of crude sutures. As if Caleb was conscious of her gaze, he unwrapped the arms of his robe from around his waist and started to thread his arms back into it. Embarrassed for him, Katya looked away. She mumbled an apology but wasn't sure that he heard.

When he had finished buttoning up his robe, Caleb turned to Katya and lifted one of the water barrels, his eyebrows raised. Without a word, she stepped forward with her hands out, palms up and one on top of the other as if she were taking holy communion. It had been many years since she had.

Caleb poured water into her palm, his eyes never leaving hers. She splashed the water on her face, gasping at its temperature.

"Oh, my, that's cold," she said with a laugh.

"Do you not want to drink some?" Caleb said. "Like I said, the barrels are quite clean." Katya put her hands back out and this time, instead of splashing water over her face, she drank from them. "More?" he asked. She nodded in response.

"Thank you," Katya said when she had finished. "That feels so much better."

"It's the simple pleasures, don't you think?" Caleb replied, looking up at the sky. "The sun's shining, it's a beautiful day." He upended the barrel and started filling the trough.

"When are we going to talk, Caleb?" Katya asked him. "About our situation?"

Caleb didn't reply at first, but focused on the task he was doing. When the barrel was empty, he glanced at her before unscrewing the lid of the second one.

"Soon," he said as the water gurgled into the trough. "There's more information I need to gather first."

"What information?" Katya shot back, trying and failing to hide her irritation. Caleb just looked at her with gray eyes. "We should just run as soon as we can."

"Where to?" His reply was simple and devastating.

"There must be something, somewhere. As you said, England's a small country." She folded her arms across her chest. "We could steal their van."

"As soon as we've got the keys, that is. Unless you can hot wire it?" Caleb was looking at her with a faint expression of amusement, which only increased her irritation. "We should head back to the farm," he said, picking up the two empty barrels.

They walked in silence for a while, Katya lost in her thoughts. A few times, she looked over at Caleb, but he didn't seem in the mood to talk. She liked him, but at the same time, he had a habit of disappearing into himself. There was a phrase for it which she racked her brain to remember. When she did, she clicked her fingers in delight.

"Are you okay?" Caleb asked, looking up at the sound.

"Penny for your thoughts?" she said, stifling a smile.

"There's plenty more than a penny in those thoughts, Katya," Caleb replied with an even expression.

Her satisfaction at remembering the phrase faded as she watched him stepping around a sleepy bee inching across the path in front of them. She watched him for a few seconds before filing back into line beside him. Within a couple of hundred yards, she had decided what she was going to do.

Caleb had until the evening of the next day to gather his information, whatever that might be. Then, after nightfall, she was leaving with the girls. With or without him.

40

Martin groaned and shuddered as, beneath him, Natalka made a series of appreciative noises that he knew were far from authentic. But, he thought as he thrust himself into her one last time, he didn't care for her pleasure, much as she didn't care for his. He just took his pleasure, anyway.

"Oh, my God, Martin," Natalka said in heavily accented English. "That was amazing." She puffed her breath out through her cheeks and smiled up at him. "I am so warm."

They were in one of the guest bedrooms of Martin's house. It was one of the few rooms without hidden cameras installed, which was why he used it when he was with her or any of the other women he wanted to entertain. Or, more accurately speaking, be entertained by. Martin rolled off Natalka, resisting the urge to slap the stupid smile off her face, and padded to the en-suite bathroom to fetch himself a towel. When he returned, Natalka was still naked on the bed, lying on one side and looking at him. She was, in Martin's opinion, one of the better looking women who had spent time as his housekeeper.

She was in her early twenties, slimmer than she had been when she'd arrived, and had been quick to learn what Martin liked and what he didn't. Despite what he, and Robert, had done to her over the last month or so, she still retained an air of innocence. At the start, it had been genuine. But now, he thought it was a carefully constructed mask she wore to garner favor which had run out.

"I'm moving you on, Natalka," Martin said. From the frown that appeared on her face, she didn't understand him, so he pointed a finger at her. "You," he said before pointing at the bedroom door, "are going to another place."

"Another place?" Natalka asked. "But I enjoy being your housekeeper." She tried for a sultry smile, but Martin had seen it before and knew it was fake. "I like what we do. The way you make me—"

"Enough," Martin said. "Get dressed."

"Where am I moving to?" Natalka said as she reached for her underwear. Martin watched as she examined her panties, realizing they were ripped, before carefully balling them up in her hand.

"I have a place near Milton Keynes," Martin replied. "A massage parlor. You'll be working there until your debt is paid." He was already bored, both of this conversation and this woman. "You said you like what we do?"

Natalka hesitated before nodding. "Yes, I do," she said in a hushed voice, picking up her jeans from the floor.

"Well, now you'll get to do it with plenty of other men."

Martin ignored the look of horror on Natalka's face as he turned and picked up his own clothes. By the time he returned from the bathroom, she was in a flood of tears. She turned to him and was about to say something when he cut her off.

"Change those sheets," he said, not even looking at her. "They're soiled."

Martin left the bedroom, slamming the door behind him, and made his way down to the lounge. He crossed to a drinks cabinet made to look like a globe and opened the lid before selecting a fine malt and a crystal tumbler to do it justice. Martin was just adding a couple of drops of water— to release the peat, according to a book he'd been reading— when Robert entered the room.

"Send Natalka to Milton Keynes," Martin said, sipping his drink. If Robert was surprised at Martin's decision, he had the sense not to show it. "There'll be a replacement in for her in a few days' time." He turned and stared at his head of security. "But you're not to touch the new girl until I tell you that you can."

"You had a phone call while you were busy, Martin," Robert replied. He handed him a slip of paper with a cell phone number scribbled on it. Martin didn't bother looking at the number. It would be a burner phone, so not a number he would recognize. Then Robert mentioned the name of a politician with wonderful connections. Martin couldn't care less about the politics, and was only marginally interested in the man's connections. He was most interested in the depth of the politician's pockets, which was substantial.

"Thank you," Martin said as he slipped the paper into his pocket. When Robert made no signs of moving, Martin took a few steps toward his office door. Just before he entered it, he turned to the other man. "When I left Natalka, she was a bit upset. Perhaps you could comfort her before she leaves us for good?"

A wry smile appeared on Robert's face at Martin's suggestion.

"I think I know exactly what she needs," Robert said.

"Just don't be too enthusiastic with her," Martin replied. "She'll need to start earning on day one." Without waiting for a reply, Martin walked into his office and closed the door behind him. He crossed to a drawer in the large mahogany desk and pulled out a brand new phone. Never used, and bought for cash by Robert at a market stall with no cameras. A moment later, he heard a familiar deep baritone voice.

"Hello?" the voice said. There would be no names mentioned on this call.

"How may I help?" Martin asked. It was unusual for his clients to call him directly. The majority preferred to hide behind the anonymity of a secure email.

"I have a proposition for those packages you have," the baritone voice replied. "One which I think you'll find most acceptable."

41

"What should we do?"

Aleksander could hear the tremor in Gjergj's voice as he asked the question. He looked down at Ana, who was still cowering in the van's footwell. He was tempted to hit her again, but that wouldn't help. They didn't have many options. They were in a van on a quiet road, with a police car behind them trying to pull them over, with a kidnapped girl.

He reached behind him for the comforting cold metal of the pistol he had in his waistband. Would he have enough time to shoot both the policemen? He knew from a television program he'd watched on the small television in what passed for a lounge in the farmhouse that police cars in this country all had cameras. But perhaps, by the time anyone watched the footage, he could be long gone? Aleksander wriggled out of his jacket. Before he draped it over the girl, he stared at her as menacingly as he could and pressed a finger to his lips. There was no language barrier with that gesture, and he saw her nodding as he covered her with the garment. At least now she couldn't be seen.

"Aleksander?" Gjergj said. "What do I do?" His voice was bordering on panic, and in the footwell the girl had fallen silent, perhaps picking up on the situation even though she couldn't understand them. Behind them, the police car siren sounded again.

"There," Aleksander said, pointing at a small driveway by the side of the road that led to a farmer's fence. "Pull in there." He was going to have to brazen this out. He would shoot the police officers if he had to. Then they could disappear. The only thing linking the van to them was Gjergj, and he could be taken care of. That would be a shame, Aleksander thought as the van slowed. He liked Gjergj, but business was business.

The van drew to a halt, tilting slightly as Gjergj pulled onto the verge. Too late, Aleksander realized he was too close to the gate to open the door. That meant he would have to shoot the policemen from the inside of the van, which complicated things. But it wasn't as if they could shoot back. The police here were so powerless, they didn't even carry firearms.

He slid his hand behind his back and pulled the pistol from his waistband before hiding it beside his thigh. The police car stopped a few feet ahead of the van, blocking the road completely. Aleksander heard Gjergj swear under his breath as the passenger door to the police car opened, and a burly police officer stepped out.

"Good morning, gentlemen," the police officer said once Gjergj, his hand shaking, had wound down the window. Aleksander looked at the officer. He was wearing a black stab vest with his thumbs hooked into it close to his armpits. Would it stop a bullet? "Lovely day, isn't it?"

"He doesn't speak English," Aleksander replied on Gjergj's behalf. "Is there a problem?" His hand tightened on the grip of the pistol and he leaned to one side to see if he would have a clear shot at the driver if he shot the officer at the window.

"Not at all, sir," the officer replied, his face expressionless. "Just a routine stop. Could you ask your friend for his driver's license, please?"

"He wants your license," Aleksander said, switching to Albanian. "Just get it for him, nice and gently." Gjergj reached into his pocket for his wallet and pulled out his license. As he handed it to the police officer, he almost dropped it.

"Thank you," the police officer replied as he looked at the plastic card with Gjergj's photo. "What are you up to today, then?"

"I'm sorry?" Aleksander replied, not understanding the question.

"Where are you going?" the police officer said. He handed Gjergj back the license. Beneath the jacket, the girl squirmed, but Aleksander wasn't sure if the police officer had noticed. He wanted to jab her with his foot, but didn't want her crying out.

"We're going to the farm," Aleksander replied.

"Which farm?"

"Er, I'm not sure what it's called."

"You don't know the name of the farm you're going to?"

"No." Aleksander pointed at the sat nav. "It's in there."

The police officer leaned forward a couple of inches to look at the small screen. The slightest movement of the girl under the jacket would give them away.

"Halliwell Farm," the police officer said, reading from the screen. "Can't say I know that one. Where is it?"

"We just follow the woman." Aleksander pointed again at the screen. "She tells us."

"You're working there, are you?"

"Yes."

"Doing what?"

Just as Aleksander was about to reply, there was a shout from the other police officer.

"Mark?" The police officer standing by the van turned to look at his colleague. Aleksander had a clear shot at the man in the driver's seat, although it would mean that Gjergj would get a red hot shell casing in his face. "We've got a shout, mate."

Aleksander's fingers tightened around the grip of the pistol as he prepared to raise it. One for the driver, one for his colleague. A quick U-turn and they would be on their way. At his feet, the girl wriggled again just as the police officer glanced back at Aleksander. This time, he had noticed the movement.

"What's under there?" he asked, staring at Aleksander.

42

Caleb remained silent for most of the walk back to the farmhouse. He knew Katya wanted to talk, but he needed time to process what was going on. When he had worn a uniform, one of things they had done a lot of was think about courses of action for any particular scenario. Caleb remembered his commanding officer asking them for courses of action. What are our COAs for this, he would ask for a variety of different situations. Some good, but more often than not, bad. It was a logical way of thinking, which he appreciated.

The first COA was always to do nothing. That was where he was at this moment in time. There was no plan, not yet, anyway. The option was to do nothing and see what happened. If he let that play out, what would be the result? The girls would no doubt be taken somewhere, probably somewhere different to where Katya would be taken. The only certainty was that the girls weren't about to be adopted, and Katya wasn't about to start work as a nanny. Would the three men leave the farm when the females in their group had gone? If so, where would that leave Caleb? He had no watch to leave behind for the pigs to snuffle about their sty.

The second COA was, generally speaking, a more nuclear option. Hit hard, hit first, and hit fast with the most weaponry available in as short a space of time as possible. Always the tempting course to take, for the commanding officers back at the firm base at least. But always the least preferable option for those on the ground. Sometimes, something would survive the onslaught, and a wounded dog bit with a vengeance.

That left the middle ground, which is what was occupying Caleb's mind. He had a mental map, with the farmhouse they were walking to at the center. Ground zero. There was a track leading two hundred and ten yards, give or take one or two, on a bearing of ninety degrees leading to the pigsty. A farther one thousand seven hundred yards on his mental map was a small collection of rectangles that showed the location of the farm complex he had seen from the tower. On a bearing of one hundred and seventy degrees from the farmhouse was the track they had driven in on. But apart from these landmarks, the rest of the map was a green forest.

Caleb had one actual weapon. The ax. Two if he included the pitchfork, but that was back at the pigsty. He was surprised they had let him use either of them, but the fact they had told him several things and hinted at several possibilities. It told him they were not expecting him to offer them any resistance and hinted at carelessness or at least complacency on their part. Perhaps they were unused to violence? Perhaps they could talk the talk, but weren't able to walk the walk? Caleb had only seen one gun, the one Aleksander had been wielding, and his impression was that he was used to using it. But any weapon, whether bladed or a firearm, was only useful in the right hands. And at the moment, the gun was in the wrong ones.

"Katya?" Caleb said, stopping when they were a few hundred yards away from the farmhouse and turning to look at her. She raised her hand to shield her eyes from the sun, and as it shone through her clothes, it rendered her blouse transparent. A sudden pang of hunger ran through him, causing him to close his eyes for a few seconds to dispel it. It had been a long time since he had been with a woman.

"What?" Katya replied. He could sense the tension in her voice.

"Have you ever used a gun?"

She just looked back at him, giving him the answer he thought he knew without speaking.

"I'm an English teacher, Caleb," she said. "So, no, I've never used a gun."

Caleb turned and continued to walk toward the building. What she had just said would make no sense at all in Texas. But they weren't in Texas.

"Caleb?" Katya had jogged a couple of steps to catch up with him. She reached out and took his hand in hers, sending another pang through him. Her fingers were soft and cool on his. "Caleb, please? We have to do something."

He looked at her, careful to keep his eyes locked on hers. To look anywhere else would only feed the hunger, and it was a distraction he didn't need.

"We will, Katya," he said, almost whispering. "I promise you, we will."

"But what?"

Caleb took a deep breath before replying.

"I'm working on it."

43

"What's going on?" Mateo barked down the phone the second after he'd answered the call. "Aleksander?"

"It's okay," he heard his brother say. "We're back on the road. The police are gone."

"What do you mean, gone?" Mateo shot back. If his stupid brother had done anything, he wouldn't hesitate to throw him to the wolves. And if he'd done anything to the police, there would be a lot of wolves. "What have you done?" To his surprise, Aleksander laughed.

"Nothing, Mateo," Aleksander said. "I've done nothing. Must you always think so poorly of me?" Mateo bit back his response as he waited for his brother to continue. "They have gone on a call somewhere. We pulled over, but then something came on their radio, so they left us alone."

Mateo breathed a sigh of relief. He crossed himself with his free hand before raising his fingers to his lips and kissing them. Then he raised his hand in thanks to the soul of their mother. She would have been looking out for them, just as she always had done.

"Where are you now?" Mateo asked.

"We're about forty-five minutes away," Aleksander replied. "Just about to pull onto the track."

"And the girl?"

"She's fine. Quiet as a mouse."

"Good. We'll have lunch when you get back. Then we'll get them back to work."

Mateo disconnected the call and turned just as the woman and the man in the robe entered the farmhouse. They both looked hot from the sun, perhaps even slightly sunburnt. He gestured to the sink.

"Get some water," he said.

As Mateo watched, Caleb crossed to a cupboard and pulled it open. He reached in and got three glasses, filling them all at the sink before placing them on the table.

"May we sit?" he asked Mateo, looking at the table. Mateo nodded and watched them sit down, the relief on the woman's face obvious. "I have poured you a glass as well, Mateo," Caleb said. He was almost smiling at Mateo, but not quite, and Mateo had to catch himself before he thanked the man.

A few moments later, with two empty glasses and one full one still on the table, Caleb got to his feet and asked if he could use the bathroom. Mateo nodded and Caleb walked past him, brushing against him with his robe as he did so. A few moments later, Mateo heard the cistern flush.

"Where is Elene?" Katya asked Mateo.

"She's upstairs, in the bedroom. I think she's sleeping."

"Why are you doing this, Mateo? Keeping us here?"

"It will only be for a day or so. Just while we're getting everything ready." He could tell from the look on her face that she didn't believe him, but he didn't care. She was about to say something else when Caleb returned.

"You may rest in the bedroom," Mateo said to them both, wanting them out of the way. "We will eat in an hour, once Aleksander has returned."

Caleb walked over to the table and collected the two empty glasses. He refilled them and walked toward the door, brushing against Mateo again as he did so.

Mateo followed them up the stairs to the bedroom where Katya collapsed onto her bed with a grateful sigh. Caleb crossed to his own bed and sat down, glancing over at the sleeping form of Elene as he did so.

"You don't have to do this, Mateo," Caleb said as Mateo picked up the ankle shackle. "I mean you no harm."

Mateo didn't reply, but placed the shackle around Caleb's ankle. Not the one that still bore the abrasions from when Aleksander had applied it, but the other one. He was careful not to tighten it too much. The man in the robe would be no good to them if he couldn't walk.

With Caleb secured, Mateo returned to the kitchen. He took a seat at the table and pulled out his phone. A few seconds later, he was talking to Gramoz, who didn't sound happy. But then he rarely did.

"There's a delay in the packages," Gramoz said. "The weather is not good. So the additional ones won't be with you tomorrow."

"When, then?" Mateo asked. The sooner they arrived, the sooner they could all be moved on. It was only then that Mateo and Aleksander would receive the rest of their money.

"They will be there when the weather's good enough," Gramoz said, growling down the line. "Just keep your head down and your brother's trousers up."

"Yes, Uncle," Mateo replied, but he realized he was talking to himself. It looked as if their guests would be with them for longer than he'd thought. That was all he needed. Aleksander couldn't even do the shopping without getting into trouble, and the more time he spent in Katya's company, the more difficult it would be to control him. Maybe it would be easier just to let his brother have his fill of the woman?

Mateo sighed and looked at his phone. Trying to control Aleksander was only prolonging the inevitable.

44

Katya lay back on the bed, pulled a sheet over her, and closed her eyes. She knew she wouldn't be able to sleep, not after napping that morning. When she opened them a moment later, she saw Caleb looking at her. He said nothing. He was just looking, but there was nothing uncomfortable about his scrutiny. If anything, it reassured her as she re-closed her eyes.

She knew she had to do something. The fact Mateo had chained Caleb up, even for a short period, told her he would also be wearing his shackles during the night. That meant if they were going to do something together, it would have to be before then. The alternative would be to leave Caleb behind, and Katya didn't know what she thought about that option. Surely he could look after himself? Katya didn't have a sense of any threat being aimed at him. It was only she and the girls who she thought were in real danger.

Katya sighed and threw the sheet off, getting to her feet as quietly as she could to avoid disturbing Elene. Caleb was still looking at her but, when Katya glanced at him, he closed his eyes and sat on the bed, looking as if he was meditating. Perhaps he was. She padded to the small upstairs bathroom and, with the door closed behind her, stood on the toilet seat to open the small window above it. The hinges were old, and it took her a couple of tries to open the window. When it did open, the movement was accompanied by a slight metallic screech. Katya paused, listening for footsteps or any other sign Mateo had heard, but there was nothing. At night, the noise would be more noticeable.

She leaned forward to look out of the window, tracing her hands over the frame. Katya could squeeze through, she was sure. The girls would be no problem. But Caleb? Katya wasn't sure. As she looked down, Katya could see a sloping roof below and then a drop to the ground of perhaps seven or eight feet. It was a long way, particularly for the girls, but it was doable. If they left Caleb behind. Katya could also just make out the gap in the trees that Caleb had pointed out to her previously.

Katya closed the window before opening it again. This time, the screech wasn't as loud, so she repeated the motion a couple more times to loosen the hinge. By the time she had finished, it was quieter but still made a noise. She needed to find out what was underneath the roof and what the ground was like. Katya thought it was the downstairs bathroom, which would make sense. If it was, then perhaps no-one would hear them. She could always throw down some bedding to help muffle any noise. After making sure the window latch was closed but not too tightly, Katya sat down on the toilet lid.

She was desperate for a shower or, failing that, a bath. Her own body odor was becoming noticeable, if not to others, then to her. Katya had asked Ana to see if she could add some basic toiletries to the shopping, but she wasn't sure whether Aleksander would allow her to or not. Maybe if she built up some trust with Mateo, she could accompany him on a shopping trip? There were some other items she needed. Not ones she was going to ask anyone to buy for her. She didn't need them yet, but she would in the coming days, and she wasn't going to ask Aleksander to buy sanitary products for her. Elene might need some too, Katya didn't know. If she didn't, then that day could not be too far away. Had anyone even had that conversation with the poor girl? As far as Katya was aware, the orphanage Elene and Ana were from was run by women from a local church. But even women who went to church had periods.

Katya got to her feet and turned the tap on, just in case. Then she dried her hands on a moldy towel and returned to the bedroom. Elene was still asleep.

"Katya?" Caleb said, looking at her. "Come and sit here." He tapped the side of his bed with his hand. She did as instructed, sitting a few inches away from him. When he reached out his hand and put it over hers, she saw him close his eyes for a few seconds. "When are you thinking? Tonight? Tomorrow night would be better. More light from the moon."

"What do you mean?" Katya replied, surprised.

"It's a long drop from the roof, especially for Ana," Caleb said, removing his hand. "But if you drop to the right-hand side, the ground there is softer. Let Elene go first and then pass Ana to her."

Katya looked at him, feeling a lump in her throat that she wasn't expecting.

"What about you?" she whispered, wanting him to put his hand back on hers.

"I'll be fine," Caleb said, smiling wryly. "God will look after me."

45

Martin watched as on the large computer monitor in front of him Robert was hard at work. When he had started, Natalka had made every effort to make appreciative noises, but within minutes they had turned to screams that were so loud, Martin had been forced to turn the volume down. Now she was silent, her eyes screwed tightly closed. Martin knew she was waiting for Robert to finish what he was doing, thrust by thrust.

With no particular desire to watch Robert and Natalka any longer, Martin switched the monitor off. He'd only watched to make sure that Robert didn't mark her. Natalka's body would need to be blemish free or she wouldn't be able to work, and if she wasn't working, she wasn't earning Martin any money. Martin's thoughts turned back to his earlier conversation with his politician client. What he had suggested was most irregular, and would irritate all of Martin's other clients to no end. But this could only happen if they knew about the politician's proposal. Martin had no intention of letting them know, not with that amount of money on the table, and with another package coming on, they would be none the wiser. All it needed was a little finesse, and Martin was very good at finessing.

Martin got to his feet and crossed the room to stand in front of his window. Beyond the leaded glass, a vast expanse of lawn stretched away to a thin strip of river at the bottom of the garden. The river hadn't always flowed across the land the way it did now, and he'd had to cross more than one palm with silver to have it diverted the way he wanted it. But now, it was perfect. There was even a small, thatched summer house next to the water that several of his guests enjoyed using on occasion. Blinds in the windows ensured secrecy when it was required.

He was going to miss Natalka, in a sense. He always missed them when he moved them on. But knowing that he had started them on their journeys gave him some comfort, something Martin was always keen to do. He enjoyed the knowledge that what they were doing with other men, they had first done with him. That was the only reason Martin tolerated Robert's extracurricular activities.

Martin crossed back to his desk and picked up the report Robert had prepared for him. He sat in the mahogany captain's chair and eased himself back a few degrees as he perused it. The report detailed two of the additional security guards that Robert had hired for the forthcoming party that weekend. A lot of the language in the report, Martin didn't understand. Too many three-letter abbreviations and unit names that he'd never heard of. But the men certainly looked the part, Martin thought as he looked at their photographs. Both were large, the type of bulk that only muscle can give. Experienced, capable, and, according to his contact within the Ministry of Defence in London, very dishonorably discharged from the British Army.

As long as they were discrete and didn't ask too many questions, Martin was happy enough. Neither of the men looking back at him from Robert's report looked to have the intelligence to ask questions, anyway. They weren't known as grunts for nothing. All they had to do was ensure that the people at the party weren't disturbed while they enjoyed themselves.

Martin put the report down on the desk and checked his calendar. He was expecting a visit from another man tomorrow, which was one reason for Natalka's departure. The visitor, his superior in a sense, would not approve of her presence in his house. Most of the people in the organization they worked for would not approve of her presence in his house, and the fun he'd had with her could lead to his dismissal. But Martin was senior enough in his organization to not be concerned about that happening.

"I think some time in the summerhouse," Martin muttered to himself. He crossed to his drinks cabinet and poured himself a large drink. Bourbon this time, just to mix things up for his palette.

Twenty minutes later, sitting by the river, Martin contemplated the fine view he had. But he was bored.

"Yes, boss?" Robert, as usual, answered his cell within two electronic rings.

"Has she washed?" Martin asked. Robert would know who he was talking about.

"Yes, she has," Robert replied.

"Send her to the summerhouse."

Martin disconnected the call and stood. He took a few steps to one of the windows and started drawing the blinds down. Martin knew the only person who could see in was Robert, but it paid to be discrete.

At least Natalka didn't scream when she was with him.

46

C aleb tore a piece of bread from the roll, grateful for the nourishment if not the flavor. Across from him, Ana and Elene were sitting at the kitchen table, while Katya was stirring a pot on the stove. Whatever was in the pot smelled amazing. Caleb was so hungry after his exertions that afternoon he couldn't wait for something to eat.

The van had returned at about one in the afternoon, but they had left Caleb and Katya with the girls in the bedroom. They could hear shouting on the lower floor, but had no idea what the argument was about. Taking her time as the brothers yelled at each other, Katya had spoken to Ana about their trip. The girl told them the van had been stopped by a police car after Aleksander—the wicked man, as Ana referred to him—had been spoken to by a security guard at the supermarket. But because Ana couldn't understand what anyone was saying and, when the police car had stopped them, she was underneath a coat, it was impossible to say what had happened. Katya had relayed all this to Caleb in English.

"It's good news, isn't it?" Katya had asked him. "The police, I mean." Caleb hadn't been as sure, explaining that the police had let them go, so they couldn't have been suspicious.

Once the shouting had stopped, Mateo had come to the bedroom.

"You," he'd said, pointing to Caleb. "Come with me." Once unchained, Caleb had followed Mateo to the front of the farmhouse. There was an enormous pile of coarse gravel with a wheelbarrow and a spade leaning up against it. Mateo had told Caleb to fill the barrow and wheel it to where the track to the main road started. Then he had pointed at a pothole. "Fill it, then fill the others."

Knowing that the task was only intended to keep him occupied, Caleb took his time. As he worked, he thought back to an article he'd read a few years previously about the Golden Gate Bridge in San Francisco. The article had been about the team of painters who constantly worked to paint it, using brushes to coat each and every one of the six hundred thousand rivets. Then, when they reached the end of the bridge, they started over.

"What's in the pot, Katya?" Caleb said. Katya looked up at him before replying. She looked very different now. Having been set to work that afternoon to clean the house from top to bottom, helped by the girls, the three of them had been rewarded with a shower. Aleksander had told Caleb that he could shower after everyone else had. In cold water, as there would be no hot water left. Caleb didn't mind that. Cold showers were character building.

"It's tinned stew, I'm afraid," Katya said with a smile. She had tied her hair up into a loose ponytail that showed off her angular face and was wearing fresh clothes. The difference, in Caleb's opinion, was massive. She looked more relaxed, more human than he had seen her so far. "I've put some extra ingredients in that I found in a cupboard to make it a bit more interesting, but it's still pretty bland."

He watched as Katya dipped a spoon into the pot and walked over to him with her hand under it to catch any drips. She pursed her lips and blew on the food before extending the spoon toward his mouth as if he were a child. Caleb opened his mouth and allowed her to feed him, locking his eyes with hers as she did so. The stew was far from bland to Caleb's way of thinking. And the way it had been delivered was almost sensual.

"We eat first, bitch." Katya flinched at the sound of Aleksander's voice, and Caleb turned to look at the Albanian. He was leaning against the door jamb and, as Caleb watched, he ran his eyes up and down Katya's body. As if she sensed the inspection, Katya turned away. Aleksander walked over to the table and lashed out his hand, knocking the bread from Caleb's hand. It rolled onto the floor, leaving a trail of crumbs. Caleb said nothing, but crossed his hands in front of him and looked down at the table.

A few moments later, having watched the Albanians file in, take bowls of stew and bread, and file out, Caleb was looking at the plate in front of him. He'd made sure his serving was last and that the girls had plenty. When Katya had put equal helpings into her bowl and his, Caleb had used the spoon to transfer some back to her. Then he closed his eyes to offer a small prayer for the souls of the animals who had made the meal possible. He was almost finished when he heard Elene say something to Katya.

"She wants to know what you're praying for?" Katya asked Caleb.

"I'm praying for the animals that made this meal," he replied. "That their journey into death was a good one, but you may not want to explain that bit." He saw Katya think for a moment before saying something to the girls in their native language. Then Ana and Elene looked at each other and burst out laughing.

"What did you tell them?" he said. Katya looked at him as the girls continued giggling. She beamed, and it lit up her entire face.

"I told them you were praying to your God for forgiveness."

"Forgiveness for what?" Caleb looked at the girls and raised his eyebrows, which only made them giggle more loudly.

"Forgiveness if my stew makes you fart in your sleep."

47

Aleksander belched loudly and sat back in his armchair. Across from him in the farm's small lounge, Mateo was using his bread to mop up the remnants of his stew from the bowl. Gjergj, almost as if he didn't want to be in the same room as the brothers, had eaten quickly and was in front of the farmhouse.

"I'm still hungry," Aleksander said, nudging his empty bowl with his hand. "She didn't make enough food."

"She made what you bought her," Mateo replied. "You'll have to go back to the supermarket if you want anything more. Here. Take the bowls out."

Laughing at his brother, Aleksander got to his feet and walked to the kitchen.

"You," he said, pointing at the two children. "Get in there and collect the bowls." The girls just looked at him with a blank expression.

"I'll get them," Katya said, starting to get to her feet.

"No, I said they do it," Aleksander replied. "Tell them what I said."

He waited as Katya translated his order. When she had

finished speaking, both girls looked at him with fear in their eyes. Elene said something to Katya, who replied in a soothing voice. As the girls stood, Aleksander could see they were scared, and Elene's fearful expression in particular stirred him. Perhaps on the next trip, Aleksander thought as he watched her walk out of the kitchen, they could bring an extra package just for him?

"Upstairs, priest," Aleksander said to Caleb. The other man regarded him over the top of his empty bowl. Aleksander couldn't read his expression at all. It was like a blank slate. The Albanian slammed his hand on the table, making Katya and the remaining girl jump. "I said, upstairs. To your bedroom. There's work to be done."

Caleb stood and placed his bowl next to the sink. Then he turned and, with his head bowed slightly, made his way past Aleksander. A moment later, Aleksander heard the stairs creaking. It was just him and Katya in the kitchen now.

Aleksander took three swift steps across the tiled floor. His hand shot out and grabbed Katya's neck, his finger digging into the soft flesh. Aleksander lifted his hand as much as he could, forcing her onto her tiptoes and back against one of the kitchen cupboards. He held her there for a few seconds, but other than air hissing through her teeth as she tried to breathe, she made no noise. She didn't even look at him, but was staring at the opposite wall, blinking furiously. Aleksander leaned in so his mouth was only inches from her ear.

"Soon, bitch," he said. "Soon it will be just you and me." Aleksander could see her face reddening as the veins in her neck started bulging. He gave the soft tissue a last squeeze before releasing her.

Katya took a deep breath as her hands flew to her throat

and she started sliding her back down the cupboard. By the time Ana and Elene returned from the lounge, she was sitting on the floor, her fingers massaging her neck. Elene said something to her, putting the bowls in her hands on the table and running across the kitchen. Aleksander ignored her and made his way to the bedroom.

When he reached it, Caleb was standing in the center of the room, facing the door. He still had the same blank expression on his face when he looked at Aleksander. Pausing at the entrance to the room, Aleksander considered pulling his pistol to make sure he wasn't about to try something. But what could he try? He was only a man in a robe.

"Those two beds," Aleksander said, pointing at the beds the two girls had slept in the previous evening. "They need to be moved into the bedroom opposite." He saw Caleb's eyebrows go up a notch, but the man had the good sense not to ask why.

Aleksander took a step back onto the landing and watched as Caleb stripped the beds. He folded the linen into precise rectangles before placing it on his own bed. Then he removed the mattresses, moving them into the other room before returning for the bed frames. Aleksander laughed when Caleb came back for the frames. They were solid wood and, Aleksander knew from when he and Gjergj had moved them previously, very heavy. But he made no move to help him, nor was he asked to.

To Aleksander's surprise, Caleb made moving the heavy frames look easy. He was stronger than he looked. When Caleb returned for the linen, having moved the frames into the other room, Aleksander followed him into the second bedroom. Caleb made the beds back up in silence, adjusting the position of the two new beds with the two already in the room so they were spaced evenly. When he had finished, the sheets were crisp and taut.

Dismissing Caleb to the kitchen, Aleksander returned to the lounge. Mateo had set a fire in the log burner for later, when it would be cold, and was sitting in an armchair, sipping from a bottle of beer. Aleksander got himself one out of the fridge and sat opposite his brother.

"The bedroom's done," he said. Mateo nodded in response.

"Good. But they won't be here until the day after tomorrow at the earliest." Mateo took a long drink from his bottle. "Bad weather."

"You could have told me that before I moved the beds," Aleksander replied. Mateo's grin told him he knew Aleksander hadn't been the one to move them. "So what now?"

"Now?" Mateo said. "Now we wait."

48

Katya sipped at the glass of water Elene had offered her. The cool water trickling down her throat was refreshing, but also highlighted a sharp pain in her neck when she swallowed. She had been on the verge of passing out when Aleksander had released his grip, and that final squeeze he had given her had caused the edges of her vision to black out for a few seconds.

"Are you okay?" Elene said, whispering although it was only Katya and the girls in the kitchen. "Did he hurt you?"

"No," Katya replied, clearing her throat. "No, he didn't."

"I don't like him," Elene said.

"He's an evil man," Ana added, also whispering. "I don't like the way he looks at you, Katya." For one so young, Ana was very perceptive.

"Neither do I, Ana," Katya said. "But listen, I want to talk to both of you."

The three of them sat around the table in a conspiratorial huddle.

"What is it, Katya?" Elene asked.

"I need you both to be very brave and very grown up

tonight, okay?" Katya said. "Can you two do that for me?" The two girls nodded their heads in unison. "Tonight, in the middle of the night, we're going to creep out of the window in the upstairs bathroom and run away."

"But it's too high," Ana said, her eyes widening. "We'll hurt ourselves falling out."

"You won't, Ana," Katya replied. "There's a roof outside that we can get on to, and then we can get to the ground from there. You might need to drop a little bit, but it won't be far.

"Where will we go?" Elene asked. Katya bit back her initial response. *I don't care. Anywhere but here.*

"We'll follow the track back to the road, and find a policeman like the ones you saw earlier, Ana," Katya said. "But it won't just be two they send to get the men who are holding us. They'll send hundreds."

"With guns?" Ana's mouth was half open, her eyes wide.

"Lots of them. And police dogs as well, I expect." Katya smiled as Ana's eyes widened even further.

"What about Caleb?" Elene asked. "Is he coming too?"

Katya paused before replying, wondering how to best answer the question. Could she tell the children that Caleb was being shackled? One thing she did know was that there was no chance he wouldn't be chained up that night. If they wouldn't even let him nap without it, they wouldn't let him sleep without it.

"I don't think so, no," she said a moment later.

"But what if they hurt him?" Katya looked at Elene's face, reaching her hand out to wipe a solitary tear away from the corner of her eye.

"They need Caleb to do all their work for them," Katya said. "But as soon as we're safe, he's going to run away too."

"Will we see him again?"

"Of course we will."

"How will we know when it's time to go?" Ana asked.

"I'll wake you, but you have to be really quiet." Katya put her hands in front of her like a pair of paws. "Like little mice." There was a glimmer of a smile from Elene at the gesture.

"I'm scared, Katya," Ana said. "What if they run after us before we get to the policeman?"

"Then we'll run quicker, Ana." It was Elene who answered Ana's question. "You always used to win the races back home, didn't you? I bet you're quicker even than Katya?"

"No!" Katya said with an expression of mock horror. "No one is quicker than me! Not even you, Ana." She paused. "Are you?"

"Perhaps," Ana replied. "I might be."

"Let's have a race, while we're escaping. The one who runs to the trees the quietest and the fastest wins."

"What do we win?" Ana asked.

"It's a surprise," Katya said, unsure what else to say. "But it's a very good one. What do you think?" She looked at both girls until they both nodded their heads.

A few moments later, when the conversation had moved away from what the surprise might be, Ana announced she needed the bathroom. Once the kitchen door had closed behind her, Elene turned to Katya.

"Katya?" she said. "What Ana said about the way he looks at you?"

"Yes? What about it?" Katya replied.

"I don't know why, but he looks at me the same way." Elene paused for a few seconds, a deep frown on her face. "May I ask you a question?"

"Of course you can, sweetheart."

"We're not being adopted, are we?"

Katya felt a sharp pain in her chest at Elene's question. She wanted to cry, to hug her, or both. But she didn't think she could do either. How should she respond to that? The look on Elene's face was different. Resolute. Almost adult, but not quite. Katya opted for the truth.

"No, Elene," Katya said, reaching out for her hand. "No, you're not."

"Then what are they planning on doing with us? With you?"

This time, Katya knew she couldn't tell the truth. Hoping that Elene wouldn't see beyond the lie, she replied.

"I don't know, Elene," Katya said. "I don't know."

Elene paused for a few seconds before replying. Her expression had changed subtly. It was now disappointment that, as Katya watched, turned to fear.

"Yes, you do, Katya," she said, her voice trembling. "Yes. You do."

49

"Tell them to hurry up," Mateo said to Katya, his irritation obvious. The two girls were in the small upstairs bathroom, cleaning their teeth. He watched as she said something through the door at Ana and Elene. They answered, but he had no idea what had just been said.

"Why have they been moved?" Katya asked. "They would both prefer to be in the same room as Caleb and I."

"Because we said so," Mateo shot back. He wasn't in the mood for questions.

Mateo took a step back as Caleb came up the stairs, followed by Aleksander who was holding the pistol loosely by his side. He caught the scent of fresh soap as Caleb passed him and wondered briefly whether there had been any hot water left. Aleksander had left the hot tap in the kitchen running to make sure there wasn't. It was petty, but his brother had that attribute in spades.

"I take it he didn't make a run for it from the shower?" Mateo said to his brother. Aleksander didn't reply, but just smirked. The two men walked into the bedroom and a moment later, Mateo heard a metallic click. He waited until Aleksander had gone back down the stairs.

Leaving Katya standing by the bathroom door, Mateo walked into the bedroom, where Caleb was now sitting on his bed. Mateo reached into his pocket for the key to the shackle and crouched down to loosen it, knowing Aleksander would have left it far too tight. He was right.

"There's no need for a shackle," Caleb said to Mateo. "If I was going to run, I would have done it by now." Mateo paused. He had a point. Caleb had plenty of opportunities to abscond and not taken any of them. "Please?"

"No, not yet," Mateo replied. "Perhaps tomorrow, if we think you can be trusted." He looked at Caleb's expression, expecting to see disappointment, but there was nothing. No expression at all. Caleb was just looking.

Mateo got to his feet and left. When he got back to the landing, the two girls had finished in the bathroom. Katya was tucking them into their beds in the other bedroom. Mateo watched them for a moment. The scene was almost homely, with Katya acting like their mother as she straightened the sheets around them.

He shook his head and trudged down the stairs. They were products, that was all. His role was to bring them to this country. What others did with them, to them, was none of his business. As long as Mateo got his money, that was the only thing that mattered.

When Mateo got to the lounge, Aleksander was sitting in his customary position in the armchair, sipping from a bottle of beer. Mateo walked to the fridge and got one for himself.

"Where's Gjergj?" Mateo asked Aleksander.

"Outside, on his phone," Aleksander replied. "He says he can't get a signal in here."

They sat in silence, both sipping at their beers.

"Is there any news on the next lot?" Aleksander asked after a few moments.

"I spoke to Gramoz earlier," Mateo replied, irritated. "I told you earlier. There's a delay because of the weather."

"How long?" Aleksander said after swearing under his breath. Mateo just shrugged his shoulders. Aleksander swore again and had just raised the bottle to his lips when there were five quick raps on the kitchen door.

"What the hell does he want?" Mateo said, getting to his feet. "What is it?" he called out as he approached the door.

"Mateo, Aleksander," Gjergj shouted through the wood. "Come outside."

Followed by his brother, Mateo opened the door to see what Gjergj wanted. There was a deep droning sound in the air, and Gjergj was pointing at the sky. Mateo followed his finger to see a speck in the sky, getting larger. It was a helicopter. A small one, perhaps with only two people. As it approached and became clearer, Mateo saw it was black with white stripes down the side. The helicopter moved slowly and in a straight line. If it continued on its current course, it would pass directly over the top of the farmhouse.

"Back inside," Mateo said, gesturing at the door. When they were standing back in the house, he left the door ajar with just enough room to watch the helicopter. "Aleksander, when you spoke to the police earlier, did you tell them where the farm was?"

"Of course not," Aleksander shot back. "What do you think I am? Stupid?"

"He saw it." It was Gjergj. "On the screen of the sat nav. The policeman saw it."

Mateo looked up at the helicopter, which was now close enough for him to read the letters stenciled on the side. It was a single word.

POLICE.

50

——————

Caleb watched as Katya leaped up from her bed and ran across to the window, waving her arms wildly at the small helicopter that was passing by. He focused on the noise of the rotors for a few seconds. There was no sign that the aircraft was slowing down, speeding up, or pitching. Without looking at it, Caleb knew it was flying straight and level. Even if one of the occupants saw Katya waving, all they would probably do is wave back.

"It's the police!" Katya said, her excitement obvious. "Caleb! It's the police!" She continued waving at the helicopter, but it was now moving away from the farmhouse. "Why aren't they stopping?" A moment later, as the sound of the rotors faded into the distance, she let her arms drop to her sides. When she turned back to face Caleb, the disappointment was etched onto her face.

"Katya," Caleb said, reaching into his bag. "I have something for you." Hopefully, it was something that would take her mind off the helicopter. "I made it this morning while you were sleeping." He pulled out a small gauze square with some green material sandwiched between the layers.

"What is it?" Katya asked, crossing to his bed and sitting down next to him.

"It's a poultice." He held it up and gently pressed it to the bruise on the side of her face, made by Aleksander's fist. "Not the best one I've ever made, but it'll help."

"What's it made from?" she asked, putting her hand over his. Caleb was reminded how cool her fingers were.

"Comfrey," he replied. "Also known as knitbone or bruisewort, but not for many years."

"It's a plant?"

"Yes," Caleb said. "It has many healing properties. Place it under your jaw when you go to sleep, and the bruise will hardly be noticeable in the morning."

"Thank you, Caleb," Katya replied. She looked at him for a few moments and he wondered what she was thinking. Then he saw her eyes drop to the shackle on his ankle. "Did you ask Mateo?"

"I did. But he said not tonight. Perhaps tomorrow."

"So we leave tomorrow." Her eyes met his, and he knew it was a statement, not a question.

"No, you leave tonight."

"But what about you?"

"I'll catch up with you."

"How?" Katya blinked a couple of times, and he sensed she was trying not to cry.

"I'll catch up with you," Caleb said again. "I'll come and find you."

"You'll go to the police?" she asked him. "Ask them to tell you where we are?"

"Yes, Katya. That's what I'll do." He smiled at her but she didn't respond.

Katya got to her feet and Caleb watched as she crossed the room to her own bed. She lay down on it and turned over so she was facing away from him. A moment later, he could see her shoulders shaking.

Caleb lay back and made himself as comfortable as the iron shackle around his ankle would let him. He closed his eyes but knew that the sound of Katya sobbing quietly would mean he wouldn't sleep. Couldn't sleep.

He focused on the noise of the forest instead. He could hear two long-eared owls calling to each other. The repetitive hoo hoo hoo of the male was answered by a single, higher-pitched hoo from the female. He tried to visualize them in his mind's eye, but he didn't think he'd ever seen one in the flesh before. Caleb tried to allow the sound to calm him as, after some moments, Katya stopped sobbing. But he knew from the way she was breathing that she wasn't asleep.

Perhaps thirty minutes later, when the night outside had fully fallen and even the owls had quietened for the evening, Caleb heard Katya's sheets rustling. He kept his eyes closed, not wanting her to think she was disturbing him as she went to the bathroom. The floorboards creaked under her weight as she crossed the room. Then Caleb heard the door open and close again. Then, a moment after that, he heard the window hinge squeak at the same time as the cistern was flushed. Caleb allowed himself a smile at her ingenuity. Now, when they did leave later in the night, the window would already be open.

The door opened again and Caleb heard Katya close it behind her, the latch clicking as she pushed it shut. More footsteps, but then she stopped. There was another rustling noise, similar to the one she had made with her sheets but much quieter. Then his bed dipped as she sat on it, swinging her legs up and lying next to him.

"Katya," Caleb said in a whisper.

"Shh," Katya replied, pressing her body against his. Caleb closed his eyes. He could feel every curve of her body through his robe, and her breath on his ear. When she brushed her lips over his earlobe, it sent a long-forgotten feeling through his core. Pure desire.

"Katya," he said again. "Katya, no." He opened his eyes and turned to face her. Their lips were only inches apart. "You don't need to do this."

51

"What the fuck are we going to do?" Aleksander shouted at Mateo, who glared back at him.

"Aleksander, would you calm down," his brother replied. Aleksander looked at him and the smug expression on his face. Did he actually realize how bad this was? "There's nothing to suggest they were here for us."

"Why else would they fly over the farmhouse if they weren't here for us?" Aleksander shot back. "There's nothing else for miles around. It's a bit of a coincidence, don't you think?"

"Why would they fly a helicopter over us if they were coming? Especially one with Police written on the side."

"It's reconnaissance," Aleksander said. "They'll be poring over the video now. The layout of the farm, the escape routes. All of it."

He walked over to the fridge and pulled out a beer, not asking Mateo or Gjergj if they wanted one. Gjergj, as usual, was engrossed in his phone. He was standing by the kitchen window, holding his phone out near the glass. A moment later, he turned and held it out toward Aleksander. On the screen was a photograph of some sort.

"What's that?" Aleksander asked him.

"It's Google Earth," Gjergj replied. "Look. It's the farm. From space."

"So what?"

"It shows what you just said they would be looking for from the helicopter. Layout and escape routes."

"You see?" Mateo said, a smile appearing on his face. "They wouldn't need to fly a helicopter over the farm."

"We should go," Aleksander said as he sat heavily in an armchair. "I don't like it."

"Go where?" Mateo replied.

Aleksander sighed and took a long sip of his beer. "We've never seen a single helicopter since we've been here," he said, staring first at his brother and then at Gjergj. "Then a police helicopter flies over the farmhouse the same day we get stopped by the police. I tell you, I don't like it."

"You don't have to like it, Aleksander," Mateo replied, using the same tone he always did when he wanted to move on from a subject. A patronizing one. "Like Gjergj said, they can see everything they need on the internet. They wouldn't waste the money on flying a helicopter over us to get it, would they?"

"If you say so, Mateo," Aleksander said. There was no point trying to argue. Mateo's mind was made up. "So we just wait here until the other packages arrive?"

"Yes, Aleksander." Mateo sighed. "Like I said, we just need to wait."

"But it's boring. There's not even a television."

"Well, go for a walk in the woods, then."

"Maybe I will," Aleksander said. "Maybe I'll take the whore from upstairs for a walk in the woods. She wouldn't forget that in a hurry, I can tell you." He got to his feet and fetched himself another beer. "I'm going for a smoke."

"You do that, Aleksander," Mateo replied with a sideways glance at Gjergj.

Aleksander made his way outside the farmhouse, considering the look the other two men had just exchanged. What was that all about? As he lit his cigarette, he wondered whether they were planning something. Cutting him out of the deal, perhaps? Aleksander laughed at the thought. Mateo was a fool, but not that much of a fool. Blood was blood, and they were brothers. Mateo was obliged to pay Aleksander his share of the proceeds, or it would dishonor him. And Aleksander didn't think Mateo had the balls for such a grave insult.

He puffed on his cigarette and looked out at the tree line, indistinct but just visible in the light of the moon. In the distance beyond the trees, Aleksander heard a low rumble of thunder and he shivered involuntarily. When he and Mateo were children, their father used to tell them tales of the Kulshedra, a terrifying female dragon with many heads who devoured humans on sight. Especially small boys. Aleksander and Mateo had spent many evenings huddled in their beds, listening to the thunder outside in the mountains. According to their father, the noise was a sign that a Kulshredra was in the area. If the noise was getting louder, she was getting closer. The legends also spoke of the drangue, a semi-human winged divine hero and protector of mankind. A drangue was the only thing that could defeat a Kulshredra but, again according to their father, none ever had.

The thunder rumbled again, slightly louder this time. Aleksander shivered as he looked at the treeline. There was a screech in the forest and he jumped, almost dropping his cigarette. An animal, not a Kulshedra. He was far too old for such stupid tales, but he still didn't like forests. Bad things came out of them, of that he was sure.

Aleksander flicked his cigarette away after one final puff and watched the flurry of sparks. With a last look at the tree-line, he let himself back into the house.

52

"I don't need to do what?" Katya asked. She leaned her head back slightly so she could focus on his eyes and let a smile play over her face. What she was doing was a risk, but she wanted to make sure that Caleb would come and find them after they had left. She liked him. Under normal circumstances, although she could barely remember what normal felt like, she wouldn't have been so forward. But she liked him a lot.

"This, Katya," Caleb said. "What you're doing now."

"I'm not doing anything," she replied, changing her smile to a mock pout. "I'm just lying here. Next to you." She watched as he closed his eyes and straightened his head. If he opened them, he would be staring at the ceiling.

"It wouldn't be right. What if Ana or Elene walk in?"

"They won't. They're exhausted." She reached up her fingers and ran them over his lips, but there was no response. Katya let her hand slip to his chest before bringing her leg up so that her inner thigh was resting on his knees. "Don't you want to?"

"It's not about want, Katya," Caleb replied, his eyes still

closed. "Or about need. It just wouldn't be right. Not here. Not now."

"Why not?" Katya said. "Do you think God might be watching?"

"God is always watching. Always listening."

"Is He?" Katya wanted Caleb to open his eyes and look at her. She liked it when he looked at her. When she realized Caleb wasn't going to answer her question, she inched her thigh up his legs, watching the expression on his face carefully. When her thigh reached what she was looking for, she saw the slightest twitch in his eyelids. There wasn't much you could hide when you were wearing a robe. "Are you sure you don't want to? Only your body is saying something different."

"Katya," Caleb said, using his arm to gently move her thigh back toward his knees. Finally, he opened his eyes and looked at her. "My body is doing exactly what it's designed to do, which is to respond to an extremely attractive woman." There was a faint smile on his face. "One who isn't wearing much."

"So it's not a no?" Katya replied. "It's a not now?"

"Perhaps, Katya," Caleb said, his smile fading. "You're vulnerable. In danger. Now is not the time for us. You need to sleep."

Katya sighed, realizing that the moment had passed. If there was indeed a moment to pass.

"I'm not tired. Besides, what if I don't wake up?"

"You will wake up," Caleb replied. "I'll wake you when it's time."

"What if you fall asleep?"

"I won't. I'm not as tired as you are and I can sleep when you and the girls are gone."

"Do you want me to go back to my own bed?" Katya

asked, moving her body closer to his. "Or can I stay here?"

"Of course you can stay here, Katya," Caleb replied, adjusting his own position slightly so they were both comfortable.

"Can I ask you something?" Katya said a moment later.

"I thought you were going to sleep?" She could tell from the way Caleb spoke he was smiling.

"I will, in a moment. But I have a question first."

"Sure. Fire away."

"What do you think about when you're meditating?" There was a long silence before Caleb replied.

"I don't really think about anything. Meditating isn't thinking."

"So what do you actually do then, if you're not thinking?"

"I'm acknowledging my emotions. Not letting them control me, but letting them pass."

"Why?" Katya opened her eyes and looked at him. "What's wrong with your emotions?"

"There's nothing wrong with them, Katya. Emotions are part of who we are. But they can control people, instead of people controlling them."

"But if they're part of who we are, then how can they control us?"

Caleb opened his eyes and turned to her with a smile.

"In a stream of water, you stand. You don't try to block it. You feel the water rush past you, but you remain strong without getting swept away," he said. "Now go to sleep." He leaned across and placed a kiss on her forehead. His lips were dry and there was nothing sexual about the gesture, but it was one of the most sensual kisses Katya had ever had.

"I like you, Caleb," Katya said as she closed her eyes and

snuggled against him. "I like you a lot, preacher. But I've never heard you actually preach."

"It's a bit like sex, Katya."

"How is preaching like sex?" she replied with a faint smile on her face.

"There's a time and a place for it. And this is neither. Now, sleep," Caleb whispered. "Sleep."

Katya smiled. It was as if he was trying to hypnotize her into sleeping. But she never heard him say it a third time. She was asleep already.

53

Caleb inhaled through his nose, counted to five, and exhaled slowly through his mouth. His body was still reacting to Katya's presence. He was uncomfortable, but it was the type of discomfort that most men, Caleb included, didn't mind. He knew he'd done the right thing. But it had been hard. Very hard.

Beside him, Katya was breathing deeply. Caleb turned his face to look at her. He took his time, taking in every inch of her face. She looked so peaceful, and he hoped she was at peace. Because what was to come would be difficult. For her and for the girls. As he watched, Caleb could see Katya's eyes flickering under her eyelids. Was she dreaming? Caleb wasn't sure if he'd ever had a dream. Perhaps when he was a child he'd dreamed, but he didn't think he had as an adult. When he slept, he slept.

Caleb adjusted his position and reached out for the poultice that was lying next to the pillow. Moving slowly, he adjusted Katya's head so the material was just under the bruise on her cheek. The fact she didn't respond to his touch in the slightest confirmed what he thought. Katya was sound asleep, her body recovering from the stresses and strains of the day. He inched his body away from hers and waited as she adjusted her position slightly, still without waking. Then he lay next to her for a few moments, a couple of inches between their bodies. If Katya was going to wake, it would be now, so he needed to wait until he could be sure she remained asleep.

As he did so, he thought about Ana and Elene. Earlier, before Katya had come to his bed, she had ushered the children in to say goodnight to him. He had laid his hands on their heads, closed his eyes, and prayed for them. Katya had already spoken to them about their planned escape and he could feel their fear through his fingertips. Of the two, Caleb thought Ana was the more resilient even though she was the youngest. She was going to need every ounce of that resilience, not just that evening but for the coming days.

Caleb looked again at Katya, who was still dreaming. He wondered what she was dreaming about as he traced her lips with his eyes. Caleb tried not to think about what it would be like to kiss them, but he gave in and allowed himself the briefest fantasy. Preacher or no preacher, he was still a man. And Katya was still a woman. A very beautiful woman. With a brief shake of his head to dispel his thoughts, Caleb slowly moved his legs so that he was sitting on the edge of the bed. As he did so, he held onto the shackle on his ankle to stop it from making any noise. Then he reached under his pillow with his other hand and withdrew the small bar of soap from the downstairs bathroom. Imprinted into the surface was an outline of the key that he'd slipped out of Mateo's pocket when he'd brushed against him earlier, only to return it a few moments later.

He studied the imprint, measuring the height of the cuts and bitings along it. Caleb had managed to press the key into the soap all the way up to the key's shoulder. It was all he needed. From the serrations on the imprint, he could visualize the internal mechanism of the padlock that secured his shackle. There were five spring-loaded pins which, when aligned, would pop out and release the locking bar.

Caleb reached back under the pillow and pulled out two bobby pins he'd removed from Ana's hair when he'd placed his hand on her head. Resting the shackle on the ground, he bent one of the pins until one end was at ninety degrees to the rest of it. It was crude, but as a tension wrench, would be effective. Sliding it into the padlock, he applied some pressure to keep the lock open, taking care not to snap the soft metal of the bobby pin. With his other hand, he slid the second pin into the padlock and gently raked it back and forth to push the pins above the cylinder. One of the pins felt stuck, and it took a few wiggles for Caleb to free it, but the padlock wasn't a complicated one. A few seconds later, the lock opened with a satisfying click.

With a last look at Katya, Caleb undid the shackle, placing it softly on the floor, and rubbed the skin on his ankle. He really wanted to kiss her, even though she was asleep. Given what had happened earlier, he didn't think she would mind. But if she woke and started kissing him back, Caleb didn't think his body would let his conscience tell him what to do.

Caleb stood and took a deep breath. He counted to five and exhaled.

It was time.

54

Mateo flicked his eyes open and groaned. His bladder was like an aching ball in his abdomen. That last beer had been a mistake. Careful not to disturb Aleksander, who was snoring softly on his bed on the other side of the room, Mateo swung his feet out and padded to the bathroom.

A moment later, his discomfort eased, Mateo walked into the kitchen to grab a glass of water. According to his watch, it was just after two in the morning, so at least when he went back to bed he had a decent stretch of sleep to look forward to. There was nothing worse, he thought as he filled a glass, than waking up at four or five and then going back to bed with only a few hours to go before the day began.

"What the fuck?" Mateo said, whispering even though it was only him in the bathroom. There had just been a flash of light in the forest to the west of the farmhouse. Only for a split second, but there was definitely someone there. Mateo concentrated hard on the treeline, lit by a faint moon. As he watched, he saw another flash. "Punë muti!" Mateo said, more loudly. Shit!

He crept across the kitchen floor and eased open the door, careful to stay in the shadows. From the direction of the flash of light, he heard a dog barking in the forest. Mateo swore again and closed the door. Half-running, he returned to the bedroom and rushed across to Aleksander's bed.

"Aleksander!" Mateo whispered, shaking his brother's shoulder. "Aleksander! Wake up!"

"What is it?" Aleksander replied, rolling over and trying to pull his bedding over him.

"Wake up! There's someone outside."

Mateo watched as Aleksander sat bolt upright in his bed, instantly awake despite the hour.

"What?" he asked Mateo. "Who?"

"I saw some flashlights and heard a dog barking. I think it's the police." It was Aleksander's turn to swear.

"I told you," Aleksander said. Even in the dim light, Mateo saw the fierce look on his face. "I told you they would come. What do we do?"

"We need to leave. I'll wake Gjergj and tell him to get the van ready. You go up and wake the girls. I'll be up in a minute to help."

Mateo crossed to the other bed and started to wake Gjergj. As he did so, he saw Aleksander pick up a roll of gray duct tape from the floor. After the incident in the supermarket, Aleksander had searched one of the farm's outbuildings before coming back with the tape. Next time, he had told Mateo, he'd make sure the girl kept quiet. Mateo had wondered how that might work in a supermarket, but had said nothing. For once, Aleksander's forward thinking might be helpful. The last thing they needed was the girls screaming while they were trying to sneak past the police cordon being put into place around the farm.

"Gjergj!" Mateo said, shaking the driver. "Gjergj, wake

up. The police are here." Gjergj wasn't as quick to wake as Aleksander had been, but when he did come to, his eyes were wide.

"Where?"

"They're outside. In the woods." Mateo tried to keep his voice down and hide his apprehension. "I saw them just now. They're surrounding the farm."

55

A leksander resisted the temptation to say something more to his brother. He had tried to tell Mateo, but no, he wasn't having any of it. That was typical, Aleksander thought as he peeled back the duct tape. Aleksander always had to do as Mateo said, just because he was the oldest. It had always been that way, even when they were children. What Mateo said happened, happened. Even when he was wrong, like now. Aleksander wanted to smile at having been right, but now wasn't the time.

He climbed the stairs slowly, not wanting to wake anyone. The first thing he needed to do was to silence the woman. If he did that, then the girls would be easier to control. If she started screaming, though, not only would it wake them up, but it would also alert the police outside. Aleksander knew little of police tactics, either back in Albania or here in England, but he knew they would take time to get ready. Their challenge was to slip away before that point. Aleksander paused outside the bedroom door and ripped a piece of tape from the roll. He wanted to get it over her mouth before she woke.

The door handle squeaked as he opened it, but Aleksander didn't think it was loud enough to wake them. He inched the door open and peered inside. There was a thin shaft of moonlight illuminating the room, but it still took him a few seconds to work out what was going on. The woman's bed was empty, but as he looked across at Caleb's, he saw her hair fanned out on his pillow.

"What the hell?" Aleksander muttered when he realized she was alone in the bed. All attempts at stealth forgotten, Aleksander strode across the room in three enormous steps. He leaned forward and picked up the iron shackle from the floor. The padlock was undone, but how? In the bed, Katya stirred. Her hand snaked over the top of the covers and, as she realized she was alone, her eyes flickered open.

Aleksander grabbed the thin sheet covering Katya and yanked it back. Then he clamped the shackle onto her ankle and, his hands trembling slightly, fastened the padlock to it.

"What are you doing?" Katya said. Her voice was slurred, almost as if she was drunk. Aleksander reached up with his hand and covered her mouth, realizing he'd dropped the strip of duct tape on the floor while he'd been putting the padlock on. As he picked it up with his free hand, he saw Katya's eyes darting around the room.

"Where is he?" Aleksander hissed through gritted teeth. He relaxed his hand slightly to allow her to speak.

"I don't know!" Katya replied. From the shocked look on her face, Aleksander thought she was telling the truth. "He was here. But I don't know where he is now."

Aleksander placed the strip of duct tape over her mouth and quickly dropped his hands to her wrists. Katya still seemed to be half asleep, and hadn't reacted to having her mouth taped. Nor did she respond when Aleksander pushed her back onto the bed and pulled one of her arms behind her back after rolling her onto her front. It was only when he started winding the duct tape around her wrist that she started to struggle, no doubt finally realizing what he was doing. But it was too late for her to stop him wrapping her wrists together with the tape.

"Stay where you are," he said to her, putting as much authority into his voice as he could muster. He took a moment to look at her, bound and secured to the bed and wearing only skimpy underwear, before leaving the room.

Pausing on the landing, Aleksander waited until he heard Mateo climbing the stairs. As he waited, he considered where the man in the robe had gone. Had he taken the girls somewhere, and was planning on returning for the woman? Aleksander's pistol was still downstairs, next to his bed. Should he go back and get it?

"Mateo, he's gone," Aleksander whispered when his brother joined him. A frown spread over Mateo's face. "Caleb. He's gone."

"How?"

"I don't fucking know," Aleksander shot back. Mateo's frown deepened, as it always did when he swore. "But he's not in the bedroom."

"Okay, if he's gone, he's gone. Let's get the girls," Mateo said. Aleksander thought for a second about raising the possibility that Caleb had taken their precious parcels, but decided against it. They would find out soon enough. "You got the tape?"

"I'll take the older one, Elene," Aleksander said. He hoped she would struggle. He liked it when they struggled.

"Okay," Mateo replied. "But don't hurt her." Aleksander

tutted under his breath. His brother was no fun. "Come on, let's go. We need to hurry."

Aleksander tore two strips off the roll of tape and handed one to Mateo.

"You ready?" he said, his hand on the door handle.

"Let's go," Mateo replied. Aleksander opened the door. All they needed was the two girls to be there.

56

B y the time Caleb reached the gap in the tree line that led to the lookout tower, he was breathing hard from the exertion. He'd not run there from the farmhouse, but moved quickly. The last thing he wanted was Aleksander and Mateo on his tail, although he was sure he'd left the farmhouse without disturbing anyone. Before he'd let himself out of the bathroom window, he'd applied some beeswax from his bag to the hinge to quieten it even more. It had been a tight squeeze through the window and at one point Caleb had thought he was going to have to find another exit.

Caleb slowed his pace as he left the track. The moonlight didn't penetrate the woods, and he made his way with his arms outstretched, letting the tall ferns on either side of the track brush over his fingers. The ladder creaked as he put his weight onto it, but Caleb wasn't concerned. He was far enough away now and, besides, he doubted the brothers even knew of the tower's existence. As he ascended the ladder, Caleb forced himself to relax. He'd made it.

In the distance, a dog barked. Caleb paused for a

moment to listen. He had been half-expecting the bark to be followed by the howling of a coyote, alerting the rest of its family to an intruder, or perhaps a kill. But this was just a single bark from, Caleb estimated, a medium-sized dog. The bark's timbre was too deep to be a fox. A spaniel, perhaps, or a retriever. The dog barked again and Caleb angled his head to locate the direction it came from. It was the same direction as the farmhouse he had just left. Frowning, Caleb continued his ascent. Unlike back home in Texas, where groups of wild coyotes prowled, England didn't have wild dogs as far as he was aware.

A few moments later, Caleb reached the top of the tower. He knew he could be silhouetted against the moonlight, but for that to matter, someone would need to be looking directly at the tower, and Caleb thought that unlikely. First, he looked at the farmhouse, but there were no signs of life. No lights in the windows, no obvious movement that he could discern. Then he turned to look at the pigs' enclosure, which was just visible in the gloom below him. Beyond it was the pig farmer's house, his next destination. There would be things there he would need. Clothes. Food, perhaps. Maybe even a weapon, although Caleb had no need for one. If there was a weapon in the house, it would most likely be a shotgun. Not the most discreet weapon to wander the land with. But there were no signs of life at this farmhouse either. Caleb wouldn't know for certain until he reached the house, but from his current vantage point, he couldn't see any vehicles. The farm machinery he'd seen earlier was still there, but where the station wagon had been was just a space.

That was a setback. Caleb had been relying on being able to take that vehicle, either by stealth or by force. Not having it would slow him down a lot, particularly because he didn't know where the next nearest vehicle would be. But on the plus side, if the farmhouse was empty, then it would make searching the building easier.

Caleb looked at the sky briefly to locate the North Star. Then he turned his eyes to the horizon and started slowly turning in a circle. Starting due north, it didn't take him long to locate what he had climbed the tower to find. Almost directly southeast from his location was a faint orange glow. It was a long way off. Fifteen miles, perhaps more. From the glow, Caleb surmised it was a small town. Perhaps a village. But definitely civilization. Sunrise would be in three and a half, perhaps four hours. If Caleb didn't take too long searching the farmhouse, he could be there by the time the sun crested the horizon.

Fixing the direction of the town in his mind, Caleb descended from the tower. He made his way back down the path, arms outstretched again to keep in the center. When he reached the road, Caleb turned left toward the pig farmer's house. It would only take him ten or fifteen minutes to reach it.

As he walked, Caleb was tempted to stop and turn around to look at the farmhouse where Katya and the girls were sleeping. But he didn't.

Caleb never looked back.

57

Katya wrenched her wrists as hard as she could, but the tape wound around them was unyielding. She tried to arch her hands forward, twisting her forearms against each other to get her fingertips into a position where she could get to the end of the tape, but to no avail. Her wrists were tied fast and pressing into the small of her back. Katya couldn't even get any purchase on the tape covering her mouth against the smooth bed sheets.

Her nostrils flaring from the effort, Katya managed to adjust her position so she could see the door to the bedroom. Aleksander had left it open, and she could see Mateo and him outside Ana and Elene's door. They were talking to each other and Aleksander was peeling strips off the roll of tape in his hands.

Katya's heart was hammering in her chest as she tried to take in what was going on. She had gone from being asleep next to Caleb to being gagged and tied, Caleb's shackle now on her own ankle. Where was he? Where had he gone? Katya felt tears building in her eyes as she thought back to the previous evening when he had rebutted her advances. Now she knew why he had turned her down. Because he was leaving. Was it some sort of warped honor? Not sleeping with her because he knew he would never see her again?

As Katya watched, Mateo opened the girls' door. The two men walked into the bedroom. A second later, there was a scream that only lasted for a second, if that, before it was cut off. Katya couldn't see inside the room, but she could hear some muffled thuds followed by a scraping noise. The next thing she saw filled her heart with fear. It was Aleksander, a twisted smile on his face. Draped over his shoulder was Elene, squirming, her mouth taped shut like Katya's and tape wound around her wrists. Elene's eyes met Katya's, and she saw the abject terror in them as Aleksander hefted the girl on his shoulder. His arm was wrapped around Elene's midriff and Katya saw his knuckles were white as he dug them into her side to prevent her moving. Then Elene disappeared from Katya's sight as Aleksander started down the stairs.

A few seconds later, Katya saw Ana through the door. Like Elene, her mouth and wrists were taped, but Mateo was carrying her with one arm looped under her legs and the other around her shoulders. He was saying something as he carried her, but Katya knew Ana couldn't understand him. Then Mateo disappeared as well.

Katya renewed her struggles against the tape binding her arms. Even if she could free them, she was still shackled to the bed. But she had to do something. Where were they taking the girls? And where was Caleb?

A few moments later, Katya lay back on the bed, exhausted. Her shoulders were aching, a deep pain that her wriggling had made worse. All she had achieved was to bunch the tape around her wrists into a thin cord that chafed her skin even more. She paused for a moment to listen. There were footsteps on the gravel outside the farm-house. Then the sound of a vehicle door opening and closing again. Katya sobbed, knowing that the girls were being loaded into the van. They were being taken away.

Katya felt herself start to well up at the thought of them being taken and her being left behind. What if they never came back? How long would she survive without water or food? Would it be days? Weeks? She swallowed, trying not to cry. With her mouth taped up, if her nose filled up with snot and tears, she might struggle to breathe. Relax, she told herself. Just relax.

But there was no way Katya was going to be able to do that.

58

Mateo paused by the van, Ana still in his arms. In front of him, Aleksander was opening the side door, the other girl still slung over his shoulder. The noise it made as it slid open made Mateo wince.

"Do it quietly," he whispered, glancing at the tree line where he'd seen the flashlights earlier. There was nothing to see other than darkness, but he knew he'd not imagined it. Ignoring Aleksander's muttered response, Mateo placed Ana on the ground. He pointed at the now open door, but she shook her head with a fearful glance at the dark interior of the van. Aleksander had placed Elene inside the van and pushed her into it. With another curse, he turned and picked up Ana roughly, one hand under each of her armpits. She squealed through the tape as he did so, and Mateo's eyes shot back to the trees.

Mateo took a few steps toward the van. The way they'd tied the girls' hands in front of them meant there would be nothing to stop them removing the tape and screaming. But the only other option was for them to sit up in the front of the van, where they could be seen. He also doubted they would all fit on the front seat. Mateo had no intention of going in the back of the van, and he was sure Aleksander wouldn't either. So they would have to take the chance.

"Go back up and get the woman," Mateo whispered to Aleksander. He was rewarded with a sneer, which he ignored. Now wasn't the time for having a pissing competition with his little brother. "Aleksander, just go." With a frown, Aleksander turned on his heel and did as instructed. Mateo watched him walking toward the farmhouse, pulling the pistol from the back of his pants as he did so.

Mateo walked up to the sliding door in the van and looked in. Both girls stared back at him, their eyes wide. Elene's face was streaked with tears. Aleksander had been none too gentle when he had been carrying her, and Mateo hoped she wasn't marked in any way. Martin wouldn't like that one little bit. He raised his index finger to his lips and made a shushing sound. Then he eased the door closed before walking to the passenger side of the van. On the front seat was a rucksack, hastily filled with as many of their belongings as they'd been able to gather. Mateo knew there was still stuff in the house, but nothing that could identify them.

"Gjergj?" Mateo asked through the open window. "Are we all set?" Gjergj nodded in response.

"Yes," he replied. "I've double checked, and it's set for electric. So no engine noise."

"Good." Mateo looked at Gjergj. He looked nervous but resolute. "As soon as Aleksander gets back with the woman, we go. Yes?"

"Where do we go?"

"Away from here is all that matters. We'll worry about that later."

"I need a smoke," Gjergj said, a faint smile on his face.

"Later."

Mateo looked out of the windshield at the tree line. A few seconds later, there was a flash of light in the woods.

"Did you see that?" he asked Gjergj. Then there was another flash. "Are they coming? Start the engine."

His fingers trembling, Gjergj pressed a button on the dashboard. An array of lights lit up in front of him, but the van remained silent.

"What about Aleksander?" Gjergj asked Mateo. What happened next answered Gjergj's question for him.

From the direction of the trees, there was a noise. Definitely not a normal one.

It was a gunshot. Very loud. Very close. Mateo turned to Gjergj, his eyes widening as the echo of the shot reverberated around the clearing.

"Go! Go! Go!" Mateo said, banging his hand on the dashboard.

59

Caleb froze at the sound of the shot. He held his breath. The sound had come from the direction of the farmhouse. It was a deep and powerful noise. A shotgun as opposed to a pistol. Caleb was too far away to hear anything else, such as the chung chung sound of a pump action being reloaded. But a shotgun was a shotgun. A persuasive weapon in the right—or wrong—hands.

He was in what he assumed was the master bedroom of the pig farmer's house. It was, as he had suspected from the tower, uninhabited. From the sparse belongings that were in the building, Caleb thought that the pig farmer lived elsewhere, and only used the farmhouse on occasion. He had spent a few moments confirming it was empty before breaking a window and clambering through it into a kitchen. Caleb had first checked the fridge for food but, other than a milk carton so old its contents had separated, there was nothing. One of the kitchen cupboards had yielded some canned food and a few packets of cookies that he was going to return for.

Caleb was wearing a pair of dark blue jeans and a thin

three-quarter zipped fleece that was also dark blue. When the shot rang out, he was rifling through a drawer, searching for a thick pair of socks. The pig farmer was slightly larger than Caleb, and his feet were perhaps a half size larger, but thick socks would mean the boots he had found would fit.

As he continued rifling through the drawer, Caleb considered what he had just heard. The brothers hadn't owned a shotgun as far as he knew. Just a pistol. There could have been one elsewhere in the house—not unusual for a farmhouse, even in England—but why would either of them be using it at this time of the morning, before the sun had even risen? It could only mean one thing. There were other people there. People who were armed. Not just armed, but prepared to use their weapons. Were there other traffickers, perhaps? Was it some sort of gang war? Caleb didn't know and, he thought as he pulled a thick pair of woolen socks from the drawer, it was no concern of his.

Caleb sat on the bed to put the socks on, followed by the boots, which were now almost a perfect fit. Then he went to a cupboard in the corner of the room to see what else he could find that would be useful. When he saw the bag stuffed in the bottom of the cupboard, he nodded in satisfaction. That would give him something to keep his own bag in, along with the food from the kitchen. He took the bag out and shook the dust from it.

In a drawer next to the bed were more items of underwear, which he placed in the bag. When he moved the socks and underwear, he saw an ancient pornographic magazine at the bottom of the drawer. A woman with peroxide-blonde hair stared at him, her impossibly pneumatic breasts clad in a skimpy bikini top. Caleb leaned forward and checked the date on the magazine's cover. It was over ten years old and the woman on the front was, apparently, a reader's wife, as were the other women inside. He shook his head, wondering how lonely a man had to be to not only look at a magazine such as this one, but to keep it for so long. His thoughts turned briefly to Katya, and the feel of her body against his earlier that night, but he closed both the drawer and the memory.

Returning to the kitchen with the bag, Caleb filled it with his own bag, the food from the table, and his carefully folded robes. There were no mirrors in the house that he had seen, but he didn't need to check his appearance to know that when he reached civilization, he would be less conspicuous than if he were wearing a robe.

Caleb hefted the bag on his back as he left the house, adjusting the straps so they were comfortable on his shoulders. The lack of a vehicle was a setback, but not one which distracted him for long. He glanced at the sky to orientate himself. The orange glow he'd seen from the tower was some way off, but he didn't mind that.

He took a deep breath and started walking.

60

With the sound of the gunshot still echoing in his ears, Aleksander crouched behind the kitchen sink. He listened intently for a few seconds, hearing several things. The first was male voices shouting in English. He couldn't make out their words, but it sounded like there were several different people. The second thing was the sound of gravel being crushed under tires. He stood, peering over the sink and out of the window. The van was leaving, the electric motor making no sound.

Aleksander got to his feet and ran to the door, flinging it open. The van was perhaps a hundred yards away and accelerating fast. Mateo and Gjergj were leaving. Without him. He considered sprinting after it, but he knew he'd never catch up. He swore under his breath, wondering what to do. Should he run?

His attention was drawn to a light in the trees. Clutching the pistol firmly in his hand, he took a few steps back into the house so he couldn't be seen. As he watched, a man emerged from the tree line and stepped out into the moonlight. He was dressed from head to toe in camouflage clothing. In one hand was a shotgun, in the other a large lamp. Aleksander saw him take a few steps forward and crouch down to examine the ground. Behind him, a second man emerged dressed in similar attire. The second man also had a lamp, but no shotgun.

"Which way did it go?" Aleksander heard the second man call out. In response, the first man pointed across the clearing to the tree line on the other side of the farmhouse.

"That way."

Aleksander started laughing. These men weren't police. They were hunters, tracking whatever they had just wounded. The large lights they used would freeze animals. Anything from a rabbit to a deer. He watched as they walked across the clearing, oblivious to the fact they were being watched. The first man stopped a couple of times, crouching again to check the ground. Following the blood.

His laughter didn't last for long, though. Although the threat of imminent capture by the police was now gone, it didn't change the fact that Mateo had run. Without him, and with their precious cargo. He would have to address that with his brother when he caught up with him.

Aleksander walked into the room the three men had been using as a bedroom to get his phone. He would call Mateo, tell him that the coast was clear. Let him come back with his tail between his legs. But when he crossed the room to get his phone, it was gone. No phone, no charger. Aleksander swore under his breath when he realized that almost all their possessions had been cleared out. He remembered Mateo telling Gjergj to collect everything together when they were fetching the girls from upstairs.

He returned to the kitchen and grabbed a beer from the fridge, sitting down at the table to drink it and think. At least Gjergj had left the beer and food behind. Aleksander knew he had a few options. He could wait, see if Mateo returned. Perhaps they were just hiding down the road until it was clear what was happening? But what if they weren't? What if they had gone with no intention of returning?

Aleksander had been watching Mateo carefully for the last few weeks. He knew he was up to something, but wasn't sure what. Maybe this was it—he was just going to abandon him. His own brother. Aleksander had noticed his newfound secretive nature when it came to money. The fact he never let his passport leave his pocket. Aleksander wasn't stupid, despite what his brother thought. If Mateo was taking the girls to their final destination, he and only he would get the money. Sure, there would be a cut for Gjergj, but Mateo could keep the rest and there was nothing Aleksander could do about it. Could his own brother really do that to him? With a sigh, Aleksander raised the bottle to his lips and took a long sip. Yes, Aleksander thought. He could.

His sadness turned to anger over the course of the next thirty minutes, and several more bottles of beer. Not enough for him to be drunk, but there was no rakia left. There was a scraping noise from above his head, and Aleksander turned to look at the door that led to the stairs.

He got to his feet, his anger bubbling up in his chest. If his brother had disappeared, then he wouldn't be back anytime soon. Which meant he was left to dispose of the woman.

A cruel smile spread onto Aleksander's face as he made his way to the door. He might as well have some fun before he fed the pigs.

ateo took a few deep breaths as the van rattled its way silently down the track. His heart was still beating fast, and his fingertips were tingling. He tried to calm himself down, but a wave of nausea hit him in the solar plexus.

"Gjergj," he said sharply. "Stop the van."

The van had barely ground to a halt when Mateo was out of the vehicle, retching on the side of the track. He spat a glob of mucus into the vegetation and took some more deep breaths, hoping that he wasn't going to vomit.

"Are you okay, Mateo?" Gjergj called from the driver's seat. Mateo nodded in response, leaning forward and putting his hands on his knees. A few moments later, the nausea almost gone, he climbed back into the van.

"Sorry," he said to Gjergj, who just looked at him with concern. "Just nerves, that's all." From the look on Gjergj's face, he didn't believe him.

"What do we do now?" Gjergj asked. "Keep going with the girls, or...?" He angled his head back over his shoulder in the direction they had just come from.

"We can't go back," Mateo said. "The place will be crawling with police."

"But what if it wasn't the police?" Gjergj replied. "I don't get why they would shoot at us. Did you see any damage to the van just now?"

Mateo didn't reply, but got back out of the van. He slowly made his way around it, looking for any signs of damage in the light of the flashlight on his phone, but there was none. Not so much as a dent from what he could see through the mud. Whatever the police had been shooting at, it wasn't the van. As he walked around the vehicle, he thought about what Gjergj had just said. Mateo's knowledge of the British police was limited to watching programs such as Police Interceptors on televisions in run-down hotel rooms, but he thought they were reasonably disciplined. Therefore unlikely to take unannounced potshots at things.

"Maybe you're right," Mateo said, joining Gjergj at the front of the van where he was having a smoke. "But after the helicopter? I don't think we can take the chance." He thought for a moment. "I say we drop them off. Perhaps we can get another vehicle from the peshkop and come back for Aleksander and the woman?"

"It isn't that far, the address you were given," Gjergj replied. "Less than an hour, according to the sat nav."

Mateo thought some more. What would Martin's likely reaction be if they only delivered the girls, and not the woman? It wasn't as if he was paying for her. Or, and this was the idea that was gathering momentum in his mind, they could drop the girls off, get the money, and he could slip away. Make the break he'd been thinking about for some time? His hand slipped to the rear pocket of his trousers, where his passport was hidden. The money could be accessed from anywhere, but what about his brother?

He watched Gjergj smoking, almost jealous at the man's ability to just do nothing but enjoy a simple pleasure. The fact it was a simple pleasure that would probably kill the man wasn't lost on Mateo, but he envied him a small bit regardless of that. Mateo needed to somehow confirm that Aleksander was in the custody of the police. If he was, then he could make his escape in the knowledge that he'd not abandoned Aleksander, but run for his own safety.

"We've got two options, Gjergj," Mateo said, a plan slowly forming in his mind. "We could take the girls to the peshkop, and then come back. Like I said just now."

"What's the second option?" Gjergj replied a moment later after grinding the cigarette out under his shoe.

"We go back now to see if the police are there. They'll be all over the farmhouse if they are so easy to spot. And if they're not, we get Aleksander and the woman and then we go to the peshkop's house."

Mateo watched as Gjergj examined another cigarette in the packet.

"When you say we go back, you mean me?" he asked Mateo.

"Someone needs to keep an eye on the girls," Mateo replied, fixing Gjergj with a look that he hoped didn't come across as smug. "You go on foot, see what's going on, and then return. We'll decide then."

A few moments later, while he was watching Gjergj trudge along the path and into the darkness, Mateo realized what he'd just managed to do. He'd not intended to, but he'd just increased his cut of the money if he took the girls to the peshkop's house by himself. And what if the police came back down this path? He would be, if he'd got the English phrase correct, a sitting duck.

Mateo returned to the van and climbed into the driver's

seat. He drummed his fingers on the steering wheel for a moment.

What should he do?

62

K atya had managed to get herself into a comfortable position on the bed, but her shoulders were so painful it felt as if they were dislocated. She had no idea of the time, but estimated that it had been at least thirty minutes since the sound of the gunshot. When she'd heard it, she'd jumped on the bed so much she almost fell off it. The sound had been followed by a period of intense excitement, mixed with fear. Was it the police? Was Katya about to be rescued? Or was it something else entirely? As the time passed with nothing else happening, her initial elation at the sound had ebbed back into despair at her predicament.

She lifted her head at a noise from somewhere within the farmhouse. It was followed a few seconds later by another sound, a creak. Katya's heart fell as she realized someone was coming up the stairs. She so badly wanted it to be men in uniforms, smashing the doors down and shouting POLICE! But it wasn't. Someone was coming, and she was sure she knew who.

When the door to the bedroom opened, her fears were realized. It was Aleksander. He was holding the pistol in one hand and the roll of duct tape in the other. He placed both items on the table next to her bed on the other side of the room and crossed to the bed she was in. Caleb's bed.

Aleksander reached down and picked at the corner of the tape covering her mouth. In a single movement, he ripped it away. Katya gasped in pain before taking a deep breath in through her mouth. As Aleksander walked back across the room and picked up the roll of tape, she took as many deep breaths as she could. He might have been about to replace it and she wanted to make the most of being able to breathe properly, even if only for a few moments. But when Aleksander returned, he produced a small knife from his pocket, using it to slice through the tape around her wrists.

Katya bit back a scream as her shoulders moved back into their normal position. The pain across the top of her back was excruciating, but she didn't want to give him the satisfaction of knowing how much agony she was in.

"Thank you," she whispered through gritted teeth.

Aleksander didn't reply, but peeled a fresh piece of tape from the roll. He grabbed her wrist, wound the tape around it, and pulled her hand toward the bed frame. Before Katya realized what he was doing, her wrist was fastened to the bed. It was followed by the other one. Her arms now formed a Y shape, leaving her body completely exposed. When he pulled the sheet she'd managed to get herself under away, a cruel grimace on his face as he did so, his intentions were crystal clear.

Katya closed her eyes, not wanting to watch his eyes crawling over her body.

"Please don't do this, Aleksander," she said. He took a

couple of steps toward her.

"It won't be like last time, bitch," Aleksander replied. She could smell beer on his breath. "There's no one here apart from you and me. That gun shot? It was hunters, looking for food. They've long gone, as has my bastard of a brother."

Katya opened her eyes to see Aleksander right next to her. He had the knife in his hand, and she flinched as he pressed it against her cheek.

"Aleksander, please," Katya said, trying and failing to keep the fear out of her voice.

"It's just you and me here," he said, stroking her cheek with the blade. "No one to disturb us." She felt the blade sliding down to her neck and shivered. It wasn't sharp, but it didn't need to be. "My brother has taken the girls and run away. He's left you and me behind." He adjusted his position and out of the corner of her eye, Katya could see that he was rubbing his crotch. "So why don't we have some fun before we say goodbye?"

Katya tensed her arms, but there was no give in the tape. She couldn't even try to kick him and, even if she did, what good would that do?

"Why, Aleksander?" Katya said, playing for time even though she knew it was futile. "Why are you doing this?"

His smile was one of the cruelest things Katya had ever seen.

"Because I can, Katya," he said with a sneer. "Because I can. Now, are you ready to play?"

The knife dropped to Katya's chest, and she gasped when she felt the metal touching her breast. Aleksander twisted it and was trying to cut through the material of her bra when Katya heard the most welcoming sound she'd ever heard in her life. Five slow knocks on the farmhouse door. It was Gjergj. That meant they were back.

"You have got to be fucking kidding me," Aleksander said as he got to his feet. He pointed the knife at Katya, who was on the verge of tears of relief. "This isn't over, bitch. You'll get what's coming to you. Mark my words."

63

"Mateo," Martin said, trying to keep the irritation out of his voice. "Whatever brings you here at this ungodly hour?" On the doorstep in front of him, the two girls were shivering behind the Albanian.

"I'm sorry, Martin, but we had to change our plans. May we come in?"

"Of course, of course," Martin replied. "Where are my manners? Please, come in. Oh my, look at you two. You're frozen." The girls just looked at him, uncomprehending.

He stepped back to allow the unexpected visitors to enter the house, closing the door behind them.

"Has something happened?" Martin asked Mateo as he led them into the lounge of his house.

"It was the police. They came to the farmhouse."

"What?" Martin said. The word came out as a bark. "What?" he said again, more softly this time.

"It was Aleksander," Mateo said. "He went shopping and ran into trouble. Somehow they found the farmhouse. From his sat nav, I think."

Martin paused, thinking hard. This was a major risk to their entire operation. Mateo opened his mouth to say something else, but Martin put his hand up to stop him. He needed a few moments to think this through.

TEN MINUTES LATER, having roused Robert from his bed, the three men were sitting in Martin's private study. He had a drink in his hand but the other two men had nothing.

"Talk us through it again, Mateo," Martin said, sipping his scotch. He listened intently as Mateo went back over the story for Robert's benefit. Back in the lounge, the two girls were curled up on sofas, wrapped in duvets.

"You're sure there's no chance the van was followed?" Robert asked when Mateo had finished recounting the events of the previous few hours.

"None at all," Mateo replied. "We left before the main assault began."

"But they'll have the number plate," Robert said, addressing the statement at Martin. "I'll deal with the van." He picked up his phone and started tapping at the screen.

"But then I'll have no transport," Mateo said. Martin looked at the Albanian and frowned. That wasn't his problem. But if the man had no transport, then he would be hanging around the house, and Martin couldn't have that. Mateo needed to be a long way away by the time Martin's guests started arriving.

"I'll lend you something," Martin said, figuring that was the best way to get rid of him. "What about the woman?"

"The police will have her and Aleksander." Mateo looked at him with a pathetic expression. It was all Martin could do to not slap him round the face. But Martin wasn't a man of violence. Not with a grown man, at least.

He swore under his breath. The farmhouse had been one of Martin's most useful assets. Ideally located, remote enough for their purposes. Now he was going to have to find another location somewhere. And he'd been looking forward to getting a new housekeeper. He swore again, realizing that he would have to get one of the women back from the establishments to service his house and his needs. But that wasn't a priority.

The woman had seen him. That was a problem. She could describe him to the police. Depending on her recall, she could give the police enough information for a sketch, or photo-fit, or whatever it was they did. Someone, somewhere, might recognize him. But denial was easy for a man like Martin. It would be his word against someone else's, and Martin's word was highly thought of. If necessary, there were several people who he could have a quiet word with. Call in a favor or two. But Martin didn't enjoy doing that. Being indebted to people went against his character. He much preferred it the other way round.

"Right," Martin said, placing his scotch down on the desk. "Robert? Deal with the van and provide Mateo here with an alternative. One of the cars." He fixed Mateo with a cool look. "But I want it back. It's a loan, not a gift. The girls can stay here. I'll need an alternate housekeeper for them, so get on the phone first thing and find a Georgian one."

Martin waited as Robert scribbled something down on a notepad he'd produced from his pocket. When he had finished writing, Martin continued. "The two girls can stay in the annex downstairs for the time being. They'll be secure enough down there. Maybe we can bring your team in early to be on the safe side?"

Robert nodded and looked up at Martin expectantly. "I'll have them here later this morning." He got to his feet. "Will that be all?"

Martin didn't reply but just waved a hand to dismiss the man. He waited until his head of security had left the office before turning his attention to Mateo.

"I suggest you lie low for a while, young man," Martin said. "If the police are as good as they are purported to be, your brother will sing like a proverbial canary." He watched as the Albanian frowned, but Martin wasn't about to explain the phrase to him.

"I'm thinking of getting out, Martin," Mateo said. "For good." It was Martin's turn to frown.

"Really?" he asked. "That's a bit extreme."

"I've been thinking about it for a while. Planning for it."

"Well, I suppose all good things must come to an end eventually," Martin said. He picked up his glass and had just emptied it when there was a soft knock at the door. "Come in?"

"Sorry to disturb you, boss, but what do you want me to do with the other one?"

"The other what?"

"The other Albanian smoking by the van."

"I'll come and get him," Martin heard Mateo reply. "That's Gjergj. He's my driver."

64

Caleb waited until the door was fully open. Then he waited for a second or two for the look of confusion to disappear from Aleksander's face. Then he drove the ax into his forehead, using a punching motion to ensure it had enough force behind it for the blade to penetrate his skull.

When he pulled gently on the ax, he knew he'd put adequate force behind the blow to embed it into Aleksander's frontal bone just enough for it to be lodged, but not so much it killed him. Guided by Caleb, Aleksander stumbled forward, blinking furiously as he did so. He made no attempt to raise his hands to the ax, not that it would have made any difference at all.

Caleb moved Aleksander to the side of the door and then pushed him back up against the jamb.

"Do you read Scripture, Aleksander?"

The Albanian didn't reply, but just continued blinking. A rivulet of blood started running down the side of his nose. Caleb watched as it ran into his eye, but again he made no effort with his arms. Perhaps Caleb's initial blow had been a little too hard if it had caused a loss of strength so quickly. But Caleb knew it could just be the shock of having an ax to the face.

"Aleksander?" Caleb said. "I asked you a question?" He increased the pressure on the ax, using the wooden jamb behind Aleksander as leverage.

"Ugh," Aleksander managed.

"I'm going to take that as a no," Caleb replied. "Which is what I thought. So you're not familiar with Deuteronomy? Specifically, chapter thirty-two, verse thirty-five?"

"Ugh." Aleksander's hands started twitching, but his arms didn't move.

"Your foot has slipped, my friend," Caleb said. "Your day of disaster is near and your doom is rushing upon you."

Caleb raised his free hand and used his palm to strike the ax head, driving it deeper into Aleksander's forehead.

"How about the Book of Amos?" This time, Aleksander made no sound at all. His eyes were fixed on Caleb's. "I am justice, rolling on like a river." He slapped the ax head again. "Righteousness like an ever-flowing stream. I'm paraphrasing, but I think you get the drift, don't you?"

Caleb paused for a few seconds, studying Aleksander's eyes as he saw them start to glaze over. Inside his forehead, the ax would have penetrated the meninges, the membranes that were supposed to protect and cover the brain. Caleb knew that if he left Aleksander now, he would almost certainly die. But Caleb wasn't about almost certainly.

"How you doin' there, big fella?" Caleb asked, his Texan accent becoming more pronounced. Inside Aleksander's brain, blood would be flowing into the epidural space between the various membranes. If untreated by a neurosurgical team, the blood would exert pressure on the brain, slowly forcing it down through the hole at the bottom of the

Albanian's skull and compressing his brain stem. Caleb could take the ax out to relieve the pressure through the fracture in his skull, but he wasn't going to. Regardless, there was no neurosurgical team anywhere nearby. And even if they were, Caleb doubted they would be able to help Aleksander even if they wanted to.

Another blow to the ax head followed. That one would render the rupture of the meninges irrelevant. The blade of the ax was now firmly in Aleksander's frontal lobe. Caleb saw his eyes become even more glazed. One of them started to drift to one side, twitching slightly as it did so.

"Prepare to meet thy maker, Aleksander," Caleb said, raising his hand again. "I'm sure He'll be delighted to see you."

Caleb put as much force as he could into the final blow before releasing his grip on the ax handle. As he watched Aleksander slump to the floor, he considered offering up a short prayer for the repose of his soul.

But Caleb couldn't be bothered.

65

The moment Aleksander had left the room, Katya started writhing desperately on the bed. He'd left the gun on the bedside table, and if she got her hands free, she thought she could reach it despite the shackle around her ankle that chained her to the bed. One thing was for sure—she was going to try her best. No way was she going without a fight, and if she had to, she would drag the bed across the floor.

Gritting her teeth, she pulled as hard as she could on the tape securing her arm. A few seconds later, she paused, panting hard. Had the tape on her right wrist just shifted a little? She thought it had, so she took a deep breath and focused all her attention and effort just on that hand. Even if she had to strip all the skin from her wrist, she was going to free herself. She had to. If Aleksander didn't kill her today, he would at some point.

"Oh, come on," Katya said, relaxing for a few seconds. She didn't know how long she had. What if Gjergj went away again, leaving her alone with that pig of a man? She would rather die of starvation in the forest than at his hand.

At least then she would retain her own self-respect. Katya pulled again at her right wrist. The tape was definitely loosening, just not quick enough.

After what seemed like the longest twenty seconds of her life, Katya felt the tape shift. She was almost there. With a grunt, she put all her energy into pulling until, finally, it had loosened enough for her to slip her wrist out. Breathing hard, she used her right hand to free her left.

Katya turned her attention to the shackle around her ankle. She reached down and pulled the padlock that secured it a couple of times, but it remained closed. How had Caleb released it? Ignoring the shackle, she reached across the room, but the bedside table was still at least two feet away from her outstretched hands. She was going to have to move the bed.

The noise when she pulled it for the first time surprised her. There was no way that couldn't be heard downstairs, she told herself. She tried to lift it, but the wooden bedstead was too heavy. Katya knew she only had a few short seconds before either Aleksander or Gjergj came running up the stairs. She dragged it another foot or so toward the bedside table. She was almost there. One more lunge with the heavy bed would do it. Katya paused for breath, composing herself for the last pull. As she did so, she heard the distinctive sound of footsteps on the stairs. She had to be quick.

Putting all her weight into it, Katya dragged the bed a final time. She was there! Her hand reached out for the pistol. It was much heavier than she remembered, and she could see her fingers trembling. Did it need to be cocked? Katya had never fired a gun in her life, but had watched enough films and television shows to know that you couldn't just pull the trigger. But if Aleksander was carrying it around, wouldn't he have cocked it already? Katya had no way of knowing.

Outside the bedroom, she heard footsteps on the stairs. There was a creak that told her whoever was outside had reached the top. She wrapped both hands around the gun and pointed it at the door. Just before it opened, she remembered the safety catch. With her left thumb, she flipped it. But was it on or off? It would depend on whether Aleksander had left it engaged or not. She thought she would have enough time if it didn't fire to flick it back to where it had been.

Katya took a deep breath and willed her hands to stop trembling. She looked at the door as it started to swing open, revealing the silhouette of a man on the landing. Aleksander or Gjergj, Katya didn't care. Forcing herself to keep her eyes open, Katya's knuckles whitened as she pulled the trigger.

The subsequent gunshot answered her question about the safety.

ateo searched with his hand underneath the passenger seat for the lever that would allow him to move his seat back. Beside him, Gjergj was studying the controls of the car Robert had given them. It was a small Fiat. Ridiculously small in Mateo's opinion, not that Robert had asked him for it when he'd handed over the keys with a warning to look after it.

In the driver's seat, Gjergj had found the switch to turn the headlights on. He then started the car, which was far noisier than the van had been.

"Where next?" Gjergj asked. "Back to the farmhouse?"

Mateo thought for a few moments before replying. When Gjergj had come back from the farm earlier, he'd reported that all was quiet. No signs of anyone at all, let alone a phalanx of police with guns and dogs. They had both made the decision to continue on their journey and get the girls to a place of safety. Relatively speaking, as Mateo knew only too well. As far as Gjergj was concerned, they were just bringing people over to England. He'd never asked what happened to them and neither Mateo nor Aleksander had ever said anything. That had been the deal when they'd taken him on board. He drove, and that was all he did.

But what should Mateo do now? He couldn't run, not yet. At least not until Martin had paid them, and that would be a few days at least. Then Mateo would need to transfer his share of the money to the bank account he'd set up back in Albania. His escape fund, as he thought of it.

He had been tempted to disappear when Gjergj went back to the farmhouse. Just go to Martin's house with the packages and ask him for help. But, as he'd reflected at the time, Martin didn't strike him as the sort of person who would help a man out like that. Not when there would be nothing in it for him. Mateo would just have to wait for his moment. It would be soon.

"I guess we should, yes," Mateo said a moment later. Gjergj gave him a curious look but said nothing as he put the car into gear.

While Gjergj drove, Mateo looked out of the window at the passing scenery. Martin lived not far from a village called Bucknall which seemed to Mateo to be not much more than a collection of farm buildings with some houses dotted amongst them. The road through the village was narrow and winding and only a few houses had lights on. It was still an hour or so from sunrise, and the village hadn't yet spent money on street lights.

"Have you heard anything more from Gramoz about the other packages?" Gjergj asked as they drove past a small, red-brick primary school shrouded in darkness.

"Not yet, no," Mateo replied. "Last he told me they were still held up on the other side of the channel."

"It'll be more difficult to get them in this," Gjergj said. "Not much room, is there?"

"We'll manage."

"I doubt I'll be able to hire another van, either."

Mateo nodded his head. Losing the van was unfortunate, especially as they'd hired it in Gjergj's name. That was, in hindsight, a mistake. The rental was due to expire the following week, by which time Mateo would be long gone and Gjergj, if he had any sense, would be back in Albania. Mateo doubted the hire company's reach spread that far.

"No, that's true. You'll probably need to head home before the rental runs out."

"Seriously?"

Mateo looked at Gjergj in the gloom. Had he not thought that through? From the expression on his face, he obviously hadn't.

"Yes, seriously. We're almost done here, anyway. We can head back to Albania, have a break, and regroup. I'll get another van off Gramoz or someone like him."

They drove on in silence for a while, passing through several more small villages. Mateo was tempted to tell Gjergj to just head to the airport, but now that he knew Aleksander wasn't in police custody, it made it very difficult to just leave. An ideal situation would have been for Aleksander to have been arrested so that he and Gjergj could have run legitimately. Getting back across the channel to France was easy enough. The authorities were only interested in people coming illegally to England, not leaving. But for him to run now would mean his brother would be in the wild, and at some point, could catch up with him. Plus all his family back home would know he'd betrayed Aleksander for money. Mateo wanted his freedom, but not to be cut off from home forever.

"Where do you think the man in the robe went?" Gjergj asked a few moments later. "Do you think he'll have gone to the police?"

"He'll have gone as far away from the farmhouse as possible, if he's got any sense," Mateo replied. "But I doubt he'll have gone to the police. He's here just as illegally as the girls and the woman." He sat back in his seat and adjusted his legs, trying to get them comfortable. "The minute he shows up at a police station, he'll be arrested. I don't think we've got anything to worry about there. We've seen the last of him, I'm sure of that."

67

"What are your thoughts, Robert?" Martin said, sipping his coffee. There was no point even trying to go back to bed now, and if Martin was going to be up, so was Robert. "On Mateo's plan?"

"Hmm," Robert replied. Martin had spent the previous few moments filling his head of security in on Mateo's wish to retire from their operation. "I can't say I like it. He could be a loose end."

"I agree. But I'd quite happily cut his brother loose. Can they be trusted?"

"No." Robert sipped at his own coffee. "Not in the slightest. But that's a risk I guess we have to take. Unless you wanted to, er, take some more affirmative action."

"Not really," Martin said. "Someone, somewhere would be sure to miss them. We only have their word that no-one knows where they are. This Gramoz fellow doesn't sound like a particularly nice chap, from what you told me." He had paid Robert a handsome sum for a background check on the man, some of which he was sure found its way into Robert's own pocket. But Martin didn't begrudge him a little markup, and the intelligence had been invaluable. "I'd rather keep him at arm's length as much as possible. I certainly don't want him turning up here looking for his nephews. Where are they now?"

Martin waited while Robert checked his phone.

"They're on the A46, just outside Market Rasen," he said a few seconds later.

"So heading back to the farmhouse?"

"It would appear so, yes."

"But why? If the place is crawling with police like Mateo said it was, why would they go back there?" Martin frowned, thinking back to exactly what Mateo had said.

"We only have his word that's the case," Robert said. "He could be lying. Perhaps something happened between the brother and the woman, and Mateo's covering for him?"

"Could be, I guess." Martin looked at his watch. "I can ask a friend, but not at this time of the morning. I don't think the Assistant Chief Constable would appreciate a phone call at this hour."

"I could send a couple of my team down there to see what's going on if you want?" Robert replied. "They're not needed until the weekend, so it would keep them busy."

Martin nodded. Robert's team, if it could be called a team, were a group of surly looking ex-military men who were providing security for the weekend's event. There would be no trouble at the party, but they would be able to ensure that there were no curious passers-by. Particularly those with cameras and long lenses.

"They'll be discreet?" Martin asked him. Robert just smiled in response. "In that case, send them down there. I think you're right. Mateo's lying about what happened at the farm. And if he's lying about that, then what else is he lying about?"

"What are their ROE?" Robert asked.

"What do you mean?"

"Rules of engagement. What they can—and can't—do."

"I'll let you decide, Robert," Martin said, tiring of the conversation. "Your judgment is always impeccable."

"And if affirmative action is required?"

"As I said, Robert, I leave that up to you. If it's required, it's required. But no trace of anything like that is to lead back here."

"Of course, Martin," Robert replied with a cruel smile. "That goes without saying. But if they get there and the woman is there?"

"She is to be brought to me. Without so much as a broken nail. I have plans for that young lady." Martin's smile met Robert's, exceeded it even. "Understand?"

68

The bullet sailed over Caleb's head, not by feet, but by inches. He felt it pass over him before the echo of the shot rang around the room. It wasn't the first time someone had shot at him from such close range, but it was the first time someone had done so and missed. Or lived to tell the tale.

"Caleb!" Katya screamed. She threw the pistol to the floor, making Caleb flinch. Even though he knew the free-floating triangular firing pin was supposed to be light enough to prevent accidental discharge, it was still a risk. But Caleb had no time to process what she had done. With the pistol still spinning on the bedroom floor, Katya had tried to run across the room, but the shackle prevented her from moving. When he crossed to her, Katya threw her arms around him. "Oh my God, Caleb. Are you hurt? Did I hit you? Are you okay?" Her voice was high-pitched, and she was talking rapidly.

"Katya, calm down. I'm fine," he said, putting his hands on her hips where they rested perfectly. "If I had any hair, I might have a parting, but it's all good."

"Oh my God, I am so sorry. I thought you were Aleksander!" Katya said, her voice catching in her throat. "I am so sorry. Where did you go? Where did you get those clothes?"

"Katya, hush. All in good time. Let's go downstairs and sit in the kitchen."

"But what about Aleksander? And the driver?"

"The driver's not here. I don't know where he is."

"And Aleksander?"

"He's lying down." Caleb could feel a smile causing the corners of his mouth to twitch. "He's got a splitting headache."

Katya took a step back and looked at Caleb. A frown appeared on her forehead and she shook her head from side to side.

"You killed him." It was a statement. Not a question. Katya knew, but Caleb didn't know how she knew.

"It was more a case of assisted suicide, Katya," Caleb said.

It was Katya's turn to smile, but he could see a sadness behind her eyes. Was that because Caleb wasn't the man she thought he was, or was it for another reason? Caleb was unsure until she spoke again.

"I'm sorry you had to do that for me, Caleb." She leaned forward and kissed him on the cheek. "But thank you."

"I didn't do it just for you, Katya," Caleb replied. "I did it for Ana. For Elene. For all the other people he has hurt. I fear there are plenty."

TEN MINUTES LATER, they were sitting on either side of the kitchen table. Caleb had sat Katya down while he made them both a coffee, putting extra sugar in hers. She had spent the previous few moments telling Caleb about her ordeal at Aleksander's hands after the hunters had left. About how she thought she was going to be raped and murdered. Caleb had listened intently, knowing that was exactly what had been in Aleksander's mind. As his last breath was leaving his body, Caleb had sensed his full depravity.

"You don't need to fear him anymore, Katya. He is no longer a concern to anyone except God. And I have no doubt God will know exactly what to do with him," Caleb said, lifting his eyes briefly to the ceiling.

Katya smiled. This time, there was no sadness behind it.

"Well, I hope he burns in Hell," she said as her smile faded away.

"Perhaps he will, Katya," Caleb replied. "Perhaps he will."

"So, tell me about your clothes. You look so different without a robe." Her eyes twinkled as she said this. "Almost normal."

"Only almost?" Caleb said with a grin.

He went on to tell her about the empty farmhouse beyond the pigsty. How he had broken in to look for supplies, weapons, whatever he could get his hands on.

"If something happens, that's where we'll meet," he told her. "I think Mateo and Gjergj are probably coming back."

"Why would they? There's nothing left behind for them here."

"There's you and Aleksander. As far as they're aware, you're still here." He looked at her, seeing the fear start to come back in her eyes.

"You think they will?" she asked him, her voice almost a whisper.

"If I were them," Caleb said, "I'd be coming back for you."

69

Mateo yawned, stretching his arms out above his head as far as the car's roof would allow him to do. A few seconds after that, Gjergj yawned as well, following it with a laugh.

"Whoever said they're not infectious was lying," he said. Mateo nodded in agreement. Ahead of them, the sky was just lightening. "You mind if we stop at some point?"

"No, good idea. I'm starving. There's a McDonald's further along here that's open twenty-four hours."

They drove on in silence until the distinctive M-shaped sign appeared around ten minutes later. Gjergj pulled into the lot, parking next to a large Harley-Davidson motorcycle. Mateo got out, stretching properly this time.

"I'm going to have a quick smoke," Gjergj said, pulling his cigarettes from his pocket. "You ordering?"

"Yep, can do. What do you want?"

"I'll have one of those sausage and egg things, please."

"Coffee?"

"Of course," Gjergj said as he lit his cigarette.

Mateo walked into the restaurant, which could have

been anywhere in the world. He tapped at the large screen to try to place his order before realizing that it was still ten minutes away from five in the morning, the time they started serving breakfasts. The only other customers were two heavily tattooed men staring into cups of coffee. He made his way over to the counter where an exhausted-looking young man, his face riddled with acne that working in a McDonald's wasn't going to help with, was staring at his phone. Mateo cleared his throat and the young man looked up.

"Help you?" he said, sounding every bit as tired as he looked.

"Can I order a couple of breakfasts, please?" Mateo asked.

"Sure, in ten minutes you can."

"Can't I order them now and you cook them in ten minutes?"

"Er, nope."

Mateo leaned forward on the counter and stared at him.

"Why the fuck not?" he hissed. The young man's jaw dropped and he took a step backward, but Mateo wasn't in the mood to be pissed about by a little self-important idiot like this one.

"I, uh, it's the tills. They won't let me put the order through until after five." The young man was looking around, no doubt for some support from a supervisor, but he was on his own.

"Two coffees then," Mateo replied. He nodded toward a table at the far end of the restaurant. "I'll be over there."

ALMOST TWENTY MINUTES LATER, after Mateo had placed his order on the screen at exactly one minute past five, he and Gjergj were looking at their breakfasts. Mateo unwrapped the paper on his muffin and looked suspiciously at the congealed mess.

"It doesn't look anything like it does on the photos," he said, prodding it with a finger. Mateo was sure it had been cooked the previous day and reheated. Gjergj, who appeared to have no such reservations, was already tucking into his own muffin.

"It never does," Gjergj said, his open mouth treating Mateo to a view of his breakfast. "But it's bloody tasty." Mateo took a bite of his roll, which to his surprise, tasted a lot better than it looked.

The men ate in silence, the only conversation being when Gjergj asked Mateo for his hash brown if he wasn't having it. Then they picked up their coffees. Gjergj started gathering the trash from the table, but Mateo stopped him.

"Leave that," he said to Gjergj. "It'll give that officious little jerk something to do."

They made their way to the exit and Mateo realized Gjergj was going to have another smoke before they set off. He thought about complaining, telling Gjergj to just get in the car and drive, but he couldn't be bothered. All he wanted to do was get back to the farmhouse and go to bed. His eyes were gritty from a lack of sleep.

Mateo just hoped Aleksander didn't kick up too much of a fuss when they got there.

70

Katya shivered in the early morning air, pulling the dark jacket that had previously belonged to Aleksander around her shoulders. It was dawn, but the light had yet to reach the area of the woods she was standing in. Katya was near the gap in the trees that Caleb had originally identified as a meeting point, were they to run. She was breathing hard, having sprinted across the clearing from the farmhouse.

She and Caleb had been talking in the kitchen when he had suddenly held a hand up to silence her. Then he had tilted his head to one side as if listening for something.

"They're coming," Caleb had said a few seconds later. Katya, who couldn't hear anything, was surprised.

"You sure?" she had asked him.

"Yes."

At Caleb's insistence, Katya had started walking across the clearing. They had briefly discussed her going to the other farmhouse, the pig farmer's, but Caleb thought that there wouldn't be enough time. So, for the time being, she was to hide close by. When she was around half-way across the clearing, she saw the distant flash of headlights through the trees. Caleb's hearing must be phenomenal, Katya had thought as she broke into a run.

She pulled the jacket closer to her body, reminding herself of its original owner. Caleb hadn't told her anything about how Aleksander had died. Just that he'd made sure he knew he was paying a price for his wrongdoing. God, Caleb had said, would sort everything else out. In her pocket, weighing the jacket down but reassuringly, was his pistol. Katya had watched as Caleb had disassembled it on the bedside table, cleaned and oiled the components with a small weapon cleaning kit he'd found in Aleksander's bedside cabinet. Once he had reassembled it, Caleb had spent a few moments teaching Katya how to use it. How to stop the natural tendency of those unused to weapons to fire high. How to compensate for the recoil so that the second and third shots would land on target, even if the first went awry. They had just been discussing a human being's center of mass when Caleb had heard the vehicle.

Katya didn't know what Caleb had planned for Mateo and Gjergj. After she'd almost killed him earlier, Caleb had disappeared for a while. When he returned, Katya had asked him what he had been doing.

"Planning," Caleb had replied, but he wouldn't divulge anything more than that.

Finally, Katya could hear the vehicle approaching. It sounded more like a car than a van and was much louder than the electric van had been. Either the approaching vehicle wasn't Mateo and Gjergj or they had changed the van for something else. For a moment, Katya was concerned that whoever was in the car—if it wasn't the Albanians— was heading straight into a trap. But Caleb didn't strike her as the type of person who would make a mistake like that.

He was completely different without a robe. She'd only been half joking when she'd said he was almost normal. What if she had actually hit him when she'd fired at him? Katya shivered at the thought. She could have killed him. Would have killed him. But what had happened had taught her one thing, as he had explained to her at the kitchen table. She had the capacity to kill.

"Everyone thinks they do, Katya," Caleb had said. "When they're threatened, or protecting someone they love. But when it actually comes down to it, most people can't." The knowledge that she was one of those who could was both reassuring and frightening to Katya. She thought back to the moment she pulled the trigger. At that split second, when she thought Aleksander was in front of her, she had pulled that trigger in the full knowledge that the action could result in the death of another human being. It was her lack of emotion at that realization that scared her more than her actions themselves. What did that say about her as a human being, she wondered as she watched the headlights slowly approaching through the trees. And what if she was put in the same situation again?

That one was easier. If she was in the same situation again, she would pull the trigger.

But next time, she wouldn't miss.

71

Martin watched through the heavy, leaded windows of his private office as, outside the house, Robert was giving some instructions to two of his team whom Martin hadn't seen before. The two men he was briefing were standing side by side, loosely in a standing at ease position, while Robert spoke to them. Every few seconds, Robert brought one of his hands down in a chopping motion which was accompanied by the other two nodding.

Behind them was a large, black Range Rover Evoque, one of four SUVs that Martin owned. He liked the boxy vehicles, and the power that sat under their hoods. Except he didn't technically own them. His company did, but to find out it was his company would take several forensic experts months if not years to discover. He'd paid a lot of money to a lot of banks in various countries to make sure there were enough layers of deniability between him and the company itself.

The two men turned, Robert's briefing seemingly complete, and one of them picked up a small gym bag that was lying on the gravel drive in front of them. As he did so, he turned and looked at Martin. The man held his eyes for a few seconds before nodding almost imperceptibly at him. Like his colleague, the man's movements were concise and considered. They both wore black from head to toe, matching the SUV and its windows that were so tinted Martin couldn't even see their silhouettes when the door had closed. After lurking on the gravel for a moment, the car crept away down the drive and toward the road. A few moments later, there was a soft knock on his office door.

"Come in," Martin said. The door opened and Robert walked in. "All good?"

"Yes, Martin, they're all set. They're taking some extra equipment with them. Just in case." Without waiting for an invitation, Robert sat down in one of the leather-bound chairs.

"Ah, I wondered what was in the bag," Martin replied, taking a seat opposite Robert. "What's their story, those two?"

"Both ex-Regiment." Martin didn't need to ask which regiment Robert was referring to. "I was in Afghanistan with them both back in the day. Just as the fun was starting. Both good lads." Robert crossed his legs. "They don't mess about, either of them."

"No, they don't look as if they do."

Martin was about to call Natalka to bring them some coffee when he remembered she'd gone to Milton Keynes the previous day. He swore under his breath.

"Any news on a replacement for Natalka, Robert?" Robert glanced at his watch before replying.

"Should be here in a couple of hours."

"Who is she?"

"A girl called Lika. She's being brought from the Nottingham parlor."

"Has she been through here?"

"No, she went direct. She's seventeen but is Georgian, so she can look after the girls. She's on the website under the name Foxy."

"Okay, well, seeing as she's not here yet, how about you rustle up some coffee for us?"

If Robert was offended at being given such a menial task, he didn't show it. He got to his feet and made his way to the door. While he waited for him to return, Martin navigated to the web page Robert had referred to and clicked on the section labeled Our Ladies.

About half-way down the page was a young woman with shoulder-length black hair. She was slim, wearing a matching set of lingerie, and was looking directly at the camera with a sultry expression. Martin knew the teams that ran the parlors often had to have several sets of such photos done, as the first few still had fear in the women's eyes.

Martin couldn't see any fear at all in this woman's eyes, which irritated him. He didn't like having girls from the parlors. He much preferred them when they first arrived. Fresh and unpolluted. Still, Martin thought as he zoomed in on the parts of her body he was looking forward to enjoying the most, there were ways of putting that fear back. As an added bonus, such exercise was good for his heart, according to the cardiologist he paid a lot of money to tell him what he already knew.

A few moments later, when Robert returned with two cups of coffee, Lika's photo was still on the screen.

"She'd do," Robert said as he placed Martin's coffee in front of him.

"Well, if your men bring that woman back from the farm then I'll have no requirement for this one," Martin replied, nodding at the screen. "Perhaps you and your team would like some pre-party entertainment? I'm sure she'd be only too happy to oblige." But he knew it wouldn't make a difference if she didn't.

"I think the boys would enjoy that very much, Martin," Robert said as he looked at the monitor. "Very generous of you." He leaned forward to get a closer look at the young woman. "Very generous of you indeed."

72

Mateo belched, the taste of the sausage and egg muffin coming back into his mouth for a moment. That was the only problem with fast food. It gave him gas and, unless he drank a load of milk, heartburn. There was a small garage just before their turn off, Mateo remembered. He would send Gjergj there for some milk and other supplies when they got back to the farmhouse. Besides, he would need some time to talk to Aleksander.

As Gjergj drove, Mateo thought back to the lies he'd told Martin back at his house. Aleksander was going to have to keep his head down for a while if Martin thought he'd been arrested. Saying that had been stupid, in hindsight. He could have come up with any number of different excuses for not bringing Aleksander and Katya with him. But it wasn't as easy to explain why he'd taken the girls there early. Mateo had never been good at thinking on his feet, but it was the only thing he could think of to say at the time. Why hadn't he just said they were sick, and he'd brought the girls early to avoid them getting sick as well?

Mateo thumped his thigh. Why hadn't he thought of that earlier?

"You okay?" Gjergj said, not looking over at him.

"Yeah, I'm just thinking about what I told Martin, that's all."

"What did you tell him?"

"That the police were at the farmhouse and that Aleksander and the woman had been taken by them."

"Ah, right," Gjergj replied. "What are you going to do?"

"I'm not sure," Mateo said. "Probably just wait for the money and disappear for a while."

They drove on in silence for a couple of miles. Once or twice, Gjergj opened his mouth to say something before closing it again.

"Spit it out, Gjergj," Mateo said when he did it again. "Just say what you've got to say."

He saw Gjergj glancing over at him with a nervous expression.

"Um, I was thinking about what you said earlier," he said, speaking slowly. "About going back to Albania?"

"What of it?" Mateo noticed Gjergj's knuckles whiten on the steering wheel.

"I don't think I'm going to come back."

"You're quitting?" Mateo was surprised, but at the same time, could see a potential opportunity. "Are you serious?"

"Yes."

"Why? Isn't the money good enough for you?" Mateo needed to be careful about how he handled this. "You think you can earn this type of money back in Albania? Delivering food or driving an Uber?"

"It's not the money, Mateo," Gjergj replied. "I just don't think the peshkop's running an adoption agency. There's more to it than that."

"Has someone said something?" Mateo asked him. "What makes you say that?"

"It's not just that."

"What, then?"

"The Bosnian."

"What of him?" Mateo studied Gjergj's face. Gjergj hadn't been involved in the disposal of the Bosnian, but he knew exactly what had happened to him. If Aleksander hadn't opened his big mouth in the van, then Gjergj would be none the wiser. Mateo cursed his brother silently.

"I'm just a driver, Mateo," Gjergj said. "That's all I thought I would be doing. Driving people around." He turned to look at Mateo and he saw the man was deadly serious. "Not murdering them."

The next few moments were spent in an uncomfortable silence. Gjergj slowed and turned the car into the track that led to the farmhouse.

"We'll talk later," Mateo said. "But if that's your decision, I won't stand in your way." He wanted some time to think Gjergj's comments through. The key problem was going to be Aleksander. Perhaps the three of them could return home and somewhere along the way, Mateo could just vanish? Go to the bathroom somewhere and never return? It would take some planning, but Mateo was good at planning. It was the spur-of-the-moment stuff that he struggled with.

The two men remained silent as they drove down the path and toward the farmhouse. Mateo knew it was his imagination, but it seemed to get longer every time they drove down it. He spent the time swiping through his phone, checking the local news back in Albania. But he soon got bored with that, so checked his text messages instead for any news from Gramoz. There was none, and he was about to compose a message for his uncle when Mateo felt the car start to slow down.

"Why are we slowing down?" he asked, not even looking up from the screen.

"Look," Gjergj replied. "There's a fallen tree. It's blocking the road."

When the car stopped, Mateo and Gjergj climbed out to examine the obstruction. It wasn't a very large tree, and they should be able to shift it between them. But Mateo couldn't work out how it had fallen. There had been no wind of note, and it was a single tree. He walked up to it to examine it more closely.

Mateo heard a thud behind him. It was followed by another similar noise a split-second later. He turned to see Gjergj lying on the road, not moving. Next to him was an ax, and next to that was a man picking it up. He was dressed in jeans and a dark blue fleece. It wasn't until the man had picked the ax up and turned to face him that Mateo recognized him.

"Mateo," Caleb said with a smile. "Welcome home."

73

Only a split second before Caleb had thrown the ax, he had flipped it round so that the first part of the ax that would strike Gjergj was the heel, not the blade. The effect was the same. Instant incapacitation. But now the driver was unconscious, as opposed to dead.

The main reason he'd flipped the ax around at the last second wasn't because Caleb didn't want to kill him. In fact, whether Gjergj lived or died was of no real consequence to Caleb at all. It was more about Mateo's reaction time. If he was quick off the mark, and Caleb didn't think he was, then it would take a few seconds to free the ax if it was fully embedded in Gjergj's skull. As Caleb had suspected, Mateo wasn't quick off the mark. But it never paid to make assumptions.

Caleb held the ax loosely in his right hand, the blade uppermost, and watched as Mateo crouched down into a fighting position. He broadened his smile.

"You don't look too pleased to see me, Mateo," Caleb said, taking a step toward him and glancing in the car's rear. There was no sight of Ana or Elene. "Where are the girls?"

"I've taken them somewhere," Mateo said. Caleb almost laughed at the way he tried to inflect his voice into something menacing. It didn't work. He could see Mateo looking over his shoulder and at the farmhouse. "Where's Aleksander?"

"He's feeding the pigs at the moment," Caleb said. It took Mateo a couple of seconds to process what Caleb had just said, and his face twisted into a mask of anger.

"You killed him?"

"Yes, I did."

"Why?"

This time Caleb did laugh.

"Seriously? You're asking me why I killed your brother? How many people has he killed? Ruined? Raped?"

Mateo didn't reply for a few seconds, but just glared at Caleb.

"I'm going to kill you for that," Mateo said. He shook his hands loosely before balling them into fists. "How about you put that ax down and fight like a man?"

"I've got a better idea," Caleb said. He ran his hands up and down the shaft a couple of times before throwing the ax onto the floor between them. Then he took a couple of steps back. "Why don't we even things up a bit and you have the ax? But we're not animals, Mateo. If I get the ax back off you, then it's over. We go to the farmhouse and talk."

He watched as Mateo took a step forward and picked up the weapon. He held it in two hands and took a couple of short swings. Caleb watched as Mateo reinforced what he had thought. He'd never fought with an ax before. And now that he had one, he would be much slower and more predictable.

Mateo's first swipe was a wild one. Caleb stepped back in plenty of time and watched as Mateo almost lost his balance.

"Hold it a bit closer to the ax head," Caleb said. "You'll get more control of it that way." Mateo swung the ax back in the opposite direction. It was another wild swing that didn't come near Caleb. He adjusted his hands as Caleb had suggested and took a third swing.

This time, as Mateo swung the ax, Caleb took two big strides forward. He was now well within the arc of Mateo's swing and, as Mateo's arms brushed against Caleb's, Caleb shoved him hard after hooking one of his feet behind Mateo's leg. Mateo fell backward, landing on the path on his backside with a grunt. Then he jabbed the ax at Caleb's foot, but all he managed to do was embed it in the soft ground. Caleb put his foot on the ax and held it there as Mateo struggled to free it.

"How d'you think this is going for you, Mateo?"

Mateo let go of the ax and scrabbled to his feet. Caleb could have just picked it up and technically ended the fight. But he wasn't sure Mateo would honor the arrangement and besides, he wanted to see what Mateo had in store. A few seconds later, a glint of light near Mateo's right hand told him. Mateo had a knife.

"So much for fighting like a man, Mateo," Caleb said, taking a step back. But he still didn't pick up the ax. He didn't need it.

Mateo lunged forward, swiping at the air between them with the blade angled back toward his wrist. He was obviously more comfortable with a knife than he was with an ax. Caleb waited until Mateo was at the very end of his swing before lifting his leg and kicking Mateo at the side of his right knee. His goal was to hyperextend the joint more than the five or ten degrees than normal. As Mateo screamed and hobbled backward, Caleb knew he'd hit the right spot. Inside Mateo's knee joint, any of the seven ligaments that held it together would be damaged. Over time, the muscles would start swelling from the strike, further limiting Mateo's range of movement. A further kick to the same area, or a low, oblique kick, could rupture the meniscus, the joint capsule that reinforced the entire knee. But Caleb wasn't going to let the fight get that far. He was getting bored.

Caleb looked at Mateo's neck and drew an imaginary line from the base of his ear to the top of his shoulder. Beneath that line was Mateo's brachial plexus, a concentration of nerves that served the upper body. If Caleb could hit him there, Mateo would drop the knife. If Caleb hit hard enough, the resulting shock to the carotid artery, jugular vein, and vagus nerve could drop Mateo.

As Mateo lunged toward him, using the knife in a stabbing motion, Caleb waited until his arm was fully extended. He snapped his hand out to grab Mateo's wrist and, with his other hand, delivered a sharp punch in the middle of the imaginary line, just in front of and below Mateo's ear.

The knife clattered to the ground. It was followed, a few seconds later, by Mateo.

74

Katya watched, swaying from side to side to try to keep the gun focused on Mateo as the two men danced around each other. She had no idea why Caleb had just thrown his weapon to the ground for Mateo to pick up, but as she watched his clumsy swings, she could see Caleb had just slowed him down, and Mateo was too stupid to realize it. When Caleb caught Mateo on the knee with his foot, an audible crack echoed around the tree trunks she was hiding behind, causing her to wince. If there was the slightest chance that Mateo got the upper hand, she was going to drop him. Even if the first shot missed, which it probably would, she could walk forward, firing as she did so, just as Caleb had taught her earlier. But in the end, the fight was over before it had really begun.

Lowering the pistol and re-engaging the safety, Katya took a few steps forward. As she stepped onto the path, Caleb looked up at her. Despite his exertions with Mateo, he wasn't even out of breath.

"I thought I said to stay at the pre-arranged meeting

place," he said, but there was the ghost of a smile on his face.

"And I thought you might appreciate a bit of back-up," Katya said, looking at the prostate forms of Mateo and Gjergj. "But it would appear not. What do we do now?"

"Let's get them to the farmhouse and secured," Caleb said. "Then we'll work out our next steps."

"We're going to get the girls?" Katya asked. He looked at her with a frown.

"I'm not sure you should be involved, Katya," he replied. "But that's my intention, yes."

"Maybe we should go to the police?" Katya didn't like the way he had just dismissed her. "Hand these two over to them and tell them everything."

"And what do you think their response would be?"

"The police, or these two?" she asked him.

"Both."

"I'm not sure, to be honest. But they're the police. With all the resources they've got, they'll be able to do something. Won't they?"

"They've not been able to stop any of this yet, have they?" Caleb replied, waving his arms at the two unconscious men. "The first thing the police will do is lock you and I up in a cell. How can we help Ana and Elene then? And these two?" He prodded Mateo as he said this. "If they've got any sense at all, they'll say nothing. There's not enough time to go to the police."

"So we'll go and get them, then. You and me."

He looked at her with a cool expression, and she wondered what he was thinking. She already knew he wasn't just a preacher. Preachers couldn't fight like he just had. Katya thought he'd just got bored with sparring with Mateo, so he'd put him on the ground. And the way he'd taken Gjergj out with the ax? No preacher Katya had ever met could do that.

"Maybe," Caleb said eventually. "Let's get these two secured first. Then we'll talk."

BETWEEN THEM, they manhandled Gjergj into the farmhouse, half-dragging, half-carrying the man across the clearing in front of the building. By the time they had duct taped him to one of the kitchen chairs, Katya was perspiring hard. Caleb, by contrast, had barely a bead of sweat on his forehead. She watched as Caleb checked Gjergj's airway before leaving the farmhouse without a word. Katya followed him, wondering if she'd upset him. He'd not spoken at all since they started dragging Gjergj across the ground, and he remained silent as they dragged Mateo from the car and toward the kitchen.

A few moments later, Mateo was in the chair next to Gjergj. Both men were tightly bound at the ankles and wrists to the heavy chairs. Their heads were lolled forward, but neither man had moved a muscle. Caleb still hadn't said anything. Even when he searched the men's pockets, pulling out everything within them, he said nothing.

"How long do you think they'll be out?" Katya asked Caleb. He pulled a chair to the opposite side of the table to the two men and indicated for her to sit on it.

"I'm not sure," he said as she sat down, placing the pistol on the table in front of her. "Could be a few more moments, could be hours. I think only minutes, though. I didn't hit either of them that hard." Katya suppressed a smile. That's not how it had looked to her.

"Okay," Katya said. "You want a drink of water? I'm parched."

"Sounds good," Caleb replied. "I'm going to go and shift that tree and bring the car to the front of the house. You keep an eye on these two."

Katya crossed her arms, tilted her head to one side, and arched her eyebrows at him.

"Excuse me?" she said. Caleb looked at her with a hint of amusement in his eyes before he replied.

"Katya, would you mind staying here and keeping an eye on these two?" He paused. "Please?"

Katya smiled as Caleb left the farmhouse. She got to her feet and crossed to the sink, where she filled two glasses with water. She drained one before refilling it and returned to the table, where she put both glasses down. Then she sat down and thought about their potential next steps. Whether Caleb liked it or not, they were in this together.

A few moments later, she heard the farmhouse door open. She turned to see Caleb's head peering round it.

"Um, Katya," he asked. "Got a question for you."

"Sure, fire away."

"Can you drive a stick?"

75

"What's going on?" Martin asked Robert, who had been engrossed on his phone.

"They've arrived at the farmhouse. My men are about twenty minutes behind them, maybe less." Robert looked up at Martin. Apart from a slight reddening of his eyelids, he looked as fresh as he normally did. Perhaps it was a military thing, Martin thought as he looked at him. Being able to stay awake for hours and hours without sleeping. Martin was already looking forward to getting his head down later in the day. Just as soon as he knew everything was in order.

"Tell them to hold fire on that affirmative action. I just want to know what's going on. Have them stay back and just observe," Martin said. He saw Robert's forehead crease in a frown, but other than that, there was no reaction.

"Yup, okay. Reconnaissance it is then." He paused for a few seconds before continuing. "You know what they say in the military, Martin?"

"No, Robert," Martin replied with a sigh. "Never having

served in the military, I have absolutely no idea what they say."

"Time spent on reconnaissance is seldom wasted," Robert replied, returning his attention to his phone. "I'll give them a call in a moment and give them the good news." Martin, not able to tell whether Robert was being sarcastic or not, sighed again.

"If it's not too much trouble, Robert," Martin said. He looked at the man, who was just staring at the screen. "That'll be all." Without a word, Robert got to his feet and left.

Martin looked at his watch, thinking it wasn't too early to call his contact with the police. He opened a drawer and pulled out a burner phone, along with a small notebook. Squinting at the tiny numbers in the notebook, he dialed the number he wanted.

"Yes?" a man's voice replied after a couple of rings. Just a single word, exactly as always.

"Are you at work?" Martin asked.

"Yes."

Martin closed his eyes, imagining the police station at Lincoln in his mind's eye. He'd been to the Assistant Chief Constable's office once, and it was almost as opulent as his own office. He needed to consider how to best phrase the next question. According to the man he was talking to, if they could be said to be talking, every phone conversation in the United Kingdom was sucked into super-computers down at Cheltenham, the home of the country's security services. They wouldn't be listened to in real time unless he used specific words, or a sequence of them, that would trigger a human listener, but they would still exist in perpetuity.

"Was there any local activity last night," Martin said, "related to our forthcoming event?"

The man at the other end didn't reply, but Martin could hear the tapping of a computer keyboard. A few seconds later, Martin had his answer.

"No."

Martin disconnected the call without a further word. There was no need to ask the man if he was sure, if there was the possibility it hadn't been entered into the system yet. What Mateo had described was a large-scale operation. If it had happened, his contact would know. Which meant Mateo was lying through his teeth. And Martin hated liars.

He sat back in his chair, steepled his fingers, and thought for a few moments. What he had just learned was good news, obviously. It meant their operation hadn't come to the attention of the authorities. Their planned event would still go ahead, so he would be handsomely recompensed for his efforts. It also meant the delectable Katya was still in play. She could be here soon, learning the ropes. Quite literally. Robert and his colleagues could have some fun with the other girl before she was returned to work. So everyone benefited from what he had just heard.

But it also meant that Aleksander, Mateo, and the driver were still in the mix. And given Mateo's lies and what he had told him about wanting to quit, that created some uncertainty. Aleksander was a wildcard at the best of times. What would be best for everyone, except perhaps the three of them, would be for them just to disappear. But that was also a risk, particularly if they didn't disappear completely.

He could change the stance he'd just taken with Robert and have them taken out. But then he could appear weak, changing his mind so quickly. Martin hated weakness, and the idea of him appearing weak to others was an anathema to him.

"No," Martin muttered under his breath as he rubbed his chest. "Hold the line, see what happens."

Given everything that had happened over the last few hours, Martin was sure of one thing.

Something would happen. It just remained to be seen what that something was.

76

Caleb picked up the glass of water that Katya had put on the kitchen table and flung the contents in Mateo's face. Nothing. No response at all. Mateo remained where he was, his head tilted so far forward his chin was almost on his chest.

"Well, it works in the movies," he mumbled under his breath before turning to Katya. "Guess we'll just have to wait."

"Guess we will," Katya replied with a grin on her face. She'd been wearing it for the last few moments since he'd asked her to drive the car back to the farmhouse. Caleb sighed. Might as well get it over with.

"What?" he asked her.

"What do you mean, what?"

"What are you smiling about?"

"Nothing," Katya replied, her smile broadening. "I'm just surprised, that's all."

"Because I can't drive a stick shift?"

"Yes," she said, picking up the empty glass and walking

to the sink to refill it. "You going to drink this one or throw it all over Gjergj?"

"I'll drink it, don't worry," Caleb said. "I just never learned, that's all. When I was younger, I was taught on an automatic. Then when I bought a car, I bought an automatic. So I've never needed to learn a stick."

"I think you're the first person I've met who can't drive one." Katya was still smiling. Caleb wasn't sure why, but he enjoyed seeing her smile so said nothing. "You want me to teach you?"

"Sometime, sure," Caleb replied.

"How about now?" Katya nodded at Mateo and Gjergj. "They're not going anywhere, are they?"

Caleb thought for a moment but was saved from having to reply to Katya's question by a soft grunt from Mateo. As he watched, the Albanian started to stir.

"Maybe another time," Caleb said, pulling out a chair and sitting at the table. It took a few moments, but eventually Mateo regained consciousness. The first thing he did was struggle against his bonds, then his head snapped from side to side as he took in where he was.

"Hey, Mateo," Caleb said. "Remember us?"

Mateo said something in Albanian. From the way he said it, Caleb doubted it was complimentary. He gave the man a few more moments to fully recover. A few years ago, Caleb himself had been dropped by a brachial stun, albeit in a training environment, but he remembered how much it hurt and how groggy he'd been afterward.

"Hurts, doesn't it?" Caleb said. "I'm guessing you've got shooting pains going down the side of your neck and that you really want to stretch out your arms. Sorry, but maybe later."

"What do you want?" Mateo said.

"Information," Caleb replied, hardening his expression. "Specifically, a location."

"Water."

Caleb turned to Katya, who obliged, crossing again to the sink to fill a fresh glass. Caleb watched as she brought it to Mateo's lips, allowing him to half drain the glass.

"A location, Mateo," Caleb said again. In response, Mateo tried to spit at him, but the globule of phlegm only just made the kitchen table. "That's not very polite, Mateo. Now, where are the girls?"

Mateo swore again in Albanian.

"If I give you the location, you'll kill me."

Caleb regarded the man for a moment, pondering the best response.

"No, I won't," he said, glancing at Katya.

"How do I know you won't?" Mateo replied.

"Because I give you my word, and my word is my bond. Katya? Could you get the bag with Mateo's phone, please?"

When Katya returned with the bag, Caleb pulled out Mateo's phone, swiped at the screen, and pointed it at Mateo's face. He was rewarded with the screen lighting up. Caleb asked Katya to turn the face recognition and pin number off and, while she was fiddling with the screen, he returned his attention to Mateo.

"Mateo, I promise you that when Katya and I leave here, I will not have killed you. I will remove the tape on your wrists and legs and leave you unbound." Katya handed Caleb the phone. "Thank you," he said as he started swiping through the phone's contents. He glanced up at Mateo a couple of times as he did this, and could tell that the Albanian was wavering. Why wouldn't he? He had nothing to lose. Mateo either lived or died. If he lived, he could run, and Caleb was sure he would. If he died? Well, he died. "Are you ready to talk, Mateo?"

Once Mateo started talking, everything came tumbling out in quick succession. In the space of a few moments, Caleb had the address where the girls were being kept, the day and time of Martin's party, and the details of their operation all the way from Albania to the English coast.

When Martin told them about the event that was planned for a few days' time, Caleb felt a shiver pass down his spine at the thought of grown men visiting the girls. He glanced at Katya, who was wringing her hands, her head down. She must realize the significance of what Mateo had just told them?

"But I'm quitting," Mateo said, an earnest expression on his face. "Me and Gjergj have already talked about it. We're out of it."

Caleb looked at him carefully. Had Mateo forgotten about his pledge to avenge his brother's death? Perhaps he had reconsidered, given his situation. That's what Caleb would have done. He listened idly as Mateo told him and Katya about their plans to sneak back over the channel and disappear, leafing through the contents of Mateo's wallet as he did so.

"Pin number?" Caleb asked as he pulled out Mateo's bank card.

"I'll need that money," Mateo said with a frown.

"Mateo, I'm not asking you for the details of the bank accounts where you've squirreled away all that cash, am I? But I could."

With a sigh, Mateo rattled off four digits. Caleb would have to trust that the man was telling the truth. He pulled out Mateo's driver's license.

"You're sure that's the pin number?" Caleb asked him.

"I've got your address here. Which I'm guessing is also your family's address. So I could pay them a visit if you're lying to me?"

"I'm not, Caleb," Mateo said. Caleb looked at him again, satisfied the man was telling the truth.

"Okay, I think our work here is done." Caleb put the phone back into the bag and picked up the pistol on the table.

He saw Mateo's eyes widen with terror. "Mateo, I gave you my word that I won't kill you. And I won't. As I said, my word is my bond." He handed the pistol to Katya. "But I didn't say that Katya wouldn't."

77

"Good morning, sir," Sergeant Mark Bush said as the driver of the black Range Rover Evoque lowered his window.

"Good morning, officer," the driver said. He was speaking in a neutral tone, almost no accent that Sergeant Bush could discern. "Is there a problem?"

Sergeant Bush glanced at his colleague, Tony, who was still sitting behind the wheel of their marked police car. They were in a lay-by on a country road near to Lincoln and had only just put the handbrake on when the Evoque had come hurtling around the corner. But the police officers hadn't yet set up their speed gun, and their dash-cam was pointing at the bush opposite their hiding spot. It was only Sergeant Bush's experience that told him the Evoque was speeding, and that wouldn't hold up in a court of law. Tony raised his thumb to let Sergeant Bush know the vehicle was kosher. The Automatic Number Plate Recognition system had the vehicle as being registered to a private company, but Sergeant Bush had asked Tony to put it through their own local intelligence system to be on the safe side. All the

ANPR would do was pull up any traffic related flags, whereas the intelligence system was much more in depth. But there was nothing. Sergeant Bush was on his own.

"Are you in a hurry, sir?" Sergeant Bush said. "Only it looked to me as if you were going a bit quick back there."

"Ah, okay," the driver replied. "I didn't think I was, but if your gadgets say otherwise, then I must have been." The man in the driver's seat was perhaps mid-thirties, stocky but not fat, and had a crew cut that matched the man in the passenger seat. Neither man showed any sign of concern about being pulled over. If anything, they looked bored with the encounter already. The driver turned to look at Sergeant Bush with pale blue eyes. "Is that what they're telling you? Your gadgets?"

Sergeant Bush was, as his father would have said, caught between a rock and a hard place. He had no legitimate reason to pull the car over, other than Tony's enthusiasm to exercise their own powerful car and Sergeant Bush's own Spidey-sense. He looked past the driver and into the car, but there was nothing to be seen apart from the occupants.

"Do you have your license and documentation for the vehicle with you?" Sergeant Bush asked.

"I have my license, but nothing else. I'd be more than happy to bring the MOT certificate and insurance within the next seven days if that would help?"

The driver's response gave Sergeant Bush pause for thought. It was the way he had worded it. Was he a copper? Ex-copper? If he was, then why not just say? The other documents weren't, strictly speaking, necessary, as the ANPR would have told them if there was an issue with the vehicle.

"Your license, please?"

Sergeant Bush watched as the man reached into his

pocket for his wallet. As he withdrew his driver's license, the police officer saw a laminated identification card behind a window in the wallet. He only saw it for a split second, but it was long enough to read the words on the top.

"Thank you," Sergeant Bush said as he took the card from the driver. "I'll only be a few seconds."

He walked back to his police car, studying the license as he did so. The driver's name was Paul Topping, a resident of Hampshire. The photograph on the license was him, and the hologram looked legitimate.

"Here you go, mate," Sergeant Bush said to Tony as he handed him the license. "Run him through the PNC, would you?"

The two police officers waited as the Police National Computer's data streams did their thing in the background.

"What do you think, Sarge?" Tony asked his boss as they waited for a result.

"The driver's got a British Army ID card in his wallet. I only saw it for a split-second."

"Posh car for a grunt," Tony replied, glancing up at the Evoque. A soft chime from the on-board computer told them that the PNC check was negative.

Sergeant Bush sighed. He had nothing. There was no point even looking at the vehicle to see if there were any minor offenses, like the tires being a couple of millimeters below the legal standard. It was only his gut feeling that the car had been speeding that remained.

"Something's not right about those two, Tony," Sergeant Bush said as his colleague handed him back the license. "But there's bugger all we can do about it. I'll just thank them for their service and send them on their way."

"We could follow them for a bit?" Tony replied. Sergeant

Bush stifled a laugh as he looked at the yellow and blue checkered livery of their police car.

"Good idea, Tony," he said with a grin. "But I think they might notice."

Sergeant Bush made his way back to the Evoque and handed the driver his license.

"We good?" the driver asked, his hands already on the steering wheel of the car. He wasn't even making eye contact.

"We're good," Sergeant Bush replied.

Without another word, the driver put his window back up and inched the car forward before accelerating back onto the road. Sergeant Bush watched the car disappear around a corner.

Something wasn't right about that vehicle or its occupants. But there was nothing he could do about it.

"I think some community engagement is called for, Tony," Sergeant Bush said as he climbed back into the car. "What do you reckon?" His colleague smiled in response.

"McDonald's it is then, boss," Tony replied. "Unless I'm mistaken, it's your round."

78

Katya took the pistol from Caleb and watched as he tore another strip of tape and placed it across Mateo's mouth, ignoring his protestations. Mateo's eyes were wide and pleading. He was blinking rapidly and shaking his head from side to side. Katya raised the pistol and glanced at Caleb. He said nothing, but just nodded in encouragement. She flipped the safety off with her thumb and aimed the pistol at Mateo's chest.

As she tightened her finger on the trigger, she saw Mateo close his eyes and lower his head in resignation. Katya looked across at Caleb, who also had his eyes closed. But from the way he had his hands clasped, she thought he was meditating. Perhaps, Katya thought as her finger tightened further, he was praying for Mateo at the moment of his death?

"I can't do this," Katya said in a whisper a few seconds later. She released her grip on the trigger and put the safety back on. "I'm sorry, Caleb. I can't do this." Her hands were trembling. How close had she just come to killing a man in cold blood? Murdering someone? Because that's what it would have been. Murder.

Caleb opened his eyes, and she watched as he picked up the pistol, placing it in Mateo's bag. He looked at her, his gray eyes boring into hers. His face was inscrutable, showing no signs of any emotion.

"Katya," Caleb said, his voice low and soft. "Would you mind going to the car with the bags? I'll just be a moment."

Katya got to her feet and picked up her suitcase and Mateo's bag, which now also contained Caleb's. She looked at Caleb, who now had Mateo's knife in his hand. He was holding it loosely, balancing it on his fingers.

"What are you going to do?" Katya asked him. Across the table, Mateo still had his eyes closed but had lifted his head back up. Katya could see the relief on his face, but perhaps he wasn't out of the woods just yet.

"Exactly what I said I was going to do," Caleb replied. Mateo opened his eyes, but Katya didn't want to look at him again. She was done with Mateo. "I'm going to release their bonds."

Katya left the farmhouse and walked to the car. She placed the suitcase and the bag in the rear and took a moment to walk around, appreciating the fresh air. Those last few moments in the farmhouse had been stifling. She had come so close to pulling the trigger all the way. But there was a massive difference between killing someone who was going to rape and kill her and killing someone who was bound to a chair. The fact it hadn't been Aleksander at the door, but Caleb, was irrelevant. Katya hadn't known that when she had pulled the trigger.

She opened the driver's door and sat in the seat, resting her head on the steering wheel for a moment. In her mind's eye, she pictured the scene that would have ensued had she pulled the trigger. The image of Mateo, sitting in the chair with his arms and legs still tied and his brains splattered over the wall of the farmhouse, sent an involuntary shiver down her spine. She could feel her heart rate starting to increase and took some deep breaths, keen to avoid a full-blown panic attack.

"You okay there?" It was Caleb, standing at the driver's side window. Katya just nodded in response, not trusting herself to speak. Caleb regarded her for a moment before walking around the car and getting in. He placed his hand on her forearm, and Katya felt the tightening in her chest start to ease. Caleb said nothing, but just sat there until she nodded her head.

"I'm good, thank you," she said, her voice quivering. "Just thinking about what nearly happened, that's all."

"But it didn't happen, Katya."

"Did you kill them?"

"No, Katya. I gave Mateo my word that I wouldn't. And I didn't. They are in the kitchen, no longer bound to the chairs."

"We should go."

Katya pressed the start button and put the car into gear. They made their way across the clearing in front of the farmhouse. Katya glanced at it in the rear-view mirror, knowing that she would never see the place again. If she had her way, at least. When they were a mile or so down the track, Caleb indicated at a place where the road widened.

"Can you pull in there for a moment?" he said. When the car had stopped, he pointed at the sat nav built into the dashboard. "Are you able to work that?"

It took Katya a few moments, but she worked out how to bring up the screen to enter a destination. Caleb read out the zip code of the address Mateo had given them.

"Are we going straight there?" she asked him.

"No. We need to rest and prepare. We have time. But let's get closer and we'll find somewhere to hole up."

Katya had just put the car back into gear when she realized Caleb had fetched the bag from the rear seat. He pulled out the pistol, disengaged the magazine, and then reached into his pocket. A few seconds later, she saw him feeding bullets back into the magazine.

"You emptied it?" she said, her voice an octave higher than normal. Caleb didn't look at her, but she could see his smile.

"I was sure you wouldn't shoot him, Katya," he said as he continued feeding bullets back into the magazine. Then he turned to her and smiled broadly. "But human nature being what it is, I didn't want to take the chance."

79

C aleb sat back in his seat and tried to make himself as comfortable as he could. The car they were in was, he thought, the smallest car he'd ever been in. It wouldn't last five minutes back in Texas. At home, there were potholes larger than this car.

He'd known that Katya couldn't kill Mateo. Removing the bullets from the pistol had been unnecessary, but he'd been certain about things before and proven wrong. Rarely, but more than once. And caution killed no one, generally speaking. But he'd wanted Katya to have the opportunity, if only to realize that while she could kill when the situation required it, she wasn't a murderer. In a sense, they were the same. Caleb had, could, and would kill when the situation required it. But he wasn't a murderer. The legal system may not take such an approach, depending on where he was, but Caleb was content that he was following His law to the letter.

Caleb could sense the relief at leaving the farmhouse behind emanating from Katya the farther away from the place they got. A few kilometers down the road from the turnoff to the farm, they stopped at a McDonalds where the young man behind the counter fell over himself to fulfill Katya's order. The restaurant was empty, save for a couple of police officers sipping coffee in one corner. Apart from a glance in their direction, the police officers' eyes much more interested in Katya than in him, they paid them no attention. It was probably just as well the pistol was still in the car. Caleb smiled as he imagined a scenario in which he had it in the back of his pants, only for it to drop out halfway across the restaurant.

"So, where next?" Katya asked him. She took a large mouthful of her burger, seemingly oblivious to the continued attention from the young man behind the counter.

"I'd like to find a sports or outdoor supplies shop," Caleb said, taking a much smaller bite of his own food. He chewed and thought before swallowing. "Then a hotel. I don't know about you, but I could do with some sleep."

"Sounds like a plan," Katya replied. She reached into her pocket and pulled out Mateo's phone. Caleb hadn't noticed her taking it from the bag in the car. She swiped at the screen. "Can you go and ask the boy behind the counter for the wi-fi password?"

"I think he'd much prefer it if you asked him, Katya," Caleb said with a grin. "Besides, I'm still eating my burger, and you've almost finished yours."

With an exaggerated sigh, Katya finished her food and got to her feet. When he saw her standing up, the young man behind the counter leaped off the stool he was sitting on. Caleb smiled as he watched them talking, wondering if Katya realized the effect she was having on the youngster. She returned a moment later, the young man grinning from ear to ear.

"I think he likes you, Katya," Caleb said with a smile. Katya gave him a withering look and turned her attention to Mateo's phone. Now her phone, from the looks of it.

"There's a big outdoors store a few kilometers away," Katya replied, "and a chain hotel maybe ten minutes down the road from there. What do you need in the outdoors shop?"

"Supplies," Caleb replied. He saw Katya's eyebrows go up but said nothing further to answer her question. "How far is the hotel from where Ana and Elene are?" She looked at him for a few seconds before replying.

"Um, maybe three kilometers?"

"As the crow flies?"

"What does that mean?"

"In a straight line. It's a phrase."

"Ah, okay." Caleb watched as she closed her eyes for a few seconds, committing it to memory. Then she looked back at the screen. "It's difficult to say, but maybe half that? The road kind of loops round."

"So we can use the hotel as a base."

Behind them, the two police officers got to their feet and, after disposing of their coffee cups, made their way toward the door. Caleb waited until they had left before continuing.

"I'm thinking early hours of the morning. You stay at the hotel, I'll go and get the girls, and bring them there."

"That's it?" Katya asked, her eyebrows shooting up. "That's your plan? Go and get the girls and bring them to the hotel?"

"Well, there'll be more to it than that, obviously, but..." He caught a warning look in her eyes and his voice tailed away. Someone was standing behind him.

"Excuse me, sir?" a male voice said. "Is that your Fiat 500

outside?" Caleb looked to see the younger of the two policemen standing behind him.

"No," Katya said before Caleb had a chance to say anything. "I'm the driver."

"Could you come with me, please, ma'am?" the police officer said, his voice full of authority. "Just step outside, if you would."

80

"Put it on speakerphone," Martin barked at Robert. They were sitting in his office, Martin behind his desk and Robert in his customary chair. Robert swiped at the screen of his phone and placed it on the desk.

"Paul? You're on speaker. I'm here with Martin. Sitrep, please?"

"We might have a problem, Robert." The man's voice was tinny and muffled. Robert leaned forward and increased the volume of the phone.

"What sort of problem?"

"We're following the car, but the two Albanians aren't in it."

"Then who is?" Robert looked at Martin, but his face was deadpan. Martin leaned forward to better hear what Paul was about to tell them.

"A man and a woman."

"Describe them," Robert said.

As Paul described the man and the woman in the car, Martin realized almost immediately that he was describing Katya and the man the Albanians had brought to work on the farm. It was only his clothing that was different. It seemed the man in the robe was no longer in a robe. But where were the Albanians, and how had these two got hold of their car?

"That's not the problem, Robert," Paul said. "They're with the police."

Finally, Martin saw Robert's face display some sort of emotion other than cruelty. His eyebrows went up perhaps half a centimeter before returning to their normal position. Martin was disappointed at the news, but not unduly concerned. There would be no way that the police could connect either the man and the woman, or the car, to him. He would be far more concerned if the police had Aleksander and Mateo. That would be a risk. Mateo, in particular, would almost certainly tell them everything. And he had Martin's address. They would need to be dealt with.

"Where are you?" Robert asked Paul.

"About a hundred meters away from the car park they're in. They're outside a McDonald's." Paul went on to describe the exact location of the restaurant's parking lot, and Martin realized they were heading in the general direction of his house. "What do you want us to do?"

"What are the police doing?" Martin said, leaning even farther forward. "Have they arrested them?"

"No, I don't think so," Paul replied. "They're just talking to them."

"Stay where you are and report back," Robert said. "Make sure they don't see you."

"Roger."

The line disconnected, and Martin sat back in his chair with a sigh. It was one thing after another. First the girls being dropped off early, then Mateo complaining, and now this. But if the man and the woman had his car, then where was Mateo?

"What do you think, Robert?" he asked his head of security.

"Not sure what's going on, Martin," Robert replied. "I don't understand why they've got the car. Would Mateo just have lent it to them?"

"He must have. Bloody idiot." Martin closed his eyes for a few seconds. "You know," he said, opening them again, "the more I think about it, the more I think those Albanians are a liability."

"I have assets in place, Martin," Robert said. Martin looked at him before replying. As usual, he was expressionless. "But my suggestion would be to leave them on point and see what happens with the man and the girl. I take it they're the other part of the package?"

"They must be. Are they coming here, do you think?"

"Well," Robert replied. "They're hardly running away, are they? Not if they've stopped to eat."

"Even people on the run need to eat, Robert."

"But it doesn't make sense. If they were running, they would go further away before stopping. I'm sure of it. And as for the police, well, they wouldn't meet them in a restaurant, would they? They would go directly to a police station."

"That makes sense. But I don't understand what they're doing."

"That's why my suggestion is to leave the assets in place. If they are coming here, the rest of my team is here."

Martin thought for a few moments. What should he do? He didn't really have anywhere to move the girls and still hold his event. Nowhere secure enough for that, and nowhere he could gather the leverage he wanted. And if there was no event, not only would he lose a significant amount of money, but he would lose face. Some of the people attending, most of them in fact, were highly influential. He could, as Robert had suggested, let things play out and see what happened.

It was a risk, but life was all about risk. And Martin hadn't got to where he had without taking any.

81

"That was a cheap shot, Tony," Sergeant Bush said as they drove out of the restaurant parking lot. "There was nothing wrong with those tires in the slightest."

"The driver's side was a bit worn," Tony replied with a grin. "That's community engagement, Sarge."

"Yeah, and I'm the Queen of England." He changed his voice to an approximation of Tony's. "Here's my card, ma'am. That's my personal mobile number, so just call if there's anything I can do."

"Well, you never know, do you?" Tony said, chuckling. "Don't ask, don't get, and all that."

"What about the bloke she was with?" Sergeant Bush asked his colleague. "You didn't think he'd mind?"

"They're not together," Tony replied. "Not together together, if that makes sense."

"How d'you know that?"

"I was watching them. No cues whatsoever that they were a couple."

"You're a response officer, Tony," Sergeant Bush said with

a grin. "Not a detective." When he saw the black Evoque parked next to the road, a hundred meters or so from the restaurant, his grin faded. "That's the Range Rover we pulled over earlier."

"So?" Tony replied.

"Bit of a coincidence, don't you think? Why are they parked up there?"

Sergeant Bush looked across at his colleague, but Tony's mind appeared to still be on the woman he'd just tried to chat up. As before, there was nothing he could do, as no laws had been broken. But there was something about the two occupants of the Evoque that he'd not liked.

As the police car passed the Range Rover, Sergeant Bush swiveled in his seat to look at the vehicle. The driver raised a hand in greeting as they drove past, but didn't look at Sergeant Bush. He was just sitting there, as was the man in the passenger seat, staring straight ahead. Sergeant Bush frowned. There was definitely something off about the two men.

"Tony? What do you think?"

"About what, Sarge?"

"For goodness' sake, Tony. About those two men in the Range Rover."

"It's common enough car around here, Sarge," Tony replied. "Proper Chelsea tractor that's probably not been off-road in its life." In his side mirror, Sergeant Bush saw the black Evoque pulling back onto the road and heading in the opposite direction.

Sergeant Bush gave Tony a fierce look that he didn't see. "Swing the car round up here, Tony." He pointed at a turn off a few hundred yards in front of them.

"We pulling them again? What for?"

"No, we'll just follow them for a bit."

"But why?" Tony's voice was almost a whine.

"How about we play a game of paper, scissors, rank?" Sergeant Bush glared at his younger colleague. "Oh, I win."

With a wry smile, Tony pulled into the turnoff and spun the car around. He remained about a hundred yards behind the Evoque. A few hundred yards in front of that was the little Fiat.

"She was well fit though, Sarge, wasn't she?"

Sergeant Bush sighed. Sometimes, working with Tony was like working with one of his own children.

"As a happily married man, Tony," he said, smiling despite his irritation, "I couldn't possibly comment."

82

Caleb sat back in the passenger seat and looked in his side-view mirror. While the police officer had been doing his best to get Katya's attention outside the restaurant, Caleb saw a large, black SUV pull onto the side of the road around a hundred yards away. There were two occupants in the vehicle, but they were too far away for him to see clearly. He couldn't even tell from that distance whether they were male or female. A hundred yards was the ideal distance for reconnaissance for exactly that reason. As the police officer drew Katya's attention to the driver's side tire, Caleb kept an eye on the car, looking for any glint of light that might reflect from an optic such as a sniper's scope or binoculars. But there was nothing.

"Where first, Caleb?" Katya asked him. "The outdoor shop or the hotel?"

"Is there much distance between them, do you remember?" he replied, still watching the car in the side-view mirror.

"I think only a few miles by road," Katya said, glancing

over at him with a smile. "But much quicker as the bird flies."

"As the crow flies, Katya." Caleb smiled back at her. "It's as the crow flies."

"Why does it have to be a crow?"

"I don't know. It's just a saying. I think probably the hotel." In the mirror, he noticed the police car, which had originally gone in the other direction, had turned around and was now behind the black SUV. They formed a rough convoy, around a hundred yards between each vehicle. But he wasn't the only one who was concerned about the vehicle's occupants. There was no reason for the SUV to have stopped where it had.

"So," Caleb said a moment later. "Are you going to call that policeman?"

Katya laughed out loud. It wasn't a sound that Caleb had heard often, but it raised his spirits.

"Why are you asking, preacher man?" she said. "Are you jealous?"

"No, I'm not jealous. Why would I be?" Caleb felt a smile spreading across his face. He would say nothing to Katya, but when the police officer had handed her his card, accompanied by a groan from his colleague, he had felt the faintest flicker of jealousy.

"You can be, if you want." Katya was also smiling. "It's not a sin to be jealous, is it?"

"Technically, it is. Proverbs, chapter twenty-seven. Verse four."

"Ah, okay." Katya's smile broadened. "You're about to enlighten me?"

"Anger is cruel, and wrath is like a flood, but jealousy is even more dangerous."

"Very, er, biblical," Katya said. "Have you memorized the entire Bible, then?"

"No," Caleb replied, his face hardening slightly. "Only the important bits. But I will tell you something." He paused, waiting for her to respond.

"Yes?" Katya asked with a brief glance in his direction.

"When the police officer gave you his card and pointed out his personal number?" He paused again.

"Yes? Come on, Caleb." Katya laughed again. "Out with it!"

"I may have sinned a little," Caleb said. Katya's laugh got louder, and a few seconds later they were laughing together. It wasn't something Caleb did often, but it felt right.

They drove on for a few moments, Caleb closing his eyes briefly to recall her laugh in his head. Then Katya put the indicator on and pulled into a parking lot. It was larger than the one back at the restaurant, was perhaps half full of cars, and adjoined a single-story structure with a line of windows evenly spaced down the side. A sign at the building's entrance said Travel Inn in large blue letters.

"Here we are," Katya said as they pulled into a parking space facing the main road. She unclipped her seatbelt and opened the door. "Oh, I'm stiff," she said. "I've not driven a car for a long time."

Caleb remained in the passenger seat as Katya put her hands on the small of her back and arched her chest forward, groaning as she did so. Just then, the black SUV drove past, giving Caleb an opportunity to see the occupants. Both male, young, crew cut hair. It wasn't what they did that concerned Caleb. It was what they didn't do.

Both men in the car, as it had driven past, had kept their attention fixed on the road in front of them.

Why had neither of them looked at Katya?

83

K atya closed her eyes, bent her legs at the knees, and slid into the tub so that the hot water enveloped her head until only her face was above the surface. It was by far the most relaxed she'd been since arriving in the country. She inhaled deeply through her nose, smelling the lavender bubble bath she had used far too much of. It was bliss. Absolute bliss.

Earlier, Caleb had used Mateo's credit card to book the only remaining room in the hotel. According to the sullen young woman working at the reception desk, there was some sort of conference on and they only had one room left. Caleb, who hadn't even looked at Katya as he agreed to take it, hadn't asked the woman how much it was. Mateo's credit card could handle it, he had said as they walked to the room. The figure on the receipt was extortionate, even if it was apparently a VIP suite.

Considering how much they, or rather Mateo, had paid for the room, it was disappointing. But after the previous few days, it was palatial, at least to Katya. There was an en-suite bathroom with an enormous tub—one that Katya was currently taking advantage of—and a lot of complementary toiletries for both genders. Bubble bath, body butter, shaving cream and disposable razors, even conditioning lotion. Katya was intending to use at least some of each while Caleb was out. After a perfunctory examination of the room, he had asked Katya to show him on the phone where the outdoor supplies shop was. Then he had told her he would be a little while. He wanted to think. To prepare. To plan.

"Fail to plan, plan to fail," Caleb had said as he had left. But he had left only after ensuring that Katya would not leave the room, and would keep the door shut to anyone but him. That was fine by Katya. The room had a bathroom, a large television, a comfortable bed, and a minibar with drinks and snacks. She could stay inside it for days if she had to.

Taking her time, Katya pampered herself. By the time she reluctantly emerged from the bathtub, the skin on her feet was wrinkled from the water. She wrapped herself in a soft, luxurious robe that was one of a pair on the back of the bathroom door and pressed the button to the remote control before looking for a news channel. What she saw filled her with horror.

Early this morning, the somber-faced newsreader said, Border Force officials recovered several bodies from a small vessel that had floundered approximately a mile from the English coast in Kent. The scene on the television changed to a beach. Her eyes filled with tears as she watched several body bags, some of them smaller than others, being transferred onto the beach while a female newscaster talked earnestly to the camera. Six bodies have been recovered so far, including at least two children, the newscaster told the studio before going to say that more fatalities were expected.

"Those poor things," Katya mumbled to herself, only too aware that could have been their fate. She sat on the bed, realizing that tears were flowing down her face. She rocked herself back and forth, sobbing for a few moments and thinking about Ana and Elene. They had survived what the poor souls on the television had not, only to find themselves in mortal danger from the country they had fled to for safety. Katya balled her fists and pushed them into her eyes to stop the tears, but they kept coming. She knew they were tears of relief for her own safety, tears of fear for Ana and Elene, and tears of grief. Both for the people on the television, but also for her old life.

Around twenty minutes later, with no more tears left to cry, Katya picked through her suitcase to find some clothes to wear for the rest of the day and the evening ahead. As she dressed, she thought about the forthcoming night. Katya was determined to have a more active role in what was to happen than staying in the hotel room and waiting.

If Caleb thought she was just going to sit about while he tried to rescue them alone, he was wrong.

84

Caleb pushed open the door to the shop to be greeted by a blast of cold air from the air-conditioning. It wasn't that warm outside, but the shop had cranked it up to the maximum, perhaps hoping cold people bought more clothes than warm people.

The shop was called Great Outdoors and, according to the signs plastered on the exterior of the warehouse styled building, catered for everything from aerobics to watersports. It was a large shop, even by Texas standards, with a lot of floor space given over to an interior display of various tents. Caleb took his time walking around. He had a good idea what he wanted to pick up, but it wouldn't hurt to see what else they had.

There were a lot of products in the shop that were sold in similar shops back home. But there was also a lot that was not. There was no firearms section. No archery section. Not even a hunting section, although the fishing department appeared to have a lot of similar equipment. Should Caleb decide to take up RV camping or horseback riding, the shop would serve him well.

Once he had oriented himself, he returned to the front of the store and picked up a basket. Over the next ten minutes, he went back around the store, slowly filling it up with items that he either knew he would need, or items he thought might come in handy. Caleb had a quick look through his basket. He had most of what he'd come for, save one or two final items, which he thought he could pick up from the garden center just next door.

"Excuse me," he asked a lithe young woman dressed in combat trousers and a tight t-shirt with the shop's logo embroidered above her left breast. "Do you sell maps?"

"Sure," the woman replied. According to her name badge, her name was Phoebe, and she was happy to help him. "Ordnance Survey ones or just walking maps?"

"Um, what are Ordnance Survey maps?"

"They're the really detailed ones. Where's your accent from?"

"Texas, originally," Caleb replied. That was the problem with talking to people. His accent made him stand out and made him memorable, which he didn't want to be.

"Oh, wow," Phoebe said, a smile lighting up her face. "How cool is that? Where in Texas?"

"Kind of all over," Caleb replied. The woman was looking at him, still smiling. She was perhaps Katya's age, or within a year or two either way. "Er, the maps?"

"I'm sorry. Please, follow me."

The shop assistant led Caleb to a rack containing an extensive selection of folded maps in clear sleeves. "What area do you need the map for?"

"Here," Caleb replied. "The local area."

"Are you walking? Touring?"

"Er, walking, I guess."

"Then you'll want the Explorer series. They're the most

detailed ones. But there are also these." Phoebe pointed to another section. "They're the Landranger ones. So they cover a larger area, but with less detail." Caleb watched as she picked out two maps, one from each section. "Here you go. Have a look at one of each and see what you think."

"Thanks."

Caleb took the maps to a display cabinet with binoculars, GPS units, and survival knives locked away behind glass. He took the Explorer map out and unfolded it. As he was studying the map, frowning at the unfamiliar symbols and lines, he realized Phoebe was still just behind him.

"Have you used a map before?" she asked him. Caleb laughed briefly before responding.

"Once or twice, yes. But not one like this. What are they called? Ordnance Survey?"

"Yes. It goes back to the eighteenth century, when Scotland and Napoleon were trying to invade England." She laughed, and Caleb immediately thought of Katya. "Sorry, I did a history degree at uni. I can be a bit geeky sometimes." Her smile faltered, and he saw her hike it back up. "Not that it's done me much good, working here."

Phoebe took a few moments to explain the key parts of the map to Caleb. Where the key to the symbols was, how the scale was calculated, what the various lines meant. None of it was new to Caleb and he could have worked it out for himself, but Phoebe seemed to want to help him, so he let her continue.

"They're kind of like our US Geological Survey maps, but a bit more detailed," Caleb said as he folded the map away.

"I'd love to go to the United States," Phoebe said with a smile. "That'd be really cool. Does everyone in Texas talk like you do?"

"Yes, ma'am," Caleb said, exaggerating his drawl. "We sure do." Her smile broadened.

"That is so cool, the way you say that. You need anything else?"

"Can I see some of the binoculars from that cabinet, please?"

"Sure." Phoebe reached down to her waist and unclipped some keys. "Which ones?" she asked as she unlocked the cabinet.

"Which are the most powerful ones you sell?"

A few moments later, with a set of binoculars in his basket, along with a spotting scope he'd seen that would be a useful backup, he only needed one more item.

"Can I take one of those survival knives, please? The large one at the back?" Caleb saw Phoebe's face light up, and he wondered if she would get a commission from his purchases. He hoped she would.

"If you're buying this one, I'd get another whetstone. The one that's included is a bit rubbish."

"Okay, but thank you. I have one already."

"You need anything else?" Phoebe asked him. Then she lowered her voice. "Anything at all you see that you'd like?" Caleb regarded the young woman carefully before deciding to take a chance. He lowered his own voice.

"Can I ask you something just between you and me?" he said. Her face lit up again, and she leaned forward.

"Sure," Phoebe said. "Ask away."

"Do you know anywhere I can get any bigger weapons than this knife?" Her face fell as he asked this, and he realized he'd misjudged the situation.

"Sorry, sir," Phoebe said with no trace of the smile on her face that had been there a few seconds before.

As Caleb paid for his shopping a few moments later, he

thought back to the police officer who had given Katya his card.

"Don't ask, don't get," he muttered to himself as he walked back into the lot.

85

"What did he say?" Martin asked Robert, who had just come off the phone with his team following the Fiat. His security director had asked if he wanted to listen in on speaker, but Martin was too busy writing some e-mails. He had a day job, after all, and needed to at least attempt to keep up appearances.

"They've tracked them to a local Travel Inn but had to break away from the reconnaissance briefly."

"Why?" Martin asked.

"Local police being nosey." Robert offered no more information, nor did Martin ask for any. "But they know where they are. It looked as if they were going into the hotel, so they can pick them up again later."

Martin frowned. He didn't like the idea of the woman in a hotel with another man. He didn't want her soiled before he could soil her. Just as he was thinking this, he heard a car approaching on the gravel. Martin stood and crossed to his window. Outside the house was another of his Range Rovers. He recognized the driver as the man who provided security for his establishment in Nottingham. The rear door opened and a young woman got out. She was slim, with black hair tied up in a ponytail that accentuated her angular face.

"And this must be Lika," he muttered.

"I'm sorry?" Robert said. Martin waved his hand to dismiss him and returned his attention to the young woman. If anything, she looked better in the flesh than on the website. Martin knew she'd been in the county for just over a month. With anywhere from ten to twenty clients a day, at least she would bring some experience. Perhaps he would keep her for a while, after all.

"I think your men need to do some cleaning up, Robert," Martin said as he watched Lika take in the house. He liked the look of appreciation on her face a lot.

"What do you want to be cleaned up, Martin?"

"The Albanians," Martin replied, still staring at Lika. She was now walking toward the house, her slim hips swinging in a most pleasing way. Martin made a decision there and then. "And the two in the hotel. Loose ends, the lot of them."

"The Albanians should be easy," Robert replied. "Assuming, of course, they're still at the farm. But the hotel might be more difficult."

"More difficult how?" Martin said, craning his neck to watch Lika walking up the steps to the front door.

"The scene will need to be cleaned after my team has done their job. Properly cleaned, and then, of course, there's the disposal." Not able to see Lika any more, Martin turned to Robert. "My team isn't able to do those elements, so we'll need to bring someone in."

"You have someone?"

"I know of people, yes. I've used them before. They're very, shall we say, forensic in their attention to detail."

"Well, bring them in, then."

"Their expertise isn't cheap, Martin."

"How much?" Martin narrowed his eyes as he looked at Robert.

"Seven grand," Robert replied, his face remaining impassive. "Per disposal."

Martin sucked his breath in through his teeth before replying.

"And how much of that is your markup, and how much is their fees?"

"Even if the police sent a full forensic team into the hotel room where they are, they wouldn't find as much as a hair follicle out of place." Robert was examining his fingernails with a nonchalant expression, but when he turned to Martin, his eyes were hard. "They're good, Martin. That's why they cost so much."

Martin knew he was being squeezed, but he also knew that was how the world worked. His best guess was that the team would cost five or six grand, with Robert taking the rest as a referral fee. But it would also keep a degree of separation between Martin and these types of people. One which Martin was keen to maintain.

"I'll send the team to the farm now, if the police are not still hanging around," Robert said. "But the hotel will have to wait until after dark."

"Make it so," Martin said, getting to his feet. "Now, if you'll excuse me, I need to go and introduce myself to someone. I'm not to be disturbed for an hour, at least."

"Okay, boss," Robert replied.

Martin crossed to the door of his office before turning back to Robert.

"Actually, make that two hours. I don't like to rush an introduction."

86

Mateo let out a loud groan, almost a shriek, as he looked down at his legs. They looked normal, but both were absolute agony. A dull but excruciating pain was throbbing in both his calves in time with his heartbeat. On the floor next to the chair he was sitting in were discarded strips of duct tape. He had nothing. His pockets were empty. His cell phone, his wallet, even his vehicle were all gone, stolen by Caleb. The only thing he had left Mateo with was pain. Mateo groaned again while beside him, Gjergj was still blissfully unconscious.

After Katya had left with the bags, Caleb had checked the tape over Mateo's mouth and placed a strip across the still unconscious Gjergj's. Then he had upended one of the sturdy farmhouse chairs and turned it upside down. Caleb used Mateo's knife to slice the duct tape securing Gjergj's legs before lifting them and placing them on one of the chair's struts. Gjergj's lower calf was lying on the round wooden strut.

. Then Caleb had turned and looked at Mateo with an expression somewhere between curiosity and revulsion.

"You disgust me, Mateo," Caleb had said. Mateo, who still had a strip of tape over his mouth, had been unable to reply. All he had been able to do was watch as Caleb walked over to a block of knives on the kitchen sideboard. Caleb had looked at each of them in turn before selecting one of them. "Did you know, Mateo," Caleb had then said as he balanced the knife on his fingertips, "that according to the book of Deuteronomy, a man whose male member is cut off cannot enter the assembly of the Lord?" Caleb had taken a few steps toward Mateo. "Or one whose testicles have been crushed?"

He had raised his foot to stamp on Gjergj's shin. There had been a muffled crack, and bile had started to rise in Mateo's mouth. By the time Caleb broke Gjergj's other leg, Mateo had been hyperventilating through his nose.

"But I doubt very much that you'll be entering the assembly of the Lord, Mateo, with or without a penis," Caleb had said. "I foresee a much darker eternity that awaits you, but you cannot go unpunished. Are you familiar with the Gospel according to Mark?" Mateo had shaken his head, trying to use his eyes to plead with Caleb. "I thought not. Chapter nine says that it is better for you to enter life lame than with two feet to be thrown into Hell."

Caleb had then dragged the chair toward Mateo.

"I promised not to kill you, Mateo," Caleb had said as he sliced through the tape securing one of Mateo's legs. Mateo had wriggled as hard as he could, but with only one leg free, he hadn't been able to get any purchase. "But I didn't promise not to hurt you. It'll only be your fibula that gets broken, but if you don't stop wriggling, then it'll be both bones in your leg. Which is it to be?"

Mateo had screwed both eyes shut as he had felt Caleb placing his leg over the chair. The pain, when it had come, had been excruciating. It had been like a white hot poker inside his leg. The second leg was worse and Mateo had hoped he might pass out, but it was not to be.

"Keep the tape on your mouth for a count of a hundred," Caleb had said as he cut the restraints around Mateo's wrists. "Then you can scream as much as you want." And with that, Caleb was gone.

With no phone, Mateo wasn't sure what the time was, but it had to be at least an hour since Caleb and Katya had gone. Gjergj had made one or two noises since they had left, but was snoring again. Mateo had sat there, trying to control his breathing. But he couldn't just sit there all day. Mateo had to do something, but with two broken legs, he wasn't sure what he could do. His lower legs were throbbing, but the white-hot pain had been replaced by a deeper, throbbing pain that was constant. If he remembered correctly, the tibia was the thinner of the two bones. Did that mean he could stand up?

A few seconds later, as he lay sprawled on the floor with the excruciating pain in his legs returning to torture him, Mateo had his answer.

87

It had taken Mateo almost ten minutes, but he had been able to crawl across the floor to the sink and haul himself up. Taking as much of his weight on his upper body as he could, he filled a glass with water and was able to drink most of it before his own body weight became too much. At least when he slumped back to the cold stone floor, he managed to not take too much weight through his legs.

Mateo needed a plan. More than a plan, both he and Gjergj needed a hospital. But how would they explain their injuries? If it was just Mateo, he could say that he fell somehow. Landed awkwardly. He sat there, wondering if he should remove his shoes. Would his feet swell up? It wasn't as if he could use them.

A few moments later, Mateo knew what he could do. At some point, the pig farmer would be bringing some feed for the pigs. Tomorrow, perhaps. If not tomorrow, then the day after. Mateo could survive until then. If he could get to the pigsty, then he could persuade the farmer to take him to a hospital. Not the closest one, where Gjergj would be taken if anyone found him, but one in the next county. There, Mateo could get treatment for his injuries and take stock. He had no money on him—Caleb had seen to that—but if he could get access to the internet, he could transfer some money into an account. It would have to be a new account because Caleb had his British bank cards. And for a new account, he would need identification. Mateo swore and thumped the stone floor, sending a jolt of pain through his legs.

Using his hands and dragging his legs behind him, Mateo made his way to the farmhouse door. He needed to stop a couple of times to rest, and every inch of ground he covered sent fresh waves of pain down his legs. By the time he reached the door, he was dripping with perspiration and had damp patches under both arms. But, he thought as he reached up for the door handle, he was making progress.

When Mateo had managed to open the door, he half-slid, half-rolled into the sunshine outside. With a final look at Gjergj, still slumped in the chair, he let the door close behind him. There was always the chance that Gjergj wouldn't come round at all. He'd been unconscious for what felt to Mateo like hours now. Perhaps he was dead? Mateo certainly wasn't going to go back and check.

With the gravel digging painfully into his hands, Mateo made his way across the clearing in front of the farmhouse. He aimed to the right, toward the track that led to the pigsty. Mateo groaned a couple of times as his legs caught against larger stones, but he kept going. He had to keep going. There was no other way. Above his head, high in the blue sky, some large birds circled. Mateo knew they were red kites, as he'd seen plenty of them since arriving in England, but their similarity to vultures was eerie. Mateo had never seen a vulture in real life, but he knew what they did, and what they did it to.

It could have been twenty or thirty minutes, but Mateo eventually managed to crawl across the clearing and into the shade provided by the pine trees on the other side. He took a few moments to relax, or at least relax as much as he could with the pain in his legs and the palms of his hands. Mateo was thirsty, but the nearest drinking water was all the way at the pigsty, and even then, it wouldn't be particularly clean. There was a stream at the side of the path, Mateo remembered. He could drink from that.

His thoughts encouraged by the prospect of fresh drinking water, Mateo was about to start crawling again when he heard a noise. A familiar noise. Tires on the path. There was a vehicle traveling down the path that led from the main road toward the farmhouse. Mateo could have cried with relief. Was it the peshkop? The pig farmer? He knew it wouldn't be Caleb and Katya. There was no reason for them to return.

Either way, whether it was the peshkop or the farmer, Mateo had some help on the way.

88

K atya peered through the spyhole in the door to make sure it was Caleb outside before she pulled the door open.

"Hey, how did you get on?" she asked as he walked in, depositing a large shopping bag next to Mateo's bag. "What's in there?"

"Supplies," Caleb replied, but didn't elaborate. He reached into the bag and pulled out two maps. "Could you lay these out on the bed?"

As Katya unfolded the maps, she could see Caleb rearranging things and taking items out of the carrier bag to place in Mateo's rucksack. He had a pair of binoculars, several items of clothing, and some other things that she couldn't see. Caleb dropped one thing on the floor. A large, plastic tent peg.

"Are we going camping?" Katya asked as he scooped it up and put it in the rucksack.

"Not just yet, Katya, no." Caleb's voice was terse, and he seemed distracted.

"Is everything okay?" Katya asked him. She watched as he forced a smile onto his face.

"Of course, everything's fine. Are you hungry? It's almost lunchtime," Caleb said. "We could order some food in while we're looking at these." He gestured at the maps on their bed. "Then we'll get some sleep."

"Sounds like a plan."

Katya used her phone to order some sandwiches and snacks to be delivered to the hotel reception. While they waited for the food to arrive, Caleb talked her through the maps.

"So we're here," he said, pointing at a small square on the map. "Our target is over here." He pointed at another square. "Which is around four kilometers." Katya frowned, trying to work out how many miles that was, but Caleb beat her to it. "That's about two and a half miles."

"As the crow flies?" Katya asked with a grin.

"As the crow flies, yes. You see these contours here?" His finger traced some thin lines on the map. "The house is in a shallow valley, which makes the best place to get an overview of it just here." Katya's finger beat his to a green oval shape close to the house.

"This wood, just here," she said, a triumphant smile on her face.

"Very good, Katya," Caleb said.

"So when is the mission?"

"The reconnaissance will be tonight, or more specifically, tomorrow very early. I want to see the lay of the land at the same time of day as the actual mission."

"So we're going to get the girls the day after tomorrow? Can't we go sooner?" Katya frowned, not liking the idea of leaving them where they were for another day. Who knew what might happen to them?

"Proverbs. Chapter nineteen, verse two, Katya," Caleb replied. Katya sighed and crossed her arms. Caleb just continued. "It is not good for a person to be without knowledge, and he who hurries his footsteps errs." Katya sighed again as Caleb slid from the bed. "I'm just going to jump in the shower."

"Whatever," she muttered under her breath as the bathroom door closed. A moment later, she heard the sound of the shower followed by something she'd not heard before that brought a smile to her face. Caleb was singing.

Katya pottered around the room for a while as Caleb showered, examining the various fixtures and fittings. She was just looking in the bedside cabinets when the phone rang, making her jump. Their food had arrived.

Leaving Caleb to finish his shower, Katya made her way to reception to collect their lunch. When she returned, Caleb was finished and had dressed in a pair of shorts and a t-shirt that he'd bought from the outdoors store.

"Go, eat your food with gladness, and drink your wine with a joyful heart, for God has already approved what you do," Katya said as Caleb smiled at her. "Ecclesiastes. Chapter nine, verse seven."

Caleb's smile broadened as he clapped his hands slowly.

"You found the Gideon bible, then?" he said.

"For a man of faith, Caleb," Katya said, grinning as she placed the food on the desk, "you have precious little in me."

ALMOST AN HOUR LATER, both Katya and Caleb were lying on the bed. Caleb had drawn the curtains, but the room was still light from the sun outside. Katya could feel the heat from Caleb's body. They weren't touching, but they didn't need to be. The bottle of wine she'd ordered with their lunch was empty. Katya didn't think she could sleep at all, but when she looked at Caleb, he had his eyes closed.

"You asleep?" she asked him.

"Not anymore," he replied with a grin as he opened his eyes.

"You remember what you said about preaching being a bit like sex?" Katya said, her voice almost a whisper.

"What, there being a time and a place for both?"

"Yes."

"Yes," Caleb said. His voice was also low. "I remember."

"Do you think now might be the time and the place?"

Katya watched as a slow smile spread across his face.

"I think it might be, yes." Caleb replied. Katya felt her heart rate increasing in anticipation. Should she make the first move? Should she wait for him to? "So, today's scripture is from the Song of Solomon, chapter seven."

"Seriously?" Katya said as Caleb turned over to face her. She mirrored his movement and looked into his eyes. "I wasn't talking about preaching, Caleb."

"How beautiful you are and how pleasing, O love, with your delights, Your stature is like that of the palm, and your breasts like clusters of fruit." Caleb leaned closer to her so that their lips were almost touching. "I will climb the palm tree; I will take hold of its fruit." She felt his hand slide onto her hip and, as she watched, he closed his eyes. "May your breasts be like the clusters of the vine, the fragrance of your breath like apples, your mouth like the best wine. May the wine go straight to my lover, flowing gently over lips and teeth."

"Caleb?" Katya whispered.

"Shh. I'm not finished. I belong to my lover, and their desire is for me."

"Caleb?" Katya whispered again.

"Yes?"

"Would you shut up and just kiss me, please?"

To Katya's relief, he did just that.

89

"Well, this is interesting," Sergeant Bush said to Tony as they made their way down the narrow path. Above their heads, the trees almost formed a tunnel and, despite the bright sunshine, it was dark enough for the car's headlights to come on automatically. "Never been down here before. Have you?"

"Nope," Tony replied, his eyes fixed on the path ahead. They had already driven over one pothole that had jarred the suspension, resulting in a loud metallic clunk from underneath the car. In response, Tony had slowed the vehicle to a crawl. "What did the call say again?"

Sergeant Bush checked his notebook. "All it said was *Halliwell Farm. Man down.* Spoken by a male, no discernible accent, but the operator said she thought he sounded a bit foreign."

"A bit foreign?" Tony replied, laughing. "Someone's out of date for their inclusivity and diversity training."

"The call was made from the payphones near the small shopping center just outside Market Rasen."

"I still don't get why we're doing it," Tony said. For such a young police officer, he'd learned the art of grumbling very quickly. "We're response officers. It should be uniform."

"There's no uniform available," Sergeant Bush replied. "Besides, we're proud to serve. Aren't we, Tony?"

"If you say so, Sarge." Tony grinned at him briefly before looking back at the path in front of them. "Looks like the trees open out just up here."

A few moments later, the police car pulled into a clearing. In front of them was a dilapidated farmhouse, seemingly devoid of life.

"Looks like the set for a horror movie," Tony said. Sergeant Bush was about to reply when a slight movement on the edge of the clearing caught his eye. It was a man, sitting on the ground with his legs straight out in front of him.

"That could be our man down, Tony," Sergeant Bush said. He unbuckled his seat belt as Tony put the handbrake on and got out of the car, putting his white peaked hat on as he did so. "You okay there, sir?" Sergeant Bush asked. The man looked neither comfortable nor pleased to see him.

"It's my legs," the man said. "I think they're broken."

Sergeant Bush looked down at the man's legs as Tony walked up to join him. Both the police officers were trained in first aid, but Sergeant Bush couldn't see much wrong with them.

"Can you walk?"

"No."

"What happened to your legs, sir?"

"I fell over."

Sergeant Bush looked at Tony and nodded at the house. "Check the house out, Tony. I'll have a look at this chap's legs and call for a big white taxi if we need one."

"A what?" Tony asked.

"An ambulance, Tony," Sergeant Bush replied with a grin. He'd forgotten how young Tony was.

While Tony walked toward the house, Sergeant Bush crouched down next to the man on the ground.

"What's your name, sir?" he asked him.

"Mateo," the man replied.

"Where's your accent from?"

"I'm Albanian."

"Right. And you say you fell over?" The man on the ground nodded in response. "Where do your legs hurt?"

Mateo pointed at the lower section of his legs, just above the ankle. Sergeant Bush, taking care to be gentle, rolled up both trouser legs to have a closer look. He couldn't see any obvious deformities or bony injuries.

"I think I'd better call you an ambulance, sir," Sergeant Bush said, standing up. "When you fell over, did you by any chance fall onto someone's feet? Only there're quite clear footprints on your shins." Mateo just grimaced in response.

Sergeant Bush was just walking back to the patrol car when he saw the door to the farmhouse fly open. Tony came running out and Sergeant Bush was about to break into a run to see what was going on when Tony stopped, leaned forward, and vomited all over the ground.

Just like Sergeant Bush had when he'd seen his first dead body.

90

C aleb hooked his arm behind his head to plump up his pillow, careful not to disturb Katya, who was sound asleep with her arm draped across his chest. He knew he should sleep, but it was evading him. Perhaps because of what he and Katya had done earlier that afternoon. Several times, as it had turned out. He looked at his watch. It was almost midnight, and he wanted to leave the hotel at four in the morning, before the dawn.

To pass the time, he wondered how many people in the world, at any one time, were being intimate with each other. Would it be thousands? Tens of thousands? When thought about in that context, there was nothing special about what they had done. But Caleb knew that wasn't the case at all. Far from it.

Caleb thought back to his youth when, as a young man of eighteen, he had met a woman named Maria who would become his first, and perhaps most memorable, lover. She had been older than him by four or five years and, although she never quantified it, had a lot more experience in such things. She had been patient with him, cautioning him to calm his urges and slow down. Focus on other things than his own pleasure. Such as hers. Although she was, by her own admission, acting selfishly, she took the time to teach him. Caleb had no yardstick by which to measure his prowess, but Maria had intimated that he was an excellent student. When they parted after a few intense months, reluctantly but amicably, she had made him promise to never forget that no matter how much society changed, there was always a place for chivalry in the bedroom.

Beside him, Katya moaned softly. Caleb turned to look at her and saw a faint smile on her face, but her eyes were still closed. Was she dreaming?

Earlier that afternoon, their needs fully sated, Caleb and Katya had lain on the bed talking. She had told him about her previous partner, a young man called Badri, who she had been with since they were at school together. One evening a few years previously, Badri had got involved in a fight in a bar between some Russian soldiers and native Abkhazians in the bar he worked at. According to those who had witnessed it, Badri had stepped in to defuse the situation. The Abkhazians had fled and Badri had been taken by the Russians to a small courtyard behind the bar.

"They beat him to death," Katya had told Caleb, her voice devoid of emotion. "Like animals. I wasn't even able to see him afterwards. His injuries were too bad." Caleb had said nothing, but let her talk. The pain was dull, she had told him, but always there. He wanted to tell her that the pain she felt was her way of keeping Badri's memory alive, but he didn't. Katya would know that without him telling her.

"But that is in the past," Katya had said eventually, tracing the puckered scar on Caleb's chest. "And this is the present."

Caleb closed his eyes, determined to sleep. He listened for the sound of Katya's breathing and timed his own to match hers. He needed to rest. There were two busy nights ahead. He knew Katya wanted to play a role in what was to happen, but Caleb couldn't let that happen. It would be too risky for her. Caleb was more than happy to act alone. He preferred it. He knew he could look after himself, but he couldn't offer Katya the same protection if things turned bad. Which they almost certainly would if Caleb had anything to do with it.

A few seconds later, Caleb's eyes snapped open. He angled his head to one side, listening. It was the sound of a car, moving slowly. No engine noise, just the quiet whisper of tires on gravel. Then it stopped and a few seconds later, there was the sound of a door closing. Then another. Not being closed the way someone would normally, but being carefully shut. Then two sets of footsteps. One getting louder, one getting quieter. Caleb's thoughts drifted back to the black SUV he had seen earlier, and the occupants' lack of reaction to Katya as she stretched her body.

Unless Caleb was mistaken, and he rarely was, he and Katya were about to have some visitors.

91

Mateo looked at his legs, now both encased in plaster casts. They were temporary ones, the technician who had applied them had told him. At some point, he would have to come back to the hospital to have them exchanged for more permanent ones. Six weeks, the technician had said he would need to wear them. Mateo had no idea how he was going to survive for six weeks without being able to walk. It wasn't as if he had travel insurance to take him home to Albania.

He was in a single room in the Emergency Department, which surprised him when they wheeled him into it after the plasters had been put on. Mateo was waiting for the doctor to come and see him so that he could be discharged from the hospital. Gjergj was in the main department somewhere, a harried nurse had told him earlier when she'd come in with some pain medication.

Mateo leaned back into his pillow and closed his eyes. What was he going to do? How was he going to get home? Would the police want to question him further about Aleksander? He'd told them everything he knew already, or at least a version of it. Mateo had described both Caleb and Katya in detail, claiming they were hitchhikers that they had picked up. Caleb had, in his version of events, robbed them and assaulted both him and Gjergj. The more times he told the story, the better it got. Even the policeman who'd scanned his fingerprints into a device that looked like a phone had sounded sympathetic to the fact Mateo had been assaulted and robbed.

When he heard the door to the room open, he opened his eyes. It was the doctor who had treated him earlier, a man who looked far too young to be a proper doctor. But his identification badge had Dr. Pete Simmons on it, as did his *Hello, my name is* badge. And just in case anyone missed it, he also wore a white coat and a stethoscope draped around his neck.

"Mr. Ahmeti?" the doctor said. Mateo smiled. Few people were so formal. "We're almost there, I think." The young doctor took a couple of steps forward and examined Mateo's toes. "Wiggle them for me, please?" Mateo did as instructed. "Any pain?"

Mateo shook his head. "No," he said. "A nurse gave me something for it."

"Can you feel this?" Mateo nodded as the doctor touched each of his toes in turn.

"Well, now the fractures are immobilized, there shouldn't be much pain, if any." Dr. Simmons glanced down at the notes he'd brought in with him. "We'll need to bring you back to the fracture clinic in a few days to have those backslabs changed to full casts."

"Sorry, backslabs?" Mateo asked.

"That's the type of plaster you have on." The doctor glanced at his watch, just in case Mateo hadn't realized how much of a hurry he was in. "I think we're okay to discharge you. Do you have questions for me before we let you go?"

"Where do I go?"

"I'm sorry. I don't understand?" Dr. Simmons just stared at him.

"I have nowhere to go," Mateo said, trying not to sound too desperate. He pointed at his plastered legs. "And even if I did, how am I going to get there?"

"Ah, I see. Well, that's not really our problem. Is there anyone you can call?"

"I have no phone. No money. Nothing." The only person Mateo could call would be Gramoz, and he could imagine his uncle's reaction if he did. There was always the peshkop, but his number was in Mateo's phone and, apart from his first name, Mateo knew almost nothing about him. He couldn't even remember the man's address.

"I, er, well," the doctor said, lost for something to say. "How about I fetch the nurse to come and help you? She'll be able to talk through your options. But as of now, you're discharged and free to go."

Mateo swore under his breath as the doctor left the room. When the nurse came in, he would ask her if he could speak to Gjergj. Perhaps he would have some ideas about what they could do? But he would be in the same situation as Mateo was, with both legs plastered to just below the knee.

The door opened again, but it wasn't a nurse who walked in. It was a man Mateo hadn't seen before. Mid to late forties, stocky, and with a face that had seen it all before. Behind him were two police officers, burly men who looked much larger than they were because of the amount of equipment on their vests.

"Mr. Ahmeti? Mr. Mateo Ahmeti?" the man said. He was

wearing a cheap suit with a polyester tie. In his hand was a small, black leather wallet, which he flipped open to reveal a silver crest. It was the second time in less than ten minutes that he had been addressed so formally, but this time, Mateo didn't smile. "I'm Detective Inspector Mahoney of Lincolnshire Police."

"Yes?" Mateo replied, his voice almost a whisper.

"I'm arresting you on suspicion of the murder of Aleksander Ahmeti," the policeman said. Mateo groaned and closed his eyes. "You do not have to say anything, but it may harm your defense if you do not mention, when questioned, something which you later rely on in court. Anything you do say may be taken and given as evidence."

"I told the other guys," Mateo replied. "Aleksander was killed by the man in the robe. The man who broke both my legs." Behind the detective, one of the police officers smirked.

"If that's the case, Mr. Ahmeti," the detective said as his uniformed colleague stepped forward with a set of handcuffs. "Why were your fingerprints all over the ax that killed your brother?"

92

K atya woke with a start and started struggling against the firm hand that was covering her mouth. She had been dreaming, and remnants of the dream were still in her consciousness as she heard Caleb making a soft shushing sound. Only a few seconds before, he had been with her in her dream. They had been standing on the very edge of a cliff, both having climbed it hand in hand. Just before she woke, they had stepped off the cliff together. But they hadn't fallen. They had soared up into the air.

"Katya," Caleb said, his mouth only inches from her ear. "Someone is coming."

"Who?" Katya whispered back when Caleb removed his hand.

"I don't know who they are," Caleb replied. "Only that they mean us harm. Get dressed. Quickly, and quietly."

Katya pulled the duvet back and started picking up her clothes from the floor where they had been discarded only a few hours previously. They had not fully drawn the curtains earlier, and a sliver of moonlight gave them just enough light to work with. In silence, Caleb picked up his own clothes. He swept around the room, putting all their belongings into Mateo's rucksack. As they got ready, Katya listened intently, but she could hear nothing. How did Caleb know there was someone coming? Perhaps, she hoped, he'd been mistaken and they could just go back to bed. But he'd not been mistaken before, and from the quiet intensity she could see in his eyes, he wasn't mistaken now.

"What do we do?" Katya whispered, trying to keep the fear from her voice. There was something unsettling about the look on Caleb's face.

"Get in the tub," Caleb said, pointing at the bathroom.

"Seriously?"

"Seriously. It's the safest place for you if they're armed."

Katya looked across at the bathroom. The tub was a large, solid one with a shower attachment over the top. She could see Caleb's logic, although she had no idea if the metal sides would deflect a bullet or not. With an uncertain look at him, Katya walked across the hotel room, entered the bathroom, and climbed into the tub. When she looked back at Caleb, he was gesturing with his hands for her to lay down. She did so, but a few seconds later peered above the rim. She wanted to see what Caleb was doing, but all she could see was the door to the hotel room.

A few seconds later, Katya heard a soft knock at the door. Caleb had been right. There was someone there.

"Hello?" Caleb called out, doing a reasonable impression of a man just roused from sleep.

"Hotel security, sir. Is yours the white Fiat 500? In the lot?" It was a man's voice, with a British accent.

"Yes, that's mine," Caleb replied. "Is everything okay?"

"There's a problem with the car, sir. Could you come to the door?"

"Sure. Just coming."

A few seconds later, Katya could see Caleb walking across the hotel room, hugging a wall to keep clear of the door. In one hand was a *Do Not Disturb* sign that could be hung over the outside of the door handle. As he passed Mateo's rucksack, Caleb stooped down to retrieve something from it. A vicious-looking survival knife with a serrated edge.

Katya watched as Caleb crept toward the door. Then he held his hand up, dangling the *Do Not Disturb* sign like his hand was the claw from a fairground claw fishing game. When he reached the door, Caleb stood to one side of it and reached his arm up. Katya saw he was about to use the sign to block the peephole in the door. She was just wondering why he was doing that when it wasn't possible to see through it from the other side, when there was a sound like someone coughing twice in quick succession.

Katya stifled a scream as two small holes appeared in the door and splinters of wood flew into the room.

93

"Have you had a chance to consider my offer?" Martin smiled at the deep baritone voice on the other end of the line. When the burner phone had rung in his top drawer, he'd known who the caller was before he'd even answered the call.

"I have, yes."

"And your thoughts?"

"It's rather irregular, my friend," Martin replied. There was a throaty chuckle in response.

"Yes, I understand. But I was hoping you might be able to facilitate it for me. I will, of course, make it worth your while."

"And how exactly would you be doing that?"

"I could double my contribution to your, er, your trust fund."

Martin's eyebrows went up a notch at the offer. Given the amount the man and his fellow enthusiasts were paying him for the event, it was a significant amount being offered.

"Two hours, you say? Of private time before the others arrive?" he asked the man.

"Yes," Martin's caller replied.

Martin paused for a moment. It wasn't just about the money. It was also about the leverage that the footage would give him. His caller was, Martin sensed, going places. If the political situation went the way everyone seemed to think it would, he could be destined for great things. Including a house on a very famous street in London. One with a shiny black door and the number ten in silver letters on the front. That, Martin knew, would give him the ultimate in terms of leverage. It might take his caller a year or two, possibly even more, to reach his ultimate goal. But Martin could wait. He rubbed his chest as he considered the proposal, wondering whether to pop some pills to dull the ache he felt. He was due another ultrasound at the hospital in the next few weeks. Even though it was a private hospital, and they treated him with the respect his money deserved, he still disliked the place.

"I think that all sounds very doable," Martin replied, deciding against any pills. It was only a dull ache, nothing more.

"The others mustn't know, of course."

"Of course," Martin said as he ended the call.

A few moments later, as Martin was updating a spreadsheet with his incoming and outgoing funds, there was a soft knock at the door. Martin waited before replying, savoring the figures he was looking at. With the additional contribution, the *Incoming* column was very healthy indeed.

"Come in," Martin said, closing the spreadsheet down. He knew it was Robert. He was the only member of Martin's staff who would knock this late in the evening. Martin glanced at his watch. It was only a few minutes before midnight. "What is it, Robert?" Martin asked as his head of security walked in and sat down, uninvited.

"Have you seen the news, Martin?" Robert said, crossing his legs.

"No," Martin replied. "Why?"

"It's not good, I'm afraid. This morning, a boat floundered in the channel. Ten dead, another two still missing."

"How tragic," Martin said. "But what of it?"

"Your packages were on that boat."

"What?" Martin asked, the pain in his chest suddenly sharpening. He reached into his drawer for his pain pills.

"The additional two children that Gramoz was organizing. They were on that boat."

"Damn!" Martin said. It was the closest he ever got to swearing, but a man in his position had to be careful. He closed his eyes. Whether the packages were alive or dead was of no concern to him. Either way, they were now beyond his reach. "We'll have to make do with the two we have. They'll just have to work harder."

He watched as Robert stayed in the chair, seemingly unconcerned about the development. Martin knew the number of packages was irrelevant to Robert, anyway.

"My assets are in place at the hotel, anyway. They're taking care of things, as we discussed."

"Good," Martin replied, although he was sad to think of Katya being dealt with. "And the farm?"

Martin couldn't be sure, but he thought he saw a flicker cross Robert's eyes.

"The Albanians were nowhere to be seen," Robert replied. "They're in the wind."

"Well, hopefully we'll never see them again."

Robert stood, said goodnight to Martin, and left the room. Martin got to his feet and poured himself a generous measure of single malt. He stood for a moment, swirling the liquid in its cut-glass crystal tumbler, and thinking.

Why had Robert just lied to him about the Albanians?

94

The last of the wood splinters hadn't even landed on the floor before Caleb was on the other side of the room. It was an L shape, and he hid behind the corner where he couldn't be seen from the door. A few glances around the room told him that his position couldn't be seen by either of the mirrors, and he crouched down.

It could only have been a few seconds, but it felt to Caleb like a full minute before there was a soft click at the door. His thoughts immediately went to the hotel receptionist, and he hoped that whoever was on the desk was merely incapacitated and had not been killed for the key card. He felt the temperature in the room change by a fraction of a degree as the door opened. Caleb closed his eyes, listening hard. Whoever had just put two rounds through the door was moving slowly. He didn't need to see them to know that they would have the silenced weapon in front of them with their arms extended.

Caleb mentally rehearsed his movement when the gun appeared around the corner he was hiding behind. Whoever was behind the gun would expect him to be there.

Simply because there was nowhere else he could be, other than the bathroom. And the new arrival wouldn't clear the bathroom until he'd cleared the main hotel room. So he would come around the corner expecting to see him. But human nature regarded people as standing, not crouching. If Caleb's plan worked, and they usually did, the fact he was crouching would give him a few extra split-seconds, perhaps even as much as a second, to rise with the knife and plunge it into his assailant.

His aiming point was the epigastric region. Specifically, the left upper quadrant of that part of the abdomen, just below the lowest ribs. The flesh there was pliable. Easy enough for a knife to slice through unimpeded. Caleb held the knife in his left hand. While it was, technically speaking, his weaker hand, he wanted the angle of the knife to be toward the assailant's left side. Then Caleb could, with a couple of focused twists of the blade, rupture many organs vital to life. Not just vital to life, but well perfused with blood. The heart was his primary target. Ventricles didn't pump so well when they were lacerated. The aorta, the inferior vena cava. All large blood vessels that took blood either to or from the heart and in the general area. There were so many crucial vessels that it would be almost impossible to miss them, and the effect would be swift and catastrophic.

When his assailant rounded the corner, Caleb intended to spring up, use his right hand to slam the hands with the pistol into the wall, and his left to deliver the coup de grâce with the knife. As the extended barrel of the silenced pistol inched into sight, Caleb adjusted his feet to make sure he had enough purchase to put all his power into his legs. The longer barrel caused by the silencer would work in his favor and make the weapon more unwieldy. But Caleb's plan didn't involve the weapon coming into play.

Caleb held his breath as the assailant rounded the corner in one swift movement, the pistol extended in front of him. In the split second before he put all his power into his legs, Caleb recognized the passenger from the black Evoque. No mask, no face covering. Caleb knew that one of them would die in that room. All he had to do was ensure it wasn't him.

He rose, his right arm coming around as he did so. With the flat of his hand, he drove the assailant's wrists toward the wall where the plasterboard of the hotel room gave in. It wasn't solid enough to break any bones in the man's hands or wrists, but just dented the plasterboard, leaving the pistol in the man's hands. Using all his strength, Caleb drove the knife into his abdomen, the tip hitting exactly the spot he wanted. But the knife didn't disappear into the soft flesh. With a jarring impact on Caleb's wrist, it stopped before entering his abdomen. Then his assailant reacted, bringing the pistol down on the top of Caleb's head with force.

Time slowed for Caleb as a blinding light appeared behind his eyes in response to the blow. He realized two things in quick succession. The first was that the man was wearing a Kevlar vest.

The second, and more concerning to Caleb, was that he could fight.

95

Mateo scratched his abdomen and stared at the two police officers sitting opposite him in the interview room. He was wearing a tracksuit top and bottoms that were several sizes too big, but had been the only ones he'd been able to fit over his plaster casts. Beside him was a disinterested-looking lawyer whose sole advice to Mateo had been to reply *No Comment* to questions that could incriminate him. He had told the lawyer, a duty solicitor, that he hadn't killed Aleksander. That it had been Caleb. But from the look on his face, the lawyer didn't believe him. Neither, it would appear, did the police.

"Tell us again why you are in the United Kingdom," Detective Inspector Mahoney said. He was still wearing the same cheap suit, but had loosened his tie a couple of inches. Next to him was a man who had introduced himself, but Mateo had already forgotten his name. In the corner of the interview room, a CCTV camera blinked a red light every few seconds.

"To look for work," Mateo replied. They'd been around this subject before, several times.

"Where?"

"Anywhere I could."

"And how did you enter the United Kingdom?"

"On a boat."

"Illegally?" Mahoney arched an eyebrow at Mateo, who glanced at his lawyer. The lawyer shook his head almost imperceptibly.

"No comment," Mateo replied.

"Where did you get the green van?" Mahoney asked.

"My friend, Gjergj, rented it." Mateo knew they would know this already.

"I am showing Mr. Ahmeti a photograph from a CCTV camera at Lincoln Sainsbury's supermarket." Mahoney put a photo on the table and swiveled it so that Mateo could see it. "What can you see, Mr. Ahmeti?"

"A van. My brother, Aleksander. And Gjergj. Talking to a security guard."

"Can you see a young girl in the photograph?" the detective asked. Mateo nodded in response.

"Yes," he said. In the still image, frozen just before Aleksander and Ana had got back into the van, the agitation on Ana's face was clear to see.

"Who is she?"

"I don't know." Mateo's lawyer nudged his arm. "I mean, no comment."

"You don't know who she is, Mr. Ahmeti? Is that correct?"

"No comment."

"Are you a kiddy fiddler, Mr. Ahmeti?"

"A what?" Mateo asked as his lawyer stirred beside him.

"Do you like children? Sexually?" Mahoney asked, his eyes hard and unyielding.

"No!" Mateo shot back. Another nudge. "No comment."

"Did you and Aleksander fall out over the girl? Is that what happened? Maybe you couldn't agree who could go first?"

"No. Not that. Never."

"Is that why you killed him?" This time, the lawyer was quicker with his nudge.

"No comment."

Mateo and the detective regarded each other for a few moments. Mateo badly wanted to scratch his abdomen again, but he didn't want to move a muscle. They both just sat there, staring at each other. In the end, it was the lawyer who broke the impasse.

"Do you have any further questions for my client, Detective Mahoney?"

"Let me just remind your client of his situation," Mahoney replied. "Mr. Ahmeti is under arrest for the murder of his brother, with clear forensic evidence linking him to the murder weapon. Charges for illegal immigration will follow, and possibly many others, depending on what we find." The detective pointed at the photograph on the table between them, resting his index finger on Ana's face. "I want to know who she is and where she is. And the other one. Do you understand?"

"No comment," Mateo replied.

"In the farm, there are two beds upstairs that appear to have been slept in by children. Where are they?"

"No comment."

"Are they trafficked?"

Mateo didn't reply. He didn't trust his voice not to break, even if all he said was no comment. How had the police gotten so far so quickly? He had seriously underestimated the man in the cheap suit.

A few seconds later, there was a knock at the door.

Detective Mahoney got to his feet to open it, exchanging a few words with the officer who had just knocked. When he returned to the table, he didn't even sit down, but just glanced at his watch.

"Interview terminated at twelve oh five." He glared at Mateo, his eyes dark and intense. "The interpreter's just arrived," Mahoney said. "Let's see what your friend's got to say for himself."

96

Katya screamed as Caleb was struck on the top of the head hard with the pistol, the extended silencer giving it an unusual appearance. Caleb staggered, but was quick to regain his footing and arc his upper body away from the second blow which glanced off his shoulder. She started scrabbling in the tub, trying to get some purchase on the slippery interior. She had to help him, somehow, but she didn't see what she could do. Was Mateo's gun still in the bag or was it in the car? As Caleb and the stocky man holding the gun grappled with each other, Katya started to stand. A split-second later, there was another cough and a loud metallic clang. She screamed again, almost diving back into the bath as the metal reverberated from the round that had hit it and had almost hit her.

She inched her head above the rim of the bath a few seconds later, just enough for her to see over it. Caleb and his attacker looked to be wrestling, neither of them able to use their weapons. Caleb had grabbed the wrist of the arm holding the gun, but the other man had done the same to Caleb's wrist, meaning he wasn't able to use the knife. She couldn't see Caleb's face as he had his back to her, but the attacker's face was a stone mask. Katya watched Caleb arch his head back, driving his forehead into his attacker's face. She heard a wet crunch and when Caleb moved his head, she saw two dark streams of blood flowing from his attacker's nose. But it didn't seem to faze him in the slightest.

The attacker dropped to his haunches, unbalancing Caleb. Then he let go of Caleb's wrist and delivered a powerful blow to the side of Caleb's face. Caleb's head whipped round, and Katya saw surprise in his eyes. His assailant's next move was a forearm strike, aimed at Caleb's neck, but before he could deliver it, Caleb jabbed at his groin with the knife. The man gasped, reaching down for Caleb's wrist.

The gun in his other hand was pointing away from Katya, so she crouched again in the tub, determined to do something. Then she stepped over the side of the tub as the two men returned to grappling with each other.

"Katya, no!" Caleb shouted. She glanced at him to see that his assailant was doing his utmost to pivot round with the pistol so that it was pointing at her. She ran to the bag as Caleb grunted with the effort of trying to stop him. But she couldn't find the pistol inside it. All that was in it were clothes. She scrabbled around, desperate to find the weapon, aware that the other gun was gradually inching in her direction, despite Caleb's efforts to stop it. Then she felt the hard metal of Mateo's pistol, right at the bottom of the bag. "Katya! Run!" Caleb shouted, an urgency in his voice that she'd never heard before.

Not stopping to think, Katya picked up the bag and tried to run for the door.

Then she heard another cough and, a few seconds later, her face hit the carpet.

97

C aleb saw Katya go down out of the corner of his eye, but he didn't have time to react. He was tiring fast, and his assailant was stronger. The jab Caleb had delivered to his groin was aimed for the femoral artery, but the lack of blood spurting from the wound told Caleb he had missed it. He needed to end this fight, and quickly.

Using all his strength, he jerked his left wrist, getting enough traction to rake the blade across his assailant's anterior forearm. The wound wasn't deep enough to damage any of the nerves or tendons in the area, but it was a sensitive part of the body and it distracted the attacker for long enough for Caleb to take further action. He jerked his wrist free of the man's hand and placed his forearm on the side of his neck, just below his ear. Then, in one seamless movement that used every ounce of the energy remaining in Caleb's body, he pushed against his head to force it to one side. At the same time, he pulled down as hard as he could on the hand with the gun with his right hand. Not expecting the movement, his attacker was caught off guard and stumbled slightly. This only served to further stress the unnatural movement of his body.

The result was exactly what Caleb had been aiming for. The gun clattered to the floor, landing with a soft thump on the carpet. Caleb's attacker, the nerves in his brachial plexus completely avulsed, had no control over his arm. He sneered at Caleb, but there was nothing he could do as Caleb raised the arm that until a split-second earlier had been holding the gun, and plunged the knife into his armpit.

Caleb held his gaze as he jerked the knife a couple of times, backward and forward, to ensure the knife transected both the axillary artery and vein. The man shook his head from side to side, but made no effort to do anything with his remaining good arm. There were a multitude of nerves also in the area, and any that hadn't been avulsed would now be lacerated. But Caleb knew it would make no difference to the outcome.

As he waited for the man he was holding to lose consciousness, he offered up a prayer for his soul. Whoever this man was, he had fought well and he would die well. Caleb spun him around gently, sitting him down on the bed and then laying him down. Twice, his assailant opened his mouth before closing it without speaking. Caleb crossed the man's arms over his chest and watched as he prepared to breathe his last breath, an expanding pool of dark liquid spreading from the wound in his axilla.

"Is he dead?" Caleb heard Katya say. She had untangled her legs from the straps of Mateo's bag and got to her feet. As she had fallen, the contents of the bag had spilled on the floor, and she was sweeping everything back into it. Caleb turned to her and placed a finger on his lips.

"The Lord is with you, mighty warrior," Caleb whispered

as the man on the bed breathed for one last time. He turned to Katya. "He is now. We have to get moving." Katya nodded in response. "Before his partner arrives."

"There are two of them?" Katya said with a gasp.

"Yes," Caleb replied. He took a step toward the door and picked up Mateo's bag.

"Shouldn't we go this way?" Katya said, picking up her own suitcase and gesturing at the window.

"No, that's where he'll be. Covering the rear."

They made their way through the hotel, moving as fast as they could. As they passed through the reception area, Caleb looked behind the desk to see the night porter lying on the floor, his arms and legs tied. His eyes were pleading with Caleb to release him, but there was no time. The man Caleb had just fought was no ordinary man, and he needed as much distance between him and Katya as they could get. Besides, if he freed the night porter, then the place would be crawling with police in no time. All looking for a white Fiat.

Caleb threw Mateo's bag into the rear of the car and got into the passenger seat. Katya started the vehicle, put it into gear, and drove out of the lot, leaving two long black trails of rubber behind her. It was only once they were on the main road a few hundred yards away from the hotel that she began to relax. But Caleb couldn't relax.

His eyes were fixed on the side-mirror, and on the large black SUV that had just pulled out of the hotel parking lot.

98

"Who was that guy, Caleb?" Katya asked, turning to look at him. "And why was he trying to kill us?"

"I don't know for sure, Katya," Caleb replied. His attention was fixed on the side-mirror. Katya glanced in the rear-view mirror and saw a large black SUV behind them, gaining fast. She moved the Fiat to the left-hand side of the road to give them plenty of room to pass. Whoever it was, it looked as if they were in a hurry.

"My best guess is they're some sort of security detail for Martin," Caleb replied. "He was good. Ex-military would be my guess. But just a little too sluggish, so probably not currently serving. You see the SUV?"

"Yep," Katya replied, glancing again at the mirror. It was now only around a hundred yards behind them.

"Think you can outrun it?"

"What?" Katya said with a gasp. "There're more of them?"

"There's at least one more, Katya," Caleb said. She

looked at him again but couldn't see any concern on his face. "I saw them earlier."

"And you were going to tell me when?" Katya asked him, her mouth a thin line. She pressed her foot on the accelerator and the compact car lurched forward. But there was no way they could outrun the powerful vehicle behind them.

Just up ahead, there was a turnoff to the right. Katya waited until the car was around twenty yards from it before shifting down a gear and hauling on the wheel. She felt the car leaning to the side, but the wheels hugged the road as they screeched around the turn. Next to her, Caleb didn't react at all. She shifted gears again and sped up. The road they were now on was much more suited to the smaller car, as it was narrower and windy. Katya just hoped they wouldn't meet something coming the other way, but she figured it was unlikely at nighttime.

"He's still gaining," Caleb said a few seconds later. Katya's rear-view mirror was filled with the headlights of the larger vehicle. Was he about to sideswipe the car to try to force them off the road? The SUV could only be a few yards behind them. Katya looked over at Caleb to ask him what she should do, but he was leaning back into the rear of the car. A few seconds later, Caleb had one of the maps unfolded on his lap. A frown was on his face as he used his index finger to trace something on the laminated paper.

"Hard left-hand turn coming up," he said. Katya's hand hovered over the gear stick as she prepared to take the turn, squinting through the headlights to make sure she timed it right. Again, the car held the road well, but she felt the back end sliding out when they were about halfway into it. As she sped up out of the turn, she glanced again in the rear-view. The maneuver had bought them some time. Only a few seconds, but the larger vehicle had to slow down much more. "About a mile down this road," Caleb said, "there's a small track on the right. We need to take that track."

Katya opened her mouth to reply, but before she could speak, there was a loud pop as the rear window of the Fiat shattered. Katya screamed as fragments of glass peppered the back of her head.

"Caleb, they're shooting at us!" Katya shrieked. "Do something!"

Her fingers whitened on the steering wheel as Caleb reached around again for Mateo's rucksack. He rummaged in it frantically.

"Katya, where's the gun?"

"It's in the bag." She rose her voice to speak over the noise of the wind rushing into the car.

"It's not." Caleb rechecked the rucksack.

"Shit," Katya said, remembering tripping over the bag earlier and spilling its contents on the floor. While it had probably saved her life, had she put the gun back in the rucksack? With a sinking feeling in her chest, she realized she hadn't. "Um, Caleb, you're not going to like this."

"Not going to like what?"

"The gun. I think it's back at the hotel."

Caleb paused for a second or two before replying. Katya's eyes darted to the rear-view where the SUV was still only yards behind them. She pressed her foot to the floor, but the small car was already going flat out.

"Not a problem," Caleb replied. He undid his seat belt and leaned around to the rear of the vehicle. "We'll just have to improvise, that's all."

99

Caleb scrabbled with his fingers to unlatch the rear seats of the Fiat. He needed to fold them forward get into the trunk, but he couldn't reach. As Katya drove, the small car lurching from side to side as she did so, he reclined his seat so he could climb over it. There was a flash of light to the left-hand side of the SUV behind them, so bright he could see it over the headlights, but it was just that. Caleb wasn't overly bothered about being shot at. And he knew how difficult it was to shoot from a moving vehicle at another moving vehicle. In Caleb's opinion, it was a waste of rounds. It was one thing hitting a window, but quite another hitting a person in a car that was being driven the way Katya was driving theirs.

"What are you doing?" Katya shouted at him. Caleb could hear the tension in her voice. He just wanted her to concentrate on driving the car. At the speed they were going, the slightest mistake could see them onto the roof or smashing headlong into a tree.

"Just concentrate on the road, Katya!" Caleb shouted back. Finally, he managed to get the rear seat to fold down.

Caleb scrabbled around in the dark until he found one of the things he was looking for. It wasn't much of a weapon and wasn't his first choice, but it was something. He scuttled back into the front seat, Katya glancing at him as he lowered the passenger window.

"What are you going to do with that?" she shouted. Caleb didn't respond, but turned around and leaned out of the passenger window. He was going to have to use his right arm, which as he was left-handed, wasn't ideal, but if his aim was true, then it wouldn't matter.

Caleb leaned his arm back, ignoring another flash of light from the car. Then he hurled the tire jack as hard as he could, aiming for the center of the windshield. His aim was off, which wasn't surprising given the circumstances, but in the end, the result was better than he had hoped. The tire jack spun through the air before glancing off the hood of the SUV and impacting the windshield almost directly in front of the driver.

The weapon wasn't heavy enough to shatter the glass, but it was heavy enough for an enormous spider's web of cracks to appear in the windshield. Caleb knew that the driver would have just lost most of his vision through the fractures. The SUV dropped back, and Caleb saw the driver was fighting to maintain control of the vehicle. The best result—from Caleb's and Katya's perspective—would have been for him to roll the vehicle, but he was able to bring the SUV to a controlled stop. His next step, if he had any sense, would be to kick the glass out and continue after them.

"Has he stopped?" Katya asked, her voice closer to normal. She still had to speak loudly to be heard over the noise of the wind in the car.

"For the moment, yes," Caleb replied. He peered

through the windshield at the road ahead. "That turn is maybe a hundred and fifty yards further, Katya."

Caleb took a deep breath through his nose as Katya eased up on the accelerator. The small car was still moving fast, but the reduction in speed reduced the wind noise. She slowed for the turn, which was sharper than it had looked to Caleb on the map. It was, he reflected, a good job they weren't traveling as fast as they had been. Katya wouldn't have made the corner if they were.

"How did they know we were at that hotel, Caleb?" Katya asked. "If they are Martin's security team, how did they know where they were?"

"Would you lend Mateo a car and not make sure you knew where it was?"

"They're tracking us?"

"I would."

The road they had turned onto was as straight as a Roman road, but much narrower than the one they had been on. It fell away in front of them, illuminated by the moonlight.

"What did you do to Mateo and Gjergj, Caleb?" Katya asked. "Back at the farmhouse?"

"I just slowed them down," Caleb replied with a wry smile. "But don't worry, they'll be okay."

"How do you know?"

"I phoned a friend." His smile extended as she looked at him with a curious expression. "About five hundred yards down here," he said, pointing at the road in front of them, "there's a dip in the road with a short tunnel under a railway line. Go through the tunnel and there's a bend in the road."

"Okay," Katya replied. "Where then? Do we need to change cars?"

"We do, yes, but later. After the bend, I want you to pull over."

"But what if they're still after us?" Caleb could hear the fear creeping back into her voice as she glanced up at the rear-view mirror. "Caleb? There're lights behind us." She looked over her shoulder briefly before speeding up.

Caleb watched the black SUV's lights in the side-view mirror. He smiled as the tunnel came into view in front of them.

"Perfect," he mumbled under his breath.

100

Mateo lay on the thin mattress and stared at the ceiling of his cell. The only illumination he had was a single incandescent bulb in the ceiling, protected by a wire guard. He shifted his legs to get them more comfortable and wondered what Gjergj was saying to the police. How much of the story he had made up would survive? It wasn't as if he and Gjergj had any time to get their stories straight.

He thought back to fighting with Caleb in the forest, before he had been sucker punched. Hardly a fair fight at all. He remembered the strange way Caleb had run his hands up and down the ax handle before he'd thrown it on the ground. Bastard. He'd been making sure his fingerprints weren't left on the handle. And now the police didn't believe a word he said. Neither, he imagined, did his lawyer. Mateo didn't know how long it took to become a lawyer, but the only advice he'd offered was to not incriminate himself. How many years had the man spent at law school to come up with that sage advice, he wondered?

Now, with time to think and no pressure other than his

own situation, Mateo ran through his options. He couldn't see any that didn't involve time in prison, either here or back in Albania. Mateo had no idea about any sort of extradition policy with his home country. If he had a say in the matter, he would much rather stay in a British prison than an Albanian one.

Mateo sighed, realizing he wouldn't have a say in the matter, anyway. He only hoped that perhaps Brexit had put a stop to prisoners being moved around Europe, but when he remembered Albania wasn't yet in the European Union, he sighed again. One thing Mateo knew for certain, regardless of whether he was in a British prison or an Albanian one was if he was there as a pedophile, his stay would be horrendous. When the policeman had asked him earlier if he liked children that way, the very thought that the police were thinking he might had sent a shiver down his spine.

His best bet was to be prosecuted as a people trafficker. That much was true. While he'd known the final destination of his packages, he wasn't complicit in the activities of those who bought them. He was just the delivery mechanism. But Mateo wasn't a pedophile, and he wasn't a murderer. Perhaps there was a deal to be made? If Mateo offered Gramoz and Martin to the police, the ends of the chain to either side of him, perhaps they would offer him witness protection?

If Mateo was going to act, he needed to act quickly. According to his lawyer, the police could hold him for up to four days before charging or releasing him if they wanted to. And if Gjergj told the truth—about the people trafficking, at least—then he would corroborate his story.

Mateo was about to get to his feet when he remembered his plaster casts. Instead of knocking on the door, he used the flat of his hand to pound the cell wall.

"Hello?" Mateo shouted. He was rewarded with a string of catcalls and obscenities from other prisoners in the cells. "Hello? Can I speak to someone, please?"

It was at least five minutes before there was any response other than the insults. A small hatch in his cell door flew open, and Mateo saw a pair of dark eyes staring through.

"What?" the police officer on the other side said.

"I want to speak to the detective," Mateo replied.

"This time of night? You'll be lucky, sunshine. He'll have gone home a long time ago."

"Is there someone else I can speak to? I've got some more information."

"No." The police officer started to close the hatch in the door. Mateo called out again, asking if there was anyone at all, but the only response was the sound of the hatch slamming shut.

Mateo lay back on the thin mattress and tried to plump up the equally thin pillow. He doubted he could sleep, but at least he had some time to think through what he could offer. He had to prove that Caleb existed, and that he had killed Aleksander. But how was he going to do that? Part of their planning had been to ensure that their packages were never in the view of a CCTV camera, no mean feat in England where they seemed to outnumber people. And, as it had turned out, that part had failed when Aleksander went to the supermarket.

He had to do something. It wasn't just his freedom that depended on it, but possibly his life.

101

Katya's fingers tightened on the steering wheel as she stared at the road ahead. She was trying to ignore the lights in the rear-view mirror, but it wasn't easy. Beside her, though, Caleb seemed unconcerned. She even thought she heard him humming under his breath.

Ahead of her, the road dipped away, and she saw the tunnel under the bridge appear in the headlights. It was a lot narrower than she'd thought it would be, and for a few seconds Katya wondered if the car would even fit through. But as they approached, she could see they had plenty of room.

Katya's stomach lurched as the car went down into the dip in the road. She tapped the brakes lightly to lose some speed, but not too much. The headlights were still behind her, after all. They were perhaps three or four hundred yards away. The car entered the tunnel with plenty of room to spare and emerged on the other side only a few seconds later. Katya slowed a bit more to take the bend that Caleb had described.

"Just here," Caleb said as they rounded the bend. Katya brought the car to a stop, and Caleb unlatched his seatbelt and opened the passenger door. Katya was just about to unlatch her own seatbelt when Caleb stopped her. "Wait here," he said, fixing her with a look that meant business.

"Okay," Katya replied, but she was talking to his back. A second later, Katya heard the trunk open and, when it closed again, she looked up at the rear-view to see Caleb running down the road, back toward the tunnel.

Katya remained in her seat, as instructed, her hands still gripping the steering wheel. She could hear the approaching SUV through the gap in the car where the rear window had been. Then she heard the screeching of brakes, followed by a sound that made her jump. A loud, metallic crash that seemed to echo off the hedges on either side of the road. Katya froze. What should she do? Had Caleb just been hit?

She waited for perhaps a full two minutes before getting out of the car. Then Katya paced for a moment, wondering how much longer to leave it before going against Caleb's instruction to stay where she was. She was about to set off toward the bridge when she saw Caleb sauntering back up the road, his thumbs hooked in his jeans, cowboy style.

"What was that noise?" Katya asked as Caleb approached. "Did he crash?"

"Kind of," Caleb replied. He had a glint in his eye. "The tunnel was a bit too narrow for his vehicle. He won't be bothering us anymore." Caleb smiled. "I gave him a pitch. He accepted it."

"What sort of pitch? Like a baseball one?"

Caleb smiled and almost laughed.

"No, like an idea. That sort of pitch."

Katya thought for a few seconds, trying to understand

the unfamiliar word use before storing it away for the future.

"So he accepted the suggestion?" she said, looking at Caleb to gauge his expression.

"Yeah, he got the point. Shall we?" Caleb gestured toward the car with his hand, and Katya knew from his indifference that the man in the SUV behind them was dead.

Katya got back in the Fiat and started the engine before turning to Caleb.

"Where now?" she asked him. She wanted to ask him how many people he had killed in his life, but knew she wouldn't get a straight answer.

"Back to the hotel," Caleb replied. "But we'll have to take the long way round."

"Why the hotel?"

"Because if they are tracking the car, and I'm sure they are, they'll know where we are." Caleb rolled his shoulders. "So we need a different car."

"Okay," Katya replied. "Then what?"

"I think we need to do a bit of reconnaissance, Katya," Caleb said.

Katya smiled as she pulled away. Caleb had just said *we*. That meant she was going with him.

102

C aleb made sure he kept his face neutral as Katya drove the Fiat back toward the hotel. Inside, he was fuming. Not with her, but with himself. Katya was a civilian. He wasn't, not really. But he had made two fundamental mistakes in the previous thirty minutes or so. It was only luck, perhaps with some divine intervention, that meant they were still alive.

He had made two assumptions, the first leading to the second. Caleb had assumed that Mateo's pistol was in the bag. The pistol that he knew was fully serviceable, having stripped it to check. And because he'd thought that, he'd not taken the gun from the man in their hotel room. Another gun that he knew was fully serviceable, as it had been fired at him and Katya. Caleb didn't like silencers. They not only played havoc with a weapon's accuracy, but they took away the shock and awe of a gunshot. Sometimes, that shock and awe was the only thing that bought enough time for a second shot. And Caleb had never missed his second shot.

When the black SUV had wedged itself under the bridge, it

had embedded itself so far inside the tunnel that none of the doors could be opened. After he had dealt with the driver, Caleb had climbed up the bank and stepped over the railway line to get to the other side. The trunk of the SUV was jammed, the impact having skewed the vehicle's chassis. So whatever was in the car, apart from the driver, would have to remain there. The only other option was to climb in through the kicked out windshield, but Caleb didn't want to do that. The interior of the SUV was not as clean as it had been and, once he had retrieved Mateo's pistol, he had what he needed in his bag.

When Caleb had been younger, he'd been drilled thousands of times on a single phrase. *Prior preparation prevents poor performance.* The five Ps. It was, Caleb reflected as Katya turned back onto the main road that led to the hotel, a shame he'd not followed this advice earlier.

Katya seemed to have picked up on his own reflection and remained silent as they drove.

A few moments later, they were back in the hotel lot. He pointed at a far corner of it, an area overhung with trees and bushes.

"Park over there," he said to her. "At least it can't be seen from the road." The police car that had been following the SUV earlier was at the back of his mind. If the police officers were attentive, they may have also noticed the Fiat in front of it.

"Okay," Katya said. She parked the car where he had showed her and turned to him as she turned the engine off. "What's wrong?"

"Nothing," Caleb replied after a brief pause. "Why?"

"Don't answer a question with a question, Caleb," Katya said with a faint smile. "What is it?"

"I should have done better, Katya." Caleb blew his

cheeks out. "I should have checked that we had the gun. It was a mistake that could have killed us both."

"That's nonsense, Caleb," Katya replied. "It was me that tripped over the bag, not you."

"Even so, I should have done better."

"Caleb, if it weren't for you, I would have been dead a long time ago." Katya stared at him, her eyes boring into his. There was an intensity in them he'd only seen once before, and they had been doing something very different at that point in time. "You have nothing to apologize for."

Caleb nodded in response, keen to change the subject from his own shortcomings. He opened the door and waited for Katya. As he did so, he surveyed the other vehicles in the lot.

"Can you hotwire a car?" Katya asked, walking over to stand next to him. Caleb's eyes swept the lot. There were a couple that he thought he might be able to start, but it wasn't something he'd done for a long time. When he had learned the art of boosting cars, they had been a lot simpler.

"Possibly," Caleb replied. He took a couple of steps toward the hotel. "But probably not. Come on, let's get the pistol and then we can worry about the car."

103

Sergeant Bush yawned, leaning his head back. There was an audible click in his neck as he did so.

"I bloody hate double shifts," he said to his colleague, a female police officer named Rebecca, who was sitting in the driver's seat. She just grunted in response. Sergeant Bush had been due to sign off at two o'clock the previous afternoon. Instead, because of someone calling in sick for the night shift, the station supervisor had offered him double time if he filled it. Sergeant Bush glanced at his watch. It was almost half past midnight, which meant he had another seven and a half hours to go.

In Sergeant Bush's pocket, his cell phone vibrated. Stifling another yawn, he wriggled in his seat to pull it out. When he glanced at the screen, he saw it was his colleague from the earlier shift.

"Tony?" Sergeant Bush said when he answered the call. "Let me guess, you couldn't sleep and were missing me?"

"Ha ha, boss," Tony replied. In the background, Sergeant Bush could hear a deep, rhythmic, booming noise. "Very funny."

"Where are you?"

"I'm in a club. Well, technically, I'm outside it in the smoking area." Sergeant Bush grinned at Tony's reply. It had been years since he'd been to a nightclub other than to pick up his children when they'd pissed away their taxi fare home. "But I've had a weird text message."

Sergeant Bush sat up a bit straighter in his seat and leaned forward for his notepad, which was balanced on the dashboard in front of him. This could be interesting. Tony wouldn't call him on duty, and so late, if it wasn't.

"Go ahead," Sergeant Bush said, his pencil poised over the paper.

"Okay, here's the number it's from. It starts three, five, five." Then he read out a further nine digits. "It's not one I recognize."

Sergeant Bush frowned. He circled the first three numbers and nudged Rebecca.

"Can you google that dialing code, Becs?" he asked her before returning to speak to Tony. "What's the message?"

"Bridge six five two, lima, charlie, hotel. Man Down."

"That's it?"

"Yup, that's it," Tony replied. "You think it's from the same person who called about the farmhouse?"

"Sounds like it could be," Sergeant Bush said. "Man Down. That's what he said last time."

"Can I leave that with you, Sarge? Only there's some bloke who's taken a bit of a shine to my Lisa. I don't want to be too long, if you get my drift?"

"Sure, thanks Tony. I'll follow it up. There's not much else going on."

"Pleased it's quiet for you, Sarge," Tony, and Sergeant Bush could hear the smile in his voice. "Hope it stays that way."

"Bastard," he replied as he disconnected the call. By saying the q word, Tony had probably jinxed his shift.

"It's an Albanian dialing code," Rebecca said as Sergeant Bush looked at the text he'd scribbled down. He frowned, realizing that Tony was probably right. But how had Tony received the text?

A few moments later, having spoken to control, Sergeant Bush had the location of the bridge. Control also had the mobile number and was trying to trace it, but Sergeant Bush knew it would be a fool's errand. It was difficult enough tracing local cell numbers, let alone foreign ones.

The bridge, according to Rebecca, was in the arse end of nowhere. She'd attended a couple of incidents where vehicles had hit the bridge there before. As she drove, he filled her in on what had happened earlier that day, giving her details that wouldn't have been in her handover brief.

"So you think we're looking for a body?" Rebecca said when Sergeant Bush told her about the use of the same phrase in the phone call about the farmhouse. "Shouldn't we call it in?"

"That wouldn't be popular, would it?" Sergeant Bush replied. "Not at this time of night. No, let's just go and have a look and see what we've got."

104

W hen they walked through the hotel foyer, the night porter was still lying behind the desk. Katya looked at him with sympathetic eyes. She knew what it felt like to be bound and unable to move. The porter had his eyes closed and a deep frown on his face. He looked to be in his early sixties, perhaps older. Katya wondered about his circumstances, and what in his life meant he had to work behind a hotel desk at night.

"Caleb," Katya said. "Should we release him?"

"No," Caleb replied. "The minute we do, the police will be on their way. Someone will find him in the morning. A cleaner perhaps, or a guest." He strode past the desk and toward the corridor that led to the room they had been in. "That will give us enough time to get away from here."

"But can't we at least make him more comfortable? Give him a drink?"

Caleb paused with his hand on the door to the corridor. He looked back, first at Katya, then at the porter, then back at Katya. As Katya watched, his face softened.

"Okay. On the way back, we'll make sure he's okay."

Satisfied, Katya followed Caleb down the corridor and to what had been their room. It was easy enough to find. Only one door had a couple of bullet holes in the wood where the spy hole had been. Caleb used the key card to open the lock and pushed open the door, walking inside. Katya hesitated for a few seconds. There was a dead man on the bed, and she wasn't sure she wanted to see him.

"Are you coming?" Caleb said from inside the room.

Katya took a deep breath and walked into the room. The man who'd attacked Caleb was still lying where they had left him. On the bed where she and Caleb had stepped off a cliff together. The contrast between the two scenes was almost too much for Katya, and she felt tears filling her eyes.

"Look away, Katya," Caleb said, his voice soft. He was standing next to the bed, his hand near the body. "You don't want to see this." Katya realized he was about to pull the knife out of the corpse.

She dropped to her knees and peered under the bed, eager to have something else to focus on. There, almost dead center under the bed, was the gun. As she wriggled under the mattress to retrieve it, she heard a wet noise above her, followed by what sounded like a gasp.

When Katya wriggled back out from under the bed, the pistol in her hand, Caleb was in the bathroom. She could hear running water as he cleaned the knife. Avoiding looking at the man on the bed, Katya cast her eyes around the carpeted floor to see if anything else had been missed, but there was nothing.

Caleb came out of the bathroom and stripped a pillow-case from a pillow lying next to the bed. Katya looked at it, remembering gripping it tightly the previous night.

"Katya?" Caleb's voice dispelled the memory. He was holding the pillowcase out to her for her to put the pistol

into. Once she had placed the gun inside, Caleb picked up
the man's gun from the bed, complete with the elongated
silencer, and did the same thing with it. "Okay?"

"Okay," Katya nodded, relieved that they were leaving.

As the door closed behind them, Katya wiped her eyes
with the backs of her hands. If Caleb noticed her distress, he
said nothing.

WHEN CALEB WOKE the night porter, the old man's eyes
flipped open and instantly filled with terror.

"It's okay," Caleb said to him, his voice soft. Katya saw
him put a hand on the man's forehead. "We will not hurt
you. You have my word." The fear in the man's eyes started
to dissipate. "I'm going to remove this tape from your
mouth, but please say nothing."

A few moments later, the night porter was lying on a
couch at the back of the reception office. His hands and legs
were still taped, but he was much more comfortable. Katya
had filled a bottle of water and made sure that he had plenty
to drink before Caleb replaced the tape over his mouth,
telling him that help would be along soon. The way he
spoke to the man was so gentle, Katya wasn't surprised how
compliant he was. The porter nodded as Caleb apologized
to him again for the inconvenience, almost as if Caleb was
apologizing for something other than leaving him gagged
and bound. Before they left the building, she and Caleb
took bottles of water and as much food from the office fridge
as they could fit in the pillowcase.

In the parking lot, Katya stood next to Caleb as he
surveyed the vehicles.

"What do you think, Caleb?" she asked him. He was staring at the cars with a frown. "Can you start one?"

"I don't think I can, Katya," Caleb replied. "It's a lot different now. It's all proximity keys, alert systems, that sort of thing." He sighed. "Not just a case of taking a screwdriver to the steering column and touching the blue wire to the red one."

"But what are we going to do?" Katya's voice was terse. They needed a vehicle to get to the girls. They couldn't rescue them without one, could they?

"I think perhaps we'll pray," Caleb said. "Matthew, chapter twenty-one comes to mind."

"You think God's going to just start us a car?"

"And whatever you ask in prayer, you will receive, if you have faith."

Katya looked at Caleb, who had his eyes closed and a faint smile on his face. To Katya's amazement, there was a bleeping sound and the headlights of a blue Nissan Juke parked a few yards away blinked twice.

"Shall we go?" Caleb said, glancing at Katya as he walked toward the car. He peered inside through the window. "Looks like you're driving. It's a stick shift."

"How did you do that, Caleb?" Katya asked him. Caleb just smiled as he pressed an electronic key fob into her hand.

"Just make sure you don't dent the night porter's car."

Caleb sat in the passenger seat, the map balanced on his knee. He had identified where he wanted to be. Less than half a mile away from Martin's house was a small hill with, according to the map, a wooded area covering much of the top. It would be, he hoped, an ideal vantage point from which to surveil the house and its surroundings.

As Katya drove, Caleb ran through the courses of action available to him in his head. The first, as it always was, was to do nothing. But in order for this course of action to have the effect Caleb desired, which was the successful and timely rescue of Ana and Elene, several things needed to happen. First, Mateo had to give up the location of Martin's house, and the fact the girls were being held captive there, to the police. Second, the police needed to believe Mateo. And third, the police needed to take decisive action, and quickly. There were, Caleb knew, too many variables in that course of action.

The second course of action was for him and Katya to go to the police themselves. As with the first option, this too had many variables. The main one was the fact that Caleb had killed three people in the last twenty-four hours. One, Aleksander, had been discovered. Another, the driver of the SUV, was about to be, and the third would be found within hours in the hotel they had just left. He considered what might happen if Katya alone went to the police, but he wasn't sure whether she would be believed, either. They didn't have enough evidence to persuade them quickly enough about the danger Ana and Elene were in.

"Take a left at the end of this road, Katya," Caleb said, glancing down at the map where his index finger was tracking their progress. She nodded in response but said nothing, perhaps sensing his introspection.

The third course of action, and the one which Caleb knew he was going to take, was for him to rescue the girls. That was the only course of action that he could fully control. But what of Katya? He knew she was desperate to be involved, but the risks would be high. Extremely high. He needed to involve her, but keep her safe. And the involvement he had in mind probably wouldn't appeal to Katya.

Caleb thought about the two men that had been sent after them. They had to be Martin's security team. There was no other reason for them to target him and Katya. Caleb knew that there would be more, and the ones who had been sent out on the previous mission wouldn't be the best of them. The best would be back at Martin's house. At least, that's how Caleb would have configured them.

"What's next, Caleb?" Katya asked a moment later. "What do we do?"

"That's just what I've been thinking about," he replied with a wry smile. "Mateo and Gjergj will be with the police by now. And Aleksander's body will have been discovered." He saw a flash of grim satisfaction cross her face in the gloomy interior of the car. "How long will it be before they link us to the farmhouse or the hotel? That's what I'm trying to work out."

"When they find the man in the hotel, it won't take them long, will it?" Katya said. "There's the night porter, for a start. Cameras in the hotel. A dead guy on our bed. Those men? Were they Martin's?"

"I'm pretty sure, yes," Caleb replied. "Who else could they be?" He paused for a couple of seconds before continuing. "Will they make the connection between Aleksander, the two men who were chasing us, and Martin?" Caleb asked. Even though he had his course of action determined, he wanted to know what Katya thought.

"That depends if Mateo blabs."

"He will."

"But will they believe him?" she asked. Caleb smiled at Katya's thinking. "And can they trace those men back to Martin?" His smile broadened.

"They will, eventually," Caleb said. He thought back to his childhood when he'd read a book by a British author named Enid Blyton. In it, if his memory served him correctly, the police were called the plod because they didn't move quickly. "But not fast enough."

"So, what do you think?" Katya asked Caleb.

"I think we need to do something more quickly than they will," he replied.

TEN MINUTES LATER, they had arrived at the hill that Caleb had identified on the map. Caleb directed Katya up a narrow path that led to the top. In the headlights of the car, he could see that on the very top of the hill were several tall trees.

Oaks, he thought, from their distinctive silhouette. Surrounding the trees were a multitude of bushes that looked to be a mixture of brambles, gorse, and other wild bushes. It was perfect.

"Katya, you see those bushes over there?" Caleb said as he looked at the map to orientate which direction Martin's house was in. It was almost directly in front of them, beyond the trees and the bushes.

"Yes," Katya replied, peering through the windshield.

"I want you to drive into them."

"Seriously?"

"Yep." He turned to look at her. "Just do it. I'm dead serious."

106

"Bloody hell," Sergeant Bush heard Rebecca say as they approached the rail bridge with the short tunnel under it. In front of them, lit up in the full beam of their headlights, a black Range Rover was stuck fast. "He's wedged that in there, good and proper."

Sergeant Bush frowned as he looked at the license plate of the vehicle. It looked familiar. He reached into his breast pocket for his notebook and flipped it open. Sure enough, it was the same car from earlier in the day.

"I know that car," he said as Rebecca flipped a switch to turn the light bar on top of their BMW on. "Me and Tony pulled it earlier."

"What for?" Rebecca asked, opening the car door.

"It was speeding, but we didn't get it on the gun." He looked down at his notes. "Registered to a private company in London. Driver was a Paul Topping."

He got out of the car and walked toward it with Rebecca. When they reached it, she tried the handle on the rear door, but it was stuck fast. Then she tried to peer in through the tinted and cracked glass of the rear window, but shook her head from side to side a few seconds later.

"What do you want to do, Sarge?" she asked Sergeant Bush. Her hand was hovering on the telescopic baton in her utility belt. "Put the window in?"

"No," Sergeant Bush replied, looking at the steep embankment that led to the railway line. It was covered in dense vegetation. "You can climb up there, nip over the railway line, and down the other side." He stifled a smile at the look on her face as he said this. "At least you can see what sort of state the driver's in."

"Why me?" she asked him, but he could tell from the look on her face that she already knew the answer. "I guess it's a rank thing, right?"

"Partly," Sergeant Bush replied. "But you're also about fifteen years younger than me and much less likely to have a cardiac arrest climbing that bank." He nodded at the embankment. "Go on, off you trot. I'll call in the usual suspects."

Sergeant Bush could hear Rebecca muttering under her breath as she walked away. He returned to the car and sat in it while he called the incident in to the control room back in Lincoln. The only bit he didn't mention was how they'd heard about the incident. That would be a lot easier to explain back at the station, and it didn't really matter at the moment. When control assured him that fire trucks and a couple of ambulances were en route, he sat back in his seat to wait for Rebecca to return. The vehicle had two occupants earlier, and as there was no way they could get out of the car, they were, by definition, trapped. Only the fire brigade would be able to free them, assuming the men were still alive. But from the way the car was embedded in the tunnel, he didn't fancy their chances of survival.

If anything, Sergeant Bush was feeling pleased with himself. He'd known there was something off about the two men in the Range Rover when he'd pulled them over earlier. Yet again, his spidey-sense was on point, something he'd tried to explain earlier to Tony.

It took Rebecca several more moments to return to the police car. Sergeant Bush heard her before he could see her crashing through the vegetation on the embankment. When she eventually appeared in the light of the headlights, her face was white, but she had two red spots on her cheeks from the exertion.

"Well?" Sergeant Bush said, getting out of the car and walking over to his colleague. "What've we got?"

"Dead guy in the driver's seat," she replied. Sergeant Bush nodded. It was what he had been expecting. "But this isn't a fatal accident, Sarge." Rebecca's voice was strained as she spoke. "It's a murder scene. We're going to need some more people."

If it had been Tony saying this, Sergeant Bush would have made a crack about leaving the detecting to the detectives, but he didn't know Rebecca well enough to know how she would take that sort of banter.

"What makes you say it's a murder scene, Rebecca?" he asked her, looking carefully at her face as she took a deep breath before she replied.

"Because the dead guy in the driver's seat has got a pitchfork sticking out of his throat."

107

Caleb pushed open his door, struggling to open it fully against the gorse bushes and brambles. Katya had done just as he'd asked and driven the car into the middle of the vegetation. She'd laughed as she'd done so, and he'd urged her to get the car deeper under cover, more to hear her laugh than anything else.

"What are we going to do now?" Katya said as she turned the engine off. Caleb reached around for Mateo's bag and pulled out the knife he'd used back in the hotel.

"Can you flip the headlights back on? I'm going to do some gardening."

He squeezed his way out of the car, grateful that he was wearing normal clothes and not his robe. The brambles tugged at his jeans as he worked to clear a path from the passenger door, around the front of the vehicle, and to the driver's side. He worked quickly, using the light from the headlights to see what he was doing. The knife cut through the briars like butter. Then he made his way to the rear of the car and pulled back some of the vegetation that had been crushed. He would need to cut a path to the small forest, but that could be done later. His last action was to cut some large gorse branches and lay them on the roof of the car. When he had finished, he was sure that the vehicle couldn't be seen from outside the bushes or the air.

When he sat back down in the passenger seat, Katya looked at him with amusement after she had flipped the headlights back off. Despite the branches covering the car, enough moonlight was filtering through to enable them to just about see each other.

"What is this, a stakeout?" she asked him.

"That's exactly what this is, Katya," Caleb replied. He put the knife on his lap and pulled out the binoculars. As Katya watched with interest, he removed the lens caps and then used the knife to cut a circle in the center of both caps. He then pulled out some garden netting and sliced two circles, both around twice the diameter of the binocular's lenses. Then he put the netting over each lens and replaced what was left of the lens cap to keep the netting in place. "It reduces glare," Caleb said when Katya raised her eyebrows at him.

"The only thing is, Caleb," Katya said, pointing at the thick vegetation in front of the windshield. "Even with binoculars, we can't actually see anything."

"Not from here, no," Caleb replied. "But from the forest? We'll have a vantage point over Martin's house." He pulled the spotting scope from the bag and handed it to Katya. "Here, your turn."

It took Katya a couple of tries to cut the right amount of netting, but a few moments later, she held up the scope in triumph, its lens covered with netting just like the binoculars.

"Can you still see through them with that netting on?" she asked.

"Yes, of course," Caleb replied. "I wouldn't have put the netting on if I couldn't." He smiled at her as he said this. "We should get some sleep. The dawn will be at about four in the morning. That's a good three hours. But first, we should eat."

Caleb let Katya get some food from the pillowcase. There hadn't been much back in the kitchen of the hotel, just chips and snacks, but it was enough. Katya was quiet as they ate and Caleb thought about asking her if she was okay, but he let her be. They washed the food down with warm soda. Then he found the lever next to his seat to recline it, pushed it back as far as it would go, and relaxed against the back of his seat.

"I'll wake you just before four," he said, listening as Katya reclined her own seat. "Eat when you can, sleep when you can." She didn't reply. Caleb wondered how long it would be before Katya said something. In the end, it was less than ten minutes.

"I can't sleep, Caleb," she said. He heard her seat being put back up. "Sorry. Too much going round inside my head."

With an exaggerated groan, Caleb put his seat back up and smiled at her.

"Okay," he said, drawing out the word. "What do you want to do?" He pointed at the vegetation covering the windshield. "Play I-Spy?"

"No," Katya replied with a laugh. Then her face became more serious. "I want you to tell me something."

"Sure, what?"

"I want you to tell me why you came to England."

108

"I came to England because I have to be somewhere, Katya," Caleb said with a slight smile on his face. "I already told you."

"Tell me the truth, Caleb," Katya said, slipping her hand into his. "Please?"

"It's not very interesting."

"It is," she replied. "It must be after you went to so much trouble to get here."

Katya waited in silence for Caleb to say something. It was a full minute before he spoke.

"I'm following in someone's footsteps. There's a place in Somerset that I want to visit," he said, not looking at her as he spoke.

"Where is that?"

"In the south-west of the country."

"No, where's the place that you want to visit?" Katya ran her thumb over the back of his hand. "What's it called?"

"Glastonbury."

"I've heard of that place," Katya replied with a laugh. "You came to England to go to a music festival?"

"No, Katya," Caleb said, also laughing. "I'm not planning on going to the music festival."

"Whose footsteps are you following?"

Caleb didn't reply at first, but then started telling Katya about a story, handed down through generation after generation, about a man named Joseph visiting Glastonbury in the first century.

"He was a metal trader from Palestine traveling with his nephew. They would have traveled from Tyre, or perhaps Sidon, and sailed up through the Mediterranean and the Straits of Gibraltar." Caleb's voice was soft, as if he was telling a story to a child. "Then through the Bay of Biscay and into the English Channel. But they ran into a problem." Katya frowned, not understanding why Caleb would be following in the footsteps of a metal trader.

"What sort of problem?" she asked, wondering where the story was going.

"They got shipwrecked," Caleb said, "off the coast of Cornwall. But they managed to get to shore where they built a shrine to thank God for sparing them."

"Right," Katya replied with a smile. He was definitely telling her a children's story, perhaps in the hope that she would go to sleep. "What happened next?"

"They traveled. Joseph bought tin in Cornwall and then they moved up to Somerset, where he could buy lead. He was a rich man, a successful merchant."

"You were right," Katya said, closing her eyes. "It's not very interesting."

"It is to me," Caleb replied and she could tell from his voice that he was smiling. "Have you ever followed a dream?"

"Yes, Caleb," Katya said. "All the time."

"There you go then." Caleb's voice was getting softer and Katya had to concentrate to hear him.

"What do you dream of, Caleb?" she asked him.

"I don't think I do."

Katya forced her eyes open to look at him. Caleb was just looking out of the windshield.

"You must," she said as she closed her eyes again. "Everybody does."

"If I do, I don't remember them."

Katya took a deep breath as she felt Caleb lean over and kiss her on the cheek.

"Tell me a bit more about Joseph," Katya said. She listened as he started telling her how Joseph, after traveling through the southwest of England with his nephew, returned to Palestine with a treasure trove of precious metals.

"Did he ever come back?" she whispered.

"He did," Caleb replied. "Much later."

If Caleb said anything else, Katya didn't hear it. She was fast asleep.

109

C aleb wriggled on the branch to get as comfortable as he could. He was sitting in the crook of an enormous branch of the oak tree he had clambered up a few moments before. Katya was still fast asleep in the car below, but if she woke, she would know where he was. To the east, the sky was beginning to lighten with a glorious selection of colors that changed by the minute. The dawn had always been one of Caleb's favorite times of the day. A new start with whatever had happened before wiped clean. Except Caleb knew nothing was really wiped clean.

He waited, admiring the colorful display in the distance as the sky lightened gradually. There were contrails of airplanes high in the sky and, just as he had done when he was a child, Caleb wondered about the people in them. Where they were going. What they were going to do when they got there. Caleb hadn't been on an airplane for many years. He enjoyed traveling, relishing the journey more sometimes than the destination, and to take a plane to a destination almost felt like cheating.

Caleb examined the tree he was sitting in while he

waited for the sun to rise enough for him to be able to see Martin's house, which nestled in a dip a few hundred yards in front of and below him. The tree had to be hundreds of years old judging by its size, and it was decorated with catkins dangling below the broad green leaves. The bark was covered in moss and lichen, some of which had rubbed off on the camouflage pattern of the clothes he was wearing. Caleb's fishing jacket and pants from the outdoors shop weren't quite the ghillie suit he would have preferred, but they were more than adequate to hide him. Around his neck were the binoculars he'd adapted the previous evening, and he had the spotting scope in one pocket.

Raising the binoculars to his eyes, Caleb started scouring the surrounding countryside, cross-referencing it against the map in his mind. Apart from a large barn in the distance, which he didn't remember from the map, it was as he had imagined. Martin's house was one of the lowest points around, with a small river trickling past it. The course of the river wasn't quite as shown on the map, but it was close. Although it had several small bridges crossing it, the river didn't look to be much of an obstacle.

He worked in a grid, mentally ticking off the squares on the map, until the only thing left unexamined was Martin's house. But before he scrutinized that, Caleb tracked the best angles of approach and retreat from the building. There were several, all with positive and negative points. He repeated this several times before deciding on the best path to take. The one which would provide him, and Ana and Elene, the most cover on their way back to the car.

With the sun just beginning to appear over the horizon, Caleb started to surveil his target. Martin's house was large and grandiose, and somehow out of place in the surrounding countryside. Caleb could see a wall surrounding three sides of it with what he thought was razor wire on the top. The river provided a fourth wall. He couldn't see any cameras but wouldn't expect to from this distance. Caleb would approach as if there were several, which there would be. Next to the river was a small summer house.

Caleb's attention was drawn to movement next to the house. He focused his binoculars on the area to see a garage door opening, its movement smooth. A light was flipped on, and Caleb could see a black, boxy SUV in the garage that was identical to the one he had left under the bridge. Two men were standing in front of it. One of them was smoking while the other was talking. They both wore black, but if they were armed, Caleb was too far away to see.

A few moments later, two more men arrived at the garage door from within the house. The four of them stood for a few moments before they split into pairs, one pair walking toward the summerhouse, the other turning and disappearing out of sight behind the house. A few moments after that, the front door to the house opened.

"Morning, Martin," Caleb muttered as he adjusted his binoculars. Martin was standing on his front step, looking out over the expansive front lawn that led to the river. He had a mug in his hand, which he sipped from. Caleb adjusted his binoculars to a point just above and to the right of Martin's head. The exact spot he would be aiming for if he had a sniper rifle. The wind and the drop would move the round right between Martin's eyes.

But Caleb didn't have a sniper rifle. He was going to have to do this the hard way.

110

Sergeant Bush watched as a convoy of emergency vehicles approached the Travel Inn hotel he was standing outside. Apart from his own vehicle, the only other one in the lot with blue lights on top was an ambulance they had called for the old man they had found in the foyer. According to the cook, who had arrived at five in the morning to start the breakfasts, the night porter had been tied up with tape around his arms and legs.

In all his years working on a response unit in Lincolnshire, Sergeant Bush had never had a couple of shifts like the ones he had just experienced. The night porter had told them about a couple who had booked a room the previous day, and the two men with guns who had come looking for them before tying him up.

One of those men was still in his black SUV, which the fire brigade was still struggling to extract, and the other was in one of the hotel rooms. The one that the couple had booked. The one with the bullet holes in the door. Sergeant Bush, after seeing the holes, had opened the door just wide enough to see the body on the bed. According to the Lincolnshire Police protocols, he should have confirmed that there was no help that could be offered before calling it in. But he'd been a policeman for long enough to know that no one could lose that much blood and still require help. At least, not the sort of help he could provide.

The lead vehicle was an unmarked police car, a jet black BMW with hidden blue lights in the grill. Following that was a white van that Sergeant Bush knew belonged to the forensic services. And following them was a marked response car. By standing at the entrance to the lot, Sergeant Bush was effectively providing the external cordon to the scene while his colleague, Rebecca, was in the corridor inside the hotel. A crude but effective internal cordon. If any of the guests decided to stick their heads out of their rooms to see what was going on, they would get short shrift from her. He knew she was still annoyed with him for making her climb the embankment earlier, and even the discovery of a third body in less than twenty-four hours hadn't mollified her.

"Sir," Sergeant Bush said as the black BMW ground to a halt in front of him. He recognized the Detective Inspector from the station, although he didn't know his name. Two uniformed officers got out of the marked car and started taping off the parking lot with blue and white *POLICE—DO NOT CROSS* tape.

"Morning, Sergeant," the detective replied. "DI Mahoney. You were at the farmhouse yesterday, weren't you?"

"I was, sir, yes," Sergeant Bush replied. "Any news on that?"

"We've got the brother in custody as the doer," Mahoney

said with a smirk. "His prints are all over the murder weapon." Sergeant Bush saw him glance at his watch. "I reckon we've got about an hour before the NCA come in with their size nines." He could see the disappointment on the detective's face. The National Crime Agency wasn't the most subtle agency in policing and had a habit of winding up the locals. "What've you got?"

"You know about the incident at the bridge?" The disparaging look on Mahoney's face answered his question, but Sergeant Bush ignored it and pointed his thumb over his shoulder. "His mate's having a little lie down in there."

"Did you enter the room?" Mahoney asked. It was Sergeant Bush's turn to look disparaging.

"Only to confirm life extinct, sir," Sergeant Bush said. "But I did it from the door. There's enough claret on the bed to make it obvious."

"The police doctor's on his way," Mahoney replied, and the two men shared a look of solidarity in that they weren't able to confirm someone was actually dead even if their head was missing. It took seven or eight years at medical school to do that.

"You got much longer on shift?" Mahoney asked.

"I have now," Sergeant Bush replied. "It'll take me hours to write tonight up." Mahoney gave him a sympathetic look.

"As soon as uniform pitch up in numbers, you get yourself back to the station."

Sergeant Bush nodded, even though as a detective, Mahoney had no jurisdiction in when he could finish up. He waited as Mahoney took a call on his cell phone. When he had finished the call, he looked chagrined.

"We've not even got a couple of hours," Mahoney said. "That was the chief's office. The NCA are almost here, complete with hard-ons. You okay keeping an entry log?"

Sergeant Bush just nodded in reply, too tired to argue with the detective. The moment one of the uniforms passed within hailing distance, they would be on the log and he and Rebecca would be heading back to the station. Then breakfast. Then bed.

He was certainly going to sleep soundly.

Martin sipped his coffee and watched as one of the security teams ambled along by the river at the bottom of his garden. The sun was almost fully in the air and he thought it was going to be a hot one. Martin gazed out over his garden for a few moments, his eyes drawn to the small wood on top of a hill that overlooked his property. If he had a dog, it was just the sort of place he would take it for a walk.

"Martin?" Robert's voice interrupted his train of thought. "You've got a call." Martin turned to see his head of security holding one of the burner phones.

"Yes?" Martin said as he held the phone to his ear.

"We need to meet. Breakfast. The White Horse at seven." The caller disconnected without another word, which irritated Martin. He might be the Assistant Chief Commissioner, but his caller should have had more respect for Martin than that.

Ninety minutes later, a few moments before seven, Martin was sitting in a secluded nook within the White Horse. While he waited for his caller, Martin read the back of the menu which detailed the history of the pub. He'd known it was old, but not that old.

"Martin, good morning," a male voice said. Martin looked up to see the Assistant Chief Commissioner standing by the table. He was around the same age as Martin and was wearing a silver suit with what looked to Martin like a Versace shirt and tie.

"Good morning, William," Martin said, gesturing at the seat opposite. "I've not ordered anything yet."

William sat down opposite him and gestured at the bartender, a woman older than both of them by some years. She acknowledged him with a wave and went back to polishing beer glasses, prompting an irritated tut from William.

"Did you know, William," Martin said, waving the menu at him, "that they've been serving pints at this place since Christopher Columbus was just an itch in his father's testicles?" If William was impressed, he didn't show it. He glanced at the woman behind the bar, who looked as if she might be gearing up to approach their table.

"Looks like she's been serving them since then," he said with an uncharacteristically wry grin.

A few moments later, having ordered their breakfasts, Martin waited to see if the police officer wanted to get straight down to business. But it seemed whatever he had to say was going to wait.

"I can't believe you've ordered a full English," William said. Martin just smiled, thinking about how much he was going to enjoy tucking into it while William ate his toast.

Bacon, fried eggs, baked beans, sausages, and perhaps a slice of black pudding were no comparison.

"Just don't tell my cardiologist," Martin replied in a conspiratorial tone. "God knows I pay him enough money, but he's always moaning at me."

"Bloody heart attack waiting to happen, you are."

"There's nothing wrong with my heart, William," Martin said. "Bit of high blood pressure, but probably not as high as yours."

"Why the cardiologist then?"

"I've got an aneurysm, apparently. Only a small one, and I'm getting it fixed in a few months. That, and an enlarged prostate."

"It comes to us all, my friend," William replied with a grin.

It wasn't until after they had eaten their breakfasts that William told Martin why he wanted to see him. Martin, his stomach much fuller than he thought William's was, listened intently.

"Do you know an Albanian called Mateo Ahmeti?" William asked after checking over his shoulder to make sure they were alone.

"I might do," Martin replied warily. "Why?"

"He's in custody after murdering his brother," William said. Martin made a conscious effort to not let his face change at the news. That was one less loose end to worry about, but with Mateo in custody, perhaps it was a new one as well. William glanced at his watch. "He'll be being charged about now. As soon as the custody sergeant comes in."

"Where will he be taken after that?"

"He'll be on the remand wing at Lincoln Prison," William said. His eyes narrowed as he continued. "He should be in the segregation section, seeing as how we think he's a nonce, but it's full. Cutbacks, you know?"

Martin nodded in reply. "Not on normal courtyard exercise," he said.

"Excuse me?" William asked.

"That's what nonce stands for. The oldest term for pedophiles there is. Surely you know that?"

"Of course I do, but I didn't think you would." William smiled at Martin, but it was a businesslike smile with no genuine warmth. "You know, for a man of the cloth, you know some very unusual things."

Martin raised his hand and made the sign of the cross in the air.

"Bless you, my child," he said before winking at the police officer.

112

"Are you planning on spending the whole day up there?" Katya called out, craning her neck to see if she could spot Caleb. A moment later, she saw him clambering down the branches. He moved as if he had been climbing trees all his life, which for all she knew, he had. But there was something quite graceful about the way he moved. Caleb jumped from the lowest branch, landing on both feet in front of her with a soft thud.

"No, I think I'm good. I'm hungry, though. My stomach's telling me it's lunchtime."

Katya's face fell. "Oh," she said. "There wasn't that much food left." Caleb crossed his arms in front of his chest and looked at her with a stern expression. "Sorry, I've eaten it all." She waited for as long as she could before she started laughing. "Joke, Caleb," she said, punching him playfully on the shoulder. "That's when one person says something to make the other person laugh?"

"Hilarious," Caleb replied, the corners of his mouth twitching.

They walked back to the car through the short path that

Caleb had cut in the vegetation. Katya had left the doors open as the air had warmed up throughout the morning, but this meant that every bug in the area had made a beeline for the vehicle. Katya swatted at some as she sat in the driver's seat. Beside her, Caleb had got the map out and was balancing it on his knee with one hand while he ate a chocolate bar with the other.

"You see this path here?" Caleb said, tracing a line on the map. Katya leaned across him to look at it, her arm brushing his as she did so. "That's the approach I'm going to take. Even if they've got thermal cameras, there's a stone wall that will shield me right up to the river." Katya followed the line on the map, not liking the way he was saying me, not us. "Then I can get across the river." He stabbed at the map with his index finger. "There's a large tree here in the garden that'll give me cover."

"But you don't know where the girls are being held," Katya said. "Won't you be discovered before you get to them?"

"Not necessarily," Caleb replied. "But they're in the house somewhere. I'll find them."

"So what do I do?" Katya asked. "Go round the back and approach from the rear of the house?"

Caleb paused before he replied, and Katya knew what he was going to say.

"No, Katya," he said, looking at her. "I need you to stay here."

"Why?" Katya asked, trying not to sound petulant. "I want to help."

"I know you do, but I work best alone. I need you to stay here." He was staring at the map, not meeting her eyes. "Once they're free, I can tell Ana and Elene to head up here. I need you to be here for them in case I get caught up." Or hurt, or killed, Katya thought, but didn't say anything. "If you're in the tree, with the spotting scope, you'll be able to see things I can't and let me know." Finally, he turned to look at her and she saw sadness in his eyes. "We've got cell phones."

"I want to help, Caleb," Katya said again, covering his hand with hers. "Not sit in a tree with a scope."

"That is helping, Katya." Caleb smiled, but it did nothing for the sadness on her face. "Besides, if something happens to me, the girls will need you to get away."

Katya felt a lump forming in her throat at the thought of something happening to Caleb, but she was determined not to cry.

"I don't like the thought of it, Caleb," she replied a moment later when she trusted her voice.

"I know you don't," Caleb replied, "but that's the way it is. No discussion."

Katya took a deep breath.

"Okay," she said, before putting more authority in her voice. "Okay." Then she let a smile play over her face. "You'd better show me the best way to get up that tree."

113

Mateo sat on the thin mattress and listened to the sounds around him. He could hear jeering, clapping, the sound of something metal being hit against bars. They were the same sounds as back at the police station, but amplified many times.

Earlier that morning, Mateo had been charged with Aleksander's murder. The red-faced policeman who had formally charged him had showed as much interest as if he had been reading from the menu of a Chinese takeaway when he read the text from a laminated piece of paper. Mateo had asked for the detective from the previous day, only to be told he was tied up at a scene. He might come and see Mateo in prison later, but Mateo had been told not to hold his breath.

His cell was much smaller than the one in the police station. When he had arrived, he'd been searched, which had included a man looking at a part of Mateo no man had ever looked at before. Mateo should have been embarrassed, but he was too scared. Then he'd been given the same clothes all the other prisoners he'd seen were wearing, a slightly more comfortable version of the tracksuit he wore back at the police station. The cell's interior was painted a utility green. It had a single bed, a stainless steel toilet and sink in the corner, and a tiny window that, even if he could stand up properly, was too high for him to look out of.

The prison officers who had wheeled him to the cell had told him that as soon as a bed on the hospital wing was free, he would be taken there on account of the casts on his legs. In the meantime, they had said, he would just have to make do with a regular cell.

"But how do I get down the stairs for food?" Mateo had asked them. Their replies were just smirks.

"We'll think of something," one of them had said before they deposited him on the bed. That had been several hours previously, and Mateo had only his own thoughts for company since they had left.

There were a series of metallic clunks, and Mateo's door swung open by a couple of inches. From the cheering that echoed around the prison's interior, Mateo guessed that all the other cell doors had also been opened. The sound of voices increased, and he was reminded of when he was at school and in between lessons.

Mateo jumped as his door was pushed open. Standing in the door was a man, heavily built and wearing the same clothes he was wearing.

"Mateo Ahmeti?" the new arrival said, speaking in Albanian. Mateo was surprised to hear his mother tongue being spoken.

"Yes," he replied. "That's me. Who are you?"

Behind the man was another prisoner, his hands on a wheelchair.

"We've come to take you to lunch," the first man said. Behind him, the other prisoner just grinned.

Mateo let out a sigh of relief. The prison guards had been true to their word. He'd imagined having to make his way down the staircase on his backside. At least that wasn't going to happen now. Mateo watched as the second prisoner wheeled the chair into his cell, taking care to put the hand-brake on before taking a step back.

"Can you help me?" Mateo asked the first prisoner.

"Sure," he replied, putting out his hands and gripping Mateo's upper arms. He pulled Mateo to his feet and swung him round so that he could sit in the wheelchair. But before the prisoner sat Mateo down, the other man punched him hard in the back, twice.

Mateo let out a breath as he was released, falling back and landing in the wheelchair with a thump. He looked at the two men, now walking back toward his cell door, and realized they were both wearing vinyl gloves. The prisoner who had punched Mateo was hiding something in the folds of his tracksuit top.

Mateo felt something warm trickling down his back. He arched his shoulders to try to reach around, and the trickle turned into a torrent.

"The peshkop says hello, Ahmeti," the first prisoner said as he exited the cell. But Mateo barely heard him.

He was already losing consciousness.

114

Caleb watched as Katya made herself comfortable in the large branches of the oak tree. She was wearing the camouflage pattern clothing he'd been wearing earlier, which hung on her loosely, but it would still do what it was designed to do. She raised the spotting scope to her eye and adjusted the focus.

"Wow," she said a few seconds later. "This is really clear. I can see Martin."

Caleb raised the binoculars to his eyes and trained them on the front lawn of the house. As Katya had said, Martin was walking toward the summerhouse by the river. A few steps behind him was a woman that he didn't recognize. She was lithe, slimmer than Katya, and had dark hair that he thought was tied back into a ponytail. Her shoulders were stooped under her white top, she had her head down, and it was obvious to Caleb that she was unhappy. Martin opened the doors to the summerhouse and stepped back to allow her to enter. Then he closed the door behind them, and a few seconds later, the blinds were drawn.

With a grim expression on his face, Caleb turned to Katya.

"This will be over soon," he said, nodding at the summerhouse. "Martin's day of reckoning is upon him. It will indeed be a day of wrath." Katya didn't reply, but when she looked at Caleb, he could see the pain in her eyes.

"Who was that with him?" she asked.

"I don't know," Caleb replied. "But her pain will be repaid a multitude of times. That is my solemn promise."

"Is that from the Bible?" Katya wiped her face with the back of her hand.

"No. It's from me."

JUST UNDER AN HOUR LATER, after Caleb had pointed out all the elements of the house and terrain that he wanted Katya to be aware of, the door to the summer house reopened. The woman stepped out and Caleb saw in his binoculars that she was disheveled. Her hair was now loose and wild, and she half-walked, half-ran back up the lawn. Caleb switched his attention to the door of the summerhouse, which was still open. Inside, Caleb could just make out Martin sitting in an armchair with a cigar in his hand. He watched as Martin leaned forward and lit it, puffing out a cloud of smoke.

"Are you happy, Katya?" Caleb asked. Katya, who was also watching Martin through her scope, nodded in reply.

"Yes, I think so." She put down the scope and turned to him. "You're going at dawn?"

"Yes," he replied. "The event that Mateo told me about is not until tomorrow night, so we have time. I need some time alone, if I may?"

"Sure," Katya said with a nod. "I'll stay here and keep an eye out."

Caleb descended the tree and made his way from the small thicket, careful to keep the bushes and trees between himself and the house. He walked for perhaps ten minutes until he found a small glade surrounded by hawthorn bushes. Then he sat, crossed his legs, and placed his hands on his knees. Around him, he could hear the faint buzzing of bumblebees as they moved from one white flower to the next. Caleb inhaled sharply through his nose, relishing the vanilla and almond smell of the flowers. It was not the most pleasant of odors. Caleb recalled the distinctive element was called triethylamine. The same chemical produced when a human body started to decay. He had heard that there was an old superstition that suggested death would follow if a hawthorn blossom was taken into a house.

He tried hard to clear his mind of such thoughts and to focus on the task at hand. As he did so, a variety of verses from scripture flashed across his mind until it finally settled on the Book of Daniel.

"Mene, mene, tekel, parsin," Caleb muttered under his breath, repeating the words that a disembodied hand had written on the wall of King Belshazzar's house in the book. Caleb breathed in again deeply, this time focusing not on the smell of death that pervaded the air, but on becoming Daniel. At dawn, he would be entering a lion's den but, unlike in Daniel's case, he wouldn't have an angel to close the jaws of the lions. That was something that Caleb was going to have to do for himself.

As Caleb continued his meditation, one thought kept returning to the forefront of his mind.

The writing was indeed on the wall for Martin.

115

K atya continued to view the house through her spotting scope, eager for a glimpse of Ana or Elene. But, apart from the security guards Caleb had pointed out to her, there was no sign of anyone. Martin had disappeared not long after Caleb had left her alone. She had watched Martin walk up the lawn, a phone pressed to his ear, and Katya had wished for a lightning bolt to come from the sky and strike him down. One guard was smoking under the single tree in the garden, using the trunk to shield himself from the house.

As she watched the guard smoking, Katya thought about the future and what it might look like. Her initial dreams of England were so far proving very different to reality. At least now she wasn't in any direct danger. Caleb had seen to that. But Ana and Elene were and, by extension, Caleb if he went ahead with his plan. She thought back to when he had been fighting with the man in the hotel room. There had been a moment when she thought Caleb had been bettered and if she'd had a clear shot at his assailant, there was a point where she would have taken it. But Caleb had prevailed.

If Caleb was able to rescue Ana and Elene, and Katya had every faith in the man that he would, what would be next for them? Where could they go? Where would they live? Even if they went to the authorities, and this was the only option that Katya thought they had, they would still be illegal immigrants. Katya thought that Ana and Elene would be treated differently, as they were children, but what about her? She was a grown woman, not related to the two girls in any way. Would they be separated? And what of Caleb? What would become of him?

With these and other, more depressing, thoughts swirling inside her head, Katya forced herself to focus on the task at hand. Which was, as Caleb had explained, reconnaissance. She switched her attention to the bridge that led across the river to Martin's house. It wasn't possible to tell how deep the river was from this distance, but it was moving slowly. A few ducks were paddling around the languid surface. The bridge itself was a simple one, not much more than an extension of the road it served. On the other side of the river was a large gate which she thought was operated from the house. Earlier that morning, she had seen a black SUV identical to the one that had chased them the previous day approach. When it got to the bridge, the gate started to swing open. She and Caleb had watched as Martin emerged from the vehicle after it parked near the house, rubbing his chest as he made his way toward the front door.

Katya hated Martin with a passion she'd never felt before for another human being. He was, in her opinion, at the root of Ana and Elene's situation. In her mind, there was no blood on Caleb's hands. It was all on Martin's. If Caleb was right, he was the fulcrum for everything that had happened to her, Ana, and Elene. She wondered how many other lives he had ruined.

Whatever Caleb had planned for the man was fine by Katya. If there was anything she could do to help, even if it was sitting in a tree, she would do it. And if, for any reason, Caleb failed in his mission, then she would walk down to his house herself. Katya summoned up an image of Ana and Elene in her mind, and remembered them laughing as they played a game of cards back at the farmhouse. Before Mateo and Aleksander had taken them away.

If Caleb failed, then she would kill Martin herself. Or she would die trying.

116

Martin sighed as he looked at the burner phone. That call had been awkward, to say the least. He used his own phone to send Robert a text message, asking him to come to his office. As he waited, he thought back over the conversation he'd just had.

The caller had told him, his distinctive baritone voice showing no contrition, that because of a House of Commons committee meeting, he wasn't going to make the event the following day. At first, Martin was pleased. The man could be a royal pain in the ass at times. He was used to having people at his beck and call and getting what he wanted, when he wanted it. But, on the plus side, he also had very deep pockets. Which he had just offered to dip into even more.

"Martin?" Robert said a moment later, after a brief knock on the door. "Everything okay?"

"We need to change our plans a bit, Robert. One of the guests wants to visit earlier."

"The politician? You already told me about that."

"No, not earlier as in earlier tomorrow. He wants to visit this afternoon."

"Ah," Robert replied. "That might be a problem."

"Robert," Martin replied, his voice short. "I pay you a lot of money to solve my problems. Have Lika prepare the girls and weigh them. I'll speak to the pharmacist, so one of your team will need to go and collect their drinks." He stared at Robert, who, as always, remained impassive.

"As you wish, Martin," Robert said a moment later. "What time will he be arriving?"

"Three o'clock this afternoon."

Robert nodded and left the office. Martin got to his feet and crossed to the door, flipping the lock so he wouldn't be disturbed. Then he crossed to the wall behind his desk and slid the painting of a random windmill to one side to reveal a safe built into the wall. There was a digital number pad in the door that he tapped a six-digit code into, known only to himself. Martin was under no illusion that Robert knew about the safe, but without the code, he wouldn't know what was in it. The safe itself was the size of a mini fridge but, because of the twin walls with a fireproof composite sodium silicate layer between them, the interior was much smaller. It only held two items. A laptop and a power cable.

Martin lifted out the laptop and returned to his desk, plugging the power cable in as the laptop booted up. He checked to make sure it was connected to the hidden Wi-Fi network that the house cameras were all connected to, and opened up the software to view them. He nodded as he cycled through the camera feeds. The one he was most interested in was in one of the basement bedrooms where his guest would entertain the girls. Martin set the camera's software to start recording at two o'clock that afternoon. His guest had an annoying habit of being early, and Martin didn't want to miss anything being recorded on the enormous twin hard drives on the computer. The footage wasn't stored anywhere else, but he'd paid a lot of money to ensure that even if the laptop was destroyed, the hard drives would survive. There was a lot of footage on them of many people. People who would pay a massive amount of money for the footage to never be seen should he ever need to exert that kind of pressure.

With the bedroom camera set up, Martin again cycled through the feeds until he reached the camera in the girls' bedroom. He watched for a few moments as Lika fussed around them. He turned the audio on for a moment, but was unable to understand anything they were saying. From the looks of it, though, the younger girl didn't want to get in the shower. It was the older girl who persuaded her, using a towel to flick at her sister.

Martin listened as the two girls squealed and laughed, watched by Lika. The woman had a strange expression on her face, somewhere between sadness and resignation. He had seen the look before in the summer house earlier that day, but had paid it no mind then.

He paid it no mind now as he closed the computer and replaced it in the safe.

"Whatever will be, will be," Martin muttered under his breath as he slid the painting back over the safe.

117

Caleb walked slowly back to the trees, feeling refreshed, both physically and spiritually. Having spent so much time focusing on what lay ahead, he allowed himself a moment to consider what would come after it. Where he would go, what he might do. But he dismissed the thoughts as too uncertain to spend any time on.

When he reached the trees, Katya was still up in the oak tree. He called up to her and, a few moments later, heard her scrambling down. She jumped off the lowest branch, stumbling as she landed, and she laughed as he put out a hand to steady her.

"Oops," she said, still giggling. Caleb was relieved to see her in good spirits. He'd been concerned earlier about her reaction to being told she would not be taking a more active role in the girls' rescue, but she seemed to have accepted it.

"Anything going on?"

"Not really," Katya replied, adjusting the spotting scope, which was slung around her neck. "Not that I could see, anyway."

"Did the guards change their pattern at all?"

"I don't think so, no," she said. Caleb nodded. That was good. "There's another man, though. Not one of the guards, but he was talking to Martin in his office. I was watching them through his window."

"Can you describe him?"

"Normal size, normal build. Maybe in his thirties? I'm not sure, it was difficult to tell."

"Hair?"

"Crewcut or shaved, I think."

Caleb nodded again. It was useful intelligence. The additional man could belong to the guards, so that would make five in total. It made sense, if they were operating in pairs, for there to be a leader of some sort.

"Thank you," he said to Katya, and was rewarded with a broad smile. He gestured at the scope. "You want me to take a stint up there?"

"No, I'm good. You need to save your energy for the morning. I'll head back up there in a minute. I just need to find a bush."

"Find a bush?" Caleb asked. He pointed at the surrounding vegetation. "There're loads of them just here."

"No, I need to find a private one."

It took Caleb a few seconds to realize what she meant.

"Ah, I see."

CALEB PASSED the next couple of hours sitting in the car while Katya kept watch from the tree. He checked and double-checked his equipment, making sure he had everything he needed in Mateo's bag. Then he dozed for a while, nodding off to the sound of the wind whispering through the leaves. But he didn't dream.

Caleb was somewhere between asleep and awake when he heard Katya calling him.

"Caleb?" Her voice was sharp and insistent. Caleb's eyes snapped open, instantly awake. He grabbed the binoculars, got out of the car, and ran to the base of the tree. "Come up here," Katya said, quietly but firmly.

He clambered up the tree until he was sitting on the same branch that she was. The branch was so thick it could have taken ten people without moving an inch.

"What is it?" Caleb asked as he raised the binoculars to his eyes, but he could see why Katya had called him. The gate to the house was slowly swinging open to allow a car through.

"One of the SUVs left a while ago, driven by the man I saw in Martin's office," Katya said. "Then it came back around thirty minutes later. But this car's just shown up."

Caleb focused on the car as it crept through the gate. It was a sleek-looking vehicle, almost like a Lincoln Town Car back home. The metallic paint was a deep green color that glinted in the sunlight. He could see Martin standing by the front door to his house to welcome his visitor.

The car stopped in front of the house and Caleb watched as a man got out. He was sharply dressed in a suit and had gray hair that he used his hands to smooth over his head.

"Who is he?" Katya said. "Caleb, what if he's here for the girls?"

Caleb had been thinking the exact same thing that Katya had just said. He closed his eyes and prayed for guidance. But none came. He was on his own.

"Katya," Caleb said, fixing her eyes with his. "I need to go." He saw fear bubble up in her eyes and he placed his hand on hers until it subsided. She nodded, blinking back tears.

A moment later, with Mateo's bag slung over his shoulder, Caleb made his way from the small copse toward the stone wall that would give him shelter as he approached Martin's house.

But Caleb didn't look back.

He never looked back.

118

K atya's heart thudded in her chest as she watched Caleb through the scope, crouching down but moving quickly, make his way toward the wall. She hadn't even wished him luck, let alone said goodbye. What if he never came back? She cursed herself under her breath. If something happened to him, she would never forgive herself. After Badri had died, the worst thing was the fact that she'd never had a chance to say goodbye to him properly.

She switched her attention to the house. In front of it, Martin was shaking hands with the new arrival. The man she had seen earlier stepped out of the house from behind Martin and the visitor handed him something. A moment later, the green car was being moved around to the back of the house as the two men spoke more. Then Martin extended his hand and the other man stepped into the house.

Katya's eyes were drawn to some movement by the garage. The four guards she had seen previously were standing in a group in front of the garage door. She refocused the spotting scope and what she saw filled her heart with dread. All four were carrying black, stubby guns slung across their chests. Katya reached into her pocket for Mateo's phone and, her hands trembling, she tapped out a message to Caleb. They had agreed that she would only text the burner phone he was carrying in an emergency. This was an emergency.

The guards have got guns.

She pressed send and held her breath as she waited for a reply. When it came, it was a single letter.

K

Katya raised the scope back to her eye and tracked the guards as they set off on their patrol. To her relief, they followed the same route they had earlier, two of them making their way down to the river and the other two disappearing behind the house. Then she switched to Caleb, but after tracing the stone wall several times, she couldn't see him. Katya forced herself to relax. If she couldn't see him, even though she knew the route he was taking, then neither could the guards. Could they?

Then she focused on Martin's office window to see if the two men were in there, but it was empty. She felt nauseated at the thought of that man and Ana or Elene with him. Him touching them. Doing things to them that they wouldn't understand. Shouldn't understand. Katya hiccoughed and, when she felt bile rising into the back of her mouth, thought she was going to vomit, but the feeling subsided as she swallowed the bile back down with a grimace.

Working methodically, Katya used the scope to inspect each of the windows in the house, in turn, to see if there was any activity inside. There was nothing until she got to the last window on the first floor. When she had looked at it earlier, the blinds had been drawn, but someone had opened them to open the window. Katya could see a man sitting at a desk, looking at a bank of monitors. He was smoking a cigarette and leaning back in the chair. Katya thought it was the man who had parked the visitor's car, but he had his back to her, so she couldn't be sure.

Katya adjusted the scope back to the stone wall. She traced it again all the way from where it began to where it ended by the bridge. When she got to the bridge, she saw Caleb. Her heart fluttered as she watched him crouching by the river, using the bridge to conceal himself. He was taking things out of Mateo's bag and placing them in his pockets. Then he turned and looked directly at Katya. She knew he wouldn't be able to see her, but it was if he had sensed her gaze.

She watched as Caleb, his eyes still fixed on her location, put both hands in front of him, clasped as if in prayer, before pointing a finger at his own chest.

"I will, Caleb," Katya whispered. "I will pray for you."

119

Caleb crouched in the shade of the bridge, safe in the knowledge that he couldn't be seen from the house or its garden. He took a moment to scour the sky above him, alert for the sight or sound of a drone, but other than a few red kites soaring in the thermals calling to each other, he could see or hear nothing. He was perspiring heavily after making his way down the side of the stone wall to his current location. Moving that way was hard work, and his thighs were still burning from the effort.

He spent a few moments transferring equipment from Mateo's bag into the pockets of his camouflage jacket, making sure the pockets were secure. The last thing he wanted to do was to reach in for something important, only to find it was at the bottom of the river. The gun he had taken from the man in the hotel was wrapped in plastic. It would get wet, but it would still work if he needed to use it. Caleb toyed with removing the silencer as it made the weapon awkward in his pocket, but he decided to keep it. The last object he removed from Mateo's bag was too large for his pockets, and since he was about to use it, he placed it down next to him.

Caleb hadn't been this close to the house before, so he took a few moments to catch his breath. Then he raised the binoculars and shuffled forward a yard or so, taking care to ensure he didn't move any of the bushes near the bridge too wildly. He pressed them to his eyes and started an in-depth look at the house, moving methodically from left to right. The first things he noticed were the cameras. There were two in each corner of the building, both looking in opposite directions. He studied them for a couple of minutes, but they didn't move. That meant they would have wide fields of view, which was good, as the picture quality wouldn't be very good. But on the downside, it also meant there were no blind spots caused by the cameras' movement. But a camera was only as good as the person watching the screen, and if no one was, then they became irrelevant.

The windows of the house were double glazed with no fittings on the outside. That would make a quiet entry through any of them impossible. The only exception was the furthest window away on the first floor, which was open. As Caleb watched, a thin wisp of smoke emerged from it before being spirited away in the light breeze. Caleb focused his attention on the area immediately surrounding the window. It was perhaps twenty feet above the ground and it wasn't obvious whether it opened all the way, or whether it had a safety device that prevented this, like many hotels he had stayed at. Running up the side of the building was a down-pipe, fitted to the wall with solid metal fastenings. There were three in total, which made them just over six feet apart. He rehearsed climbing the pipe in his mind and tried to calculate how long it would take him to climb from the ground to the window. If anyone saw him doing this, he would be a sitting duck. There was also the problem of whoever was smoking inside the room. But before he could even begin to climb the pipe, he had to get there.

Two of the guards were walking away from him along the front of the lawn by the river. They already had their backs to him by the time he received Katya's text, and he wasn't able to tell what type of guns they had. But he could see the slings across their backs, which made them larger than pistols.

Caleb checked his pockets were secure once more. He then placed the binoculars on the ground, as he wouldn't be needing them anymore. He picked up the item he had placed on the ground and crept to the edge of the river where bulrushes helped conceal him.

With a gasp at the coldness of the water, Caleb slid slowly into the river.

It was time.

120

"How is our guest?" Martin heard Robert ask as he walked into the CCTV room. The head of security's eyes were fixed on the bank of monitors on the desk in front of him, and a cigarette was smoldering away in the ashtray. It was the only room that Martin allowed Robert to smoke in on the grounds that if the cameras were being monitored, he could hardly slip away for a cigarette.

"He's having a shower in the guest suite," Martin replied, looking at the screens. There were eight in total, two for each side of the house, and they gave Robert a three hundred and sixty degree view of the exterior. The only internal cameras were Martin's.

On one screen, Martin could see two of the guards ambling along the rear wall of the property, while on another, their colleagues were about to pass the summerhouse where he and Lika had enjoyed themselves that morning. Or at least, where Martin had enjoyed himself.

Martin crossed to the window, eager for some fresh air. The smoke from Robert's cigarette was irritating his eyes.

There was a dull ache behind Martin's sternum, which he knew was from the stress of his visitor arriving early. Martin's plans were so detailed—they had to be—that any deviation stressed him out. He watched as a solitary duck made its way down the river and cast his mind back to the menu at the White Horse.

"Duck, with quince purée and orange infused endive," Martin muttered under his breath.

"Excuse me?" Robert said.

"That's what I'm having for dinner," Martin replied, waving a hand at Robert to dispel another cloud of smoke. "Any problems, just let me know."

Martin left the CCTV room and walked down the main staircase to get to the kitchen and find Lika. When he walked into the room, the lights were off. Martin tutted under his breath. He'd told her to start preparing some food for his guest as soon as the girls were ready. The guest would no doubt be hungry later.

"Alexa, turn the kitchen lights on," Martin said. They flickered into life and he made his way across the kitchen to the door at the end that led to the basement. Down a further flight of stairs, he walked to the girls' bedroom and rapped on the door.

"They're not ready," Lika's voice came from inside.

"Open the door!" The ache in Martin's chest pulsed in time with his heartbeat. A few seconds later, the door swung open. "What's going on?"

"She didn't want her drink," Lika said, pointing a finger at Ana who was sitting on her bed with her head lowered. Beside her, Elene was curled up in a ball. She raised her head at the sound of Martin's voice, but soon put it back down again.

"Has she had it now?"

"Yes, but only a moment ago."

Martin looked at his watch. The drugs in the syrupy drinks his pharmacist had prepared would take at least twenty minutes to kick in. It wouldn't do to keep his guest waiting, but he had no choice. One of the advantages of the pharmacological concoction Martin paid so much for was that it wiped his packages' memories.

Martin couldn't care less if they remembered what happened to them. He just didn't want them telling anyone else, in this case, his other clients.

That wouldn't do at all.

121

Caleb kept his lungs half-inflated to maintain a neutral buoyancy in the water, breathing shallowly as he lay on his back at a forty-five degree angle. His feet were on the bed of the river, and only his face was above the surface. Caleb had one hand out to the side to balance himself, and with the other he was holding a plastic decoy duck from the outdoors shop between the house and his face to hide the only part of his body that was above the water. He propelled himself with his feet, trying to gauge how quickly a duck would move through the water.

It took Caleb around five minutes to make his way along the front of the river, past the summerhouse, and into the lee of the oak tree in the corner of Martin's garden. The house and the tree were the only two blind spots where he could climb out of the river unseen by the cameras. Another reason for moving slowly was to stay behind the guards. If they followed their normal routine, they would turn at the end of the garden and walk up to the other corner of the grounds. But the other two guards were also walking along the rear wall of the garden, and they might be able to see him clambering out of the river if he didn't time it right.

Caleb angled himself to see round the decoy duck. He'd almost gone too quickly, as the men were only just turning to walk up the side of the garden. He gave it a few moments, moving the plastic decoy a few times, so it wasn't too static, and then approached the side of the river.

The blind spot from the house created by the oak tree was only as wide as the trunk itself and, because of the dual cameras, there was a risk it was even thinner than that. But there was nothing he could do about it. He placed the duck in some bulrushes and eased his way through them. Caleb peered through the tall stalks at the backs of the two men, who were now around ten yards away from the tree. He had perhaps thirty seconds before the other guards appeared at the top of the garden.

Caleb parted the bulrushes and slipped through them, keeping a close eye on the retreating guards as he did so. Moving as quickly as he could without making any noise, he made his way to the large base of the tree. Just above head height was a branch about the width of his forearm. He could use it as purchase to lever himself up into the relative safety of the tree's canopy.

He jumped, grabbing the branch with both hands so he could pull himself up. When he had got his chest on the branch, Caleb started to swing his legs up. There was what seemed to Caleb like a resounding crack and he felt himself falling back to the ground. He managed to pivot before he hit the deck so that he landed feet first, cushioning the impact with the soles of his feet.

Caleb paused, crouching down. He looked back up at the tree. There was an alternate route into the canopy, knots and whorls in the bark providing hand and foot holds.

But had the guards heard the branch snapping?

122

K atya stifled a scream as she saw Caleb fall from the tree and land on the ground. He stayed stock still for a few seconds, his arms out to the sides. Beyond the tree, the guards had stopped walking and one of them had half turned back to look in the direction of the river. To Katya's horror, the guard who had turned took a couple of steps back toward the tree.

"Climb the tree, Caleb," Katya said, her teeth gritted so hard her jaw was aching. "Climb the tree."

As Katya watched, Caleb did just that. She saw him turn and place his hands on the bark of the tree, then raise a foot to lift himself off the ground. It was going to be close, but Caleb was swift. Once he started ascending, he moved like a cougar, never letting more than one hand or foot stay where it was for more than a second. By the time the guard was a few yards away from the tree, Katya could no longer see Caleb. She exhaled hard through her cheeks, not realizing she'd been holding her breath.

Below the tree, the guard stopped for a moment. He looked down at the broken branch and kicked it with his foot. But he didn't look up into the canopy itself. As she watched, he leaned back against the trunk while beyond him, his colleague continued ambling up the side of the garden. The guard under the tree reached into his pocket, and when he pulled his hand out, he was holding a pack of cigarettes. He pulled one from the pack and lit it before tilting his head back and exhaling a cloud of smoke with what Katya imagined to be a sigh of contentment.

Katya scoured the leaves of the tree for any sign of Caleb, but he was invisible to her. But all the guard had to do was look up and he might be able to spot him. Katya could feel a bead of perspiration rolling down between her shoulder blades, but she knew it wasn't from the heat. This wasn't, she was sure, part of Caleb's plan.

She used the spotting scope to scour the garden quickly, just to see if there had been any other reaction to the branch breaking. In the far corner of the garden, the top right from her vantage point, the remaining guard had met with his two colleagues. They were standing, guns slung over their chests, and appeared to Katya to be having a conversation. Nothing in their body language or demeanor gave Katya cause for concern.

When Katya returned the scope to the oak tree, the guard who had been smoking looked different. He had dropped his cigarette and was leaning up against the bark of the trunk. His hands were scrabbling at his neck and when Katya moved the scope to his feet, she saw they were almost a foot off the ground. His entire body was shaking and his feet were drumming against the base of the oak.

Ten, perhaps twenty seconds later, the guard's hands dropped to his sides. His feet stopped drumming and became still. Katya could see that his head was at a strange angle in relation to the rest of his body, but his feet were still some distance from the ground. Then, with a jerk, his body moved up the trunk by a foot, perhaps more. There was a pause, then he moved again.

Up, and over the course of a perhaps a minute, he disappeared into the canopy of the oak tree.

123

Every muscle in Caleb's upper body strained as he hauled on the paracord to drag the guard up into the canopy of the tree. One end of the cord was looped over a branch above his head to form a crude pulley system, but he was battling against both the weight of the man and the friction between the rope and the rough bark. He hauled again before glancing down. The man below him was only a few feet below the branch Caleb was standing on.

Caleb had initially thought about using a heavy duty fishing line for this task but had soon realized that it wouldn't work. Not only would he be unable to spool the line over the man's head, but he wouldn't be able to haul him up into the tree without either lacerating his own fingers or decapitating the guard. So he had opted for para-cord instead. According to the packaging, it was good for up to three hundred and fifty pounds, if not more, and he'd been able to tie a Honda knot in it with ease. The rope wasn't quite as stiff as he would have liked, but he'd been able to twirl it into a lasso to drop over the guard's head.

"Like ridin' a bike," Caleb had muttered as he'd pulled the rope tight before the guard had even realized it was around his neck. With one last haul, the muscles in his shoulders and upper arms screaming in complaint, he pulled the guard up high enough for him to grab him by the scruff of the neck and pull him onto the branch.

Caleb looked down at the young man. He'd noticed him earlier, using the tree as a smoking shelter while his colleague completed the patrol. The fact he did so told Caleb many things. The guards were nowhere near as disciplined as they should be, and they were complacent. The regular patrols, so similar they were predictable, made them vulnerable. But, Caleb thought as he looked at the sub machine gun slung around his neck, they were far from powerless.

He reached down and unslung the weapon, examining it carefully. It was a variant of the Hekler and Koch MP5, a short-barreled carbine chambered with, Caleb confirmed as he disengaged the magazine to examine the rounds, five point five six by forty-five millimeter NATO rounds. The rounds and the collapsible stock told Caleb his earlier instinct about a military connection was correct. He reinserted the magazine, pushing it home with a quiet click. If he was correct, he had perhaps two or three minutes before the second guard returned. Caleb was counting on him not to look up when he realized his colleague wasn't smoking behind the tree.

When the second guard eventually made his way back to the tree, he stopped directly under Caleb and looked around.

"Dave?" Caleb heard him say in a soft voice, no doubt not wanting to get his colleague in trouble. Caleb looked down, judging his jump carefully. By the time he landed a few inches behind the guard, another length of paracord was already around the man's neck. This time, the cord was wound around two unbreakable tent pegs to form a garrote.

Caleb dropped to one knee and twisted his body, pivoting the man over his shoulder and face first onto the ground. The guard landed with a grunt, his weapon pinned between his body and the ground. Caleb put a knee in between the man's shoulder blades and pulled hard on the pegs. A moment later, when it was all over, Caleb rolled his body into the bulrushes next to the river, taking care to ensure it couldn't be seen from the house or the garden. Then he leaned the first guard's sub-machine gun against the tree and collected the magazine from the second before pitching it into the river's edge next to the body. Thirty rounds would be more than enough. He wasn't planning on firing a single one, though.

Caleb looked down at the cigarette butts sprinkled around the base of the tree and then up at the canopy where the body of the first guard could just be seen.

"Did no one ever tell you smoking's bad for your health?" he said under his breath as he slipped back into the water beyond the bulrushes. Caleb retrieved the plastic duck and prepared to make his way to the summerhouse.

It was time for a diversion.

124

K atya lowered the spotting scope, her heart racing. In the space of under two minutes, she had just watched two men die at Caleb's hand. Neither of them had stood a chance, and she wasn't sure how she felt about that. The other two guys, the one in the hotel and the one in the car, had at least had a fighting chance. She put the scope down on a branch and took a few deep breaths, trying to reconcile Caleb's savagery with the tenderness he had shown her.

Forcing herself to think about Ana and Elene and the predicament they were in, Katya took a few more deep breaths to calm herself. The men that Caleb had killed were all part of the system that had put them into that situation. They were hardly innocent bystanders. Those men were armed mercenaries who were being paid to facilitate pedophilia. They had chosen that course, not Caleb. If they hadn't, then they would still be alive.

She watched as Caleb slipped back into the water and held the decoy up to disguise his face. If the situation hadn't been so desperate, it would have been comical. He started making his way back down the river and she raised the scope to her eyes, determined to play her part in the mission. The man in the camera room was still there, staring at the screens. The tree had done its job and hidden Caleb from his view. But Katya couldn't see Martin. She found him a few moments later, back in his office. He had retrieved the laptop from his safe and was looking at it on his desk. There was nothing else that she could see, so she switched the scope to the decoy duck.

A moment later, shielded by the summerhouse, Caleb slipped out of the water. He crawled to the summerhouse and slipped inside, closing the door behind him. Perhaps three minutes later, he emerged and crawled back to the water's edge, this time leaving the door open a couple of inches. Then he was back in the water and the duck was making its way back to the tree. A moment after that, Caleb was back in the relative safety of the tree's canopy.

Katya returned the scope to the summerhouse. There was a thin wisp of smoke coming through the gap in the door. As she watched, it thickened and grew, becoming denser.

"Fire!" a man's voice shouted. "Fire!"

Katya brought the scope away from her eye for a moment and saw the remaining two guards running across the lawn toward the summerhouse. They ran past the tree and she brought the scope back up to her eyes, searching for the camera room. When she found it, she saw the man who had been looking at the screens standing at the window, staring out at the summerhouse, which now had thick smoke billowing from the gap in the door. Then he disappeared back into the house somewhere.

As both the guards reached the summerhouse, Katya saw Caleb drop from the far side of the tree and sprint toward the corner of the house. The guards, their attention focused on the summerhouse, didn't see him as he leaped onto the drainpipe and started shimmying up it, his hands and feet moving quickly as he propelled himself up the side of the house.

Katya held her breath as she watched Caleb reach the window and tug at it. For a heart stopping second, she thought the window wasn't going to open. But then he tumbled through the open window, reaching back to pull it back to where it was originally.

Caleb was inside the house.

125

"What's going on?" Martin shouted at Robert, who was sprinting down the stairs. He'd heard the guards shouting outside and looked up to see some smoke coming out of the summerhouse. Martin had slammed his laptop closed, cutting off the footage of his politician client as he made his final preparations to meet the girls. The man had been in the ensuite bathroom, brushing his teeth, as the two girls sat on one of the beds in the main bedroom. They had both looked groggy, but compliant, when Lika had brought them into the room a few moments earlier while the politician showered.

Martin had watched as she hugged them before leaving the room. He wasn't planning on watching when things got started, though. He wasn't that sort of man at all. He just wanted to ensure that his cameras were up and running before the fun began.

"The bloody summerhouse is on fire!" Robert shouted back, running past Martin and into the kitchen. When he returned, he was carrying a large red fire extinguisher. "Your cigars, probably."

"But that was this morning," Martin said, his voice plaintive. It couldn't have smoldered in the ashtray for hours, could it?

"What else would it be?"

Martin followed Robert at a distance. When he reached the front door, he could see smoke billowing out of the summerhouse. When he had looked a moment before, through his office window, he'd only seen a small amount. Now it looked as if the small wooden building was well on fire, but he couldn't see any flames. Only smoke.

By the time Martin reached the summerhouse, the pain in his chest was sharp. His cardiologist had told him to avoid any strenuous exercise, and Martin had never been a runner, anyway. The guards had opened the doors, and Robert was directing the spray from the fire extinguisher into the building's interior. A few seconds later, he peered inside the building before disappearing for a moment. A metal container came flying out of the summerhouse, thick smoke pouring from it. As the smoke inside the summerhouse dissipated, Martin saw Robert staring at the container. It looked like a small saucepan, like one a camper would use.

"What is it?" Martin asked as Robert directed a jet of water into the pan. Robert didn't reply, but was staring at the object on the ground, which was still smoking despite the water. In the summerhouse, one of the guards shouted.

"Nothing in here."

Martin took a few steps toward the small wooden structure. He looked in the door and saw the guard, but it was what he couldn't see that surprised him. There were no signs of a fire at all. No blackened wood, no scorch marks. Nothing. He turned his attention to Robert, who was still staring at the pan. Finally, he looked up at Martin and, for the first time since he'd met the man, Martin saw concern on his face.

"Where are the others?" Robert shouted at the two guards. He pointed at one of them. "You. Find them. And you?" Robert looked at the other. "Come with me to the house. We've got a problem."

"What sort of problem?" Martin asked, putting his hand on Robert's forearm. "What's going on?"

"It wasn't a fire, Martin," Robert replied. "It was a distraction. Someone's here."

"Who?"

"I don't know," Robert said, and Martin saw a look that hovered between disappointment and resolve on his face. Then Robert reached behind him and when his hand reappeared, it was clutching a large pistol. "But I intend to find out."

126

Moving as fast as he could, Caleb made his way out of the camera room after a cursory but fruitless search for anything useful. Perhaps he should have just burned the summerhouse down properly instead of planting a smoke bomb, albeit a carefully constructed one, but he needed the time to get back to the tree.

The previous day, he had spent some time mixing some stump killer, which was almost pure potassium nitrate, and sugar together over a small camping stove. When it was a thick gloppy mixture, he put a shoelace into the pan for a few moments before pulling it part way out and hanging it over the pan's side to form a crude fuse. The fuse had given him more than enough time to get back to the oak tree, and the contents of the pan had done what he intended. But Caleb knew it wouldn't distract the security detail for long. He needed to hurry.

The door in the camera room led to a long corridor that looked as if it ran the width of the entire house. Several doors led off the corridor, but Caleb paid them no heed as he made his way through the house the sub-machine gun in front of him. Ana and Elene would not be in an upstairs bedroom, of that he was sure. Caleb was betting they would be in a basement. Somewhat perversely, he realized he knew that because that would be where he would put them if he were Martin.

In an ideal world, Caleb would know the interior layout of the house well before he breached it. But there had been no time for in-depth research, searching for architects' plans or real-estate listings to orientate himself. He was going to have to work it out the hard way.

At the top of a winding staircase that led to the lower floors, Caleb paused for a few seconds to consolidate what he knew. By now, the guards would know that the smoke was a decoy and would be on their way back to the house. He didn't have long. They knew he was here. They might not yet know their numbers were diminished, but Caleb knew that was irrelevant. He needed to get to the basement and secure Ana and Elene. The rest he could worry about later.

Caleb sprinted down the stairs, taking them two at a time. He was in a large hallway, with an open door that led to the garden. As he ran past the door, he glanced through it to see two men running up the lawn toward the house. He thought for a split-second about putting a burst through the open door. If he didn't hit them, and he rarely missed, at least it would give them something to think about. But Caleb decided against it. He didn't think there were any close neighbors to hear the distinctive brrr of a sub-machine gun, and they would have to recognize it to call it in to the authorities, but his priority was the girls. The entire British police force heading for Martin's house wouldn't help them if they got there too late.

It was a fifty-fifty decision. Left or right? Caleb chose left. In his experience, evil graduated toward the left. Satan didn't baptize people with his left hand for nothing, nor was salt thrown over the left shoulder to blind him by accident. The door he ran through led to a large kitchen, full of industrial, sleek aluminum cupboards. He ran past a large stove, complete with eight gas rings on the top. At the end of the kitchen was a door with a frosted glass window. Through the glass, he could see a figure moving, but it was indistinct. Had he been surrounded?

Caleb paused as he watched the figure through the glass. He shifted his position so he was behind one of the counters, and slid the sub-machine gun behind his back. Then he pulled the pistol with the silencer from his waistband and raised it. Focusing on the figure beyond the glass, who could only be an adversary, his finger tightened on the trigger.

127

Katya watched through the scope as the three men started running toward the house, leaving Martin standing by the summerhouse. It was only a few seconds before she wasn't able to keep all three of them in her field of vision, but that wasn't important. What was important was that Caleb knew they were coming. Her hands shaking, she placed the scope on the branch to pull her cell phone from her pocket. As she did so, the scope tumbled off the branch and fell to the ground, bouncing off another branch as it did so. It took Katya a couple of attempts, which used up precious time that Caleb might not have, but she managed to send a message.

3 men coming

She waited until the phone pinged to let her know the message had been sent and started climbing down the tree. At least Caleb was inside the house. But would he be able to find the girls before the guards found him? At least he was now armed with something more substantial than a pistol. Her ears alert for the sound of gunfire, Katya jumped from the lowermost branch to the ground below.

Katya landed on the soft earth but, when she picked up the scope, she realized that the scope hadn't landed as softly as she had. The front lens was cracked, courtesy of a stone on the earth below the tree. She swore to herself. How was she going to be able to undertake any reconnaissance now?

"One job, Katya," she muttered to herself as she looked at the ruined lens. She held the scope to her eye anyway, but the field of vision was completely fractured. Katya stood where she was for a moment, considering her options.

Caleb had asked her to remain at the vehicle in case anything happened to him. He could send the girls to her location. But how was he going to tell them where she was? They didn't speak English, and he didn't speak Georgian. She cursed herself for not thinking that through and wondered why Caleb hadn't made that connection either. Unless he was so determined to keep her out of danger that he had given her a powerful reason to stay away from the house. He would know she would do anything not to jeopardize Ana and Elene's safety.

Katya remained where she was for a moment, thinking hard. Perhaps she could make her way to the bridge? She could hide at the spot where he had slipped into the water. It was the most natural escape route from the house. If the girls were running for their lives, with Caleb dead or wounded behind them, they would surely try to cross the bridge, somehow, wouldn't they? But how would they get over the gate? It was too high for them to climb, as was the wall, and Katya didn't know if they could swim.

She was on the verge of tears, unsure of what to do. Every scenario she thought about had holes in it. Some of the holes were enormous. There was so much that could go wrong. But she, too, had a pistol, and thanks to Caleb she knew how to use it, although she had actually fired a gun only once in her life. But to her relief, and Caleb's, that time she had missed.

Katya couldn't stand by and do nothing. The idea of staying at the car, unable to help Caleb at all, was not an option. She crossed to the vehicle and withdrew Mateo's gun from the bag. Then she made her way to the edge of the clump of bushes the car was hidden in. Her eyes traced the path that Caleb had taken, down the side of the stone wall and to the bridge. She could follow in his footsteps and at least be closer if he needed any help.

Katya just hoped that he didn't need any.

128

Caleb's finger was perhaps an ounce or two of pressure away from pulling the trigger when something made him pause. The figure he could see through the frosted glass appeared to be wearing white. But Martin and the men he had seen tackling the fire at the summerhouse had not been. He waited for the door to open and to confirm that the person on the other side was a bad guy before he sent a bullet in his direction.

The door flew open, and a woman rushed through. When she saw Caleb, his arms extended with the pistol in front of him, she stopped dead and opened her mouth. Caleb waited for her to scream, raising the pistol toward the ceiling so she could identify he was no threat, but she didn't. Caleb had killed many times before, but he had never killed a woman. Nor would he, unless the situation absolutely dictated that there was no other course of action. And there usually was. To his surprise, the woman asked him a question in a voice that was almost normal.

"Who are you?" she said, her voice accented. Caleb looked at her angular face and black hair tied back in a ponytail and recognized her as the woman he had seen running from the summerhouse earlier that day. She stared at him, and he saw a short lifetime of pain behind her cold eyes.

"I'm here for the girls," he replied, keeping his voice neutral. She regarded him for a split-second before nodding her head sharply.

"Follow me."

The woman turned and made her way back down the corridor. She led Caleb to the very end, passing the top of what he assumed was the main staircase to the lower level of the house. At the end of the corridor, she opened a door that led to a much narrower staircase. Her ponytail bobbing, the woman ran down the stairs, closely followed by Caleb.

As he followed the woman, Caleb tried to figure out where the guards had gone. They would know by now that the smoke was a decoy, which meant they would also know someone was probably in the house. Caleb was hoping that was the case, at least. He was betting that the security detail wouldn't have expected an intruder inside the house itself. They would have been anticipating an assault from outside the grounds, but that boat had sailed. What it meant was that they would have to regroup, reconsider, and re-plan. At least, that's what Caleb hoped for. It would buy him time. Not much, but perhaps enough to get the girls to relative safety.

The woman led Caleb down a further flight of stairs and half-way down another corridor. She stopped outside a door and nodded at it.

"In there," the woman said. "He's in there. With the girls."

"Is it locked?" Caleb asked her. She shook her head no in response. There were a myriad of other questions that Caleb wanted to ask before he opened the door. Where were the girls situated inside the room? Was the man with them armed? Where were the exits from the room? But there was no time.

Caleb regarded the door handle. It was a simple one, just a lever that would open the door. He motioned to the woman to step away from the door and depressed the handle, flinging the door wide open.

It took Caleb less than a second to orient himself to the interior of the room. It was a bedroom. Ana and Elene were sitting on a large bed, the man he had seen earlier standing over them with his back to Caleb. Both girls were fully clothed, and Caleb felt a rush of relief wash over him, followed a split-second later by a tide of anger and wrath. Elene raised her eyes to meet his, but her dilated pupils and lack of response told him everything he needed to know.

The man, whose life expectancy was now a lot shorter than threescore years and ten, turned to see who had entered the room. As he did so, Caleb rolled his weight back so that it was on his back foot. Then he raised his other leg from the floor, keeping it loose at the knee.

The strike, when it came, was quicker than a scorpion. Caleb extended his hanging leg, his foot connecting with the cartilage in the front of the man's neck. Caleb felt rather than heard the crunching of the structures in the soft tissue. The man staggered back a couple of steps, staring at Caleb with wide eyes.

"Take the girls, get them out of the house," Caleb said to the woman who looked just as surprised as the man who Caleb had just kicked in the throat. To Caleb's relief, she recovered quickly, barking instructions to the two girls that Caleb didn't understand. When they began to move, she hurried them first with words and then with her hands. A few seconds later, both girls were stumbling toward the door. Just before she left, the woman turned to look at Caleb. She reached out her hand and placed it on Caleb's forearm.

"Thank you," the woman said as Caleb closed his eyes to see a faint image of a man who had hurt her. Not Martin or the man in the room with them, but someone else.

When he opened them, the hardness behind her eyes that he had seen earlier was gone and had been replaced with something else that he couldn't process. Was it fear? Anger? Relief? He saw her eyes change again as she glanced at the other man in the room. This time, Caleb recognized the expression.

It was hatred. Pure hatred.

M artin watched as the three men ran up the lawn and toward the house. He could feel a tight band across his chest, a sure sign of stress. What was going on? He didn't understand what Robert had meant when he had said that the smoke bomb was a diversion. A diversion from what? And by whom? The Albanians were out of the picture. One was dead and the other, if his instructions had been followed, soon would be if he wasn't already. And if Mateo had said anything to the authorities, then he would have been informed by his sources. So who was it who had planted the device?

Frowning, he made his way up the lawn. To the side of the front door, he could see Robert giving the other two men instructions, using his hands in some sort of military sign language. His movements were direct and exaggerated, and he saw the two men nod before they split up, each one heading in a different direction. One went left, the other went right, their sub-machine guns held out in front of them in a determined fashion. Robert remained where he was by the front door, apparently waiting for Martin to reach him. Or was he, Martin considered, letting the two men go first in case there was trouble? Perhaps Robert wasn't the man he made himself out to be.

By the time Martin reached Robert, he was out of breath, despite the short distance he had just walked.

"You okay, Martin?" Robert asked, a momentary look of concern on his face. Martin just waved his hand.

"I'm fine. What's going on?" he asked Robert.

"I can't raise the other patrol," Robert replied. "The other two are searching the house. We're being attacked, Martin."

Martin wasn't convinced that they were actually being attacked. Someone planting a smoke bomb was hardly an all-out assault, and Martin hadn't seen or heard anything. But Robert was his head of security.

"Are you sure, Robert?" Martin asked. "Have you considered that perhaps your two missing men are playing games with you?" He saw a flicker of uncertainty on Robert's face. "How well do you actually know them?"

Robert's face said it all. His usual stoic demeanor was flaking.

"They both came highly recommended," he said a moment later.

"So you didn't actually serve with them? In Afghanistan, or wherever you said you did?"

"We should check on the girls," Robert said. Martin sighed, noting the change in the subject. Perhaps, once all this was over, he would need a new head of security. But men like Robert, men with no apparent scruples at all, were hard to find.

"We can't disturb our guest," Martin replied. "He could

withhold payment if we do. But I have a way of checking on them."

"The cameras?" Robert asked. Martin looked at Robert carefully. He knew? If he knew about the cameras, did he also know about the recordings? If he did, then the dynamic had just changed significantly between them. "I'm not stupid, Martin."

Without a word, Martin stepped past Robert and through the main door of the house. He made his way to his office, followed by Robert. As they entered the room, Robert made his way to the painting behind the desk, slid it to one side, and entered the combination to the safe. Martin was horrified. Not only did Robert know about the cameras, but he also had access to the safe. When Robert turned around, the laptop in his hand, there was a faint look of amusement on his face.

"What?" Robert said as he placed the laptop down and flipped the screen up. He pressed the power button and a few seconds later, entered the BitLocker code that was supposed to secure it. "Something wrong, Martin?"

Martin could feel the resentment building in his chest as he watched Robert enter his password to the main operating system. The password he'd been careful not to write down anywhere.

"In case you're wondering, Martin, I have copies. I've even got some footage of you enjoying yourself in the summerhouse." Robert's fingers flew across the keyboard. Martin saw his face, illuminated by the laptop screen, fall as he stared at it. "Ah," Robert said a moment later. "Martin? We've got a bit of a problem."

"What is it?" Martin replied, all thoughts of Robert's treachery temporarily forgotten. He took a couple of steps around the desk to see the screen. Robert had brought up the camera to the guest room in the basement. On the screen, he could see the politician sitting in a chair. It seemed as if he was looking at someone out of the shot of the camera.

But there was no sign of the girls.

130

"You've probably got about two or three minutes left of your miserable life," Caleb said to the man sitting in the chair. "So I would suggest you make the most of them. Reflect, perhaps, on your time in this world before you pass over into the next." He regarded the man, who had taken a few steps back and sunk into a chair. The only sound Caleb could hear was a high-pitched wheezing as he struggled for breath.

Caleb thought for a few seconds about whether to say anything more. Whether to tell the man in front of him that his trachea was fractured? That if he felt the skin around his neck, he could feel the air bubbles underneath crackling. That his airway was going to close up completely as the swelling from the injury compressed his airway. But, given what he had been about to do to Ana and Elene, Caleb wasn't going to waste another second of his own time in this world on a pedophile.

He turned on his heel and hurried into the corridor, pausing for a split-second to identify which direction the woman had gone with the girls. He angled his head on one side and heard a shuffling noise from the right-hand side, so he made his way down the corridor. When he caught up with the woman and the girls, they were climbing the staircase back up to the floor above. But their movement wasn't the only sound Caleb could hear. He could also hear footsteps, moving slowly and deliberately, from elsewhere in the house.

"You need to hide," Caleb said to the woman, who looked back at him with fear on her face. By contrast, both the girls were almost expressionless. Caleb knew they had been drugged with something from their dilated pupils and the lack of any response to their situation. They barely seemed to recognize him. "There's no time to get away."

The woman nodded and grabbed the girls' hands. She led them toward a door, opening it with her hip. The interior was dark and foreboding.

"Alexa, turn the kitchen lights on," the woman said. A second later, there was a flicker of light before the fluorescent tubes in the ceiling buzzed into life. Caleb looked past them to see a large kitchen lined with cupboards. The woman led the girls to the cupboard nearest the cooker which was, like the rest of the kitchen, enormous. Caleb counted eight gas rings on top of it, but the adjoining cupboard was empty. The woman shepherded the girls inside the cupboard before turning to look at Caleb. He raised his finger at the lights on the ceiling.

"Turn them off," he said, listening as the footsteps got louder. Caleb flashed his eyes around the kitchen, fixing in his mind the locations of the cupboards, the stove, and the large central food preparation counter.

"Alexa," the woman said, her voice trembling. "Turn the kitchen lights off."

The lights went off, leaving the kitchen in absolute

silence and darkness. Caleb heard the cupboard door close, and he took a few steps back toward the door they had entered through before taking a couple of steps to the side.

He was exactly where he wanted to be. In his mind, he counted down from three.

Three. Two.

Just as he imagined the word *one*, the door began to open.

131

The band across Martin's chest tightened further as he flipped through the camera feeds. There were none in the corridors of the house, only the rooms, but as he cycled through them, there was no sign of anyone. He returned the feed to the basement bedroom and looked at the politician who was still sitting in the chair. His head was slumped forward as he if was asleep.

"Could they be in the bathroom?" Robert said, glancing at the screen.

"What? Both of them?" Martin replied, his voice terse. But Robert was right. There were no cameras in the bathroom, and the door was closed, so they could be. "Come on, we'll go and look."

"No, Martin," Robert shot back. "You should leave."

"What do you mean, leave?"

"You should go. Once my men have neutralized the threat, you can come back. But it's not safe here. You should get to a place of safety."

Martin paused before replying. What Robert said made

sense, but at the same time, he wondered if he wanted to get himself to a place of safety.

"Where are you thinking?"

"Anywhere but here," Robert replied. "Somewhere we can take stock and plan our next steps." There was a faint smile on Robert's face as he said this, and Martin knew he wasn't just talking about their current situation, but the fact he had what Martin had. The footage of his clients.

Martin had an elaborate plan for a situation such as this, where his house was compromised. There was a safe house, an apartment technically, that he maintained in secrecy in the middle of Lincoln. It was clean, with several layers of deniability between the rental agreement and himself. He could, if necessary, hole up there for weeks. Or he could use it as a springboard to leave the country to get to any one of three or four countries he considered as friendly. Mostly because of their lack of extradition agreements with the United Kingdom. But if Robert knew of the cameras and his passwords, would he also know about the safe house? Martin had no way of knowing, short of asking him directly.

"You're right," Martin replied a moment later. "Do you have any ideas about where to go?"

"No, Martin," Robert replied. Martin studied his face for any signs that might tell him the man was hiding something. But he couldn't tell if he was or not. "Just get away. I'll call you when it's clear here." Robert reached into his pocket, and when he withdrew his hand, he was holding the key fob for one of the SUVs. "Take this," Robert said as he handed Martin the key.

Martin closed the screen of the laptop and reached back into the safe for the power cord. Then he put the key in his pocket and looked at Robert.

"We need to talk, Robert," Martin said. Robert's faint smile returned.

"Yes, I think we do," Robert replied. "I'm sure we can come to a mutually beneficial arrangement."

Without another word, Martin left the office with the laptop tucked under his arm. He walked out of the hall before deciding to leave through the main door and walk around the house to where the cars were parked. If Robert was right, and there was someone inside the house, he didn't want to bump into them.

Martin hit the key fob and one of the black SUVs responded with a flash of its turn signals and a clunking sound. He opened the driver's door, sliding the laptop onto the passenger seat. As his finger hovered over the start button, Martin thought back to watching the security detail searching underneath the cars with a mirror on the end of a long stick a few days previously. For all Martin knew, there could be an explosive device under the vehicle.

He paused for a moment, thinking. Was this all an elaborate sting by Robert? Perhaps he, Martin, was the ultimate target? Robert also now had the leverage that was on the laptop. But he wouldn't be able to exploit it in the same way that Martin could. Robert also had leverage on him as well. His superiors in the church wouldn't look too kindly on his activities in the summerhouse. Bishops weren't, after all, supposed to do that sort of thing with women, regardless of whether they consented.

Martin closed his eyes and pressed the button. To his relief, the only sound he heard was the powerful engine of the SUV rumbling into life. There was no explosion, no mighty roar that lifted the car from the ground with a billowing cloud of smoke.

As he put the car into gear and started down the drive,

Martin let a smile play across his face. It wasn't ideal, but he could work with Robert as a business partner. At least until he found out more about the man. And then, when the time was right?

Boom.

132

C aleb's first rule of combat, drilled into him first as a child by his father, and then by various other teachers, was to hit first and to hit hard. The best fights to be in, his father had always said, are the ones where only a single blow is thrown.

He waited until the door had opened by a couple of inches, a narrow shaft of light illuminating a triangle on the floor, to see if the man outside would do what he expected. When he saw a hand snaking into the gap, patting the wall inside the kitchen, he readied himself. Wherever the light switches were, they weren't there.

Caleb used the point of his elbow to drive hard into the man's wrist. The crumpling sensation he felt in his elbow, accompanied by a loud scream, told him he had hit the spot he'd been aiming for. Caleb wasn't sure which of the eight bones in the man's wrist had just broken, or whether it was more than one. The scaphoid was likely, as was the unusually shaped hamate. They were two of the largest bones, and consequently the most commonly injured. The others, such as the much smaller pisiform bone and the triquetrum that it sits over, were less likely to fracture but equally disabling if they did. But with enough force concentrated through a hard and unyielding weapon such as Caleb's elbow, all that mattered was the effect.

But a broken bone or two in a man's wrist wasn't the disablement that Caleb was searching for. He wanted something more permanent. A broken wrist would stop the guard using his gun, but as Caleb knew having once finished a fight with a similar injury, but it wouldn't stop him completely. Depending on the man's skill as a fighter, there was a lot he might still be able to do.

Aware that the scream could have alerted someone, Caleb opened the door with his other hand and half pulled the guard through it. Then he slammed the door as hard as he could, trying to adjust the man's position. The door bounced back off his sternum, protected by Kevlar plates, but it meant Caleb was able to move him so that the next time he slammed it, it was the guard's head that was between the edge of the door and the doorjamb. There was a sickening crack, and Caleb realized that he'd overdone the maneuver as the man slid to the floor, unconscious before he even reached it.

With a silent apology to the man on the ground, who had dark rivulets of blood streaming out of his ears, Caleb dragged him inside the kitchen and let the door close. He stood, waiting for his eyes to adjust to the darkness, when something happened that he wasn't expecting.

The lights flicked back on again. Caleb's head darted around. By the door at the other end of the kitchen was the other guard. He must have slipped in while Caleb was dealing with his colleague. And this man knew where the light switch was. He was clutching the sub-machine gun, aiming it directly at Caleb.

Then the interior of the kitchen got very noisy.

133

Katya lay in the vegetation next to the river, peering through the bulrushes at the upper stories of the house. If she hadn't broken the spotting scope, she would have been able to see into the upstairs windows. As it was, she could just make out the top of Martin's office window, but the wall prevented her from seeing inside the room.

She looked at the wall that ran around the outside of the house. It was constructed of brick, the sides smooth and without purchase. From her vantage point, she wasn't able to see the top of the wall. There could be broken glass set into the top. There could even be barbed wire. Even if she could get her hands on the top of it, which she thought she could probably do with a running start, she doubted she would have the strength to haul herself up and over, glass or no glass. And even if she conquered the wall, there were still the cameras that Caleb had pointed out to her. Cameras which would also see her if she crossed the river. There was no way for her to tell whether the man in the camera room had returned.

Katya sighed. She wasn't any better than she had been back up in the copse. At least up there, even without the scope, she could see if people were moving around. But here, the bridge and the gate prevented her from seeing anything.

She looked over the small road at the bulrushes and bushes by the river. Katya would have a better vantage point if she hid in them, instead of her current location. At least then she could see across the lawn and up to the house. She wouldn't be able to see inside any of the upstairs windows— the angle would prevent that—but she could see the approaches to the house.

Katya got to her feet and, moving slowly while she was crouched down, she inched across the road and into the bushes. She wasn't as well concealed, but she had a much better view. She remained where she was for a few moments, surveying the front of the house for any signs of movement. But there was none. It was almost as if the house was deserted. Then she saw a familiar shape appear from behind the house. A black, boxy shape.

She watched the SUV come down the track. It was moving slowly, its driver apparently in no hurry. When the vehicle was around fifty yards from the gate, she recognized Martin behind the wheel. He had a look of intense concentration on his face. Katya saw the car approaching the gate and, as it did so, the gate started to swing open. Martin slowed the vehicle to wait for it to fully open.

Katya wasn't sure what to do. She didn't know what was happening up at the house. She'd seen or heard nothing since the guards had run up toward the house. For all she knew, Ana and Elene could be in the back of the SUV being taken away. Although she could only see Martin in the vehicle, they could be lying down on the rear seat. Or tied up in the trunk. If she didn't stop Martin, and he had the girls, who knew where they would end up?

It only took her a couple of seconds to decide. As the car passed through the gate, still moving slowly, she emerged from the bulrushes with the pistol in her hand. Katya walked into the middle of the road and stood facing the car with one hand out in the universal symbol for stop. His face full of surprise, Martin did just that. Then he raised his hand and waved it to one side to motion Katya out of the way. When she remained where she was, he revved the engine a couple of times, as if to indicate that if she didn't move, he would drive over her.

Katya, her thoughts full of Ana and Elene, wasn't going to budge a single inch. When the car moved forward another foot, she raised the pistol. The look of surprise on Martin's face only increased at the sight, but he kept moving.

Using her thumb to flip the safety catch, Katya pulled the trigger and smiled as Martin disappeared behind the shattered windshield.

134

Caleb dove to the floor a split-second before the contents of the MP5's magazine tore a left-to-right line of holes in the wall behind him. Small puffs of plasterboard coughed into the air, but Caleb's attention was on what he could hear. Keeping low behind the row of counters, Caleb shuffled forward to close the distance between him and the security guard. Was the sub-machine gun empty? The other guards had been carrying fifteen round magazines, which emptied in a matter of seconds from a gun that could fire eight hundred rounds a minute. But Caleb couldn't take the chance that this guard had a larger, thirty-round magazine. Not when the gun delivered such a devastating amount of firepower.

As he shuffled forward, Caleb picked up a pan from a countertop, throwing it to the other side of the room. It hit the wall with a loud clang, that was followed almost immediately afterward by two shots in close succession. Caleb got to his feet as he heard a magazine paddle being depressed, followed by a clattering noise as the empty magazine hit the floor. Knowing he had a couple of seconds before the guard could reload, even if he was using the much derided HK slap method of reloading, Caleb sprinted forward, putting as much power into his legs as he could muster.

Just as Caleb got to the end of the counter, the guard stepped into view. He was still struggling with the magazine when Caleb barreled into him, his head down like a battering ram. The guard slammed back and into the wall behind him with a grunt. To Caleb's satisfaction, he dropped the magazine, but he used the empty gun as a club, bringing the stock down hard on the back of Caleb's neck.

Blinking away the pain in his neck, Caleb swept his foot out and hooked it behind the guard's before bringing it back to force his legs out from under him. The guard slid down the wall as Caleb rose, using his knee to drive toward the man's face. Caleb's intent was to use his knee to drive the man's nasal bones into his forebrain, but at the last minute, the guard moved his head and Caleb's knee hit the wall. Then the guard used the stock to drive it into the side of Caleb's other knee.

Caleb needed to re-evaluate his tactics. This man could fight. Caleb stumbled back, both knees screaming in pain, as the guard started struggling to his feet. Caleb thought about kicking him as he did so, but the man could grab Caleb's legs and force him back, off balance, and to the floor. He still had options, despite the guard's body armor. Eyes. Ears. The face. The genitals. All were exposed and vulnerable. But not as vulnerable as Caleb was.

Just as the guard got his balance, Caleb stepped forward and grabbed the top of the body armor beside the man's neck. He used the guard's rising momentum to pull him across the kitchen before slamming him into the stove. Then Caleb shoved hard, bending the man in the middle and smashing his face into the unyielding metal of the largest of the burner grates on top of the stove. Caleb put all his weight on the man's back to stop him from getting any purchase on the stove, and he reached down for the dial. Realizing what Caleb was about to do, the guard redoubled his efforts to shift Caleb's weight from pinning him down, but Caleb had his forearm on the back of his neck and his entire body weight behind it. His arm shook with the effort of keeping the guard in place and, with this other hand, Caleb pressed the ignition switch.

The guard screamed as the blue flames enveloped his face, which Caleb knew, while involuntary, was the worst thing he could do. He kept the pressure on the back of the guard's neck for a few more seconds, but he could feel the heat from the burner on his own skin on his forearm. Not wanting to burn himself, Caleb released the pressure and took a few steps away from the stove. The guard slumped to the floor, a mewing sound coming from his mouth as the burner continued to hiss.

Caleb looked at him, not without sympathy. The guard's face was reddened all over, the painful first-degree burns obvious as was the faint smell of roasting pork. One or two facial areas had the yellowed look of deeper burns, and the man's nasal hairs were all singed away. He had no eyebrows or eyelashes left, but the sclera of his eyes appeared undamaged. Not that it would do the man any good at all. The moment he had screamed and inhaled the hot gasses and flames from the stove, he had burned the inside of his airway. Over the next few moments, the delicate tissues would swell as a response to the damage. Until they closed completely.

He reached down and hauled the guard to his feet.

"No, no, no," the man said as Caleb led him across the

kitchen. His voice was high-pitched, and Caleb could already hear a wheeze in his voice.

"I am being merciful, my friend," Caleb said as he turned the faucet on and gently pushed the guard's face under the cold water. "Just as He is merciful. Luke, chapter six."

He left the guard where he was, slumped over the sink, and returned to the cupboard where the woman and the girls were hiding. Caleb tapped softly on the door.

"It's all clear," he said. A moment later, the door opened, and Caleb saw three frightened faces peering out. "Come on," he said, smiling at Ana and Elene. "It's time to get you out of here." He waited a few seconds for the woman to translate what he had just said. Then he saw a sight that filled his heart with love.

Both Ana and Elene smiled back at him.

135

M artin screamed as small slivers of the windshield glass bit into his flesh. He tried to slump down in the driver's seat in case the lunatic woman shot at the car again, but a few seconds later, he heard the car door open.

"Get out!" Katya screamed. "Get out of the car!"

He turned to look at her. She was standing a few steps back from the door, the gun aimed squarely at his head. From the expression on her face, she wasn't in the mood for a discussion. Martin took his hands from the steering wheel and raised them in the air.

"Okay, okay," he replied. "I'm getting out."

Moving slowly, Martin got out of the car. Katya stepped back further, keeping at least a yard between them. Not that Martin was about to try to disarm her. He knew he was far too slow for that. He saw her glance around him and into the car.

"What's that?" she asked him, nodding at the interior. He turned to look in the car. "On the passenger seat?"

"That's my laptop."

"Bring it."

Keeping his arms aloft, Martin turned and reached back into the vehicle for the computer. As he did so, he wondered if there was a gun in the glove box. He knew Robert often kept a backup piece in there. But Martin also knew that he would have a bullet in him long before he could open the compartment and get a gun out. Besides, he had never fired a gun in his life. It wasn't something the Church taught its ministers to do.

"Slowly," Katya said, her tone taut and menacing.

Martin picked up the laptop and tucked it under his arm. He turned to look at Katya, who angled the gun toward the house. Martin set off, walking slowly, with Katya a couple of yards behind him.

"The girls?" Katya asked. "Ana and Elene? Are they safe?"

Martin thought for a moment before replying. Should he tell her the truth? That he had no idea where the girls were?

"The last time I saw them," he replied, "they were both fine."

"If anything's happened to them, Martin," Katya said, "I will shoot you like the dog you are. Do you understand?"

Martin turned and laughed at Katya. But his laughter didn't last long when he saw the look of resolution on her face.

"I don't think you'd be able to shoot a man in cold blood, Katya," Martin said, trying to inject some authority into his voice. It wasn't easy when a gun was being pointed directly at your face.

"You're not a man, Martin." Katya's face hardened. "Even calling you a dog is an insult to them. Now, move!"

Katya gestured again with the gun. Martin turned and

resumed walking, keeping his pace slow to give him time to think. Somehow, he was going to have to negotiate his way out of this situation. He wondered how much it would cost to make Katya go away. Not just to go away, but to keep quiet. The alternative was to have her and the girls disposed of. Not impossible, but difficult. And what if there was someone else in the house, as Robert had said? If that was the case, then he was walking back into danger.

Martin knew he had no choice but to keep walking. Hopefully, by the time he and Katya reached the house, Robert would have dealt with whatever the problem was. Perhaps he would also be able to deal with the problem walking a few yards behind him?

The band across Martin's sternum tightened even more as he approached the front door. While they had been walking toward the house, Martin had heard and seen nothing untoward. He stepped through the front door and stood in the middle of the hallway. Martin turned around to see Katya, a look of uncertainty on her face, glancing around from her position in the doorway.

She doesn't know what to do next, Martin thought as he watched her. No idea at all.

"Where now?" Martin said, trying to take advantage of her uncertainty.

Katya took a few tentative steps into the hallway. Martin caught some movement from the direction of his office door. Keeping his head where it was, he swiveled his eyes to see Robert inching through, a squat black pistol in his hand. Katya hadn't seen him, and Martin closed his eyes as Robert raised the pistol.

The sound of the gunshot, when it came, still made Martin jump even though he'd been expecting it.

136

Katya jumped so much at the sound of the shot that she dropped her own pistol. A few yards away from her, Robert did exactly the same thing. Then, as she watched, he clutched at his groin before slumping to the floor. On the other side of the hall, Caleb stood with a dark gray gun in his hand.

"These are much more accurate on single-shot," he said, smiling at Katya. There was a low moan from Robert as he brought his knees up into a fetal position.

"Oh, Caleb, thank God you're okay!" Katya said, forgetting about her gun on the floor and running over to hug him. She threw her arms around his neck as Caleb repositioned the gun to point at Martin, who was eyeing both Katya's and Robert's pistols on the floor of the hallway.

"Don't move an inch, Martin," Caleb said. Katya could hear the steel in his voice.

She disengaged her arms from Caleb and took a step back, looking at him to see if he was injured. He had a graze on his forehead, but other than that, he seemed unharmed.

"Ana and Elene? Are they safe?" she asked him.

"They should be. There's a woman with them. I told her to head for the car behind the building." Katya saw him looking at Martin. "Your guest's car?" Martin just nodded in response. "He won't be needing it anymore."

"What happened to him?" Martin asked. From the look on Caleb's face, Katya knew the man who had come to visit the girls was dead.

"He got something stuck in his throat." Caleb gestured toward the door of Martin's office, which Katya could see over Robert's prone form. "Let's go in there. Make ourselves comfortable." He nodded at Robert. "Who's this? I think I've seen him before."

"His name's Robert," Martin replied as he rubbed at his chest.

Katya watched as Martin stepped over Robert and walked into the room. Caleb gestured to her, indicating that she should follow him. As Caleb stepped over Robert, he reached down and grabbed the man by the scruff of the neck.

"Come on, Robert," Caleb said as the man groaned. Katya saw blood on his hands, which were pressed tightly against his groin. "Man up. It's only a soft tissue injury."

When they were in Martin's office, Caleb dragged Robert into a chair next to the large mahogany desk Katya had seen through the spotting scope. He threw him into it before turning to Katya with a grin.

"I just wanted to make sure he didn't try to sneak into the Lord's assembly house," Caleb said before turning his attention to Martin, who was still rubbing his chest. "What's the matter with you? Your ticker not good with all this excitement?"

"I have an aneurysm," Martin replied. Katya watched Caleb's eyebrows go up a fraction.

"Well, bless your heart," Caleb drawled. "You think He might be trying to tell you something?" he asked, raising his eyes to the ceiling for a second or two. Martin didn't reply.

"What's on the laptop?" Katya asked, looking at the computer that Martin was still holding under his arm. "Must be pretty important if you were taking it with you?"

She watched as Martin's eyes bored into hers. Then a look of resignation passed over his face.

"Everything," he said a moment later.

"Open it up," Caleb said. "Let me see."

"No," Martin replied, his look of resignation deepening. Katya looked at him and saw a defeated man. He knew that if he opened the laptop, his life as he knew it would be over —one way or another. "It's password protected. If I tell you what they are, you'll kill me."

Katya waited to see what Caleb's response would be. She thought back to Mateo, and Caleb's promise to him he wouldn't kill him. But it appeared Martin was to be offered no such mercy.

"I can open it," Robert said, his voice tremulous. "If you let me go, I'll open it. I know the passwords."

Katya turned to look at Robert. He still had his hands clutched to his groin, but he was looking at Caleb with a determined face. Caleb took a few steps across the office and took the laptop from Martin, who was just glaring at him. He placed the laptop on the desk in front of Robert.

"Open it," Caleb said. Robert's hands were trembling as he fumbled with the screen. "Katya, could you write any passwords down?"

Katya took a pen from Martin's desk and a small notepad. On top on the notepad, in cursive black text, were some words. She tore the top sheet off and handed it to Caleb.

From the Office of Bishop Martin Lockwood.

She saw Caleb's face darken as he read the header on the notepad before turning her attention to Robert. As he prodded at the keyboard, she wrote each character down. When the operating system whirred into life, she showed him what she had written on the pad.

"Are those correct?" Katya asked. Robert just nodded in response, so she tore the top sheet off and handed it to Caleb. "Are you going to see what's on there?" she asked him.

"No, Katya," Caleb replied. His eyes were so dark they were almost black, and she felt a shiver running down her spine. It was as if the temperature in the room had just dropped by ten degrees. "I have no interest in looking at their depravity. There are others who would find that useful, no doubt. Why don't you go and see Ana and Elene?"

"Can't I stay here?" she asked him.

"No, Katya," he replied. "Bishop Lockwood and I have some things we need to discuss."

As Katya left, she felt the temperature drop even further.

137

Caleb waited until the door closed behind Katya. Then he waited for a few more seconds before turning to Robert. Caleb had watched him close the laptop, leaving bloody fingerprints on the case, and his face was gray. Caleb wondered how long it would be before he passed out from shock. When he had grabbed the man a few moment's previously, his hand had brushed against Robert's skin. The slight touch had been enough for Caleb to sense a lifetime of people hurt at his hands and had confirmed Robert's journey.

"Robert," Caleb said, knowing that the man wouldn't be able to go anywhere under his own steam. "Feel free to leave whenever you wish." As Caleb had thought, Robert made no effort to move. He turned his attention to Martin, who, although he wasn't quite as gray as Robert, was looking pale. "So, Bishop Martin, is it?"

Martin nodded in response.

"How much?" he said. Caleb threw his head back and laughed.

"How much? You think you can buy your way out of this?"

"Every man has a price," Martin replied. "Name yours."

"How's your knowledge of the Good Book, Bishop Martin? It should be rather good, I would have thought?" Caleb waited for Martin to respond, but he said nothing. "I'm thinking Timothy. The first book. Chapter six?"

"Enlighten me," Martin said through gritted teeth. Behind the desk, Robert had pushed the laptop away from him and was resting his head on his arms.

"Command those who are rich in this present world not to be arrogant nor to put their hope in wealth," Caleb said. "Does that sound familiar? Bishop Martin?" Martin shook his head. "Why, Bishop Martin?"

"What do you mean, why?"

Caleb threw his hands out to take in the opulent office.

"Why this?" His face darkened. "Why do you do what you do? Are you a pedophile?"

"No," Martin replied. Caleb looked at his face. To his surprise, the bishop was telling the truth. "But you are a rapist." It wasn't a question. "What's the woman's name? The one I found in the house earlier?"

"Lika."

"You have lain with her. Violated her."

"Let he who is without sin cast the first stone," Martin replied. "You, too, have lain with women. I saw how Katya looked at you."

Caleb felt his anger building at Martin's words, but he pushed it back, suppressing it in his mind and his heart. It wasn't his anger that he was about to deliver. It was His.

"I am not without sin, Bishop Martin. I am a man, a humble man. But what you have done? That is beyond sin." Caleb focused on the man in front of him. "That is surely the devil's work. How many lives have you ruined, hiding behind the cloth of the Church?"

Martin said nothing. Caleb knew there was nothing he could say. He reached out his hand and pressed it to Martin's sternum. He could feel his heart beating through his fingertips. It was racing, as well it might. The time of Martin's deliverance was upon him. Caleb closed his eyes and focused on what he could feel, fighting against the bile rising in the back of his throat at the revelations. So many women and children in horrific pain. So many lives ruined by greed, both monetary and carnal.

"I am an agent of wrath, Bishop Martin, sent by Him to bring punishment to the wrongdoer," Caleb said, his voice low and monotone. "Which, in this case, would be you. He put me here on this earth to seek people like you. He put me here in this country for a reason. Here in this room for a reason. To search for people who are beyond evil. People who are Satan's acolytes." Caleb took a breach to calm and channel his anger. "You are not a bishop. You are not even a man. You are an abomination."

Caleb closed his eyes as he withdrew his hand from Martin's chest. He kept his hand flat in front of him, a few inches from Martin's sternum.

"Leave room for the wrath of God, for it is written," Caleb said, intoning His words carefully. He paused for a few seconds before he opened his eyes and looking into Martin's, drinking in the evil that the man emanated. Caleb raised his voice. "Vengeance is Mine, I will repay."

With that, Caleb drove his palm forward and into the soft flesh just beneath Martin's sternum.

138

"Ana! Elene!"

At the sound of their names, Katya saw both girls throw the car door open and scramble out. They ran toward her, throwing their arms around her when they reached her. Katya felt tears stinging her eyes as she held them to her body. Behind them, a woman got out of the car and approached them, a broad smile on her face.

"Hi," the woman said in Georgian. "You must be Katya. They've told me all about you. I'm Lika."

Katya kept her arms where they were, not wanting to let the girls go for a single second.

"Are they okay? Did anything happen to them?"

Katya saw a dark cloud cross Lika's face and, for a horrifying few seconds, she thought they'd been too late.

"They are fine," Lika replied, causing a sob to escape from Katya. "Your friend got here just in time. The girls were saying he's some sort of monk?"

"He's a preacher," Katya replied. "Of sorts, anyway."

"Are we safe now, Katya?" Elene asked, her voice muffled by Katya's clothes. "Is it over?"

"Yes, Elene," Katya said, tears now streaming down her face. "Yes, it's all over."

"Then why are you crying?" Ana asked. Katya looked down at her, and the innocence in her eyes just made her want to cry even more.

"Sometimes," she replied, "people cry when they're really happy."

A FEW MOMENTS LATER, with both Ana and Elene back in the green car, Katya and Lika walked out of their earshot. They talked for some time, Katya listening as Lika told her a familiar story. It was only familiar up to a point, though. Lika's story was much, much worse than Katya's.

Like Katya, Lika had traveled to England on a small boat with promises of a new job and a new life. Both had come true, in a sense, but not in the way that Lika had imagined. When Katya told her of Aleksander's death at Caleb's hand, Lika had laughed before she had cried.

"Thank God that pig is dead," Lika said as she looked at Katya. "Did he...?"

"No," Katya replied. "He tried, but nothing happened." She reached out and took Lika's hand. "But it's over now, Lika. For you as well as for the girls."

"I feel awful," Lika replied, glancing at the car. "If anything had happened to them, it would have been my fault. But I had no choice."

"I know, I know," Katya replied as she pulled Lika into a hug. "There was nothing you could have done to stop them, Lika, believe me."

"I could have tried," Lika replied through her sobs.

"They would have killed you, Lika," Katya said, rubbing

the other woman's back. "It was you who brought them out of the house. To safety."

"It doesn't feel that way to me, Katya."

"It will, Lika. Give it time."

"What will become of us now?" Lika asked. "Will they send us back home?"

"I don't know," Katya replied. "We'll have to wait and see. Caleb will know what to do. He always does."

139

M artin staggered back and sat down heavily in the chair behind him. The blow had punched all the breath from his body. He looked up at Caleb who was just standing there, looking at him. Martin closed his eyes for a few seconds and saw movement behind his eyelids but, when he reopened them, Caleb was where he had been.

"They are coming, Bishop Martin," Caleb said in a whisper that Martin struggled to hear.

There was a tiny pinprick of pain between Martin's shoulder blades.

"Who is coming?" he asked. The pinprick grew stronger, driving all the way into his chest.

"The Dark Ones," Caleb replied.

Martin closed his eyes again and saw more movement. He could hear a rushing sound that he realized was his own heartbeat. The movement started to coalesce in his mind. Martin saw powerful legs. Heard snarls. He opened his eyes. Caleb was looking at him with a serene expression.

"You don't really believe all that nonsense, do you?"

Martin said, trying to ignore the pinprick of pain. It was now starting to spread beneath his shoulder blades. Caleb said nothing.

Martin had never been a man of faith. He had simply seen an opportunity within the Church. There was a game to be played in that establishment, and it was one that he played very well. Once all the pomp and ceremony had been stripped away, the rituals that gave men and women hope where there was none, all that was left was a means of social control. But that wasn't an opinion that Martin had ever voiced.

There was a sudden wrenching sensation between Martin's shoulders, and the rushing noise in his ears got louder. Every time he closed his eyes, the visions got clearer. He saw creatures of some description, like nothing he had ever seen before. Jagged teeth, eyes with gleaming red spots. Martin struggled to keep his eyes open. To keep them away from him.

He blinked a couple of times, looking at the man in front of him. Caleb was just staring back, his own eyes dark and full of anger. There was a grayness encircling Martin's field of vision. He saw the creatures starting to dance into the darker edges of the grayness.

Martin knew what was happening inside his chest. Caleb's blow had ruptured his aneurysm. One evening, when he had been feeling particularly morbid, Martin had looked up on the internet what might happen in that situation. He knew every heartbeat was sending blood, not to his vital organs, but into his thoracic cavity. He was bleeding to death without spilling a single drop of blood.

Martin's eyes were becoming heavier. The ripping sensation between his shoulder blades had given way to the most unimaginable pain, but Martin didn't have the strength to cry out. The gray circle was getting darker and darker, the creatures becoming more distinct. He could still make out Caleb's form in front of him, but it had changed. Martin realized Caleb was no longer facing him, but had turned and was walking away. Martin tried to say something as the dark circle closed and the creatures got closer and closer to the center of what was left of Martin's consciousness.

But Caleb never looked back.

140

Katya was sitting in the plush leather seat of the green car, almost asleep, when she heard Ana and Elene's excited squeals.

"Caleb!" one of them shouted. She thought it was Ana but couldn't be sure. "It's Caleb!"

Exactly as they had done when Katya had walked over to the car, the girls leaped out and ran to Caleb. As they approached, he dropped to his knees and held his arms out to envelop them both in a hug. He had been carrying Mateo's bag, which he had put on the ground beside him.

"You came back for us!" Katya heard Ana say, her voice high. Caleb didn't reply—he would have no idea what she had said—but he just smiled at both of the girls as he ran his hands over their heads. Then he closed his eyes as a brief expression of what looked like pain appeared on his face. At the same time, Katya saw Ana's and Elene's faces relaxing.

Holding both Ana and Elene by the hands, Caleb made his way over to the car. Katya looked at him and knew Martin was dead before he said a word. She just hoped it was painful. A faint smile played across Caleb's face, the previous trace of pain having vanished.

"It was," he said to Katya. She frowned, not having said anything. "And he will hurt for eternity."

Katya took a step toward him and he let go of the girls' hands to put his arms around her. When he pulled her tight to him, she felt a wave of relief coursing through her body. It was over. Finally, it was all over.

"Katya," Caleb said a few moments later after she had properly introduced him to Lika. "Could you and Lika take the girls to the copse, like we agreed?"

"Of course," Katya said. "What about you? You're coming as well, aren't you?"

"I need to run back to the house to get the laptop," Caleb replied. "You and Lika can take them there, yes?"

Katya looked at him for a few seconds, wondering if he was actually going to join them. When he had hugged her just now, the sense of finality had been about more than Martin and the others. To her relief, he smiled at her.

"Yes, I'll be there soon."

She watched as he walked around the car and flipped down the sun visor over the driver's seat. A key fell down onto the upholstery.

"Take the car," he said. "The gate is still open." Then he turned and walked back toward the house.

AROUND TWENTY MINUTES LATER, Katya was sitting in the tree from where she and Caleb had surveiled the house. Ana and Elene, having pleaded with both Katya and Lika to let them, were sitting on the branch next to her. They had both solemnly promised not to wriggle, dance, or mess about. Elene had the binoculars to her eyes and was looking through them at the house.

"I see him!" she said, her voice excited. "I can see Caleb coming."

Katya looked down at the house to see Caleb making his way down the path. It looked as if he had a shopping bag in his hand.

"Pass me those, Elene," Katya said, gesturing at the binoculars.

She raised them to her eyes and adjusted them so she could see properly. Caleb was just making his way across the bridge, a large shopping bag in his hands. She saw him checking his watch before he looked up at the copse. Caleb raised a hand in greeting, although he wouldn't be able to see them. Then he continued walking up the path. Katya watched him, his focus on what was in front of him, and she felt a lump in her throat. A few seconds later, tears started streaming down her face again.

"Katya," Ana said from her perch on the branch. "Are you crying because you're happy, or sad?"

Katya ruffled the girl's hair before she replied.

"It's because I'm both, Ana," Katya said with a smile.

141

Caleb sat on a small tuft of grass in front of the copse. Beside him were Ana and Elene, and Katya and Lika were sitting next to them. In front of them was a veritable feast that he had told them he had liberated from the kitchen. Also in the shopping bag was Martin's laptop, wrapped in clingfilm and with the piece of paper with the passwords clearly visible through the transparent wrap. Caleb was talking to the girls, with Katya and Lika taking it in turns to translate.

"So," Elene said, her mouth half-full of chips. "They're all gone, the evil men."

"Yes, Elene," Caleb said. "They've all gone a long, long way away. You'll never see them again." As he waited for Katya to translate, he watched her and could see her beauty shining through. No matter what she had been through, Katya had never lost that. But it wasn't just physical beauty, Caleb knew. It ran far deeper than that. As she spoke, Caleb saw the look on Elene's face change. The girl understood exactly what Katya was telling her. Elene looked at Caleb with eyes wise beyond her years as she said something to Katya.

"She wants to know if God will be angry with them?" Katya explained, prompting a smile from Caleb. He glanced down at his watch.

"Tell her that yes, he will be angry. So angry that he's going to send a thunderbolt down to Martin's house."

Katya returned his smile as she translated for Elene. Both Elene and Ana started laughing. Ana said something to Katya.

"Ana says don't be silly," Katya said. "She says you're making fun of them."

"Tell them to look at the house," Caleb replied with another glance at his watch. Any second now.

The explosion, when it came, wiped the smiles off the girls' faces in a heartbeat. They stared at the house as the windows blew out, the glass being propelled by roaring flames, and several large holes appeared in the roof. A few seconds later, the roar of the blast hit them, a low rumble full of power. Below them, the house started to fall in on itself and Martin's car, still parked near the gate, was hit by several pieces of falling masonry. It rocked on its suspension as, behind it, flames poured out of the house.

Caleb tried to hide his smile as the two girls turned to him, openmouthed. He could also see Katya and Lika staring at him.

"Tell them I told them so," Caleb said, the smile breaking onto his face. "Now, nature calls."

He got to his feet, leaving the women to stare at the house below, which was now billowing acrid black smoke into the clear air. He walked around the bushes, thinking back to when he had gone to the kitchen to find supplies, and the clingfilm to protect Martin and Robert's fingerprints. Just as he had left the darkened kitchen, after turning all the gas dials on the oven to full blast, Caleb had, for the second time in his life, spoken to a machine. The first time had been a few moments earlier, when he had asked Alexa to turn the kitchen lights off.

"Alexa," Caleb had said. "In thirty minutes' time, turn the kitchen lights back on."

142

K atya sat in the uncomfortable armchair, watching the news scrolling across the screen. Ana and Elene were sitting on a sofa opposite her, and to one side, Lika was in another armchair. The woman who Caleb had introduced them to—Joan—was making a drink, and Caleb had gone to use the restroom.

They were sitting in the offices of the British Red Cross in Lincoln. Caleb had brought them there straight from the scene of the explosion. They had left soon after the house had been destroyed because Caleb wanted to avoid the firemen and police officers. When they had arrived, he had introduced them to the woman who worked there, explaining that they were seeking refuge in England. The woman, a small but energetic person who must have been in her sixties, had welcomed them with open arms.

"You've come to the right place," she had said as she had bustled them into the room where they were now sitting. Then Caleb had asked for a stamp and an envelope, and Katya had watched as he placed the night porter's key into it along with a piece of paper with the office's address on. His car was in the lot outside.

"So," Joan said as she walked back into the room. She was carrying a tray with soda for Ana and Elene, and mugs of tea for Katya and Lika. "We'll need to take some details from you before we move you to our center. It's ever so nice, though. You'll be able to stay there until your asylum claims have been processed." On the television screen, Katya could see an aerial shot of what was left of Martin's house. The ticker tape running across the bottom was telling viewers about a potential gas explosion at the house of a prominent bishop. Katya listened with half an ear as Lika translated for Ana and Elene when she heard Joan calling her name.

"I'm sorry," Katya said, turning to look at Joan. She had gray hair, tightly permed against her head, and the kindest eyes Katya thought she'd ever seen. "I wasn't listening."

"I asked you where your friend was, my dear. The American chap who brought you here?"

"He's gone to the restroom, I think."

"He's been an awfully long time."

Katya nodded in agreement and turned to look out of the window. She saw people walking past on the street, going about their daily business as if there was nothing wrong with the world. Which, perhaps for them, there wasn't.

Then Katya saw a familiar sight on the other side of the street. It was Caleb, back in his gray robe and with his small bag slung across his shoulder. He was staring at her and she could feel the intensity of his gaze, even from that distance.

She watched as he raised his hands and clasped them in front of them, as if in prayer. Then he pointed at her. She could see his lips moving and then, in her head, she heard him speak.

"I will pray for you, Katya."

Katya repeated the gesture, tears in her eyes, as Caleb nodded in confirmation. Then he turned and walked away. She willed him to turn and look at her one last time.

But Caleb never looked back.

143

S uzy Whittle sat back in her seat, pleased that she and her daughter had managed to get two seats next to each other. The bus was crowded, as the ones to London normally were, but at least Leanne, her six-year-old, wasn't acting up. But it was a long way to go until they reached their destination.

"Mummy," Suzy heard her daughter say, tugging at her sleeve.

"What?" Suzy sighed. Perhaps it was going to be a long day after all.

"Mummy, look at the funny man."

"Shh," Suzy replied instinctively as she looked up. A man had just climbed on the bus. He was wearing a gray robe, sandals, and had a small cloth bag slung over one shoulder. As he made his way down the bus, he looked at Suzy and Leanne and smiled before he sat behind them.

THE BUS HAD JUST PULLED out of Lincoln bus station and the driver was using the public address system to welcome them aboard, tell them of his hope that they enjoyed the journey, and to give them their arrival time in London. Suzy was looking out of the window when she heard Leanne speak.

"Are you a monk?"

"Shh, Leanne," Suzy said, turning to look at her daughter, who had turned to speak to the man behind them. "Don't be rude. Leave the man alone."

"Are you a monk?" Leanne said again, ignoring her mother. Suzy sighed and started to apologize.

"I'm sorry," she said to the man in the robe. "She's just curious, that's all."

"That's fine," the man replied, and Suzy caught his American accent. She'd not been expecting that. "I know. I look a bit different."

"Are you a monk?" Leanne asked for the third time.

"No, I'm not a monk," the man said with a smile at the girl.

"But you're dressed like a monk."

"I'm not a monk."

"So why are you dressed like a monk?" Leanne asked him, making Suzy sigh. She was just about to apologize again when the man in the robe cut her off. He smiled at her, and she felt a peculiar sense of calmness.

"I'm a preacher," he said, closing his eyes to ward off any more question.

"You hear that, Mummy," Leanne said in a conspiratorial whisper as she turned away from the man in the robe.

"Hear what?" Suzy replied, trying to work out where all her stress had just gone.

"He's The Preacher."

Printed in Great Britain
by Amazon

22075848R00280